www.MinotaurBooks.com

The premier website
for the best in crime fiction.

Log on and learn more about:

The Labyrinth: Sign up for this monthly news-letter and get your crime fiction fix. Commentary, author Q&A, hot new titles, and giveaways.

MomentsInCrime: It's no mystery what our authors are thinking. Each week, a new author blogs about their upcoming projects, special events, and more. Log on today to talk to your favorite authors.
www.MomentsInCrime.com

GetCozy: The ultimate cozy connection. Find your favorite cozy mystery, grab a reading group guide, sign up for monthly giveaways, and more.
www.GetCozyOnline.com

MINOTAUR
BOOKS

www.minotaurbooks.com

Cooper woke abruptly, her body trembling with dread. Even in the comfort of the morning light, she could still smell the scent of rain. And when she stood in the shower and closed her eyes, she could see the black horizon and the tongues of lightning, waiting for her imminent arrival.

Placing the last cup on a drying rack, Cooper exhaled, trying to calm the drumming of her heart as she recalled the feelings of fear instigated by her dream.

"Lord, are you trying to tell me to prepare for a difficult time?" she asked into the silence of the kitchen. "Tell me please, so I won't be taken by surprise."

She stared at the last drips of water as they slipped into the drain and then shut her eyes. Alone in the stillness of the small room, Cooper strained to listen. An answer came then, as though whispered into her inner ear. *Prepare yourself. Hardship is coming. . . .*

Hope Street Church Mystery Titles by

JENNIFER STANLEY

Stirring Up Strife

Path of the Wicked

The Way of the Guilty
(coming in September)

Available from St. Martin's / Minotaur Paperbacks

PATH OF THE WICKED

Jennifer Stanley

St. Martin's Paperbacks

For Grandma, who passed on while I was writing this book.

Her faith in me never wavered.

This is a work of fiction. All of the characters, organizations, and events portrayed in this novel are either products of the author's imagination or are used fictitiously.

PATH OF THE WICKED

Copyright © 2010 by Jennifer Stanley.
Excerpt from *The Way of the Guilty* copyright © 2010 by Jennifer Stanley.

For information address St. Martin's Press, 175 Fifth Avenue, New York, NY 10010.

ISBN: 978-0-312-37683-3

Printed in the United States of America

St. Martin's Paperbacks edition / May 2010

St. Martin's Paperbacks are published by St. Martin's Press, 175 Fifth Avenue, New York, NY 10010.

10 9 8 7 6 5 4 3 2 1

The author would like to thank the fine men and women of the Henrico County Sheriff's Office, especially Dawn Watson-Browning for answering questions and directing me to the correct personnel and Major Carlos Talley for giving me a fascinating and informative tour of Jail West. It has been one of the highlights of my writing career.

Do not set foot on the path of the wicked or walk in the way of evil men.

Avoid it, do not travel on it; turn from it and go on your way.

For they cannot sleep till they do evil; they are robbed of slumber till they make someone fall.

They eat the bread of wickedness and drink the wine of violence.

Proverbs 4:14–17 (NIV)

1

*In the month of Nisan in the twentieth year of King Artaxerxes,
when wine was brought for him, I took the wine and gave it to the
king. I had not been sad in his presence before; so the king asked me,
"Why does your face look so sad when you are not ill? This can be nothing but sadness of heart."*

Nehemiah 2:1-2 (NIV)

Cooper Lee was not having a good day. She had spent the
morning at an elementary school in the Far West End, trying to coax their aged copier, a Toshiba e-Studio28, back
to life. But the machine had given its all and no amount of
replacement parts, duct tape, or prayers were going to keep
it running.

Kneeling on the floor next to her toolbox, a soiled rag,
and the copier's rectangular back panel, Cooper examined
the dirty developer tray. In removing the part, her hands
and forearms had gotten covered in toner. As she worked,
she'd rubbed her face in vexation, knowing that it would
be impossible to resuscitate the spent machine.

Unaware of the splotches of gray and black ink on her
cheeks and nose, Cooper sighed. She knew that the school
didn't have the funds in their budget to purchase a new

copier, and they'd desperately need one soon as summer break was ticking to an end.

"Hey!" a voice nearby whispered. Cooper looked up to see a girl dressed in a Hannah Montana T-shirt and white shorts standing over her.

"Hi." She smiled. "Aren't you supposed to be on vacation?"

"My mom works here," the girl replied. "I had to help her carry stuff into her office." She continued to study Cooper's face with interest. "You look like you have the boooooobonic plague. I learned all about that for my summer reading assignment." She crossed her arms across her flat chest and peered at Cooper intently. "Are those black *boils*?"

Cooper laughed. "No, I do not have the *bubonic* plague. I probably smeared some ink from the copier on my face. Happens all the time."

The girl frowned. "Gross. *I* don't want a dirty job when I grow up. I'm going to be a famous singer and I'll live in a *huge* house, get driven around in a super-big limo, and own, like, twenty horses." She stretched out her skinny arms to emphasize her point. "Then my mommy can quit her job. She's the school nurse and *I* think what she does is gross, too!" The girl lowered her voice to an awed whisper. "She gives people *shots*! With *needles*!"

Examining her reflection in the shiny surface of an adjustable steel wrench, Cooper grinned and began to wipe away the ink on her face using a clean rag. "Well, *I'm* happiest when I'm getting messy. My hands are usually covered in ink, garden soil, or cookie dough."

"You're weird," the girl whispered and then looked back over her shoulder as though her mother might be close enough to overhear her rude remark. "But you're still pretty," she amended and then skipped away.

Cooper replaced the back panel of the defunct machine, taking her time turning the screws. This was the only part of her job at *Make It Work!*, an office-machine sales and repair company operating out of Richmond, Virginia, that Cooper disliked. She hated telling nice people, like the secretary in the front office, that she had been unable to fulfill their expectations and could not repair their machine.

Dusting off her uniform shirt, Cooper snapped her toolbox closed and stood. She patted the lid of the copier. "You've given them your best. Time for you to retire to the greener pastures of the recycling facility."

Gathering her tools, Cooper steeled herself and walked down the hall to the front office. The secretary took one look at her doleful expression and said, "Oh, dear. You don't look like you've got happy news for me."

"No, ma'am, I'm afraid I don't."

The secretary paused for a moment, unable to keep herself from staring at the repairwoman's unusual eyes. The left eye was blue, but such a pale shade of blue that it was almost colorless. The right eye, however, was startlingly green. It immediately called to mind a meadow of emerald grass in the peak of spring, dappled by sunlight and bright circles of marigolds. The woman's face was quite lovely, though her nose was a bit too long and angular and her dirty-blonde hair, which was cut in a flattering style, could do with some highlights. The secretary took in Cooper's athletic figure with a prick of envy.

She could *use a bit of makeup*, the secretary thought and then blinked, embarrassed at having stared at the repairwoman so blatantly.

"Oh, my." The secretary shook her head slightly as the enormity of Cooper's prognosis sank in. "Are you sure you can't fix our copier? We really need to get a few more months out of that machine."

"It's totally gone, ma'am. I would have been lucky to get you two or three more minutes, let alone months. It's got nothing left to give."

The secretary nodded, unsurprised by the revelation. "I know you did your best. You always do and we appreciate the extra time you've given us by keeping that 'ole dinosaur runnin' on a wing and a prayer." She rose and, signing Cooper's work order, walked her to the front door.

"It's going to take more than a bake sale to raise funds for a new copier." The secretary's expression was bleak. "And with school starting in two weeks, I don't know what we're going to do." She wrung her hands anxiously.

"The way I see it—you've got two choices. You can soak a mess of cakes in a barrel of rum and hope that the folks who show up for your bake sale write you checks with a whole lot of zeroes. Or," Cooper smiled wryly, "you could lease one of our machines until you raise the money for a new one."

The secretary brightened. "A lease?" She paused to consider the idea. "I'm fond of the rum cake plan, too, but a lease just might get us through the crisis. Thank you, Ms. Lee. You're an angel! *Please* call me with the rates as soon as you're able. We need a copier in here as of yesterday." Then her face grew solemn and she lowered her voice. "And you'll take away the old one for us?"

Cooper nodded to the older woman, said she'd call back later with leasing options, and hopped into a black van with the *Make It Work!* logo splashed across both sides in bright red lettering. As she drove back to the office, she remembered that the new employee Mr. Farmer had hired to handle the document-shredding side of the business would be at work today. Initially, Mr. Farmer had filled the need by having the son of his widowed next-door neighbor work over the summer, but the young man was returning to college for the fall, so Cooper's boss had placed an ad in the *Richmond Times-Dispatch* ten days ago. However, he'd ended up hiring a cousin recently relocated from northern New Jersey. As a result, no one had met the mysterious new addition to their team, and all three of Mr. Farmer's staff members were curious to discover what kind of person would become their coworker.

"Thank goodness he didn't hire some pageant princess," Angela said, giggling as she told Cooper about meeting the new employee while Cooper was at the elementary school.

Angela, the office manager at *Make It Work!*, wore a typically tight pencil skirt, a low-cut blouse, and an armload of vintage bangles. As Cooper looked at Angela's platinum-blonde bob, held firmly in place by a wide pink headband and half a can of Aqua Net, she noticed the presence of a beauty mark on Angela's cheek that had never been there before.

"I'm not sure there are too many pageant princess interested in a career in document shredding," Cooper said. Tapping her own cheek with her index finger, she teased Angela. "You're really channeling Marilyn Monroe today, huh?"

Angela batted her false eyelashes as she examined her reflection in a compact that was never far from reach. "I wanna see if Mr. Farmer notices." She leaned over her desk and whispered, "And if *he* doesn't, then I sure hope that *gorgeous* creature gettin' dressed in one of our uniform shirts does." Her eyes gleamed.

"So tell me about the new guy." Cooper leaned comfortably against Angela's desk. "I can see you're fit to burst over him."

Angela placed her hands over her ample bosom. "Lord, I don't know what I did to deserve such tasty eye candy! This boy is a stud cocktail made up of one part soap opera star, one part professional baseball player, and three parts Chippendale dancer." She frowned. "He's a bit too young for me, unfortunately. You know you're old when you wish you were forty again, but I can still *look*." She wiggled her pencil-drawn eyebrows. "And if he asked me to dinner, I wouldn't be in any hurry to say no."

At that moment, Mr. Farmer stepped out of his office at the end of the hall. The owner/manager of *Make It Work!* was a short, stocky, balding man resembling the actor Danny DeVito. A quiet, reserved individual, he was a kind and generous employer. Angela had been flirting with him for years, and though he occasionally displayed a hint of fondness for her in return, he had never officially asked her out on a date.

"Good morning, Cooper." Mr. Farmer straightened his tie, which was embroidered with cobalt computer monitors on a field of yellow. "Our new employee is in the locker room. His name is Emilio Calabria and word has it that this young fellow is an exemplary salesman. He's sure to increase our burgeoning secure document-destruction division. Ben will be showing him the ropes over the next few days." He smiled shyly at Angela. "Let's all go out of our way to make him feel at home."

"Oh, I'll make him feel *real* welcome, sir." Angela saluted their boss, her cherry-red nails brushing her powdered forehead.

"Ah, yes . . ." Mr. Farmer shuffled his feet, looking

slightly daunted by Angela's enthusiasm. Hearing foot-steps approaching from down the hall, he turned and held out his hand. "And here he is now. Emilio, you've met the rest of our small staff except for Cooper Lee. Cooper, this is Emilio, the man who'll soon be shredding paper all over town."

The first thought that ran through Cooper's mind was that Angela's assessment of their new coworker was completely accurate. Emilio wasn't tall, but his lean and muscular build gave him the appearance of height. His black hair fell in shiny waves that framed his olive skin and twinkling dark eyes. When he smiled at Cooper, flashing a row of square, white teeth and sensuous lips, she decided that his was a face meant for television and movie screens or the pages of *GQ*. His hands were wide and strong and as he crushed Cooper's in a steely, wet grip, his smile turned to a snort.

"Lady, you've got some *awesome* eyes!" He laughed as they shook hands. "Man, I mean they are wicked cool. They remind me of that pretty blonde actress—she was in the *Superman* remake."

"Kate Bosworth?" Angela guessed.

Emilio pointed at her. "Smart *and* classy." He turned to Mr. Farmer. "I can see who runs *this* show."

"And *I* can see why you're such a good salesman. You're just as smooth as a stick of butter brought to room tem-perature." Angela batted her false eyelashes. "I'd never have taken you for kin of Mr. Farmer's. Just *how* are you related again?"

"Emilio's my aunt's boy," Mr. Farmer answered, clearly displeased over being so overshadowed by his cousin. "My own folks died when I was in my early twenties. Now all I've got left is my big sister and Aunt Mildred."

"And me!" Emilio clapped his employer on the back with enough enthusiasm to jostle a few teeth loose. "You're not gonna be sorry about bringin' me aboard, boss. I'm gonna work my ass off and bring in so many new clients that you won't know where to spend all your money!"

"I could think of a few ways to spend it," Angela murmured coquettishly.

Emilio beamed at Mr. Farmer and then slung his arm around Cooper's shoulders. In a conspiratorial fashion, he whispered, "This man hired me when I was down on my luck. Is he awesome or what?"

"Best boss I've ever had," Cooper replied, inhaling Emilio's powerful cologne.

She extricated herself from her hunky coworker's semi-embrace and feigned the need to grab a tissue from Angela's desk. As Cooper pulled a few from the floral box, she noticed the secretary was gazing at Emilio with adoration. Mr. Farmer also seemed to have taken note of Angela's demeanor, for he hurriedly took Emilio by the elbow and offered to accompany him to where Ben waited in the garage.

"Catch you beautiful ladies later!" Emilio said in his thick, Jersey accent and strutted off.

Angela watched the men walk away. "Ain't he somethin'?" She panted, fanning herself with a brochure from an ink cartridge and toner company.

Cooper shrugged. "Yeah, he's something, all right." She shouldered the woven straw bag she had recently purchased from Target and told Angela she'd be back in an hour.

"You meetin' that nice boy from your Bible study for a steamy lunch date?" Angela puckered her lips.

Cooper's neck grew pink. She put a hand over the telltale flesh and shook her head. "No, he's been real busy lately. And like I told you last week, I'm not sure if we're dating. We've only been out together a few times."

Angela waved her off. "You've kissed, honey. On the lips. *More* than once. So if that ain't datin', then you're the *friendliest* friends I've ever heard of!"

Cooper ordered a Happy Meal from McDonald's and took hungry bites of her cheeseburger with extra pickles with one hand while manipulating the traffic around Short Pump Town Center. The mall was unexpectedly busy for a weekday, but then Cooper realized that the mothers disembarking from their SUVs and plush minivans were no doubt shopping for back-to-school supplies. As she parked her red pickup truck, which she had fondly dubbed Cherry-O, Cooper watched a pretty woman of about the same age press a button on her car key, causing both of her minivan's rear doors to slide open. Her two young children hopped inside, relieved to be out of the scorching August sun. Each child held onto a balloon from the shoe store and as the mother lifted her daughter into her booster seat and carefully tied her purple balloon to the armrest, the little girl threw her arms around her mother's neck and covered her face with tender kisses. The mother laughed and kissed her daughter back on the bridge of her small nose. Witnessing this sweet exchange, Cooper felt a twinge of sadness stir in her heart.

"That's what I want, Lord," she whispered into the quiet of her truck cab. "I want to love someone like that. I want to be loved like that." Surprised and irritated to find herself fighting back tears, she stuffed the last four French fries into her mouth, grabbed her Coke from the cup holder, and marched into the mall.

Almost furtively, she pulled open the heavy door to the nail salon next to Macy's and, after being greeted by the receptionist, mumbled, "I'm here to see Minnie."

"We know you." The Vietnamese woman behind the reception desk smiled as Cooper retrieved a pair of flip-flops from her handbag. "You a regular customer now." She then led Cooper toward the back of the salon and gestured at one of the voluminous leather pedicure chairs. "Pick your color and sit in second chair on left," the woman directed her. "Minnie coming soon."

Cooper selected a conservative mauve polish and then settled into her chair. She pressed the red button on the attached remote in order to start up the chair massage and gazed at the other women in the salon. Only months ago, Cooper would have laughed to consider herself among the women who routinely sought a beauty treatment for their feet. However, once she had been initiated into the world of pedicures, she quickly became a bit of a junkie. She now had a pedicure twice a month and had bought several pairs of sandals to show off her neatly polished toes. One of the first things she did after work was to kick off her heavy boots and slide her colorful toes into a pair of sandals or flip-flops.

"Hello, Miss Cooper," a petite young Vietnamese girl greeted her and then turned on the water in the pedicure tub. She shook a jar of green granules into the water and then accepted the bottle of nail polish Cooper handed her. "Your sister come, too?" she asked.

Cooper nodded and then glanced in the direction of the front door. "Here she is now."

Ashley Lee Love strode into the salon like a supermodel flaunting her stuff on the catwalk. She was wearing pink Capri pants stitched with navy blue whales, a wide leather belt that accentuated her narrow waist, and a flimsy white blouse. Her accessories included three strands of pearls, matching pearl earrings, a glimmering diamond tennis bracelet, and a Versace hobo purse that looked as though it contained a bowling ball.

Flipping a shimmering lock of golden blonde hair over her tanned shoulder, Ashley inspected the array of available nail polish colors as though she were a surgeon selecting the appropriate instrument for a complicated case. She held up a pair of pale pinks in almost identical hues to the light and then meticulously painted her big toe with a stripe of color from each bottle.

"Should I pick Italian Love Affair or Argenteeny Pinkini?" she called across the salon to Cooper.

For some reason, the first name caused Cooper to think of Emilio, her new coworker. "The second one," she replied firmly.

Ashley handed the bottle to her nail technician and then slipped off a pair of elegant sandals with a wedge heel. Sliding gracefully into the pedicure chair, she opened her purse, pulled out one of several magazines rolled up inside, and showed it to her sister.

Cooper stared at the beautiful little girl gracing the cover of *Parents* magazine. She was blonde, freckled, and had the deepest dimples that Cooper had ever seen. "Cute kid," she said and then looked at Ashley's expectant face. "Why are you showing me that?"

"I need to start doing some research," Ashley answered with an enigmatic smile.

"On parenting?" Cooper was confused.

Ashley wiggled excitedly in her seat. "Of course, silly. How else am I going to get ready for when the baby comes?"

Cooper's mouth came unhinged. She stared at the

angelic, pig-tailed child on the cover of the magazine and felt a stab of jealousy. Ashley, who was exactly a year, a month, a week, and a day younger than Cooper, was married to a handsome and wealthy husband and lived in an elegant mansion in the most desirable section of the suburbs. She divided her time between playing golf and tennis, shopping at boutiques and high-end department stores, and organizing an endless parade of philanthropic events. And now, the woman who already had looks, love, and luck was going to have a baby.

What about me? Cooper asked silently and stared forlornly at the bubbles surfacing around her feet. *I'm the older sister! I have no husband, no children, and I spent five years of my life with a man who dumped me for another woman! When will it be my turn?*

"It feel okay?" Minnie inquired as she rinsed Cooper's feet and began to massage her calves using a fragrant orange lotion.

"Yes." Cooper forced a smile to her face. She suddenly felt ashamed of being envious of her sister. Touching the cover of the magazine Ashley held, Cooper looked into her sister's lovely cerulean eyes and said, "A baby. That's wonderful, Ashley. I'm real happy for you."

2

Those who look to him are radiant; their faces are never covered with shame.

Psalm 34:5 (NIV)

Ashley reached over in her massage chair and swatted Cooper with her magazine, causing her nail technician to look up in alarm.

"I'm not pregnant *yet*, Coop," Ashley hissed. "Don't go jinxing me!" She returned her feet to their former position without even glancing at the befuddled technician. "But Lincoln and I have decided it's time. Daddy and Mama would be so tickled to be grandparents and . . . Oh!" She jabbed her fingernail at an ad in the magazine. "Look at this adorable bassinet! I am going to have the most *beautiful* nursery in the whole city! I've already brought home a dozen wallpaper samples to try out. I'm leaning toward green toile with the—"

Cooper interjected with a shake of her head. "Aren't you putting the cart just a bit in front of the horse?"

Ashley paused and then narrowed her eyes defensively. "Lincoln and I are young, happy, and in love. What's going to stop us from having the most *perfect*, *precious* little baby anyone's ever laid eyes on?"

Ignoring Ashley's testiness, Cooper replied, "Nothing, I suppose."

After all, you've always gotten everything you've ever wanted, Cooper thought sourly, reflecting that while the Lees hadn't had the means to spoil their youngest child, Ashley had managed to charm people into buying her sweets and trinkets from the time she could talk. At school, she had always been the prettiest, most popular girl in the class. With each report card that came home, Cooper waited for her chance to finally outshine her sister, but it had never happened.

After high school, Ashley's partial scholarship to Hollins University allowed her to cross paths with her future husband, Lincoln Love, at a polo match attended by central Virginia's most affluent and influential families. Naturally, Ashley had been invited by a sycophantic sorority sister who also happened to be a congressman's daughter. The poor girl had hoped that by bringing Ashley along, the young men who couldn't get near Ashley would settle for flirting with her. Ashley was in her element and had no difficulty juggling a dozen coquettish conversations until Lincoln rode up on his sleek gray mare. The horse cleared a path through other would-be suitors and Lincoln offered the lovely and popular co-ed a glass of champagne from a bottle tucked in his saddlebag.

"It was love at first sight!" Ashley always said upon telling strangers about meeting Lincoln. "He even had a crystal glass in that bag!"

Now, Ashley was happily established in a mansion off the elite River Road corridor. From the outside, it seemed that Ashley's life was nearly perfect. A baby would be the jewel in the crown of an already charmed existence.

"I wonder if I'll get really fat when I'm pregnant," Ashley mused, breaking Cooper out of her envious trance.

Watching as Minnie deftly applied a clear topcoat to the toes on her left foot, Cooper frowned. "I doubt you'll get fat. You work out five days a week." For a moment, Cooper allowed herself to picture Ashley at three times her normal weight, wearing sweatpants with an elastic waist and a pullover top that strained across her bulbous bosom and belly. She guiltily acknowledged that it was quite pleasant to conjure up such an unflattering image of her sister.

"You're right!" Ashley declared. "I won't let my body control the situation. I'll enroll in prenatal yoga and follow a *strict* pregnancy diet." She rubbed her hands together. "It will be so much *fun* to shop in the new maternity boutiques, too. Styles for expectant mothers have *finally* caught up with the times. Did you know that nothing's returnable at those places?" Without waiting for Cooper to answer, Ashley wriggled her newly painted toes and asked, "When's your Bible study group starting up again? You didn't meet at all this summer, right?"

"We start again this Sunday and I haven't done all the homework yet." Cooper flushed, as her answer wasn't entirely honest. In truth, she had bought the workbook called *Joseph: Amazing Dreamer* at the LifeWay Christian bookstore the day after she had received Savannah's letter in the mailbox announcing the topic of their next study. The following weekend, after spending the morning weeding the vegetable garden, Cooper had immediately settled onto the couch with her workbook and Bible and had completed all of the blanks in the reading with the exception of a single question, which she put off answering day after day.

Still, Cooper had missed the members of the Sunrise Bible study during the summer and couldn't wait to resume their meetings. She vowed to fill in that one blank before she saw her friends again on Sunday.

Checking her watch, she jumped up and then paused to carefully ease her sticky toes into a pair of flip-flops. "I need to get back to work."

"Don't put your work boots back on 'til the last second and don't worry, this is my treat!" Ashley patted her purse gaily. She was always generous with her money. "Go on now," she teased as Cooper carefully took a step. "You don't want to keep those copiers waiting. Why, I can practically feel the toner running low somewhere in the city!"

Cooper could hear her sister's snigger all the way to the parking lot.

"Now she'll add a baby to all her other blessings? And me? I live with my folks, am thousands of dollars in debt, and still want a cigarette months after quitting! It's just not fair!" she complained to the heavens before sliding into her truck, and then immediately asked for forgiveness for her childish outburst.

Eyeing the clock, Cooper realized that her lunch hour was nearly expired. She quickly drove back to work, accelerating through two yellow lights—one of which switched to red just as she passed beneath it. Spying a police car in the opposite lane, Cooper's heart lurched into her throat, but the officer was looking out his passenger window and had apparently not witnessed Cooper's blunder. She exhaled in relief and eased her foot from the gas pedal.

I've been so unsettled lately, she thought as she pulled into the parking lot in front of her office building. Even though she was already five minutes late returning from lunch, she picked up her Bible study workbook from the passenger seat and opened to the question she had yet to answer. Gripping a pencil in her hand, she read the italicized words for the tenth time in a matter of days.

What are you seeking most at this time in your life?

Cooper stared at the letters for a long moment, remembering a time when she had been Drew Milton's girlfriend. He had broken up with Cooper nearly a year ago and was engaged to Anna Lynne White now, but Cooper still missed being loved and cherished by a man. She missed making pancakes for Drew, reading the newspaper in their pajamas, and sharing a blanket as they cuddled on the sofa watching reality shows. She missed the smell of his cologne, the sight of his electric razor on the sink, and knowing that she was claimed by someone.

What are you seeking? Cooper asked her heart and then hastily scribbled: *I want to fall in love again. Really, God. I'm ready. I want myself a man.*

"Whoa! What happened to your face?" Jake the plumber exclaimed as Cooper entered the Hope Street Church Christian Academy classroom where her Bible study group gathered.

Cooper immediately reached up to touch the swath of red bumps covering the left side of her face and neck. The rash had almost kept her from coming to the meeting she had so looked forward to, but her desire to see her friends—Nathan in particular—had overwhelmed her embarrassment.

"It's poison ivy," she mumbled, her hand lingering on her itchy cheek. She had covered the area with clear Calamine lotion and had then applied a layer of foundation on top of that, hoping to camouflage the rash. Instead, she had created a kind of flesh-colored paste that cast a bright sheen beneath the morning light streaming through the classroom windows.

"I thought you were a gardener," Trish stated a trifle wryly and absently touched a strand of her shellacked copper hair. "I don't know anything about most plants, but when I schedule an open house I always check the yard for poison ivy the week before. There's nothing like toxic plants to turn off a potential buyer." She smirked. "Unless the grass is loaded with dog poop. That's even worse. Could you imagine roaming around your future dream home when, all of a sudden, the heel of one of your new patent leather pumps sinks into a pile of . . . ew!"

"You're still beautiful to me." Savannah, the legally blind folk artist and leader of their Bible study, reached out for Cooper's hand. "It's good to have you with us again, my dear."

Grateful for the gesture, Cooper squeezed her friend's hand in return. "What painting are you working on these days?" she asked Savannah.

"A scene of Noah gathering all of the animals," Savannah replied and began to re-braid her long, black hair as she spoke. "I'm using an old door as my canvas. Jake found it for me during a water heater installation. He said it was salvaged from a home destroyed by the downtown flooding we had several years ago. That's why I chose to paint an ark on it." She smiled in Jake's direction and his eyes glimmered with pleasure.

"So how *did* you end up getting that on your face?" Bryant Shelton, Richmond's best-known meteorologist, persisted.

"My grammy's taken in a stray cat. It's a longhair and I

was petting it the other night right after it came back from the woods. The oil from the plant must have been on its fur, and I had it on my fingers when I touched my face." Cooper resisted the urge to dig her nails through the prickly skin on her cheek and instead slid into a seat next to Quinton, who was furiously writing something on a yellow legal pad. "Are you writing a new song?" she inquired loudly, hoping that the questions about her grotesque rash would cease if she continued to change the subject.

Quinton, a wealthy, plus-sized investment banker with an aptitude for baking and penning the lyrics to praise songs, nodded. As he did so, his heavy cheeks shook slightly. "Something just came to me and I wanted to get it down before we start talking about Joseph."

"Speaking of faces," Trish said and Cooper held her breath, but the realtor turned a pair of violet eyes on Bryant. "I think I saw you and, was it your girlfriend, at the movies last week."

Bryant flushed. "You found out my dirty secret. I'm a Harry Potter fan. I've see all the movies on opening weekend."

Trish stared at Bryant with undisguised disapproval. "Your *date* appeared to be about the same age as our babysitter."

"Missy? She's a grad student. I met her here at church a few weeks ago," Bryant declared casually. "That's a better start than most of my relationships have had." In addition to his incredibly vague forecasts, Bryant was notorious for his series of failed marriages to similar-looking young blondes. Though he wasn't her type, Cooper could see why women were attracted to the handsome and charismatic meteorologist. Still, she knew that Bryant's Bible study friends were worried about him rushing into one more doomed marriage and often prayed for him to proceed with more caution before making promises to another young woman. So far, Bryant had avoided proposing, but he seemed to have a new girlfriend every month and showed no signs of being aware of what he wanted from a relationship other than fun.

"And does the future Mrs. Shelton know you're wearin' makeup?" Jake teased Bryant.

Shrugging nonchalantly, Bryant replied, "I get so used to applying a little foundation before going on the air that I just started putting it on every morning." He grinned, displaying his bleached veneers. "I think my pores look smaller when I use it."

"As long as you don't come in here with lipstick and purple eye shadow." Jake winked at his friend. "I might start hittin' on you then." Cooper laughed as Jake made kissing gestures with his lips, but before Bryant could respond to Jake's good-natured barb, Nathan Dexter walked into the room carrying a large, white bakery box.

Quinton forgot all about his song lyrics. "What did you bring us, Nathan?"

Carefully balancing the box, Nathan moved forward in his customary near-lurch. His enormous feet seemed to force him into ungainliness and his long body, coupled with a pair of wide shoulders, only increased the appearance of clumsiness. Nathan had a kind, open face, and though his forehead was too high and his chin too angular to produce a perfectly attractive visage, he was smart and generous and funny and Cooper felt her blood rush a little faster through her veins as he turned a sunny smile in her direction.

"What happened to you?" His tone was filled with concern as he noticed Cooper's splotchy skin.

"A cat gave her poison ivy," Trish answered before Cooper could reply. "What's in the box?"

"Well, since our fearless leader is here and looks ready to get started, I'll let her tell you." Nathan opened the lid beneath Savannah's highly sensitive nose.

"Are those strawberry cupcakes from The Mixing Bowl?" she asked as the Sunrise members clapped in delight.

Jake stared at her in awe. "Lady, I knew your nose was good, but I had no idea it was such a fine-tuned instrument."

"If someone will pour me a cup of coffee," Savannah said, "then the Lord can call me right up to heaven. Coffee, cupcakes with real pieces of strawberry in the icing, and my dearest friends gathered around me . . . Who could ask for more?" She smiled. "I can. My motto for this study is to pray big, my friends. Let's ask for a session this morning that will really wake up and *stir* our faith. Will you join hands with me?" Savannah gently commanded. "We'll begin with a prayer."

As Savannah prayed aloud, Cooper couldn't keep herself from stealing little glances at Nathan. *Does he think I look totally hideous?* she wondered fearfully and then chastised herself for not focusing on Savannah's words.

"Any announcements before we begin discussing the amazing, and sometimes not-quite-so-amazing, Joseph?" Savannah asked the group.

Trish raised her hand and a trio of thick gold bracelets clanked on her wrist. "Tyler Fine Properties will be sponsoring a Door-2-Door Dinners route for two months. It's a great program that serves a lot of needy people here in Richmond." She twirled her bracelets around, looking pleased. "Because of the sponsorship, *I* get a magnetic sign with my business logo placed on the delivery vehicles and a few *dozen* housebound people get home-cooked meals." She examined her stop-sign red nails. "The thing is, Door-2-Door could use more food packers and drivers. I was wondering if you all would be interested in helping out with some of the weekend preparation and deliveries."

Everyone nodded or murmured their willingness to help, though Cooper felt a bit anxious over the idea of carrying on conversations with a group of housebound strangers.

Trish glanced at her friends. "I know that visiting the elderly isn't everyone's forte. I'm good at it because I know how to talk to all kinds of people, but if anyone prefers not to do the deliveries, you can still make a difference by packing food at the distribution center instead."

"We might all be more comfortable volunteering in pairs," Nathan suggested as though he could sense Cooper's unease. "I know I would."

"It'd be a cinch to make fast friends of the elderly," Quinton mumbled through a mouthful of strawberry cupcake. He contentedly brushed crumbs from his expensive Italian suit and shifted in his chair. "Could you guys imagine what a treat it would be if we brought them some of these cupcakes? We'd be more popular than the Domino's guy showing up at a fraternity house with a truckload of pizzas."

"Door-2-Door delivers *healthy* foods to those in need," Trish stated acerbically.

Nathan had finished serving cupcakes to the group and settled into the chair next to Cooper. As he opened his workbook, she reached up to cup her bumpy red cheek with her hand and turned her face away from his.

Unobtrusively, Nathan leaned over her desk and whispered, "My sister is really allergic to poison ivy, too. Believe me, I've seen worse." He brushed the hand covering her rash with his fingertips and then took a sip from his coffee cup. "One time, she had such a bad case that I had to take her to the ER. Her face was all puffy and her eyes had swollen shut. She couldn't even open her mouth all the way. I had to cut up pieces of hot dog for her lunch and push them into her mouth with a toothpick." He grinned. "At least you can see and eat, right?"

Cooper smiled in return. "Besides," Nathan continued, his tone playful. "Your new ruddy complexion really compliments your blue eye."

Swatting at his elbow, Cooper realized that their flirtatious behavior was being watched with great interest by the rest of the Bible study members.

Savannah, who hadn't seen their display but could sense that the embarrassed silence meant that she should proceed, cleared her throat and placed her hand on her worn Bible. "Let's start our discussion, friends. It is my goal this session not to be late for worship service. Please help me stop by ten twenty-five so we can calmly make our way into the auditorium before the first song begins instead of racing down the hall and sneaking into seats in the back like a bunch of kids who've spent too long coming in from the playground." She opened her workbook. "Now, I don't know about you all, but I find Joseph fascinating! Who wants to talk about the first feature question— about parents playing favorites?"

"Well, Joseph was the son of Jacob and Rachel. Jacob loved Rachel more than any other woman on earth, so it's no surprise that Joseph was his favorite son," Trish stated. "I'm an only child and my parents were older, just like Jacob was when Joseph was born. I guess my parents felt like he did about *my* birth. They made me feel special every day, and I imagine that's how Joseph must have felt." Tears appeared in her eyes. "This lesson made me realize how good they were to me and just how much I miss them." She blotted at her eyes with a leopard-print handkerchief as Bryant squeezed her shoulder in compassion.

"I'm sure Joseph had very high self-esteem," Quinton murmured as though he was jealous of Joseph's self-confidence. "Though his brothers certainly resented him."

"In *my* family, we wouldn't call it *self-esteem*," Jake barked. "That Joseph kid was a brat—straight and simple—and Jacob was pretty much settin' the scene for the brothers to do somethin' about it! Shoot, if my pop had given me a fancy robe like Joseph got and I went around flauntin' it in front of my older brothers while they were workin' hard out in the hot sun all day—probably wearin' scratchy brown robes full of holes—they'd have given me a healthy beatin'!" Jake's face looked stormy. "Sorry, but that's just how I see it."

"And we welcome your opinion," Savannah said softly. "I have a sister. We're very close, but she often got frustrated with the amount of extra attention I received because of my blindness. One night, she told me that she had prayed to lose her sight so that our parents would notice her more."

"Whoa." Nathan looked at their leader with sympathy. "What happened?"

"Well, she didn't go blind!" Savannah laughed. "But, a few weeks after she told me about her prayer, she fell off a horse and broke her leg in three places. She got plenty of attention, all right, but said it wasn't worth lying up in bed for almost two months. Turned out, she preferred less attention to an infirmity any day, which is a good thing because she's a horse vet with a busy practice and she needs both her vision *and* her legs."

"Sounds like God answered her prayer, but in His own way," Quinton said. "He can certainly be creative at times."

"Yes, indeed, Quinton. Any other comments on favoritism?" Savannah asked as she stroked the worn cover of her Bible. When no one spoke, she said, "Then let's move on to Joseph's dreams. There was an assignment in this week's lesson that asked you to record your dreams and see if you could find any message in them." She looked up. "I can hardly ever remember mine. They just disappear like mist by the time I even sit up in bed, so I didn't have much to say. Anyone else?"

"I had a cool dream the other night," Bryant began eagerly. "I was a kid of about six or seven, and it was a really hot day, like that string of hundred-degree days we had this past July. I could hear the music that the ice cream truck plays, but I couldn't see the truck. I ran all around the neighborhood and couldn't find it. Then, this lady who works at the station with me—she's about my age, divorced, has two kids and isn't my type at all—pointed out where the truck was and I ordered my favorite kind of ice cream. An orange creamsicle." He sat back in his chair. "Didn't get to eat it, though. My alarm went off and that was that."

"Perhaps *someone* is trying to tell you that your coworker might be worth having as a friend," Trish suggested. "Even though she's probably ancient—what is she, thirty?"

Bryant was nonplussed by Trish's mocking tone. "Paige is almost maybe thirty-five. But she's funny and she comes up with great story ideas for the news desk. Maybe I'll take her and the kids out for ice cream. Missy, that grad student I've been seeing, and I haven't been getting along too well lately. It might be nice to go out with a woman and do something quiet."

"There's nothing quiet about two kids," Quinton remarked. "You should spend some time with my nephews. They can make more noise than a jungle teeming with animals," he added proudly.

"I know, but that kind of noise won't hurt my ears like that techno music Missy likes," Bryant answered, wiggling his left earlobe. "My head is still ringing from taking her dancing last night. If I asked the woman from work out, I could be in bed by ten!"

"Maybe then you wouldn't need to wear all that foundation," Cooper teased and Bryant balled up his napkin and tossed it at her.

Nathan got up to refill his empty cup and as he was stirring cream into the dark, rich coffee he said, "I've had a recurring dream that's kind of creepy. No slashers or monsters or anything, just that someone is knocking on the back door of my house and I can't decide whether to let them in."

"Can you see their face?" Savannah asked.

"No. Just a dark shape out in the night repeatedly knocking on my door." He stared at his coffee cup, tracing the gilt *Hope Street* letters with his index finger. "I sense the person's a man, though. And I don't fear *him* exactly, I just don't know if I want to invite him into my home."

"If you're hesitating, you probably don't want him

around," Quinton said. "Is there anything going on with your work? A project or new client that's worrying you?"

Nathan snapped his fingers. "There is! You're so intuitive, Quinton! There's this guy who wants me to design a website for him—a commercial one where people can buy muscle-building vitamins. I guess he's made a nice pile of money as a chemist, because he drives a yellow H2, has one of those fancy gold watches, and a serious golf tan." He flicked his eyes at Bryant. "He even out-bronzes you, my friend."

Bryant pretended to be crestfallen. "First George Hamilton and now a chemist. Shocking."

"So this is a big project for you?" Savannah inquired and Nathan nodded.

"Sounds lucrative, too," Trish added.

"It sure would be," Nathan agreed. "He wants top-notch graphics, a flash video on the home page, shopping-cart features, you name it. And since my older-than-dirt A/C and heater units are on the fritz, I could sure use the cash."

Jake perked up at the mention of the units. "You're gonna call Mr. Faucet to replace 'em, right? You know we're doin' that stuff now besides the regular plumbin' jobs."

Nathan smiled. "I wouldn't think of calling anyone else, Jake, but unless I accept this project, I won't be able to shell out seven grand for new units just like that." He shrugged. "It sounds like a treasure chest has just fallen in my lap, but I just have a funny feeling about this guy."

"Why don't you try to get to know him?" Quinton recommended. "Take him out for coffee and see what your gut tells you. I don't think it's right for us to judge others on their appearance. Listen to the man talk. He might surprise you."

Nathan nodded. "That's good counsel."

"I agree with Quinton." Savannah placed both hands over her Bible. "Deuteronomy chapter one, verse seventeen says, 'Do not show partiality in judging; hear both small and great alike. Do not be afraid of any man, for judgment belongs to God.'" She smiled at Nathan. "Let Him be your guide."

The Sunrise group members murmured in agreement and then closed their workbooks as the chimes announcing the commencement of the worship service echoed into the classroom.

"Oh, good! We're going to be on time!" Trish exclaimed.

"I'll take everyone's cups to the kitchen," Cooper volunteered, wanting to be alone with her thoughts for a moment. "Would someone save me a seat in a dark corner?"

"Nah. We're going to put you front and center," Nathan teased with a smile.

"I think we should volunteer her to sing with the band," Jake called over his shoulder as he sauntered out the door.

"You'd better not!" Cooper yelled back, but the room was already empty.

Gathering napkins for the garbage, Cooper piled the empty cups and coffee carafe on a tray and carried them into a small kitchen area used by the academy teachers. She washed the cups with careful deliberation, her hands enjoying the feel of the warm water and the lemon scent of the dish soap. As she rinsed the last cup, her dream from the night before came back to her with vivid clarity.

In the dream, Cooper had been heading for the banks of Gum Creek, the stream that wound lazily through the woods far behind her house before meandering westward into Louisa County. She'd been barefoot and had continuously stepped on the prickly gumballs that fell like small bombs from the leafy canopy above. Finally, after picking her way over twigs, sharp pebbles, and scratchy plants, Cooper reached the narrow creek.

A rowboat sat expectantly in the placid water, as though awaiting her, but when she reached down to grab its side, it shifted sideways and was caught up by the slow current of the stream. Within seconds, it was out of reach, floating away from her. Longing to reclaim the little vessel, Cooper moved alongside it on the bank, but the current kept racing faster and faster, bearing the boat further and further away, and she couldn't keep up.

Suddenly, the space of sky above the stream where the boat was heading turned dark and a fork of lightning fractured the clouds just above the horizon. Cooper's dream self halted, afraid. And then, in a blink, she was *in* the boat, barreling straight for the storm. There was no rain—just black clouds, jagged lightning, and an eerie silence. Again and again, Cooper reached out and tried to grab onto the plants growing on the creek banks, but they slipped from her grasp as though made of fog.

Cooper had woken abruptly, her body trembling with dread. Even in the comfort of the morning light, she could still smell the scent of rain. And when she stood in the shower and closed her eyes, she could see the black horizon and the tongues of lightning, waiting for her imminent arrival.

Placing the last cup on a drying rack, Cooper exhaled, trying to calm the drumming of her heart as she recalled the feelings of fear instigated by her dream.

"Lord, are you trying to tell me to prepare for a difficult

time?" she asked into the silence of the kitchen. "Tell me please, so I won't be taken by surprise."

She stared at the last drips of water as they slipped into the drain and then shut her eyes. Alone, in the stillness of the small room, Cooper strained to listen. An answer came then, as though whispered into her inner ear. *Prepare yourself. Hardship is coming.*

3

He humbled you, causing you to hunger and then feeding you with manna, which neither you nor your fathers had known, to teach you that man does not live on bread alone but on every word that comes from the mouth of the LORD.

Deuteronomy 8:3 (NIV)

Cooper opened the cupboard in her tiny kitchen and inspected its contents. She had twenty minutes to cook and eat something for breakfast, but she had forgotten to restock bananas as well as maple and brown sugar oatmeal from Food Lion after work yesterday. She was also fresh out of eggs and Honey Bunches of Oats. Luckily, her mother lived mere yards away and was likely to have some leftover breakfast available for her oldest child.

Closing the door to her apartment, which was located above her parents' detached garage, Cooper walked over the flagstone patio toward the back door of the Lees' cozy, one-story house. She noted that the herbs in her mother's container garden just outside the kitchen were starting to look tired. The rosemary was leggy, the basil was stringy with brown-pocked leaves, and the oregano still seemed parched, even though it was clear that it had been recently watered.

"The end of summer," Cooper remarked to Columbus, their caged hawk. Columbus blinked his eyes lazily at her. "You must be full because you're not giving me your special 'let's go hunting' look. Daddy must have taken you for an early walk, huh?"

The red-tailed raptor turned his head away as though bored by Cooper's presence. "You must have found a nice, fat field mouse to be giving me such a cold shoulder." Cooper smoothed down the silky feathers on the back of the hawk's neck and then moved away from the aloof bird, who had become a member of the family two years ago. Columbus's wing had been fractured by a bullet while he was roosting at one of the county airports. The hawk's assailant was never found, but the heartless attack on the majestic bird had been written up in *Richmond Times-Dispatch*. Within minutes of reading the story, Grammy was on the phone to the authorities at the airport, demanding that they allow her to adopt the injured bird.

"Earl," Grammy had said upon replacing the receiver, "you gotta build me an aviary. And I mean right quick."

Cooper's father, Earl, was Grammy's only child. He was a gentle, taciturn man who rarely denied his mother anything. When she wanted to live in his den instead of a retirement community, he agreed. When she wanted to go to bingo on Wednesday nights, he drove her and waited in the car until she was done. When she attracted every stray dog, cat, or turtle as well as all the injured birds, rabbits, and baby squirrels into their rural home, Earl simply sighed and drove to Wal-Mart with a list of the supplies his mother needed in order to nurture and heal each animal.

Grammy's current menagerie of wounded creatures included a cat blind in one eye, a Canadian goose that had nearly been strangled by one of the plastic rings from a six-pack holder, and a motherless fox cub that had quickly become addicted to scraps from the Lee dinner table. The only animals ever to become permanent members of the family were Columbus and an enormous, tetchy, and tailless orange tomcat called Little Boy.

The injured animals were only given temporary haven with the Lees as Grammy intended for them to either return to their natural habitats or be adopted by local families. In order to avoid becoming too attached to her dependents, Grammy never gave names to the animals she cared for. Naturally, the rest of the Lee family applauded her knack for attracting all creatures great and small. The only time Earl ever commented on the furry, feathered, and scaled friends gathered in his yard was when Grammy fed the fox cub her son's serving of crisp bacon.

"I'll tolerate everythin' but the givin' away of my bacon," he announced at the table as Grammy sheepishly wiped her greasy hands on a paper napkin. Since then, the fox cub had to make do with less sumptuous fair such as chicken thighs or portions of fat trimmed from Maggie's rump roast.

There was no sign of the fox cub as Cooper entered the kitchen that morning and, though she could smell cookies baking, no scent of Earl's bacon lingered in the air.

"'Mornin', my girl," Maggie Lee greeted Cooper while removing a tray of round cookies from the oven. "You on the prowl for some breakfast?" she asked as she placed the tray on a wire cooling rack.

Grammy looked up from her *Reader's Digest* and pointed her thick magnifying glass at her granddaughter. "You see Columbus? He's lookin' mighty pleased with himself."

Cooper sat across from Grammy and smiled. "He fluffed his feathers and looked at me like I was chopped liver."

"He woulda looked at you with a whole lot of interest if you *were* a slab of liver," Grammy countered.

"Good point. Then he made me feel like a piece of broccoli." Cooper reached for the word-scramble puzzle book Earl routinely kept at the center of the table. "What'd he catch this morning?"

"A rabbit the size of a Thanksgivin' turkey," Grammy replied with a proud cackle. "Not bad for a bird that can barely get high enough in the sky to make a real dive."

"He must've killed hundreds of pigeons when he lived at the airport," Cooper remarked.

"Their best hunter. Not a doubt in my mind." Grammy picked up her magnifying glass and shook it angrily. "Whoever shot him will have to face judgment one day, along with all folks who are wicked to God's innocent creatures!"

"There, there." Maggie put a soothing hand on Grammy's bony shoulder. "Would you like to sample one of today's bakin' mistakes, Ma?"

The wrath in Grammy's hazel eyes drained away immediately. "What kind've you got?"

"Iced lemon cookies," Maggie replied, placing several chipped cookies in front of Grammy. As Grammy began to eat, Maggie returned with two slices of raisin bread coated with a generous layer of cream cheese and a cluster of plump, green grapes.

"Thanks, Mama." Cooper squeezed her mother's flour-and sugar-dusted hand. "This is much better than anything I'd have dug up at my place."

"You'd best fine-tune your cookin' skills, girlie," Grammy

stated, her mouth stuffed with cookie. "You gotta get that boy from your Bible study on the line and reel him in. Best way to do that is to feed him and make him dream of more meals to come."

Cooper's neck turned pink, a telltale sign that she was embarrassed. She put a hand over the heated skin and looked at her mother, who was sliding the cooled cookies onto a large sheet of waxed paper.

"What else are you bringing to the sandwich shops today?"

"The regular stuff," Maggie answered. "Chocolate chip, oatmeal raisin, and some white macadamia nut, but I figured some folks would prefer a lighter cookie, so I'm adding the lemon. It might be the end of August, but the air still feels like the inside of a fryin' pan to me."

As Cooper ate, she watched her mother slide two chocolate chip cookies into a plastic bag decorated with a *Magnolia's Marvels* gold foil sticker. She then tied the bag with a thin, gold ribbon and placed it into her delivery basket. Maggie hummed as she worked, and though she rose before dawn every morning to bake the gourmet cookies that were purchased by several cafés around Richmond, she looked as fresh, red-cheeked, and round as one of the McIntosh apples on the windowsill.

Cooper finished her breakfast and brought her dishes to the sink, but her mother waved her off before Cooper could even turn on the tap. "Go on, honey. I know you gotta get to work and you *know* I've got a system for everything that goes on in this kitchen."

"Yes, Mama." Cooper kissed her mother's cheek, which smelled like milk chocolate and cinnamon.

"You gonna see that Nathan boy this weekend?" Grammy asked before Cooper could get out the door.

Cooper hesitated. "Not on a date or anything. We're volunteering together at Door-2-Door Dinners on Saturday."

"Oh, how nice!" Maggie exclaimed, removing another batch of lemon cookies from the oven.

Grammy tossed her magnifying glass down in disgust, her wrinkled face creasing further as she frowned. "You callin' that 'nice'?" she argued. "Ain't nothin' like a bunch of cranky old folks to douse the heat risin' between a man and a woman." She fluffed her sparse hair, which had been recently been given a loose-curled permanent in order to appear thicker. Cooper thought her Grammy's white locks now resembled a cumulus cloud and tried not to grin as her grandmother dispensed advice with a wiggle of her gnarled finger.

"You listen to me, granddaughter. I've been around for near eighty years now and I know a thing or two. If you're gonna run around town deliverin' food to old coots, fine. But afterward, you make sure you go eat somewhere with that Nathan. Someplace filled with young folks in the prime of their lives. Last time I checked, you were thirty two years old and livin' with your parents. If you wanna change that, then change yourself." She pulled out a catalog from beneath her pile of newspaper pages. "I've been savin' this for you. Thought it might give you some ideas."

Cooper accepted the catalog without looking at it, kissed Grammy's forehead, which felt a bit like Maggie's parchment paper, and headed out to Cherry-O. Inside the cab, she took a quick glimpse at the catalog Grammy had given her before turning on the engine.

The cover portrayed a woman with impossibly long and perfectly tanned legs leaning against an open window as a pair of sheer white curtains lifted in the breeze. Her arms were raised gracefully above her head and her hips were cocked to one side, as though she were about to sit down in a chair. Her sun-kissed hair flowed over a pair of narrow shoulders and barely covered the black ruffles of her lacy bra. Her panties were made of the same black lace, and were so miniscule that they failed to cover most of the seductive curves of the woman's smooth, round buttocks.

Feeling her neck grow warm again, Cooper dialed up the air conditioning and tossed the catalog onto the floor in front of the passenger seat. "Only *my* grandmother would give me a copy of *Victoria's Secret*," she muttered.

When she pulled into the Make It Work! parking lot, Cooper decided to shred the catalog using the machine kept in the break room, so she stuffed it into her workbag and, after greeting a daydreaming Angela, headed into the locker room to change into her uniform shirt. Both male and female employees shared the locker room, so Cooper always changed her clothes inside one of the bathroom stalls. As she busied herself transferring the silver butterfly pin her grandmother had given her from her T-shirt to her uniform shirt, Emilio strutted into the locker room.

Without bothering to see whether anyone else was present, Emilio peeled off a dingy white T-shirt that emphasized his developed pectoral muscles. After taking an appreciative sniff of the scent of his cologne trapped within the cotton fibers, Emilio hurled the T-shirt into an open locker. He then stood, bare-chested, and, after rubbing his hands up and down his six-pack abs, decided to examine the contents of Cooper's workbag.

"Lunch, books, pens. Boring," he mumbled to himself and then came across the *Victoria's Secret* catalog.

Flipping through the pages, his eyes grew bright. "Whoa! Now we're talkin'." He nodded in appreciation over the photographs of sexy women in skimpy lingerie.

"Cooper, you little minx," he murmured in pleasant surprise as he pushed the catalog back into her bag. "Kinda makes me wonder what *you're* wearing underneath your uniform." He looked at himself in the mirror hanging from the inside of his locker door. "Look out," he announced smugly to his reflection, licking his full, sensuous lips in anticipation. "Emilio's on the prowl."

After an uneventful week of repairing seven copiers, four fax machines, and two laminators, Cooper was ready to socialize with her Bible study friends. They had helped her finally get over her breakup with Drew by offering comfort, advice, and prayer. Not only that, but they had solved a murder together, and that experience had strengthened their bond to the point where they trusted each another absolutely.

In addition to the Sunrise members, Cooper's closest confidante was Angela. Lately, however, the perky secretary seemed completely absorbed in attracting the attention of their hunky new coworker. Even her customary flirtation with Mr. Farmer had waned, and Cooper worried that Angela might genuinely be interested in Emilio.

"He's all right," Cooper had responded after Angela spent their entire lunch hour singing Emilio's praises. "But he acts a bit vain, don't you think?"

"He's just young and sure-footed," Angela had replied in Emilio's defense and reapplied a fresh coat of cherry-red lipstick. "He's asked me a few questions about *you*," she said with a hint of crabbiness. "If you were single, for instance."

"What did you tell him?" Cooper couldn't hide her surprise.

"The truth," Angela had shrugged. "That you had a crush on someone but things were progressin' mighty slow. That all y'all had done was kiss each other—and with every stitch of your clothes on, too."

Cooper's cheeks had flamed. "Angela! I don't want everybody knowing about my life outside of work! Don't talk about things I tell you in confidence to anyone in this office!" She felt bad about snapping at her friend, but she also didn't like that Angela had been acting like a different person since Emilio joined their small crew. Cooper secretly wished Mr. Farmer had hired someone a little less attractive. Maybe then, the family-like atmosphere that had existed at the office could have stayed the same. With Emilio, however, Cooper sensed impending trouble.

Shaking away negative thoughts of her coworkers, Cooper met her fellow Sunrise Bible study members on the front steps of the downtown headquarters of Door-2-Door Dinners. The squat, concrete building was teeming with activity. People streamed in and out of the double set of front doors, large trucks pulled up to the back of the building to deliver supplies, and meals were being loaded into an assortment of vehicles lined up along the entire western side of the building. Cooper looked around nervously. She wasn't accustomed to such a hubbub and wanted to locate a familiar face.

"You look like you're about to jump out of a plane," Jake said with a laugh as he joined her on the stairs. "I wasn't always a big people person, either, but in my line of work, I've learned how to deal with all kinds of folks. All ya gotta do is smile at them and you'll be okay."

Cooper couldn't imagine having to work in people's

homes like Jake did. "At my job, folks don't talk to me much once they've shown me which machine needs fixing," Cooper said. "A lot of the offices where I work seem to encourage anonymity. I'm surrounded by people who sit within two feet of each other, but are all talking on the phone to someone else."

"You're lucky that you can cruise under the radar!" Jake snorted. "Me? I get dozens of bored women who want to tell me their life stories. If it's not the ladies, then it's a bunch of soft-handed men that want me to show them exactly how I do the repair like I'm some kind of home-project TV show host or somethin'. And if it ain't the house or business owners hangin' around, then I get the family pets all over me instead. Fido and Fluffy just *love* to smell me in all sorts of embarrassin' places just when I've got my head wedged in a dark, skinny cabinet under the bathroom sink."

Cooper tried to shake off an image of Jake's pants falling down as he bent his body in two, but he caught the look on her face and shook his pointer finger at her. "I know what you're thinkin', but no one sees my butt. I make sure my belt is *real* tight before I bend over, you got that?"

From behind them, they heard Savannah's clear laugh. "Housewives, husbands, and dogs watching your every move while you fight against the stereotype about plumbers and their descending pants." She chuckled and shook her head, her long braid swinging like a pendulum down her back. "No wonder you were a smoker, Jake!"

Jake's dark eyes twinkled as he looked at Savannah, who held onto Quinton's arm. "I'm not in the clear yet," he admitted. "I still gotta wear these patches—'specially if it's been a rough day."

"I eat sweets when I'm grumpy," Savannah confessed. "I might be blind, but I can find my way to a cookie jar or my secret stash of candy bars like nobody's business."

"You and me both." Quinton shook his head in agreement.

Jake took Savannah's free arm. "Well, maybe you two will get lucky and I'll treat you to an ice cream after our hard day of work."

"But I'm not even driving or loading," Savannah protested. "I'm just going along to talk to folks. You can hardly call that work."

"Sometimes that's what our clients long for the most," a female voice said from the top of the stairs. A beautiful woman with lustrous locks of black hair and green eyes the shade of peridots smiled at them. "Are you here for the volunteer orientation?"

At that moment, Nathan appeared around the corner of the building with Trish and Bryant in tow.

"We're here!" Trish called out and then noticed the lovely woman with the nutmeg-colored skin standing at the threshold. "Hello! I'm Trish Tyler of Tyler Fine Properties, formerly Tyler Realty. My company is sponsoring a route for two months."

"Yes, of course. I'm Lali Gupta, the volunteer coordinator." The two women shook hands warmly. "Won't you all please follow me inside? There's a buffet table in our gathering room with coffee and cookies if you'd like to get a snack before we begin."

The group silently fell into step behind Lali. She led them to a large room filled with rows of folding chairs and asked them to have a seat. Even though she had already consumed two mugs of coffee at home, Cooper helped herself to a large Styrofoam cup, filled it with dark coffee and powdered cream, and gazed around at the other volunteers.

She was surprised at the diverse spectrum of age, economic status, and race within the room. It seemed like a representative of every walk of life in the city of Richmond had chosen to volunteer for Door-2-Door Dinners that Saturday. It touched Cooper's heart to see a wealthy white woman draped in expensive jewelry sharing a laugh with a young African-American man wearing a shirt that was covered in paint splatters and riddled with small holes, an elderly man wielding a cane and wearing a brown fedora whispering to a young woman with Down syndrome, and a trio of older ladies talking in fast-paced, excited sentences to a pair of middle-aged Hispanic men.

"I can't believe how many people come out to volunteer," Nathan commented from his seat next to Cooper's. "It feels good just to sit here. Makes you realize that there's a lot of kindness where we live."

"That's true." Cooper gestured at the wall behind them and took a sip of coffee. "I also like the photographs."

Nathan nodded in agreement, taking a few minutes to gaze at the oversized black-and-white portraits of some of the elderly Door-2-Door Dinners clients. The portraits were headshots, and in each one, the subject stared directly at the camera. Each expression was different. Some of the men and women seemed happy and even smiled a little. Others were somber or deeply sad, but an elderly African-American lady was laughing with her mouth open, her wrinkles spread out in a fanlike pattern as she displayed her four remaining teeth. The one that Cooper kept returning to was of an emaciated old man who rested a sunken cheek against his palm as though he was too weary to hold his head up without the help of his hand.

He refused to return the camera's stare and instead, gazed into the distance. His skin seemed stretched across his gaunt face and his pale eyes were tinged with an anguish that made Cooper want to reach out to him.

Beside her, Nathan swallowed hard and nodded toward the man's portrait. "I lost all four of my grandparents in the space of two years. None of these people look like them, but these pictures remind me of how much I miss them."

Cooper turned to him, but Nathan had averted his eyes. "Remember how we visited Eliza last year? At first, she was just a shut-in and a stranger, but she became one of our friends." She touched his hand lightly. "I bet we make new friends here as well."

"You're right," Nathan said with a sigh. "I'm just not the greatest at dealing with new situations, but I'm glad Trish got us involved. At least I get to spend more time with you." He pivoted toward her, his brown eyes eager. Cooper lowered her coffee cup as though she might suddenly lose control of her fingers and drop it. Her heart drummed faster as Nathan draped his arm around the back of her chair. "I've been so wrapped up with this demanding client that I haven't had time to do anything fun. I feel like I've kept you on hold and you deserve better than that." His hand brushed her left shoulder. "How about, after we're done here, we—?"

"Welcome, friends." Lali Gupta spoke in a clear, mellifluous voice from the front of the room and Cooper reluctantly turned toward her. "Thank you for coming to our volunteer orientation. Door-2-Door could not succeed without consistent help from generous members of the community such as you. You will become one of over two thousand people who package, load, and deliver meals to our clients. Last year alone, we delivered over two hundred and fifty thousand meals throughout the city of Richmond and its environs and I think we'll top that number this year."

A few of the volunteers tittered among themselves over the staggering number of meals delivered each day. Cooper stared at the photographs again and finished drinking her coffee.

"It just goes to show you," someone mumbled amiably. "Nobody likes to cook anymore."

"In addition to our elderly clients," Lali continued, "we also serve younger adults with disabilities and community members who have recently been discharged from the hospital and only require our services on a temporary basis. Those of you who have elected to adopt a route," she nodded in Trish's direction, "will get to know a handful of our clients on a personal level. This can be an extremely rewarding experience."

A giant of a man appeared through a doorway on Lali's left. His black T-shirt, which was decorated with an iron-on of a wolf riding a motorcycle, was stretched over his skin so tightly that it seemed to be digging into the flesh of his thick arms and neck. He wore pants with an elastic waist, undoubtedly because regular pants couldn't handle the circumference of his meaty legs. His huge feet, which were even bigger than Nathan's, were encased in construction boots and he had grown out his brown goatee long enough to fasten into a two-inch braid. The end of the braid was held by a pink rubber band. Cooper was intrigued by the man's appearance.

Noticing the burly biker out of the corner of her eye, Lali beckoned for him to join her. "Meet Campbell Perkins. The kitchen is his domain." She smiled at him fondly. "He's going to review how to load and label the prepackaged meals and go over any questions or concerns you might have about how long to spend at each stop, what to do if a client seems unwell, or any other issue of concern to you, our volunteers. It is our goal to do whatever we can to make our clients *and* our volunteers happy."

She touched Campbell on his upper arm, which was as thick and powerful as the body of an anaconda, and bowed her head. "Again, thank you for being here today. Your gift of time, and of costly gas, will fill the hungry stomachs of our neighbors. More importantly, your friendly faces will light up what might have been a lonely day for our clients. Bless you all."

As Lali walked away, Campbell cleared his throat and began his lecture on packing food into the red-and-white-checked Door-2-Door soft cooler bags. His posture and tone were reminiscent of an army drill sergeant training a fresh battalion of recruits.

"First!" he barked. "You must label *every single* thing that you pack with your client's name. You don't want to give a vegetarian client a hunk of meatloaf and you don't want to give a diabetic client the meal that comes with cranberry sauce, baked apples, and chocolate mousse with whipped cream. Got it?"

The volunteers nodded meekly, silently wondering how the brawny young man had come to find employment with Door-2-Door. As Campbell held up some examples of properly labeled meals for the crowd to see, Cooper felt an uncomfortable tightness in her bladder. Glancing at the sixteen-ounce cup she had just finished, she tried to ignore the call of nature and focus on Campbell's instructions. However, when he began to discuss the types of liquids the clients were served, absently jiggling a full liter bottle of spring water as he talked, a small groan emanated from between Cooper's clenched lips.

"Be right back," she whispered urgently to Nathan and then left the room by the door they had entered. Returning to the main hall, her eyes darted around in search of a sign indicating that one of the many closed brown doors concealed a restroom. As they all looked the same, Cooper began to open the doors. One revealed a closet, another was locked, and the third led to a new hallway.

Something about the sudden stillness in the hallway caused Cooper to momentarily pause, as though she might be intruding into an area not open to the public, but the mere sight of the water fountain a few feet ahead urged her onward. Finally, she found a door bearing the placard of a woman's outline. Cooper practically ripped the door handle off in relief, only to discover that it wouldn't turn at all. It was locked and therefore already occupied.

"Arrggh," she moaned and continued her quest until she ended up at a stairwell. Praying that the ladies' room on the second floor was vacant, Cooper took the stairs two at a time and found a restroom a few doors down from the stairway. All four stalls were empty and, out of habit, she chose the stall furthest from the door.

Cooper's good fortune in finding a bathroom was quickly forgotten as she reached for the toilet paper; only a shredded square remained on the roll. *This would do if I were a Lilliputian,* Cooper thought wryly and opened her canvas purse, hoping to find some clean tissues inside.

As she rummaged around, relieved to find a squashed

package of travel tissues wedged in between the pages of her checkbook, the bathroom door opened and two women engaged in a whispered conversation entered.

"Not again!" exclaimed a voice that sounded like Lali's.

"Mrs. Jensen's daughter called. She said her mother's gold and diamond necklace is gone. It was the most valuable thing in the house."

"Is she sure?" Lali sounded desperate for the information to be incorrect.

"Positive," the other woman answered. "Mrs. Jensen kept it hidden inside a box of Ritz crackers. According to the daughter, the necklace has been there for over ten years. The daughter cleans it whenever she visits and Mrs. Jensen tries it on in front of a mirror. It's one of their regular routines. Lali, both of them are really upset."

"What is going on, Anita? This is the fourth call about missing items this summer!" Lali's voice trembled. "Nothing like this has ever happened to our clients before."

There was a pause and Cooper was afraid to move. If she made a sound now, it would be obvious that she had listened to the entire exchange, so she raised her feet off the ground and tried to be as inert as possible, praying for forgiveness for her subterfuge.

"It's not necessarily one of our volunteers, Lali. Yes, we've got people bringing those clients meals every day, but that doesn't mean that one of them is a thief. It's just a coincidence that the folks missing things are all clients of ours."

Lali sighed. "We bring them meals, fix things around the house, do yard work, light cleaning, and deliver pet food as well. Come on, Anita. None of the clients who have noticed things disappearing from their homes have anything else in common besides us. Door-2-Door is the only common denominator, so that means *someone* from this organization is stealing from our clients."

"But that's unthinkable!" Anita couldn't contain her anger and forgot to whisper. Her voice reverberated off the bathroom tiles and, after being shushed by Lali, she immediately softened her tone. "To steal from the old and the infirm! Who would do that?"

"They're easy targets," Lali replied, sounding sorrowful but unsurprised. "*I* can't picture a single member of our regular volunteer group doing *anything* cruel. I've seen all of their faces—have come to know personal things about most of them, but I guess we don't know enough. *Someone* is hiding their true character from all of us."

One of the women turned on the water in the sink and then quickly turned it off again. "I'd better clean these glasses," Anita remarked with ire. "From now on, I'm going to make it my job to keep both my eyes on all the volunteers over the next few weeks. I'm going to chat with them until I know them better and I'm going to watch them like a hawk. We can't let anything else get stolen!"

"I appreciate your help, Anita, but what about your other responsibilities?" Lali asked. "No one can get to know *all* of our volunteers. We operate on trust here."

Cooper heard the sound of a paper towel being balled up and tossed into the trashcan. "My other tasks can wait. I've got to figure out which one of our volunteers is the thief. I can't have this program's reputation tarnished because of one wicked individual. Somehow, I'll think of a way to flush the snake from the grass."

"I hope so," Lali agreed without sounding very optimistic. "I don't want our clients to suffer."

The women stopped talking and left the restroom. Cooper washed her hands and hurriedly followed suit.

As she headed back downstairs to rejoin her friends, she wondered whether to mention the thievery to them. After all, she was not meant to have heard the conversation between Lali and Anita. On the other hand, she knew that if the Sunrise members became aware that one of their fellow volunteers was an immoral scoundrel, they would do their best to uncover the mystery surrounding the thefts.

Guide me on this one, Lord, Cooper prayed silently. *If we can do some good, have me tell them. If we're going to make things worse, then I'll just stay quiet.* Cooper waited for a moment, but no inner voice spoke to her, so she hastily added, *You can get back to me on this one, Lord. I'll be listening for your answer.*

4

Then the LORD said to Cain, "Why are you angry? Why is your face downcast?"

Genesis 4:6 (NIV)

The Sunrise Bible study members spent the remainder of the morning learning how to properly load coolers with prepackaged client meals. As the Door-2-Door Dinners facility was closed on Sunday, many clients received food boxes in addition to their regular Saturday meals to help see them through the twenty-four-hour stretch when no meals would be delivered to their homes.

Because she had never volunteered there before, Cooper was paired with an older woman named Penny. Penny, who had dove-gray eyes and an open, gentle face, showed Cooper how to check the shrink-wrapped trays for holes in the plastic, how to pack the food in order, and the proper technique for stacking the coolers onto wheeled carts so they could be delivered to the volunteers waiting outside in their cars.

"Checking for holes and making sure that nobody will miss a meal are the most important things," Penny explained as she gestured at one of the trays. "If Mr. Joseph here is going to be having fish for dinner tonight, we don't want it to start rotting before he can get it in his fridge. Most of us drive routes when we're done with our packing, so we've gotten to know all the names listed on these labels." She showed Cooper the name and route numbers located on each meal.

Nodding, Cooper glanced at Penny as they worked, thinking that the soft-voiced woman seemed so intent on getting things perfect for the Door-2-Door clients that she simply couldn't visualize the older volunteer pocketing jewelry or other valuables from one of their houses.

Looking around the kitchen, which was spotlessly clean and perfectly organized, Cooper studied the other volunteers. According to Campbell, there were seven "regulars" who showed up every Saturday morning. In fact, Campbell stated with pride as he pulled on his braided beard, "The 'Super Seven' haven't missed a single Saturday in a year's time."

The Super Seven were made up of four women and three men, all of whom moved about their tasks with chipper efficiency. Not one of them had shifty eyes, a nervous stare, or the guilty visage of a heartless villain. They were completely normal people. If anything set them apart, it was their willingness to give up fifty-two Saturday mornings in order to load and deliver meals to those in need.

Cooper zipped up one of the coolers for Route #4 and then took a moment to look around the kitchen. She watched Erik, an attractive man in his mid-sixties, slide a crayon into Savannah's hand so that the artist could decorate a few of the plain cardboard food boxes as the others busily packed. Nathan was paired with a woman near Penny's age and he seemed to be charming her with his quiet ways and sincere manner, for the two of them were muttering to one another and laughing as though they were old friends.

One of the younger male volunteers, who was very short in stature and had Down syndrome, was partnered with Jake.

"I'm Eugene!" the young man announced to Jake. Jake shook hands and smiled as Eugene proceeded to tell him all about the action movie he had seen on TV the night before. Jake listened patiently for several minutes and then kindly redirected his boisterous partner back to the job at hand. Each time he and Eugene were finished prepping coolers for a route, Jake had to roll up his sleeve and allow Eugene to touch the Celtic cross tattoo on his sinewy bicep before the young man would consent to return to work again.

On the opposite side of the kitchen, Bryant was busy flashing his famous meteorologist smile at both of the woman assisting him. One was a large African-American woman named Brenda who shouted and guffawed in response to everything Bryant said. The other woman, who seemed content to stand in Brenda's shadow, was a timid, mousy, middle-aged woman whose nametag read "Madge." Cooper didn't hear Madge utter a word all morning, but the plain-faced volunteer seemed to glow whenever Bryant paid attention to her.

Trish and Quinton were being mentored by Warren, a thin, rather nondescript man in his mid-forties with a blondish beard and weary-looking eyes. Cooper couldn't hear Warren's quiet instructions, but from the look on his face, he clearly took his job seriously. Though he smiled from time to time, it was evident that Warren didn't want any mistakes to occur with the routes he and the new volunteers were packing. Trish still did her best to impress her teacher by mentioning more than once that her company was sponsoring the food for an entire route for two months. When Warren didn't seem overly dazzled, she began to ask him if he was happy with his current residence.

"You're always a saleswoman, aren't you?" Quinton gently teased as they loaded two sets of coolers onto wheeled carts.

"Yes, I am!" Trish declared. "If you want to be the best at something, you've got to work at it every minute of the day. Take your song lyrics, for example."

A blush immediately appeared on Quinton's doughy cheeks. He was still shy regarding the subject of the praise songs he had been writing over the past year, preferring to show them only to Cooper, for she was the first person to compliment his lyrics.

"If you ever want to get paid for those songs or hear them sung by a band, then you've got to get yourself a music agent. You need to write letters and bang on doors and get in people's faces. In an entirely professional manner, of course," she added.

Quinton shrugged. "I'm not sure if the songs are ready for an agent to see."

"*They're* not ready or *you're* not ready for the feedback?" Trish demanded. "How many have you written by this point? How many have you allowed other people to read?" she continued doggedly. "How will you ever—?"

"LADY!" a deep voice roared, interrupting Trish's barrage of questions. "Lay off the man, for cryin' out loud. It's too damn early for all that naggin'. What are you, his mama?"

The kitchen fell silent as the new arrival dropped a black bag onto the counter with a loud thud. Without greeting anyone, he grabbed one of the empty food trays and slung it onto a stack of other empty trays and then began to pack one of the larger coolers.

Cooper scrutinized him out of the corner of her blue eye. He was of average height but his hunched shoulders made him seem shorter than he really was, and every muscle in his body seemed tense with anger. His dark hair was cut close to the scalp and his eyes were deep brown with large, black pupils. The skin of his entire right arm, which was the shade of roasted pecans, was covered by an intricate tattoo. It took a moment for Cooper to see that the colored shapes curving up his forearm to his shoulder portrayed a panther locked in combat with a cobra. The panther's mouth was open in a fierce snarl and its claws were unsheathed into deadly points. The cobra's fangs dripped venom and its eyes were blood-red as it reared back a hooded head in preparation to strike. Cooper was unnerved by the intensity of danger reflected in the ink's scene and couldn't imagine why anyone would want to mark themselves with such a violent image.

"What are y'all starin' at?" the man demanded, standing erect and balling his hands into fists. All of the volunteers quickly averted their eyes, except for Eugene. Even though he was a good four inches shorter than the newcomer, Eugene strutted confidently up to the man and punched him lightly in the stomach.

"You grumpy again, Leo? Why are you always so grumpy?" Eugene frowned. "Do you need some coffee or a cookie or somethin'?"

Leo's hard face softened a fraction as he issued Eugene a mock right hook, which ended up barely grazing the bottom of the smaller man's chin. "Ain't no cookie gonna help. I got me a lifetime of worries, little man.

You *wanna* be here, but I *gotta* be here. That makes me mad. Get it?"

Eugene was befuddled. "You don't like to help people?"

Leo shrugged. "I like to help myself to people's stuff, but that's it."

"That's not the same!" Eugene responded indignantly. "I know you got in trouble, Leo, but it doesn't mean you're bad." Eugene focused his eyes on Leo's tattoo and his voice trembled slightly. "At least, I don't *think* you're bad."

Leo raked his dark eyes once around the room as if determining whether he had an audience, but most of the other volunteers were still pretending to concentrate on packing food or whispering with quiet deliberation to one another.

"Eugene, I've gotta drag my sorry ass in here for six months like the judge says, but I won't be here a day after that, you hear me? There's nothin' in it for Leo, see what I'm sayin'?" Leo grudgingly entered the walk-in fridge and reappeared with a wheeled cart that reached to his shoulders and was filled with twenty rows of steel trays. Eyeing the lunch sitting on the nearest tray, Leo grimaced. "Man! Not this nasty fish again. How these folks supposed to live on this crap? Why can't they have fried chicken or pot roast or something? No wonder they can't get better so's they can make their own food. I wouldn't feed this shit to a dog."

"The dieticians know better than you do about nutritious meals," Campbell replied as he entered the kitchen, a clipboard held in his right hand. "So don't go insulting my flounder. It's good when it's heated. Has a nice, light lemon-butter sauce and collard greens to go with it. Baked apples for dessert and a thick, whole-wheat roll besides. It's a good, solid meal, so don't knock it," he added defensively and then put his hands on his hips and glowered. "And

don't you ever use that kind of language in front of the
ladies again or I'll have you gutting fish instead of packing it."

"Well, *I* don't wanna look at it." Leo pushed the cart to
the middle of the floor, where Campbell stopped it from
crashing into one of the stainless steel counters by blocking
it with his boot-encased foot. Visibly trying to control his
temper, the muscular commander of the kitchen pointed at
the side door.

"Leo, why don't you take your cheery self outside with
some carts and start loading people's cars? I'm sure
they'd love a taste of your special brand of perkiness on
this fine Saturday morning."

"Ain't you worried that I'll get invited into the car of
some fine-lookin' lady who's afraid to drive all alone into
the rough parts of town?" Leo wiggled his eyebrows. "And
then I'll never come back?"

Campbell delivered a tray of packaged meals to Cooper and Penny's station. "I'll take my chances," he said,
without bothering to meet Leo's challenging stare.

Deflated by the kitchen manager's lack of reaction,
Leo grabbed the cart for Route #21, flung the side door
open, and pushed the cart down the concrete ramp, muttering under his breath as he exited.

As soon as he was outside, the volunteers resumed their
boisterous chitchat. Cooper, on the other hand, recalled
what she had overhead in the restroom upstairs and felt
inclined to question Penny in a hushed tone.

"Penny?" she leaned closer to the older woman. "What
did Leo do? I mean, did he commit a crime or something?"

"To earn community service hours, you mean?" Penny
asked and Cooper nodded in assent.

Checking the door in order to ensure that Leo would not return within the next few minutes, Penny answered, "He was arrested for disorderly conduct. I know he had to pay a pretty steep fine and work here every Saturday for the next six months. He just started a month ago. I don't know what kind of work he's doing to pay the fine, either, but I get the sense he has to come up with a certain amount every month." Penny glanced at Eugene and sent a warm, maternal smile in his direction. "Eugene's the only one Leo will talk to. The rest of us have tried to be kind to him, but as you can see, he's not the easiest person to converse with." She gave an amused shake of her head. "But he sure keeps Saturdays lively around here."

"I bet," Cooper mumbled as she watched Leo reenter the kitchen. He shot her a menacing glance and she hurriedly looked away, before he could see that "lively" was not the word she would have chosen to define Leo's behavior. She loaded a cooler onto a roll cart and embarked out the side door, in search of the driver of Route #4.

Hostile, she thought. *That's the word I'd use. But even if he's aggressive and unfriendly, he can't have done all the stealing. Mrs. Jensen's missing necklace was the fourth item stolen from clients' homes over the summer. Leo's only been here a month. Maybe he's got a partner.*

"I think he bears watching," Cooper said aloud and then nearly upset the cart as she pushed it too quickly over the curb. Luckily, Nathan was close by and was able to grab a corner and steady it before all the coolers and Sunday food boxes skidded to the ground.

"Thanks." Cooper smiled gratefully and then helped the route driver place the food inside his old station wagon. Rows of cars filled with volunteers awaited the receipt of food for the Door-2-Door clients and Cooper felt her heart swell with happiness.

"Wouldn't this be a great photo for the front page of the *Times-Dispatch*?" she said to Nathan as they headed back up the ramp. "Why does everything printed on the front page of the paper have to be negative? I'm sick of reading stories about drug busts, arson, and crooked politicians. Wouldn't it be nice to read a headline about places like Door-2-Door?"

"The sensational grabs people's attention. It sells better," Nathan replied with a grin. "It's captivating. Personally, I'd like to read a story about a woman with one green eye and one blue eye. I was wondering if such a woman would care to have dinner with a boring, *Star Wars*–obsessed Web designer this evening so I could conduct some research for a future article."

Cooper beamed. "I'd love to, but I doubt you'd find a publisher for my tell-all biography. I'm hardly a Tom Cruise."

"Well, I won't really be in a position to ask too many embarrassing questions anyway," Nathan added hesitantly. "Because we won't be alone. I was hoping you could help me get a feel for this new client of mine. He's the one I told you all about in Bible study last week."

"The guy you're not sure you should work with?" Cooper inquired quickly, hoping to mask her disappointment over not being asked out on a proper date.

"Yeah. His name's Tobey Dodge and he's from L.A." Nathan parked his cart inside the kitchen and began to load it with the food for another route. "I just don't speak his language, you know?"

"I don't speak L.A., either," Cooper reminded him, feeling unsure about whether or not she felt like socializing with a man she knew nothing about, even if it meant spending time with Nathan. She fingered her butterfly pin. "I've never had Botox, been in a tanning salon, or had my teeth whitened until my smile looks like a super-nova."

"I know, I know. I just feel calm when you're around, Cooper. I can think more clearly if you're sitting beside me." He looked away, slightly embarrassed by the admission.

The feeling of regret Cooper had briefly experienced over having to share Nathan's attention with a stranger instantly dissipated. "Then I'll be there," she answered softly. "Right beside you."

Resuming her work, Cooper thought about how lovely the phrase "beside you" sounded. It made her think of a bride and groom standing at the altar, of a couple married for fifty years seated next to one another on a porch swing, of a future filled with companionship and love.

Humming softly, she began to imagine herself at a candlelit dinner table with Nathan, their hands clasped as they planned a life together. Strangely, no businessman from L.A. appeared in her fantasy. There was no one named Tobey present to witness Nathan lean over to give Cooper a tender and lingering kiss.

Cooper spent Saturday afternoon taking Grammy to Tom Leonard's Farmer's Market so that her grandmother could pick out some locally grown tomatoes and green beans. Normally, fresh vegetables were supplied by the Lees' own garden, but Maggie had harvested the scant remains of their crop and had already pickled or frozen the choicest produce. And since Grammy preferred to support local, family-owned businesses whenever possible, she asked to be taken to Tom Leonard's. There, she purchased bacon and pork chops from the butcher counter, fussing over the butcher as he chopped and trimmed to her specifications. "I ain't payin' for fat, young man," she chided.

Grammy also spent an exceedingly long time perusing the labels of several loaves of bread. "I don't want any of that low-fat crud," she told Cooper, tossing a loaf back onto the shelf. "I want my bread to taste like bread. The last time I let your father buy me bread, he got some healthy stuff that sat on my tongue like a square of cork-board. I told him to eat if he wanted to. *He's* got the big belly, not me. Shoot, I wasn't gonna ruin perfectly fine pieces of bacon, lettuce, and tomato by laying 'em on that tasteless junk."

Finally, Grammy selected some oatmeal bread and, after insisting on buying a paper bagful of peaches for Cooper to give to Nathan, they returned home. Grammy dumped her purchases in the kitchen for her daughter-in-law to shelve and went to her room for a catnap. Dismissed, Cooper puttered about in her greenhouse, feeding and watering containers of young chrysanthemums, sedum, and asters that would soon be planted by the circular mailbox bed and in dozens of pots outside the front door.

By late afternoon, as a nearly colorless sun sank lower in the sky, Cooper was ready for an iced coffee and a few of her mother's cookies. Sifting through the chest freezer in her parent's garage, she helped herself to three ginger molasses chocolate chip cookies and folded them into a napkin. After brewing coffee, pouring it over a large tumbler of ice followed by an inch of cold half and half, Cooper defrosted the cookies in her microwave and finished the find page of homework in her *Amazing Joseph* workbook.

She penciled in the last question of the exercise and found that her mind was filled with the profoundly disconcerting image of Joseph's brothers dipping his glorious robe in goat's blood so that they could allow their father to believe that wild animals had devoured his favorite son. Cooper couldn't begin to wrap her mind around the excruciating horror Jacob must have felt upon seeing his beloved child's bloodstained garment.

Glancing at her kitchen clock, she knew she should think about getting in the shower and commencing the lengthy process of trying to style her hair like the beautician who first cut it in so many layers had taught her. It would take an equal amount of time to struggle with the assortment of makeup Ashley had been instructing her to use on special occasions, too.

"How can women be bothered with so much nonsense every day?" she asked when Ashley had first brought her the products. "Can't I just stick with a little mascara and lipstick?"

"No, because these products can hide flaws and enhance attributes," Ashley had answered seriously. "And you need to *enhance* each and every time you see Nathan."

Even though Ashley's words echoed in Cooper's memory, she decided to delay her beauty regime a little longer by taking Columbus to the clearing behind their house so he could catch his supper. Something about witnessing the hawk's lazy ascent into the clouds always brought a feeling of peacefulness her, and as her apprehension over her dinner with Nathan's client returned, she sought get all the serenity she could.

"Oh, I wish it could just be the two of us!" Cooper exclaimed to Columbus, who replied with an unsympathetic blink of his amber eyes.

As Cooper walked with the hawk on her arm, his talons sinking into Earl's thick leather gloves, shadows from the trees and split-rail fence began to invade the golden grass of the field. Columbus dove twice from the heights and then alighted on his favorite fallen tree in order to swallow the rodent he had plucked from a tangle of weeds. Once his meal was consumed, Cooper allowed him to preen for a few minutes, and then she returned the satiated hawk to his cage. She completed her bath and beauty routine in record time and dressed in a chocolate-brown, knee-length skirt and a chartreuse sweater set. Placing the butterfly pin through the cardigan's silky material, she studied herself in the mirror.

"Not bad for a thirty-something. Still don't have L.A. boobs, but there's always *Victoria's Secret*," she stated jauntily to her reflection and headed out to her truck.

Nathan was waiting for her outside the restaurant, looking dapper in a fawn-colored button-down, checkered blazer, and dark brown pants. His tie was a shade of deep mustard stitched with dozens of russet-hued leaves. Each leaf was cupped like a hand and appeared to be falling down the length of the material. It reminded Cooper that autumn was right around the corner.

"You're lovely," Nathan said, holding open the heavy wooden door to Hondo's, one of Richmond's finest steak restaurants.

Cooper smiled at the compliment, but secretly wished that Nathan had kissed her by way of greeting.

"Let's wait for Tobey at the bar," Nathan suggested. "He won't be here for another half hour. I wanted to spend a little time alone with you first." He brushed her hand with his and then perused the wine list. He ordered a glass of Merlot for himself and then asked Cooper what she felt like drinking. Unsure, she reread the cocktail menu, but nothing seemed to grab her interest.

"We've got a special tonight," suggested the bartender. "It's an autumn margarita. It's made with fresh cranberries, cranberry juice, and Grand Marnier. It's really smooth."

"Now that sounds like a combination I've got to try," Cooper replied gratefully and then looked away as the bartender remained immobile, staring at her eyes. "Thanks for the recommendation," she prompted and her words caused him to blink and finally turn away in order to pour Nathan's wine into an elegant glass.

"So what did you think about your first day at Door-2-Door?" Nathan asked as his wine was placed in front of him. "I liked everyone, except I'd prefer not to have to work with that angry Leo guy every weekend."

"It's too bad that the volunteers seemed reluctant to laugh or joke around with him nearby," Cooper answered. "He blows in there like a hot wind and everyone goes quiet. They shouldn't let him bring them down."

"Except for Eugene. He's the only one with the guts to look Leo in the eye." Nathan grinned and then took a sip of his wine. "I really had a good time this morning and I'm glad Trish got us involved. I've been so busy with work that months have flown by without me having a social life. Being in the middle of that group and back at Bible study reminded me how much I missed my friends."

Nathan stopped talking as the bartender placed a hand-blown martini glass filled with crimson liquid on a coaster and waited for Cooper to sample his concoction. She took a sip and tasted cold, fresh cranberries and lime. It was sweet and tart and utterly refreshing.

"Delicious," she told the bartender. Pleased, he moved to the other end of the bar to serve two businessmen who placed their orders while conducting simultaneous conversations on their cell phones.

"Cooper." Nathan stroked the stem of his wineglass as he glanced sideways at her. "I've wanted to call you a bunch of times over the past few weeks. I feel like we had something growing between us and then, I don't know, I let all my work stuff interfere." He focused on his glass again. "If I take Tobey on, it's going to get even crazier, but I'd like to go out with you more. Make it a priority. See where things can go." He returned his gaze to her face.

The sincerity and hopefulness in his warm brown eyes made Cooper long to stroke his high forehead, bring the tip of her finger down his pointed nose, and trace the curve of his strong jaw. She had never felt such a crushing urge to kiss someone before, especially not in public, but as they stared at one another, Cooper began to force her body to close the gap between them.

"I'd like to go out with you more often, too," she whispered, her voice husky. Feeling her body prickle with heat beneath her clothes, she parted her lips and closed her eyes.

At that moment, a very short and stocky man swaggered into the restaurant and called out Nathan's name. He wore a silvery suit that cast a sheen even in the dim light of the bar, an eggplant-colored shirt, and black shoes polished to a high shine. He had on a silver and purple striped tie, a gold watch on one wrist, and a gold link bracelet on the other. Cooper assumed that Tobey was in his early thirties, but his thinning hair made him look a lot older.

Irritated by Tobey's arrival, Cooper drank the rest of her margarita in three gulps. She caught the bartender's eye and pointed at her empty glass and he appeared as suddenly as a lightning strike with a fresh drink. "Bad timing, huh?" he murmured and Cooper wondered how many of the bar's patrons had seen her mouth hanging open and her eyes shut, awaiting a kiss that didn't happen.

Unaware that he had interrupted a romantic moment, Tobey pumped Nathan and Cooper's hands in greeting, complained about the traffic on Broad Street, slipped off his jacket, and ordered a Jack and Coke from the bartender without pausing for breath.

"What's with all the fish on people's cars in this town?" he asked Nathan while the bartender fixed his drink.

"Fish?" Nathan was perplexed.

"You know. Jesus fish. Or whatever they're called. Guess I shouldn't be surprised. You can't turn a corner in this city without bumping into a church. In L.A.," he babbled on, "it's more bars or Starbucks or music stores than anything else. My city's bigger. Glitzier. Like a woman on the red carpet. You guys ever been?"

Nathan and Cooper shook their heads.

"You should. It's a cool town. Totally hip. Lots of gorgeous women. Kinda like you." Tobey smiled warmly at Cooper.

As Cooper recognized the compliment with a slight nod, the restaurant's hostess suddenly materialized in order to show them to their table. Tobey grabbed a second Jack and Coke, tipped the bartender generously, and immediately launched into amiable small talk with their hostess while she tried to review the specials. When she was done, a pretty young waitress appeared and recommended the shrimp cocktail to start followed by the filet accompanied by lobster tail. As she departed to collect a loaf of homemade bread and honey butter, Tobey gestured at the leather-covered menus and said, "Please order anything you'd like. This meal's on me."

Cooper thanked him for his generosity, silently noting that the cost of her meal would equal half a week's grocery bill. When their waitress returned, all three of them ordered the shrimp cocktail. Nathan and Tobey also chose the cowboy-cut rib-eye with Caesar salads and roasted mushrooms, while Cooper opted for the petite filet and the house salad.

"Would you like a side of Béarnaise with your steak?" the waitress inquired.

Tobey leaned forward and gave Cooper an encouraging smile. "You look like you're in pretty good shape. You can afford the boatload of fat and calories in the sauce. Go on, live it up!"

The waitress looked expectantly at Cooper, who had no idea what Béarnaise sauce tasted like.

"It's a buttery sauce with tarragon, shallots, egg yolks, and a hint of white wine," the waitress murmured to Cooper. "It's really good. I'll just bring it to you on the side so you can taste it before pouring it all over your filet. I bet you'll love it."

Cooper nodded gratefully and then listened to Tobey as he explained his product to Nathan.

"I sell natural muscle-building vitamins and herbs called Big Man Products." He turned to Nathan. "I'd like the website to have the domain name BigMan.com and I want a cool video showing before-and-after footage of a guy who used my stuff to build bulk. I have just the male model in mind, too. He's pretty skinny, like I used to be, but I'm going to swap him free merchandise in exchange for his appearance in the video."

"Do your vitamins work fast?" Cooper asked as their shrimp cocktails were served.

"Hey, *I'm* my own client!" Tobey laughed and then held out an arm, unbuttoned his sleeve, and pushed the purple fabric toward his shoulder as far as it would go. He then performed a bicep curl. Cooper watched in repulsed fascination as branches of blue veins popped into relief against the bulge of his muscle.

"Whoa!" Nathan breathed, clearly impressed. "Didn't you have to lift weights in order to get that kind of result?"

Tobey shrugged. "Some, but not as much as I'd have to without my Big Man pills. Can you believe I used to weigh one-twenty-eight and was as weak as a little girl?" He bit a piece of shrimp in half and chewed with gusto. When his mouth was empty, he continued. "I want guys who look like total wimps, like I used to, to be able to hold their heads up high. They just need to know how to get their hands on my stuff and I can fix their bodies up. With a whole new attitude, their lives could change forever!"

Their appetizer dishes were cleared away and Cooper occupied herself by slicing bread for her tablemates. Tobey ate his with the same speed with which he had devoured his shrimp. All his motions seemed hurried and his words spilled out of his mouth as though the barrier of his teeth couldn't hold them back.

"I didn't realize that natural herbs and vitamins could really change someone's muscular makeup," Nathan commented as their salads were served. "Are they safe?"

"Yes, absolutely! I wouldn't have used them myself if they weren't. I'd like to offer my clients safe, effective products that won't break the bank. There are too many fake health-care products in L.A. That's why I relocated. This is a fresh market. It's not overloaded with merchandise that glitters like gold but won't do a thing to change how you look! " Tobey exclaimed as he used his fork to skewer a stack of lettuce pieces, which he then shoved into the inside of his cheek until it bulged like a chipmunk's. "Ummm. This is *so* good."

Nathan concentrated on sprinkling black pepper onto his Caesar salad. "And do you make your own products or does someone manufacture them for you?"

"I make them. Well, me and my girl, Sheila." He crunched energetically on a crouton. "We purchase the raw materials, of course, but we grind the herbs and fill the capsules in a lab so clean you could serve Thanksgiving dinner on the floor. I do get the labels printed by a professional, because, as I'm sure you both know, packaging is really important. What I *don't* have," he said, pushing more lettuce onto his fork with the aid of his thumb, "is a killer Internet site where men can buy Big Man."

Cooper watched Nathan as he finished his salad. He seemed to be contemplating Tobey's request. "What kind of features are you looking for?"

The waitress appeared and silently removed their salad plates.

"I want it all!" Tobey paused a moment to pick something out of his teeth. "Shopping cart, promotional videos, banner ads on some of the top search-engine sites, pages on MySpace, Facebook, and YouTube. Everything!"

The waitress returned and held a white porcelain platter just out of Tobey's reach. He eyed the mammoth bone-in rib-eye with eagerness and reached for the plate.

"It's hot," the waitress cautioned and slid Tobey's entrée in front of him. She withdrew her hand quickly, as though fearing he might saw through her wrist if left within reach of his steak knife. Tobey at least had the good grace to thank her before cutting into his meat.

"The only thing I *don't* want on the site," Tobey continued, "is a way for people to pay with credit cards."

Nathan looked at him in surprise. "Really? That's kind of standard with business websites. Lots of folks pay with credit cards. It's convenient."

"No plastic," Tobey insisted. "I'll take PayPal or whatever program you've got that will put money straight into my bank account, but that's it. For a small-business guy like me, those credit card company fees are too steep. They really bite into my profits."

Nodding, Nathan turned his attention to Cooper. "How's the Béarnaise?"

"It's really good. I can't believe I've never had it before," she said. "My daddy would love it."

"Your *daddy*?" Tobey mocked her good-naturedly. "That is *so* Southern." He dropped his cutlery on his plate and leaned back in his chair with a satisfied sigh. "Awesome steak. So, Nathan Dexter," Tobey picked up his water glass and drank greedily. "I thought this whole interview thing was kind of weird. Most people dream of getting a client like me who wants the works and has the money to pay for it, but I guess when you're the best, you can do things your way." He looked at Nathan as he signaled for the waitress. "And I could tell right off, by checking out your other sites, that you're the best."

Nathan's cheeks grew warm at the compliment, but he said nothing. Tobey didn't seem to notice. He kept right on talking.

"I don't do dessert as a rule, but why don't we have some Irish coffee? I can see you need a few more minutes to make your decision." Tobey signaled to their waitress.

"Just decaf for me," Nathan said as she appeared with the dessert menus. Cooper followed suit, too satiated to consider ordering key lime pie or chocolate crème brulee.

"An Irish coffee for me." Tobey smiled at the waitress and then added, "And bring me the check, okay? I'm doing my damnedest to impress this man." He wiped his mouth with his napkin. "Seriously, Nathan. My product gives stringy, wimpy guys some confidence. Sometimes it helps them land a better job. Sometimes it gets them the girl. Sometimes they can finally stand up to the loser who's been bullying them for years. It's good stuff, I'm promising you that. Nothing slimy. Nothing illegal. Just a confidence boost. Everyone can use one of those once in a while, am I right?" He stood. "I'll go powder my nose and when I get back, I hope you'll tell me that we can work together."

After he left the table, Nathan looked at Cooper. "What do you think?"

"I guess I'm convinced. Like Tobey said, there are lots of people out there who could use a fresh dose of confidence. If the product is safe and effective, maybe it could help some of its users improve their lot in life."

Nathan nodded. "That's what I think, too. It's just that Tobey can be a little pushy, so I wanted to make sure I was going into this venture on my own terms, and I'm really glad I had you here to help me come to a decision." He leaned over and kissed her on the cheek, just as the waitress placed their beverages on the table.

Cooper and Nathan were stirring cream into their coffees when Tobey returned from the restroom. Nathan held his hand out to Tobey. "I'll build you your Big Man site, Mr. Dodge."

"Awesome!" Tobey laughed and then slapped Nathan vigorously on the back just as Nathan picked up his coffee cup. The liquid sloshed over the white cup and spilled onto his yellow tie.

Cooper stared at the stain spreading out on the silk. It called to mind the image of the dark thundercloud from her dream. She shivered and then cupped her hands around her coffee cup in search of warmth.

5

Those who walk uprightly
enter into peace;
they find rest as they lie in death.

Isaiah 57:2 (NIV)

Cooper felt as though she were floating into work on Monday. She kept rewinding the scene at Hondo's bar when Nathan had told her that he wanted to make more of an effort to see her. Though he hadn't *exactly* said as much, she assumed he wanted her to be his girlfriend, his significant other, the woman he thought about when he was alone. Cooper figured he wanted to test the waters together as a couple and, perhaps, even wondered whether she could possibly be the woman he wanted to spend the rest of his life with. After all, they were both well above the average age at which most people married, and Cooper knew that his thirty-ninth birthday was only a month away. It made sense that Nathan finally wanted to get serious.

"You're grinnin' like a child on Christmas mornin'," Angela said as Cooper walked into Make It Work! "I'm wearin' an equally smug smile as well, in case you didn't

notice. I suspect we've both got our minds on a fine man."
She gestured at her desk. "See anythin' unusual?"

Cooper examined Angela's tight, canary-yellow sweater,
her bulbous white necklace made of plastic beads, her
bouffant platinum-blonde hair, and her customary cardinal-
red lipstick.

"Don't look at *me,* sug!" Angela redirected her. "Look
on my desk!"

"Ah-ha. You've got two vases of roses today." Cooper
smelled a cluster of beautiful amber roses. The dignified
flowers had yet to unfold their clenched petals and the
scent was barely detectable. She then inhaled deeply from
a vase of delicate peach roses, which had enormous petals and a heady fragrance.

"I picked out the yellow ones from Costco," Angela
explained. "To go with my sweater, of course. There wasn't
any note with these other ones, but I think *Emilio* put
them on my desk." She said his name reverently.

"Emilio?" Cooper was doubtful. "Why not Mr. Farmer?"

Angela shrugged and removed an emery board from
her desk drawer. "Except for my birthday, he's never gotten me flowers. Why would he start now?"

"He's probably seen how you look at Emilio. Maybe
he's jealous," Cooper answered, firmly believing that their
boss returned Angela's affections but was too reserved to
show her how he felt.

While considering this possibility, Angela filed the
edge of her pointy right thumbnail. "I dunno. I've dropped
Mr. Farmer *plenty* of hints that I'd like to be a whole lot
more than his secretary. Maybe it's time to set my sights
elsewhere."

Cooper couldn't understand why she resisted the idea of

Angela pursuing Emilio, but she had a strong feeling that the younger man wasn't a good match for the cheery, optimistic Angela, and Cooper didn't want to see her friend get hurt.

"Just follow where your heart leads you," Cooper advised as she stroked the velvety petals of one of the peach roses. "And remember, Mr. Farmer is quite shy. He probably needs a lot of persuading to pry him all the way out of his shell. Besides, on top of all the regular complications between men and women, Mr. Farmer's your boss. It makes things even more challenging, but don't give up on him."

At that moment, Emilio sauntered in from the parking lot, smelling strongly of musky cologne and gasoline. Angela wriggled in her chair. "'Mornin', handsome."

"Good morning, sunshine," Emilio replied and winked at her. He then leaned on her desk and crossed one foot over another, as though he planned on settling in for a nice, leisurely chat. "So, what did everybody do this weekend? Go clubbing? Shake your stuff on the dance floor? Get a little *wild*?" He raised his eyebrows and threw Cooper a searching look.

"Cooper volunteered at Door-2-Door Dinners packing food," Angela stated with pride over her friend's charitable spirit. "*I* was much more selfish. I shopped, went to the doggie bakery with Betty Boop, and had a glorious brunch at the Jefferson Hotel with some friends."

"Who's Betty Boop?" Emilio inquired, turning his attention back to Angela.

"Oh, you really are a young thang." Angela giggled coquettishly. "Betty Boop is my Yorkshire terrier. She's named after the famous cartoon character from the 1930s.

She's funny, sexy, and has giant eyes, jet-black hair, and a body with hourglass curves. Kinda like mine."

Emilio blinked. "So how is your dog like a cartoon lady?"

"My Betty is very sassy, just like the other Betty. Plus, I dress her up in little doggie outfits so she looks just as glamorous!" Angela declared. "Folks are always stopping me and askin' for my Betty to give them her paw or one of her sweet, little doggie kisses."

"You dress her up and you take her to bakeries? Like Paris Hilton does?" Emilio questioned.

Angela frowned at him for the first time. It was clear she didn't find the comparison to the hotel heiress complimentary. "Betty Boop gets a Drooly Dream Bar from Three Dog Bakery every Saturday, rain or shine." Angela glanced up at Emilio from beneath a curtain of false eyelashes. "Doesn't everybody deserve treats? Like my beautiful peach roses here." Her stare was intense enough to penetrate through steel.

Emilio considered this. "Sure they do, but my idea of a treat is watching a football game while drinking a coupla cold Heinekens. Then, after the game, having a giant bacon and onion burger and, if I'm lucky, finding a Stallone or Chuck Norris movie on high-def. Kick off the shoes, stretch out on my leather sofa, and polish off the rest of the beer while the good guys mow down the bad guys with AK-47s!" he shouted exuberantly. "Of course, it's more fun to do any of these things with some company. And my favorite company is the female kind." He smiled disarmingly at both women.

Flustered, Angela turned to Cooper in order to read her reaction, but Cooper made a big show of checking her watch. "Time for work, y'all," she mumbled and hustled off to the locker room. When she emerged from the stall, having changed out of a garnet-colored pullover into her uniform shirt, Emilio was rubbing a polishing cloth over the shiny surface of his black work boots.

"So what about you?" he asked, his back and shoulders pressed against a row of lockers. Cooper wondered if it was a habit of his to constantly lean on whatever object was at hand.

"What about me?" she replied while hanging her pullover inside her locker.

She could feel Emilio studying her. "You like flowers?" he inquired.

"Yes. I love all plants." Cooper bent over, laced her work boots tightly, and checked to make sure she had additional rags in her toolbox. "Except poison ivy."

"Which flowers do you like best? You a rose girl, too?"

Cooper shook her head and picked up her toolbox. "No. I like wildflowers better. Roses are too, I don't know, *domesticated* for me. I like things a bit messier, a bit more like nature in the raw." Cooper looked up as Ben entered the locker room.

He seemed tired, as though he had slept poorly, but he drummed up a smile for Cooper. She was certain he knew that she was the one who had hidden a brochure written for loved ones of alcoholics in his gym bag a few months ago. Still, she was glad she had taken the chance. Ben had acted more like his old, happy-go-lucky self lately, and Cooper continued to pray that he and his wife were getting the help they needed.

After greeting both of his coworkers, Ben moved over to the sink and began to wash his hands. Cooper stared after him a moment, wondering if she should talk to him about how things were going. Deciding that he would approach her if he wanted to open up about his private life, Cooper realized that she didn't wish to linger in the midst of Emilio's domineering presence. Gathering up her toolbox, she yelled out, "See ya!" and left the room.

As the door to the locker room swung closed, Emilio rubbed his hands together and mumbled under his breath, "She's like a wildflower. One that I'd like to pluck." He turned his attention to Ben. "What's up, man? Things goin' all right?" He walked over to his coworker and slapped him rather roughly on the back.

Ben nodded. "Yeah. Busy, too. You've brought in quite a few accounts. I guess you *are* as good a salesman as Mr. Farmer said you were."

Emilio preened. "And I'm just gettin' started. More money for the boss man means more for us. Right?" Ben looked pleased by the idea and Emilio smiled winningly. "Hey, since we're workin' with one another, I was wonderin' if I could ask you for a little *inside* information."

"About what?" Ben responded as he dried his hands.

"Cooper. The prettiest repairwoman I've ever seen," Emilio said with a lustful glance toward the door. Suddenly, his gaze turned sly. "And her so-called boyfriend. I wanna know who I'm up against."

After work on Friday, Ashley called to see whether Cooper was free for dinner.

"Lincoln working late again?" Cooper asked when Ashley pulled up in front of the Lees' garage an hour later.

"I don't know why I have the car washed before I come here," Ashley complained instead of answering. "Why can't Mama and Daddy get this stupid driveway paved already?" She examined her lipstick in the rearview mirror of her convertible Lexus coupe and then blew a speck of dust off the dashboard. "Lincoln's kicking off some big Labor Day Sale-a-Thon down at the dealership. He was busy tying balloons to a bunch of Suburbans last time we talked."

Cooper slid into the passenger seat and prepared herself for her sister's scrutiny, but her fawn-colored pants and rust-colored blouse must have met with Ashley's approval.

"Are you still afraid to accessorize beyond that brooch?" Ashley eyed Cooper's butterfly pin and Cooper realized she hadn't successfully escaped a fashion critique. "I know Grammy gave you that and all, but it *does* look kind of old-fashioned and retro isn't in just now. Why don't I show you some of the cool faux gemstone pieces out now?"

"I'm not getting into all that stuff, Ashley," Cooper protested. "And I love this pin. It's not just a piece of jewelry. It represents a story and . . ."

"And Grammy's love. I guess faux gemstones can hardly compete with that," Ashley added, resigned. As they drove with the top down, there was no chance for further conversation until Ashley parked in front of Five Guys, where they planned to gorge themselves on burgers and spicy Cajun fries. Cooper saw her reflection in the eatery's glass window and noted that her hair, which had been relatively flat at the end of the workday, was now a tangled mop of dull blonde strands.

"Sorry I didn't have an extra scarf," Ashley said and giggled as she watched Cooper try to comb through a knot above her left ear. "I usually keep a floral one in the glove box, but it blew right out while I was trying to dig around in there for a CD as I was merging onto 95."

The sisters wolfed down their dinners and then stopped by Barnes & Noble so Ashley could purchase a book on pre-pregnancy health routines. By the time they returned to the car an hour later, Cooper carried a small bag containing a historical fiction novel set in medieval Scotland while her sister had an entire shopping bag filled with reference books on conception.

Ashley showed two of the larger tomes to her sister. "Aren't these babies adorable?" She pointed to the smiling, fat-cheeked infants gazing from the glossy covers of *Getting Pregnant: What You Need to Know Right Now* and *From Conception to Birth: Life Unfolds.*

"Don't you know how conception works by now?" Cooper teased as Ashley loaded her bag into the trunk.

Slamming the trunk closed, Ashley snapped, "I've had more practice than you, that's for darned sure." Cooper was surprised by the vehemence in her sister's tone, but Ashley's voice softened slightly as she changed the subject. "So what *is* your story with Nathan? I thought you were going to, like, become a couple. Have you gone out again since that night you made out on his porch swing?"

"No," Cooper admitted, "But we're talking on the phone a lot more."

Ashley sniggered. "Phone sex, huh?"

Cooper's neck turned pink. "Lord, no!"

Gunning the Lexus's engine, Ashley nearly backed into a knot of teenagers meandering toward the sidewalk. They made faces and a few rude hand gestures at her, but she didn't even notice.

"You'd better start thinking about sex," Ashley stated as she tied on her houndstooth silk scarf. Even when the traffic light turned green, she continued to fiddle with the fabric until it looked exactly how she wanted it to. "For example!" she yelled over the wind noise. "Have you bought any lingerie? You can't have Nathan take all your clothes off only to find you're wearing some ratty old bra and white cotton underpants that go two inches above your belly button."

Cooper pretended to feign interest in the scenery.

"I knew it!" Ashley hollered triumphantly. "I probably just described what you've got on this very instant! You'd better hit the stores, Coop. You want a boyfriend? Dress the part. And I mean right down to a pair of silky black panties and a black bra with some white or red lace on it. Do you want to ruin the big moment by looking like an old lady?"

"I can't believe it," Cooper muttered, thinking back to the *Victoria's Secret* catalog stuffed to the bottom of her workbag. "My baby sister and my grandmother are both trying to embarrass me into dressing like a hooker."

But that night, Cooper resolved to at least examine the lingerie for sale in the catalog. In the five years she'd lived with her last boyfriend, she'd worn pajamas to bed every night, so her experience with sexy lingerie was limited. Still, she decided that it wouldn't hurt to be prepared in case her next date with Nathan progressed beyond feverish kissing. Flipping through *Victoria's Secret*, Cooper picked out a few pastel ensembles with a more feminine cut than anything she'd ever had in her underwear drawer. She spent the rest of the evening fantasizing about Nathan slowly peeling her clothes off, his eyes widening in surprise and pleasure as he saw the matching bra and panties revealed beneath her simple skirt and blouse.

"I'll take that Boy Scout motto to heart," she whispered as she circled her choices in the catalog. "Be prepared."

* * *

The following Saturday at Door-2-Door, Cooper had just finished loading the last of Route 10's pair of coolers when Lali entered the kitchen and informed the busy group of men and women that they had an extra volunteer on hand that morning.

"And because of that, I was wondering if anyone might be willing to stuff envelopes in lieu of delivering food to our clients?" She gave Campbell a look of appeal. "If that's all right with you, that is."

"Of course." Campbell beamed at her and Cooper was reminded of the looks Jake gave Savannah from time to time.

Cooper's arm shot into the air. "I'll do it," she said eagerly.

"Great. Let me just check on something in the fridge first," Lali said and wandered off.

"You sure you don't want to come?" Penny asked Cooper for the second time as they loaded coolers and three weekend food boxes into Penny's Buick.

"I'm sure," Cooper answered. "I might go with Nathan when he drives a route on his own next week. People usually deliver in pairs, right?"

Penny nodded. "It gives one person the chance to talk to the client while the other unloads or prepares the food. We don't have much time at each stop because folks at the end of the route are hungry and waiting for their meals, so it's nice for one of us to focus on the client's general well-being while our delivery partner takes care of business." She pointed to the names on her delivery list. "Sometimes the food is secondary to the socializing. Our clients wait anxiously for us to arrive every day. Some of them are right there at the window when we pull up."

Thinking about the thefts that had occurred over the

summer, Cooper said, "Does every volunteer always drive the same route?"

"No. We drive a route until we get to know the folks well enough and then switch. That way, our clients get to be friends with lots of people and don't get too . . . attached. You see, we only have a little bit of time to spend with each client and if they're real familiar with one of us, they'll want us to visit, to do lots of little chores, and things like that. Problem is, we've gotta keep a tight schedule so everybody gets fed."

"I guess that's the most important job," Cooper remarked.

Penny smiled. "I know just about all the clients on the Saturday routes by now because I come every week. Of course, they change, too. Some pass away, some go into nursing homes, and some are lucky enough to move in with family members."

"It must be hard to get close to people and then have them up and disappear from your life," Cooper remarked sadly. "I think that's why I'd rather not go on the routes."

Penny's pale blue eyes were sympathetic. "We can only do what we can while we can. It's enough to bring them food and company for a little while. It's a gift for them, but for all of us, too." She put her hand on the door handle. "But if you want to stick with a route that seems unchanging, then you should drive number nine. Those twelve souls have been there for a year." She lowered her voice to a whisper. "Unlike Route Six. Three people died over the summer. We all knew them and it was pretty difficult to lose several of our friends so close together."

"That must have been awful!" Cooper edged the cart away from the car as Penny attached a magnetic Door-2-

Door Dinners sign emblazed with the logo and contact information for Tyler Fine Properties.

"It's just life, dear," Penny responded and waved good-bye.

Cooper watched the old car chug off and then wheeled the cart back up the ramp. Looking around for Nathan, she saw him talking with Lali and couldn't help experiencing a prick of envy as she observed the other woman's graceful mannerisms. Every movement of Lali's feminine body seemed to carry a calm fluidity, as though she moved in time to a languid song. Her lustrous hair, curvy form, and lovely face could captivate any man, but it was the serenity one felt in her presence that was the strongest draw. Even Cooper was pleased to have been chosen to help her with such a mundane task as envelope stuffing.

"Drive safely," Lali told Nathan as Cooper drew alongside the pair. He thanked her politely and then issued an exaggerated wink at Cooper in passing.

Once all the drivers had departed on their routes, Lali led Cooper back to a warren of cubicles. Every desk was stacked with piles of paperwork and oversized calendars filled with appointments. Myriads of colored Post-it notes covered each wall. Photos of loved ones, movie ticket stubs, handwritten letters, and children's drawings were fastened by thumbtacks to the surface of each desk's bulletin board not already papered by phone lists, Excel spreadsheets, and typed memos.

"I don't know if we have a cleared space to work in this whole building!" Lali laughed melodiously. "I suppose I could move my broken printer off my desk and let you work there." She sighed. "That printer has bested me. I thought that if I took a good look inside I could figure out why it kept jamming. Now it's totally useless, just like I am when it comes to technical repairs."

"I could take a look at it for you," Cooper offered. "It's what I do for a living—fix office machines."

"That would be such a better use of your time than filling envelopes," Lali answered happily. "It's one of our laser printers and we're really hurting without it. We use every piece of equipment for all it's worth." She directed Cooper to a set of larger cubicles toward the back of the room. The desks were all unoccupied except for one. Hunched over a list of figures, a plump Hispanic woman was clearly deep in concentration despite the fact that her right hand was flying over the keys of an adding machine as though it were working independently of the rest of her body.

"That's Anita," Lali whispered. "I never talk to her when she's in math mode." She pointed to the next cubicle back, which shared a common wall with Anita's. "Here's the printer. I just shoved it to the side and have been trying to work around it all week."

"I've got a toolbox in my truck," Cooper said, her attention fixed on the partially dissected machine. "I'll go get it and see what I can do."

"Thank you. We are so lucky to have you volunteering today!" Lali smiled and Cooper felt infused with warmth. "I'm going to drum up a little snack for the three of us." Lali peered around the cubicle in order to watch Anita. "She's going to require something to lift her spirits if she's going over the budget. I'll meet you back here in a bit." Lali walked off, humming a tune that sounded exotic in its dissonance.

After collecting her toolbox, Cooper examined the HP 2100 printer. Its LED screen flashed a neon-green error code, but Cooper knew that the jam could be connected to an assortment of different parts. She checked the most obvious area—the paper roller—in hopes of finding a small scrap of paper lodged there, thus preventing any fresh sheets from feeding through smoothly. However, there were no bits or shreds hiding in the recesses of the printer.

Retrieving her screwdriver, Cooper removed the paper roller and laser-scanning device in order to peer further inside the printer. It quickly became obvious that the problem had occurred around the fuser rollers, the part of the printer that melted the toner and transferred ink to paper. Pieces of thick cardstock had become wedged at both ends of the fuser, keeping the paper from sliding over the rollers.

As Cooper carefully removed the scraps using a pair of long tweezers, the phone on Anita's desk rang. The sound of the keys being punched stopped and Anita sighed. It sounded as though she didn't appreciate the interruption.

"Anita Elmont speaking," Cooper heard her say, and then, "Oh, Lord. Oh, the poor thing. How did it happen?" Her voice was heavy with worry.

Cooper dropped the last remnant of cardstock into Lali's garbage can. She watched it flutter down into the dark receptacle like a broken butterfly falling through the night sky. The anxiety in Anita's tone alerted Cooper that the news the woman on the other side of the cubicle was receiving was deeply troubling.

"And our volunteers found her? Oh, Lord," she repeated with a little moan. "One of them is delivering for the first time today!" She paused, listening. "Yes, I'll tell Lali. We'll call the family, too. What should I say as far as how she . . . how the end came?" She grew quiet again. "Oh?" she whispered as though faintly surprised and then added, "Thank you."

Cooper heard footsteps heading their way.

"Campbell made us pumpkin raisin bread," Lali announced cheerfully. "It's literally right out of the oven. Mmm. The smell makes me feel like fall is really here. Now all we need is a dish of candy corn." She hesitated as she reached Anita's desk. "What's wrong?"

"Mrs. Davenport has died," Anita answered somberly. "Brenda found her and she had the new volunteer along with her. The weatherman fellow from TV."

Bryant! Cooper thought.

"Oh, dear." Lali set a plate down roughly on Anita's desk. "What happened?"

"One of the paramedics called over here on the way to the hospital—that nice young man who picked up Mr. Manningham last month."

"But Mrs. Davenport was just fine yesterday," Lali's voice trembled. "How can this be? I've got déjà vu between now and the morning we got the call about Mr. Manningham! Anita, how can they both have been in perfect health one day and . . . be found dead the next?"

Anita remained silent for several moments. Cooper felt as though her heartbeat was surely loud enough for the other women to hear.

"Did the paramedic know the cause of death?" Lali asked quietly.

"Not at this point, no. But Lali, Mrs. Davenport was sitting upright in her chair."

"Just like Mr. Manningham," Lali breathed.

"Yeah. Just like that," Anita said and Cooper heard her wheeled desk chair roll backward on the carpet. "Lali. I have to say this, even though I know it sounds crazy."

Lali didn't prompt Anita to continue.

"What if these deaths weren't natural? Two folks dyin'

upright in their chairs. Two folks who were fine and dandy the day before?" Anita's voice rose shrilly. "What if some-one helped these two into the next world? Someone who didn't get all they wanted from them?"

"As in our thief? You think the person that took Mr. Manningham's coin and Mrs. Davenport's ring crossed that final line? Are you saying that these clients were in-tentionally killed?" There was fear lacing each of Lali's words.

"I'm sorry to say it, but I am." Anita sank back into her chair, her weight causing it to creak slightly. "Lord help us, but I don't think there are any lines left that this man or woman won't cross. Shoot, Lali. This devil, disguised as a saint, is jumpin' over every line I know of. I don't know how you stop somebody so blindly determined to be evil."

6

When Jacob had finished giving instructions to his sons, he drew his feet up into the bed, breathed his last and was gathered to his people.

Genesis 49:33 (NIV)

Bryant was unusually subdued during the social time preceding the discussion segment of the Sunrise Bible study group's *Amazing Joseph* homework. Trish had asked her housekeeper to bake something for that Sunday and the aroma of the goodies she had produced filled the classroom.

"My housekeeper's Brazilian," Trish explained, removing layers of plastic wrap from a plate of cookies. "Barely speaks a word of English but my house is always spotless, and let me tell you, that woman can cook!" She spread her hand out over the food. "These are her coffee cookies, a *bolo* cake, and some fried plantains."

"I'll sample one of everything," Quinton stated. "This *bolo* cake's a little like my mama's pound cake, but it's even more moist. Now don't any of you tell her I said that." He speared a plantain with a plastic fork and shook it off onto his plate. "Yum. Thank you, Trish."

"Just coffee for me," Bryant said as he gestured at the

carafe in Cooper's hand. "Would you hit me with a shot of that, Cooper? I swear my hands have been shaking since yesterday."

Cooper examined Bryant to determine whether he was being theatrical, but he seemed genuinely unsettled.

Bryant met her eyes. "It's a good thing I'm not on air tonight. Seriously. Look at me. Even my George Hamilton tan has faded since I saw poor Mrs. Davenport."

"Did she at least look peaceful?" Jake wanted to know. "I'd feel better about findin' someone like that if I could just picture them bein' asleep."

"That's the thing. Her mouth was hanging open a bit, like she *was* sleeping. But she was slumped sideways in her chair and she was so . . . pale. Her skin was white, her hair was white, her housedress was white. She really looked like a ghost." Bryant took a grateful sip of coffee. "I always pictured older folks, like my parents, dying in their beds surrounded by family." He stared forlornly at the Noah's ark coffee cup Cooper held. "I believe that's what got to me. Thinking of my own mama looking like Mrs. Davenport one day. It scared me."

Savannah had entered the room on Nathan's arm while Bryant was talking. She whispered something to Nathan, who placed her Bible on a desk and then led her to Bryant's side. Savannah put a maternal arm around his waist. "Dear friend," she said, her gentle voice filled with affection. "In Isaiah 46, God says, 'Even to your old age and gray hairs I am he, I am he who will sustain you. I have made you and I will carry you; I will sustain you and I will rescue you.'" She squeezed Bryant lovingly. "The Lord came to bring Mrs. Davenport home. She may not have looked restful when you found her, but her spirit was long gone by the time you got there. Shoot, she probably looked down from heaven and felt sorry for *you*!" Savannah laughed, released Bryant, and reached outward with her cane.

"And she'll be feasting with the angels instead of on Door-2-Door Dinners fare," Quinton added as Nathan helped Savannah to her seat. "No more worrying about hunger or poverty or loneliness. All her bodily worries are over."

"Hope there's plenty of steak and beer at my future feast!" Jake raised his coffee mug.

Bryant grinned. "Okay, folks. I'm fine now and ready to focus on Joseph. I don't want to take up any more time on me, but I've got to say that the last night of our homework bothered me a bit."

"Are you referring to the questions on Jacob's grief, which we read about after his sons brought him Joseph's bloody robe?" Nathan asked, and Bryant nodded.

Savannah accepted a cookie from Trish and then gestured for everyone to take their seats. "I think that's my cue to take over. Let's begin our session with a prayer for Mrs. Davenport's family and for Bryant's quick recovery from the shock and sorrow he is experiencing over discovering her. Are there any other prayer requests?"

Trish mentioned the name of an injured neighbor and Quinton asked for a prayer for a coworker going through a divorce. The Bible study group bowed their heads as Savannah led them in a short prayer. After they had all said their amens, they opened their workbooks and began to discuss the anger they felt over how Joseph's brothers had caused their father such poignant heartbreak.

"I can't believe they lied to their father and shoved that blood-stained robe in his face. They made him believe his son was dead and yet Joseph was very much alive!"

Nathan exclaimed. "I know things weren't peachy for our guy Joseph. I mean, he was sold into slavery for crying out loud, but at least wild beasts hadn't ravaged him. Can you imagine Jacob, an old man, lying in his tent night after night, his dreams haunted by the violent death of his favorite son?"

"Shouldn't have placed one son over another, though." Jake clicked his tongue as though scolding Jacob in person. "Ruins families all the time."

"Those brothers must have been on the verge of boiling over for years," Trish commented. "I think having Joseph tell them about his dreams of the sheaves of wheat and the eleven stars bowing down to him was more than they could take. The idea of being subservient to a spoiled brat must have made them see red."

Jake snorted. "And not the fancy red of Joseph's fancy robe, either. Goat's-blood red."

"But I simply can't imagine how they could watch as their father tore his clothes and cried out loud in his grief," Cooper said with feeling. "How could those brothers return to tending the flocks, to their regular lives of eating, sleeping, working, and trading stories around the fire while their father suffered like that?"

Quinton turned his coffee mug around in a circle on his desk. "I guess they just buried the subject among them—pretended that Joseph *did* simply disappear and that it was all for the best. In fact, they probably thought that they had showed restraint by not killing Joseph. You can fool yourself into believing a lie you've told over and over, don't you think?"

Nathan nodded in agreement. "When I read Genesis thirty-seven, I started to imagine my own father and how he'd feel if my sister or I were killed. It's hard enough for a parent to lose a child, and Joseph's death was sudden and brutal. No wonder Jacob aged overnight."

Cooper pictured her own parents settled at their kitchen table, drinking coffee and reading different sections of the newspaper. She imagined the phone ringing, her mother answering and listening to the kind of heart-rending news that no parent can bear to hear. She clearly envisioned how her mother's strong hands would grip the receiver as her face crumpled in pain. Cooper then saw her father, never a large man to begin with, suddenly shrink in stature until he was almost invisible, struck to the core by loss.

Unbidden tears sprang to her eyes as she visualized her parents' grief and she quickly brushed them away. After all, she and Ashley were healthy as a pair of oxen, but Jacob's anguish was genuinely felt by Cooper and her friends. That was what she loved so much about getting to know the people in the Bible. They were so much like the people she encountered on a daily basis—filled with pride, hope, flaws, faith, love, desire. It was their human qualities that caused generations of readers to turn to them again and again in search of wisdom and comfort.

Cooper was not the only one moved by their discussion. Trish also looked tearful. "When I think of *anything* bad happening to one of my beautiful and precious princesses, oh, I just can't even say it! Poor Jacob! That poor daddy!"

"The worst thing is how many years passed until he was able to hear that Joseph was actually alive and well," Savannah said. "But that's getting ahead to next week's lesson."

The group shared the remainder of their homework answers and then closed their workbooks. Savannah asked if anyone had announcements to make or final prayer requests before they concluded.

Quinton cleared his throat. "If y'all don't mind, I wrote a song last night." He turned to Bryant. "I was thinking about you, Bryant, and how upset you must have been yesterday. So it's kind of a comfort song for you and everybody else that might need a dose of holy TLC. It's called *I Am With You*."

Trish sat up straighter in her chair. "You mean, you're going to read it out loud to us?"

Quinton picked at some crumbs on his plate. He squished them between his fingers and then wiped them onto his napkin. He seemed to be coming to some kind of decision. "Um, I was hoping someone else would read part of it. I'd rather not recite my own words."

"*I'd* volunteer," Savannah joked, "but that won't do you much good."

"I ain't got a very nice readin' voice," Jake said and then nudged Cooper in the elbow. "You've got a good voice. I've heard you singin' in church. Give it to Cooper," Jake ordered, and Quinton responded by handing the paper to her.

Cooper rose from her chair and edged away from her desk by an inch. "I feel like I'm reciting a poem for school," she murmured with a goofy smile and read:

With every sunrise that stirs you awake
With every fresh start, each new mistake
Take me with you, take me with you

On the train, in the car
As you're gazing at the stars
Take me with you, take me with you

At your desk, standing in line
Making lists, wishing for time
Take me with you, take me with you

Turn your face toward the sun
Mine is not a lukewarm love
I am with you
I'm always with you

When you're dancing in the rain
When you're huddled up in pain
Take me with you, take me with you

With your toes dug in the sand
As you journey through the land
A day of work, of joy or strife

When you kiss your child good night
When you laugh, when you cry
When you bid a friend good-bye
Take me with you, take me with you

I am here, touching your skin
I am knocking, now let me in

Turn your face toward the sun
Mine is not a lukewarm love
I am with you
I am always with you

Cooper folded the paper and sat back down. Her group offered Quinton a smattering of applause.

"I could almost hear a melody in my mind," Nathan

said. "Too bad we don't know someone who could put your words to music."

Jake, who had been strumming invisible guitar strings with his eyes closed, sat up and gave his friend a thumbs-up. "It could use a bit of tweakin', my friend, but I like it. I 'specially like that line about the lukewarm love, 'cause real love ain't lukewarm one bit."

"Genuine love is more like a hearth fire," Savannah agreed. "That steady warmth of home."

Bryant reached over his desk and clapped Quinton on the back. "Thank you for the song. Can I keep a copy?"

Looking pleased, Quinton handed him another piece of paper. Cooper folded her copy and placed it inside her workbook.

"I sure hope old Mrs. Davenport felt someone with her at the end," Bryant said, his tone noticeably less despondent than at the beginning of their meeting.

"I'm sure she did," Nathan gave Bryant's shoulder a comforting squeeze.

As the group finished off their coffee and threw away their trash, Cooper returned to her desk and absently began to cut a plantain into tiny pieces.

"You look like you're planning to feed a toddler. Or do you just like your food smashed into little bits?" Trish asked wryly. "You don't have to eat it, you know. *I* won't be offended. *I* didn't even cook this stuff."

"The food's delicious, Trish. It's not that," Cooper answered with a start. "I'm just wrestling over whether to tell you all something."

"Well, it's too late now for sure!" Jake declared. "You can't say somethin' like that and then go all quiet. No way. Come on, out with it!"

Cooper hesitated. Her friends grew silent, gazing at her with a mixture of expectancy and impatience.

"Service is gonna start," Jake reminded her. "Do I have to go out to the Mr. Faucet van for my toolbox and torture the secret outta you?"

"Hey, I've got a toolbox, too, buddy." Cooper tried her best to look tough.

"Yeah, but have your tools been where *my* tools have been?" Jake countered.

"Okay, you win!" Cooper held out her hands in supplication. "It's just that I overheard some things both times we were at Door-2-Door's headquarters," she confessed. "And what I heard was kind of awful. I wasn't sure if I should say anything but . . ."

Reluctantly, she told her friends about the thefts and the similarities between Mrs. Davenport's and Mr. Manningham's deaths.

"So what are you implying?" Trish asked dubiously when Cooper was done. "That someone *deliberately* harmed these elderly people?"

"Seems clear as glass to me!" Jake roared. "Stealin' from folks who've got no one livin' with them for protection! Findin' the one or two precious things they've tucked away like a crow hidin' a piece of tinsel." He balled his meaty hand into a tight fist and the cross on his bicep rippled. "That's a lowlife scumbag to take from the helpless. I'd like to meet him in a dark alley."

"Lali said that both clients died suddenly, in their chairs? With no signs of illness the previous day?" Nathan asked Cooper, his long face sorrowful.

Cooper nodded.

"And they were both victims of the Door-2-Door volunteer burglar?" Quinton inquired.

"Wait a minute," Bryant interjected. "We don't know that the thief is a volunteer. I mean, *other* outsiders must go inside these people's homes."

"Like who?" Trish demanded. "You heard what Lali told us during orientation. Door-2-Door arranges for food delivery, light housekeeping, yard work, and home repair. They even take care of driving their clients to important appointments and seeing to their pets' needs. That's why I wanted to sponsor a route. Door-2-Door does so much more than provide nutritious meals."

"What about medical treatment?" Bryant argued. "These folks need regular check-ups, right? My mother sees a doctor all the time and she's fit as a fiddle. These folks can't get driven to doctor's offices that regularly, can they? Do they even have the money to pay for health care?"

"I think Medicaid pays for a nurse to come to their homes, but I don't know how often," Savannah said. "I could ask Pearl, the woman who helps me with my errands. Her daughter's a nurse."

"The point is, *someone's* mighty shady!" Jake exclaimed. "And it's *our* duty to make sure that no one hurts any more of these folks. I don't wanna hear about another robbery or . . . anything worse. We've got to figure out just who we're workin' with every Saturday and sniff out the dirty rat that's hidin' behind a mask of charity."

Most of the Sunrise members nodded in agreement, but Trish looked unhappy. Cooper suspected that the Realtor was concerned that they wouldn't be subtle enough in their investigations and that the reputation of her company might suffer as a result. "They're all lovely people," she said defensively. "We can see that for ourselves."

"But think of Joseph's brothers," Jake calmly replied.

"Look what they did because they felt slighted. People haven't changed much since Joseph was betrayed by his own family. What do you think, Savannah?"

Savannah ran a hand over her long, black braid and sighed. "What is happening to those people is certainly unjust. Our elderly should be given all the love, dignity, and respect they deserve."

"But do you believe we should get involved?" Quinton asked timidly.

After a long pause, Savannah nodded. "A line from the fourth chapter of Genesis comes to mind: 'Sin is crouching at your door; it desires to have you, but you must master it.'" She looked intently at her Bible study group. "Someone has opened the door wide and invited sin to step on in. My friends, sin has become this person's master. I believe we have been called to get involved—to find out who this wolf in angel's robes is before someone else falls prey to their poisoned heart."

Cooper hesitated before the entrance to Blythe, a West End boutique featuring delicate lingerie, fine linens, and unusual soaps and body oils.

"Come on." Ashley pushed her sister through the door. "Nothing's going to bite you in there."

The store's interior was a haven to all things feminine. Silk nighties hung from scented fabric hangers, lustrous cotton robes and towels were draped over iron headboards, sheer panties were fanned out across an exquisitely embroidered coverlet, and bras in all shapes, textures, and hues were tidily arranged along the length of one of the side walls. Candles, bottles of lotion, massage oil, and special bath treatments released a mixture of fruit, floral, and musky aromas into the air. Cooper paused to inhale a lavender candle, but Ashley grabbed her by the arm and pulled her over to where the store manager waited by the dressing rooms.

"You have to get measured, Coop." Ashley pointed at the curtained stall. "Get in there and take your top off. *And* your bra. Whatever you're wearing under that shirt is no good, so there's no sense in seeing what size it is. Sarah here will give you your *true* size."

Seeing no means of escape, Cooper removed her shirt and white cotton bra. She balled the bra inside her T-shirt, folded the ensemble in half, and placed it on the chair inside the dressing room. Then, crossing her arms over her chest, she reluctantly mumbled, "Ready."

Sarah stepped inside the stall and gently wrapped a sewing tape measure around Cooper's chest. She then brought the end of the tape under Cooper's arm and repeated the process, measuring a few inches higher on Cooper's breasts than she had before. The moment she dropped the tape, Cooper covered herself with her arms again.

"You're between an A and a B cup," Sarah told her. "Are you looking for a bra that can provide more definition?"

"Yes, she is!" Ashley declared and burst into the dressing room, which now felt rather crowded. She brandished a red and black bra trimmed in lace. "Something like this."

"No way," Cooper interjected. "I'd like a plain color, please. And no lace. It's too itchy." She turned to her sister. "Get out of here, Ashley!"

"Well, since I'm treating, I get final veto power!" Ashley called from the other side of the curtain and then she and Sarah began to confer over which bras to give Cooper to try on. As they whispered and giggled together, Cooper sat on the dressing room chair and hugged her T-shirt to her chest.

After a few moments, Sarah put an arm through the curtain, respecting Cooper's obvious desire for privacy, and offered her a selection of ten bras.

"The green one is a water bra," Sarah explained. "It's very comfortable and will really enhance your natural shape."

As Cooper pushed on the padded cups of the green bra, which was a lovely shade of pale jade, the material gave way as though it were stuffed with Jell-O. "Weird," she murmured suspiciously, but decided to humor Ashley by trying it on. Surprisingly, Sarah was right. It was exceedingly comfortable and for once, Cooper looked like she had some curves.

"Feel free to try it on under your shirt," Sarah suggested, "so you can see how seamless it is."

Following her recommendation, Cooper unfolded her T-shirt and pulled it on, pivoting sideways in the mirror as she admired her fuller, more rounded breasts. With her narrow waist and flat stomach, the bra gave her a more marked hourglass shape. Cooper stared at her enhanced feminine figure, feeling a blush creep up the smooth skin of her chest and neck as she admired her alluring reflection. Stuffing her old bra into her pocket, she pushed the curtain aside and collided into Ashley, who held three more bras in her hand.

"I'll take this one." Cooper turned to Sarah. "Can I just wear it out?"

Sarah nodded and retrieved a pair of scissors. "Certainly. Let me cut the tag off for you."

As Sarah wrapped up a matching pair of pale green

panties in tissue paper, Ashley sulked. "No one buys the first bra they try on. You are *so* not fun to shop with."

Cooper kissed her sister on the cheek. "I know. Thanks for putting up with me." Sarah then announced the total cost of their selections and Cooper's jaw dropped in shock. "Ashley!" she hissed urgently under her breath. "I could get two entire outfits for that amount of money. I can't accept this kind of gift."

"Yes, you can." Ashley handed Sarah her gold card with a flourish. "Just make sure you get some use out of these. And I expect to hear all the juicy details. That's the price of my generosity."

"*If* there are any, you'd be the only one I'd tell," Cooper said, and then she and Ashley headed back to Gum Creek. Ashley planned to join the Lees for their customary Sunday dinner while Cooper dined with Nathan at Can Can Brassiere, the trendy French restaurant in the heart of Carytown.

"Don't you meet him there, girlie," Grammy advised with a wiggle of her finger. "It's best you leave your truck at his place. That is, if you wanna put that new figure of yours to work." She cackled and pointed at Cooper's chest.

Cooper's neck grew warm. "He asked me to meet at Can Can, so I can't change plans now. It would be kind of pushy."

"So be pushy!" Grammy declared with a smile. "But you don't need to worry, granddaughter. You're lookin' just like a flower this evenin'. He won't be able to let you go home, anyhow."

Stroking her butterfly pin, Cooper blushed. "Thanks, Grammy."

"Oh, and you need to take my cardboard cat carrier with you," Grammy ordered as Cooper turned to leave.

"What? Why?"

Grammy shrugged. "I've got one of those feelin's that an animal's lookin' for me. Just take it and set an old lady's heart at ease, would you?"

"Sure, Grammy," Cooper answered and gave her grandmother's withered hand a light pat. "Though I expect all I'll be bringing home in the carrier is a Can Can doggie bag."

Cooper was wrong about the cat carrier. She met Nathan at Can Can's bar, where they shared half a bottle of white wine and an artichoke-and-goat-cheese tartine. Even though it was a Sunday evening, the restaurant was packed. The café chairs set around white-clothed tables and all of the tall barstools were occupied. The noise of the boisterous diners echoed loudly throughout the eatery as the sound of laughter, clanking silverware, and raised voices bounced from the mirrored wall behind the bar to the dark wood paneling separating the dining areas, and finally roosting in the high, chandelier-covered ceiling.

"Not really a place for quiet talks, huh?" Nathan shouted.

"Good thing you made a reservation," Cooper yelled in return.

A glamorous young hostess approached the bar and made hand signs indicating that their table was ready. Cooper and Nathan were fortunate to be placed right against the front windows, where they could watch passersby whenever they needed a respite from the escalating energy within the restaurant. In turn, those strolling on the sidewalk, enjoying the refreshing late-September air and the pumpkin-glow of a full harvest moon, could pause and gaze at the entrées Nathan and Cooper had ordered. Nathan chose the Sunday special, which consisted of Salmon au Poivre accompanied by roasted root vegetables, pickled beets, and horseradish potato purée.

"You're welcome to my beets," Nathan offered when his artistically displayed entrée arrived.

"No thanks. I'm mighty pleased with mine," Cooper said with a smile, observing the beautiful arrangement of her own dinner—grilled lamb chops with beans, roasted red peppers, olives, and garlic sausage.

"I love a woman who drinks wine and eats red meat." Nathan raised his wine glass in her honor.

Nathan talked about how time-consuming his project involving Big Man Products had become and admitted that he had seriously been considering bowing out of his Saturday volunteering.

"But after this morning, I know I've got to be there," he said, laying his fork onto his plate, which had been completely cleaned with the exception of the pickled beets. "We need to get to know the other volunteers and quickly."

An idea came to Cooper. "Maybe we should host some kind of party and invite all of them. We don't really have enough time to talk to one another on Saturdays."

"That's a great plan! What kind of party? A potluck or something?"

"I'll ask my sister for suggestions. She's the queen of organizing social events."

As the waiter removed their plates, Nathan gestured to the dessert menu. "Want to split one?"

Cooper nodded. Although she was stuffed from her dinner as well as multiple glasses of wine, she didn't want the evening to end. "You pick, though. I like all sweets."

Nathan deliberated over his choices for several moments. "How about the apple split with maple ice cream and praline sauce?"

The dessert was smooth and rich and Cooper enjoyed every sugar-laden mouthful. Finally, their decaf coffees were drained, their table was cleared, and Nathan insisted on picking up the check. The noise level in the restaurant had dropped several decibels as though in tune with the deepening darkness beyond the front window.

"Guess we should roll our full bellies out of here," Nathan said and held Cooper's chair for her as she rose.

Outside, he took her hand in his. "There's something different about you tonight," Nathan whispered as they walked through the parking lot. "You've got this glow."

Throughout the meal, Cooper had been keenly aware of the silky material of her new lingerie against her skin. Every time she moved and her arm brushed against the swell of her rounder breast, she blushed, wondering whether Nathan had noticed her plumper cleavage. Wearing only a simple black dress and Grammy's butterfly pin, Cooper had tried to sit up straight and carry herself as gracefully as possible all evening. It had been a long time since she had set out to seduce someone, but she was determined to claim Nathan Dexter as her own.

Fortunately for her, Nathan seemed eager to take over the role of seducer. For when they reached her car, his hand suddenly grew tighter around her own. "I don't want you to go," he said, his voice thick with unspoken desire.

Cooper turned and wordlessly pressed her body against his. Immediately, his arms encircled her back to pull her in even closer, and she released her breath into his open mouth. Their kiss was strong and filled with hunger. It bore no resemblance to the tender, hesitant kisses they had shared up to this point. Before Cooper knew what was happening, her hands buried themselves into Nathan's thick hair and his lips began to travel down the side of her neck. She moaned softly.

"Get a room!" someone yelled from the sidewalk across the street and Cooper sprang away from Nathan, her face flushed. When she realized that the voice belonged to one of two teenage boys on skateboards, she began to laugh.

"I felt younger than those kids for a moment there," she said as Nathan's baritone laughter mingled with hers.

"Why don't you leave your truck here?" he asked her, growing immediately serious. "This lot is patrolled regularly but my car's in a dark parking area behind the shopping center. I can always bring you back . . ." he trailed off and began to fidget with his keys.

"In the morning?" Cooper whispered and was pleased by her own forwardness. It must have been the empty canvas of night sky, the crackle of the autumn air, and the way her blood was warmed by wine and Nathan's touch that allowed her to speak with such confidence.

Silently reclaiming her hand, Nathan led Cooper to a narrow alley behind the restaurant. A sense of awkwardness settled between them as they passed the rear entrances to stores and several groupings of parked cars.

Being caught in the moment is one thing, Cooper thought. *Postponing it until we can resume it in privacy feels mighty different.*

Suddenly, a dark, four-legged shape darted in front of Nathan. The animal tried to scamper up the nearest tree, but it couldn't hold onto the bark and slid down to the bottom. Blinking at the pair of humans with frightened yellow eyes, the black kitten mewled and then slunk into the shadows created by a tower of cardboard boxes.

Unable to help herself, Cooper pulled her hand free from Nathan's and followed the kitten.

The frightened feline had run into one of the overturned boxes. Cooper slowly knelt on the ground and peered inside the recesses of the damp box. She noticed two pairs of wide eyes staring frightfully at her from within the dark shelter.

"Will you get the cat carrier from my truck?" Cooper laid the keys gently into his palm.

Nathan sprinted off, returning less than a minute later with the carrier. "Do you always carry this around with you?" He stooped down next to her, breathing hard.

"No," Cooper whispered. "My grammy said I'd need it. She was right again." She opened the carrier and noted that Grammy had lined the bottom with the unused grocery store circulars from the Sunday paper. "She says that all women who have widow's peaks, which are kind of V-shaped hairlines, possess a generous helping of intuition."

"I take it she's got a widow's peak. Do you?" He peered at her in the dim orange light cast from the streetlamp at the edge of the parking lot.

Cooper pulled back her bangs. "Guilty. Now, hold this open and get ready to close it up again quick. I think these kittens will freak out when I touch them, so I'm going to try to move as fast as I can."

She was right about the kittens being less than receptive about being handled. As she grabbed one by the scruff of its neck and prepared to hoist it into the air, the second one tried to shoot past her, sticking close to the side of the box. Using her free hand, Cooper pinned it down, feeling guilty about the cries of terror emitting from the tiny creatures.

Just as she raised them over the open carrier, a man walking an enormous dog passed within a few feet of the pile of cardboard boxes. The dog spied the kittens, began to bark, and stretched his retractable leash to the limit. The kittens squirmed and jerked in Cooper's hands and she accidentally kicked the carrier out from under them. Panic seemed to grant the tiny cats the slippery skin of a jellyfish, and they writhed and bucked in her hands, their claws bursting from their paws and raking whatever surface they encountered. As they flailed wildly in the air, Cooper found that the only way she could avoid dropping them was to press their little bodies against her chest. Finally, the dog's owner dragged his reluctant canine away and Cooper was able to push the kittens safely into the carrier.

Nathan quickly closed the top and then they both sat back on their heels as the agitated meowing of the kittens echoed down the alley.

"Are you okay?" Nathan inquired hesitantly.

Cooper examined the scratches on her forearms and shrugged. "Yeah, thanks."

Nathan stared at her chest dubiously and then met her eyes, looking utterly dumbfounded. Cooper glanced down at her dress, which had been punctured by claw marks in about thirty places. Suddenly, she realized why Nathan wore an expression of complete puzzlement.

To her horror, the contents of her water bra, which, according to its label, contained forty-five percent water and fifty-five percent body oil, was draining out over the surface of her breasts and staining her dress with a shadow of slimy moisture.

"Um." Nathan averted his eyes and then stated the painfully obvious. "I think you're leaking."

7

When Cooper opened her locker at Make It Work! the following Tuesday, she was surprised to see a gift-wrapped box sitting on the top shelf. She picked up the package, taking note of the leopard-print tissue paper, the clumsy wrapping job that utilized unnecessary amounts of tape, and the handwritten note that read: *For Cooper, my wildflower.*

She stared at the unfamiliar handwriting, heat prickling her neck, and then hesitantly tore the tissue paper. Examining the cellophane-covered fuchsia box, which contained a fluid ounce of Wild Orchid Musk Perfume, Cooper shook her head. *Was this a surprise from Nathan?* She didn't think so, for she had seen Nathan's handwriting in his Bible study workbooks and it was not nearly as serpentine as the messy script on the gift tag.

"What ya got there?" Ben asked as he hung his jacket in his locker.

Startled, Cooper attempted to shove the perfume out of sight, but Ben's arm shot out and grabbed the pink box from her hand.

He took a quick glance at the perfume and then smiled. "Never saw you as the Wild Orchid type," he teased.

Cooper blushed. "I'm not."

"Never thought of you as the perfume type at all," Ben added with a smirk and Cooper couldn't tell whether he was being playful or not.

"And why not?" Cooper grew irritated. "Just because I don't bathe in it doesn't mean I don't wear it sometimes. You wear a lot of cologne for a gym addict, by the way. Maybe you should shower more often."

Ben's eyes grew dark with anger and Cooper took an uncertain step backward. She immediately regretted having uttered such a nasty retort. After all, she was the one who suspected that Ben's wife was battling alcoholism and now, instead of being sensitive to what he was going through, she had offended him.

"Don't *ever* use that word in a sentence about *me*!" he snarled and Cooper knew that he was referring to the word "addict."

"I'm sorry." Cooper did her best to infuse her voice with apology.

Ben slammed his locker shut. "You've got no idea what an addiction is until it tears your whole life apart! *I'm* not the one with the addiction. I just go to the gym to get away from it!"

"Oh, Ben. I'm truly sorry." Cooper grabbed his arm. "I was hoping things were better for you at home."

Inhaling deeply, Ben looked at the floor. "They are. We're working on it." He ran his hands through his unruly hair. "It's a process, though, and not an easy one. I guess I thought we could just talk to some folks and she'd be done with booze, but it's not that simple."

Cooper nodded vigorously to show that she was listening carefully and that his willingness to confide in her had meaning. "I can't imagine what you're going through, but if you ever want to talk about it, we could grab coffee or lunch sometime."

"Thanks, but I'd rather just have you on stand-by, if that's okay." Ben shrugged. "You know, this is the only place that's still kinda normal in my crazy life. Well, except for the addition of Ape-Man Emilio. So I'd prefer not to talk about what's going on at home if I don't have to. Is that cool?"

"It's cool." Suddenly picturing Emilio as King Kong reaching out to grab beautiful blondes by the fistful, Cooper laughed. She slapped Ben good-humoredly on the back and collected her toolbox while he teased her about her perfume some more. After exchanging some light-hearted jibes, she wished Ben a pleasant day and then stopped by Angela's desk for her work order before heading out to her first assignment at Wachovia Bank.

Angela's pencil-drawn brows were bunched together as she frowned over a work order for one of Ben's completed jobs. "Even when that man is here he's not all here," she complained to Cooper and jabbed at the paper work with a red pen. "He's called out three times in four weeks. He comes in late, leaves as early as he can, and goes to jobs without the right parts more than I'd care to mention. I can't think of what is goin' on in that boy's mind!"

Cooper stared out the front door as Ben drove by in a Make It Work! van. "We can never tell what's happening in people's lives after the work day's done, can we?" she said enigmatically. "He only talks about this job and the gym, so those are the things we're familiar with when it comes to Ben." She added the latter phrase in order to discern whether Angela was aware of the issues Ben faced at home.

"Well, *I* can tell you a thing or two more about him, like who wears the pants at his house. *I've* answered the phone when he's callin' in *sick*," the secretary huffed. "And his wife's got a set of lungs on her, let me assure *you*."

Disconcerted by Angela's comment, Cooper shoved aside images of Ben's wife as a screaming harpy and opened her toolbox. She showed her friend the bottle of Wild Orchid. "What do you think of this perfume?"

Angela's crimson lips curled in distaste. "Well, hon. If you wanna smell like flowers and kerosene, that'll do the job. That's the problem with most of them drugstore perfumes. They always come on a little too strong." She took the box from Cooper. "Since you haven't opened it yet, why not run back to CVS, get your money back, and get somethin' nice from Macy's or Dillard's? Shoot, Bath & Body Works has a real sweet perfume called Midnight Path. It's about twice the price as that there perfume but'll work double the magic on your man."

Cooper shifted. She didn't want to have to tell Angela how her last date with Nathan had ended, but Angela didn't seem interested in her coworker's love life at the moment. Running her ruby nails over her cheek, she frowned again and quickly removed a compact from her top desk drawer. After applying a layer of powder over her smooth skin, she beamed at her reflection and held out her wrist. "Smell this scent, Cooper. I'd been wearin' warm vanilla sugar 'cause I thought Mr. Farmer had a sweet tooth and would find it irresistible, but lately I've taken to wearin' wild honeysuckle instead."

"Why?" Cooper placed the perfume back into her toolbox.

"'Cause Emilio says he likes his girls a bit unpredictable.

If I'm gonna catch his attention, I'm gonna have to prove I've got me a wild side."

Cooper looked at a pile of work orders on the far side of Angela's desk. "Is that Emilio's handwriting?" she inquired.

Angela grabbed the top sheet from her metal tray and stroked the meandering letters that formed Emilio's full name. "His signature's so manly, isn't it?"

Feeling slightly nauseated, Cooper nodded. The handwriting on the work order matched the scrawl on her gift tag. Why had Emilio given her a bottle of perfume? What message was he trying to send her?

"Yes, indeed. Every single thing about Emilio is manly. I bet every inch of him is red-blooded, American male." Angela licked her lips and uttered a sigh of longing.

It was then that Cooper became aware of the presence of their boss.

Mr. Farmer stood in the hallway behind Angela's desk as though he had been struck in the chest by a heavy implement and was too stunned to move. Angela, who couldn't see him until he rounded the hallway's corner, prattled on about Emilio's physical attributes. In vain, Cooper tried to interrupt her, but it was too late.

With a bowed head and a slump to his narrow shoulders, Mr. Farmer shuffled silently back to his office.

"Penny's got pink eye," Lali informed the Saturday volunteers as they packed the black Door-2-Door dinner coolers for the day's delivery. "Can anyone stay and help with her route? It's only four stops, so one person can do it alone."

Nathan raised his arm in the air. "I'll take it!" he shouted and Cooper smiled at him in admiration. She knew that he was as reluctant as she was to visit a group of strangers, but he had assisted with a route last weekend and was now taking one alone. Between the two of them, Nathan had come a lot further toward placing the needs of others above his own doubts and fears.

Thinking about his selflessness caused something to stir inside Cooper and she found that she suddenly wanted to step out of her comfort zone. "I'll help you with your route," Cooper said to Brenda, who was now without a partner as Nathan had agreed to be her route partner that Saturday.

"Thank you, sweetie!" Brenda's voice boomed. "And here I thought you was scared!" Her enormous bosom wobbled as she chuckled. "Ain't nothin' to worry about from these folks, darlin'. Biggest problem on this route is Mr. Crosby, and since you ain't wearin' any yellow, we'll be just fine."

"Yellow?"

"Yes, ma'am. As in any shade of the color yellow." Brenda nodded seriously. "And my dark chocolate skin looks so nice in bright lemon, too. But Frank can't stand it. The boy will go out of his head if he sees so much as a yellow polka dot. We can't serve him yellow squash or corn or anything butter-colored. Sweet potatoes is as yellow as we dare go."

Cooper swallowed. Volunteering for the route seemed like an especially bad idea at the moment. "Why does he hate that color so much?"

Brenda shrugged and hefted one of the coolers onto a rolling cart. "No one knows, honey, save the Lord and *He* ain't tellin'. Mr. Crosby ain't a big talker, either, so don't expect him to explain himself to you. Hasn't got much sense left in that old head of his, I'm afraid. Half the time, he answers the front door wearin' his underwear and not a lick else. And the underwear's usually on backward." She giggled again.

"What does he wear the *other* half of the time?" Cooper asked fearfully.

"Nothin' but his birthday suit!" Brenda answered and then roared with laughter. "Come on, baby! It ain't a pretty sight, but it won't kill you. Now, help me roll this cart on outside."

Gulping, Cooper pushed the cart down the ramp. "Which stop is Mr. Crosby's?"

Brenda halted the cart in front of a dark blue Cadillac peppered with dings and scratches. "We save the best for last, sug. Figure it gives him all morning to find a pair of tighty-whities." She flashed a wicked grin at Cooper.

Lord, give me strength, Cooper hurriedly prayed before sliding into the cracked leather passenger seat of Brenda's car.

Brenda rolled down the windows, cranked up the radio, and began to bob her head from side to side as she hollered out hip-hop lyrics.

"Hope you don't mind if I smoke!" she shouted as they paused at a four-way stop. Before Cooper had a chance to respond, Brenda popped the fat stump of a partially smoked cigar into her mouth, ignited the end with her car's lighter, and then shoved the gas pedal to the floor. Blue smoke billowed out from the muffler as the Caddy shot through the intersection.

Brenda drove past Richmond's minor-league baseball stadium, the Diamond, at such a breakneck speed that the giant structure passed by before Cooper had the chance to get her bearings. "Where are we going?"

"We're headin' to Highland Park," Brenda explained. "Bet you don't get over to this part of town too much, do you?"

Cooper shrugged. "My boss used to take us all to two baseball games every season. That is, before the Braves moved to Atlanta."

"That's not what I mean, sug." Brenda barely paused next to a stop sign before driving over the curb as she made a sharp right. After passing by a dozen run-down houses, Brenda parked in front of a tiny bungalow with a cracked cement path and chipping paint. Brenda pushed a weekend food box into Cooper's arms and, carrying the black cooler in her right hand, pounded on the metal security bars covering the front door with her left.

"Mrs. Donaldson!" Brenda called out. "It's Door-2-Door! We got some lunch for you!"

Brenda dropped the cooler on the porch floor, which was littered with brown leaves and coupons for goods and services Mrs. Donaldson could never afford.

"How often do clients get their yards or houses cleaned?" Cooper asked softly.

Kicking a crooked stick away from the threshold, Brenda clucked her tongue. "Not often enough, honey. Folks only have so much time to give, I reckon."

As the two women gazed at the layer of flaking paint over the wood siding, the door opened several inches and the wizened visage of Mrs. Donaldson peered at them from behind smudged glass.

"I'm Brenda!" Brenda held up the cooler for the client to see. "And this is Cooper. She's got your weekend box, ma'am."

Wordlessly, the old woman unlocked a bolt, removed

the chain with shaky, age-spotted hands, and then backed away from the door. Brenda opened it slowly and gestured for Cooper to go in ahead of her.

The home was so dark that Cooper could barely tell which way to turn, so she simply scooted to the right and allowed Brenda to push past her and take charge.

"You watchin' *I Love Lucy*?" Brenda cackled. "Lord, that is one funny redhead. I always liked Fred the best, myself. Now, let's get your lunch heated." Brenda prattled on while Mrs. Donaldson shuffled behind her, mumbling something unintelligible. Cooper admired Brenda's calm, noting that her mentor acted as though she was an old friend of Mrs. Donaldson and had just dropped by to say a quick hello.

In the dingy kitchen, Cooper couldn't help but focus on the stained and cracked linoleum, the peeling wallpaper of white daisies on a field of blue, or the threadbare curtain covering the tiny window above the rust-rimmed sink. The refrigerator made churning noises as though it had been worked beyond its abilities and the stovetop was covered with a pile of dishes crusted with old food. Several flies buzzed around the fractured ceiling light

Cooper looked back and forth from the flies to the dishes to Mrs. Donaldson's lined and weary face. "Brenda? Do we have time for me to clean those dishes?" she whispered.

Brenda swiveled her massive head around toward the stove. "Ew!" she squealed and then wagged a finger at the old woman standing meekly beside her. "You need to let those soak in the sink, ma'am, if you don't feel like cleanin' them. You gonna get bugs! Now come on, sit on down in front of the TV and eat. We'll tidy up for you real quick before we go."

As Brenda served their client her lunch, Cooper began scrubbing at the dishes with a tattered sponge that disintegrated piece by piece as the friction of Cooper's efforts wore it to a nub. Using her fingernails instead, Cooper chipped at the food under scalding water. Her hands quickly became red and raw, but she barely noticed her own discomfort.

"We ain't really got time for this, sug," Brenda scolded when she returned to the kitchen, but she rubbed vigorously at several dishes with Mrs. Donaldson's only dishtowel until the chipped plates gleamed in the weak light.

After the dishes were laid out neatly on the countertop to dry, Brenda asked Mrs. Donaldson if she needed anything else. The old woman looked up at her from her faded green recliner and shook her head, as though she knew that she had already received all she could expect from the pair of women standing before her.

"All right, then. Don't forget to lock up after us, ya hear?" Brenda smiled and suddenly they were back in the car, heading for the next stop. "You okay over there?" she asked Cooper as she gunned the Caddy's engine beneath a traffic light that had just changed from yellow to red. "You're awful quiet."

"I'm fine," Cooper mumbled, unable to keep from dwelling on the state of the old woman's house.

"I know what you're mind's fixin' on, but that's what poor looks like, honey," Brenda said cheerfully. "Most of our clients are scrapin' by on ten grand a year. Now, we've got some like this next lady in Ginter Park, who pays for meals 'cause she don't wanna cook no more and she ain't got anybody to cook for her. They're not all poor, but at least half of 'em are livin' just like Mrs. Donaldson. Some worse."

Cooper followed Brenda into three more houses. After Mrs. Donaldson, they made a delivery to Mrs. Gates. Mrs. Gates had a tidy, light-filled home right near the park and hobbled to her front door using a walker. She barked a series of orders at them the entire time and then seemed disappointed that they had to leave again. "But aren't you going to water my plants?" she called after them as they trotted back to Brenda's car.

Next, they visited a brother and sister living in a small home a few blocks away from Mrs. Gates and then delivered to a Mr. Sears, who was nearly deaf and smelled as though he were in desperate need of a bath. Even though they still had one stop to go, Cooper felt totally spent.

"Still got Mr. Crosby!" Brenda chirped. "Wonder what he'll be wearin' today?" She wiggled her black eyebrows suggestively.

Mr. Crosby's house wasn't much larger than Mrs. Donaldson's. Like hers, Mr. Crosby's home had been painted white many years ago and was now stained with mold and had lost at least half of its outer layer of paint. A chain-link fence surrounded the property, and patches of parched grass intermingled with loose dirt served as the front lawn. The house had two windows flanked by blue shutters so camouflaged by cobwebs that they practically blended into the rest of the house.

"A little early for Halloween, huh?" Brenda giggled and removed the mail from Mr. Crosby's mailbox. She jabbed at the illuminated doorbell with a long, plum-colored nail and then shouted, "It's Door-2-Door, so you'd best be puttin' some clothes on, Mr. Crosby!"

Cooper picked up a newspaper from the top step as they waited for Mr. Crosby to appear.

No one answered. Brenda rang again and then asked Cooper to peer in the front window. "You see him?" she asked and Cooper shook her head.

"Damn," Brenda muttered. "We're supposed to call Lali when nobody answers, but Mr. Crosby does this from time to time. I'm gonna go in. You can stay out here if you want."

Without waiting for Cooper to reply, Brenda pushed Mr. Crosby's door open and then gasped. "Oh, sweet Jesus!" she wailed and then lunged forward to where a shriveled old man sat, upright but inert in a brown leather chair. Her purple fingernails pressed against his throat and she exhaled in relief. "He's alive. He's got a pulse and he's breathin'." She then took a step back and examined Mr. Crosby with her eyes.

"Could he be asleep?" Cooper asked as she watched the rise and fall of the man's bare chest. Mr. Crosby wore a filthy red and white striped robe, a pair of ratty underwear, and black ankle socks riddled with holes. She thought she detected the scent of urine rising from the chair.

"Looks more like a skinny bear hybernatin' than an old man takin' a nap." Brenda was still panting over her fear that Mr. Crosby had expired in his chair. After fanning her dewy face for a moment, she prodded Mr. Crosby's arm with her hand and spoke his name loudly into his right ear. "Go wet a cloth in the kitchen, Cooper. We may need to shock him outta this daze."

Cooper hustled into the kitchen, which bore a sad resemblance to Mrs. Donaldson's. Seeing no paper towels or wash rags in sight, she filled half of a plastic tumbler with water and brought it back to the front room.

Brenda eyed the glass, shrugged, and then splattered the contents into Mr. Crosby's face. He jerked awake with a start, but only opened his eyes for a second before squeezing them shut again as though the daylight was painful.

"He was yellow," he muttered. "Didn't deserve no honor. Yellow, yellow, yellow." Mr. Crosby's bald head swiveled from side to side in agitation. He gripped the arms of his chair until the blue veins on the tops of his hands throbbed in exertion. "You can't have it. It's our secret! He was yellow, but it's *our* secret!"

"Mr. Crosby," Brenda said his name firmly in an attempt to fully wake him.

"It's our secret. Yellow, yellow, *YELLOW*!"

Brenda leaned over the old man's thin frame. "Mr. Crosby!"

"Whatdoyawant!" he shouted in return and opened his eyes wide. His gaze focused on the Door-2-Door sticker over Brenda's large left breast and recognition flooded over his pallid features, replaced almost instantly by an expression of irritation.

"Did you spill somethin' on me?" he demanded angrily.

Brenda stood up, squared her shoulders, put her hands on her expansive hips, and pursed her full lips. "You looked like you was a goner for a minute, but we fixed you up all right. Now, how about some lunch?"

That perked him up. "Yeah, yeah. I'm starvin'. Feel like I haven't eaten for a week. But there'd better be no corn in there. Somebody brought me corn in July." Mr. Crosby craned his neck in order to peek into the black cooler.

"There's nothing yellow on your tray," Brenda answered softly. "Now, are you feelin' okay or should I call somebody?"

Mr. Crosby looked confused. "What day is it?"

Brenda and Cooper exchanged nervous glances. "Saturday, sir," Cooper answered and handed Mr. Crosby the newspaper that she had removed from the front stoop. He anxiously turned the pages until he had reached the section containing the comics and crossword puzzle.

"Blank," he muttered, shaking his head. "Last thing I remember, I was sittin' right here doin' the puzzle. Now you tellin' me it's a day later?"

"What time do you usually do the crossword?" Cooper inquired as she pushed a folding tray table closer to the elderly man.

Mr. Crosby scrutinized her carefully, as though searching for any indication that she might be concealing a hint of the dreaded color yellow. Satisfied, he accepted the fork Brenda handed him with a grunt and began to shovel mashed potatoes into his mouth. "I only get the paper when the neighbor lady's done with it," he answered Cooper after several swallows. "She's got a son who buys her stuff. Guess she feels sorry for me with my boy bein' in jail and all."

He stabbed a green gelatin square and pushed it in his mouth. "She spends most of the mornin' drinkin' that fancy coffee that comes outta a bag. Wish I had some of that coffee," he murmured crossly. "I don't get the paper 'til she's done. Least she never does the puzzles."

Cooper stared at Friday's newspaper, which seemed to have fallen from Mr. Crosby's lap and landed in a loose pile next to his chair. "So you were probably working the puzzle about this time of the morning?"

Mr. Crosby paused in order to sip some iced tea. "Yeah. I was waitin' on *you* folks. That's the last thing I recall. I was waitin' for my lunch. Next thing I know I wake up to find it's a whole 'nother day." Suddenly, he shoved the tray away from him. "And I gotta go!"

Brenda helped the old man stand. As he hastened away, Brenda winced. "I think he's gone in that chair already. Good thing this cushion's covered with plastic." She sighed. "I'm gonna see if there's anythin' to clean this up with."

After Brenda disappeared into the kitchen, Cooper examined a black-and-white photograph of a young man standing in front of the barracks at Virginia Military Institute's campus. She was so absorbed by the handsome soldier that she didn't hear Mr. Crosby reenter the room.

"It's *gone*!" he cried and Cooper spun around to see that his wrinkled face was streaked with tears. "Gone, I tell you!"

Cooper took his arm and led him to an upholstered wing chair. He sank down into the floral material and covered his face with his hands. He made pitiable sounds that sounded like a mewling cat.

"What's gone, Mr. Crosby?" Cooper prodded gently. "Is something missing from your house?"

"Now everyone will know," Mr. Crosby moaned. "Yellow, yellow, YELLOW! Someone stole our secret. Someone was in my bedroom. I can tell." He covered his face with quivering hands and cried like a child. His shoulders shook as he whimpered, "It's gone. It's gone," over and over.

He fell silent and no matter what questions Brenda or Cooper asked, he would say nothing more. Brenda wiped off Mr. Crosby's plastic-covered leather chair, put him in a clean T-shirt, and washed his face as tenderly as a mother would clean her own child's. All the while, Mr. Crosby gazed unseeing at a football game on the television screen.

Back in the Caddy, Brenda was worried. "I've never seen him like that. He hasn't got any memory problems— somethin' happened to him yesterday."

"And I'm going to try to find out what," Cooper declared angrily. "I don't think he just lost track of time, Brenda. And now he says something's missing, too. I overheard Lali say that there have been several robberies from client homes this summer. It looks like the thefts are still going on."

Brenda stared at Cooper in shock, even though the traffic light had turned green. As the car behind them laid on the horn, Brenda frowned in thought. "You mean . . . it's one of us? A *volunteer* is messin' with these folks?"

Cooper nodded. "Seems that way."

"Lord in heaven! What is this world comin' to?" Brenda waved at the driver behind her and gunned the engine. "You just tell me how to help and I'll do it. I'm not gonna stand for folks givin' our program a bad name. I'm mild as a kitten most days, but I got claws and a big, strong body, and I'll use them both if I find out that someone I know is dopin' up old folks just so's they can rob them blind."

"Doping them?" Cooper asked and then fell silent. "That would explain how Mr. Crosby lost a day, I guess. But how would someone drug the clients?"

Brenda clucked her tongue. "Are you listenin' to yourself, girl? *We're* the ones packin' and bringin' them their food, right? Now, I ain't no college professor, but I can put two and two together and figure out how easy it would be to stir a little somethin' into the mashed potatoes."

"I need to figure out what that something is, but my experience with drugs doesn't go past Robitussin."

"Go see Mr. Crosby's son, then," Brenda suggested as she merged into the next lane without using her signal. "That's why the boy's in jail. Probably knows more about drugs than anybody in Richmond. Just wasn't smart enough to figure out he was sellin' heroin to an under-cover cop."

"Jail?" Cooper swallowed hard. She tried to envision the members of her Bible study sitting across from a con-victed drug dealer in an attempt to elicit information from him. Not one of them seemed fit for the job at hand.

"But if you're gonna go, you'd better take somebody," Brenda advised as she pulled into the Door-2-Door park-ing lot. "And you'd better pick wisely. Those prison boys don't see many women and that Crosby boy might wanna talk to you about things you don't wanna talk about. You hear what I'm sayin'? Take someone with you."

"I hear you," Cooper replied aloud. In silence, she prayed, *Lord, can you send me someone who can interrogate a man wearing an orange jumpsuit?*

8

For sighing comes to me instead of food;
my groans pour out like water.

Job 3:24 (NIV)

Brenda dropped Cooper off at Door-2-Door's side entrance and sped off to attend a fall festival at her church. After replacing the black cooler beneath one of the lengthy stainless steel counters in the kitchen, Cooper located her friends. All six of them were contentedly snacking on ham and cheese biscuits and Costco cookies in the volunteer lounge.

"How'd it go?" Jake asked. "You look a bit green around the gills."

"Not green. Pink." Trish eyed Cooper's flushed neck and handed her a cup of water. "Maybe you're dehydrated. You got back later than everyone else, too. Did you and Brenda have a really long route?"

Cooper accepted the water and looked around the lounge. The other volunteers had left for the day with the exception of Eugene. He was sprawled out on two folding chairs in the back of the room munching on a biscuit. An empty chair in the adjacent row served as a table for his can of Pepsi and a paper napkin piled high with chocolate chip cookies. A comic book was open on his lap and the young man laughed heartily as he ate and read.

"I think one of the clients on my route was drugged," Cooper announced in a low voice as she took a seat among her friends. "A man named Mr. Crosby."

"Oh, I've heard about him," Trish said dismissively. "Isn't he a little batty?"

"A bit," Cooper agreed. "But I'm not talking about how he acted. When we first saw him, we actually thought, well, that he might be dead. He'd been sitting in the same chair for twenty-four hours and he was still sitting there when Brenda and I went inside. The poor man has no memory at all of what happened to him."

Quinton helped himself to a handful of cookies and offered one to Cooper. "Lots of older folks have memory issues. Mr. Crosby probably just forgot to go to bed and fell asleep in his chair. Why do you think he was drugged?"

Cooper lowered her voice even though Eugene was clearly absorbed in his comics. "Fell asleep for twenty-four hours? No." She shook her head. "He was really upset about something that was taken from his house. I don't know what it was and he wasn't really making sense. He kept repeating how his secret had been stolen."

Holding up a finger to stop Trish from interrupting, Cooper continued, "It's clear that Mr. Crosby is wired differently than the rest of us, but he was thinking straight enough to be bothered that he had lost a whole day *and* that someone took an object from his bedroom." She broke her cookie in half and stared at the crumbs on her lap. "Brenda's delivered to this man before and she says he's never had problems with his memory. And I'm no doctor, but Mr. Crosby just acted, you know, doped."

"I trust your instincts," Nathan stated loyally. "How did Brenda react?"

"She was amazing," Cooper replied. "She revived Mr. Crosby by tossing water in his face, changed his clothes, got his lunch ready, and tidied up the house within fifteen minutes. Thank God she was there."

"Thank God is right," Savannah agreed.

"She's also the one who suggested he'd been drugged and she was mighty mad about it," Cooper added.

"So Brenda's probably innocent, unless she's a great actor," Bryant said.

"I think we need to have a little chat with Lali," Jake said, his strong arms folded across his chest. "We gotta have all the facts if we're gonna be of any help to these folks." He tossed a napkin into a garbage can several feet away. "Time to storm the castle, folks. Who's with me?"

When Anita heard about the impromptu meeting between Lali and the Sunrise Bible study members, she insisted on being present. Cooper began by telling Lali about her delivery to Mr. Crosby and her concern that his physical condition was related to the thefts, and possibly the deaths, that had occurred with other Door-2-Door clients over the past few months. Of course, she also had to confess that she had inadvertently eavesdropped on two of Lali's conversations.

"I'm not concerned that you overheard us talking about the thefts," Lali let Cooper off the hook gracefully. "I'm concerned about Mr. Crosby. You say that the last thing he remembers is being visited by one of our volunteers?" Lali's dark eyes were liquid with worry.

"He remembers working a crossword in the newspaper as he waited for his lunch to be delivered," Cooper replied.

"He doesn't actually recall eating lunch, but an empty tray was in his garbage can."

"Maybe we should get a hold of that tray," Savannah suggested softly. "If something was mixed in his food . . ."

Lali covered her face with her hands. "I just can't believe it!" She then pushed back a strand of glossy blue-black hair and smoothed a wrinkle in her skirt, as though gathering strength to face the truth. "Okay. This is what's going to happen. Anita and I will contact one of our nurse practitioner volunteers and all three of us will visit Mr. Crosby this afternoon. If the medical professional believes Mr. Crosby was drugged, my next step will be to contact the police. I'm sure they'll know how to proceed."

Jake, who restlessly drummed his fingers on the conference table, suddenly pushed his wheeled chair backward. "This whole thing should be easy enough to deal with, ladies. Just find out who delivered Mr. Crosby's food yesterday and you've got your man."

Lali shook her head. "We can't accuse one of the volunteers without proof. Besides," her voice grew heavy, "the volunteer sign-up sheet from yesterday is gone. Someone took it or threw it out or who-knows-what." She was clearly disturbed about the missing document. "The bottom line is that it never got filed, so short of asking everyone who volunteers here, I have no record of who drove where." She sighed. "The Saturday crew is fairly regular, but the weekday volunteers change all the time."

"That's the truth," Anita said. "We'd be on the phone all day asking folks, and if someone was guilty, they wouldn't tell us what we'd want to know anyhow."

"All I can do is review every detail with the police and allow them to conduct their investigation as they see fit.

I'm sorry you've been exposed to all this." She gestured at a handful of manila folders.

Anita rose and placed a protective hand on Lali's shoulder. "Thank you all for coming to talk to us, but please don't repeat details about the missing items or Mr. Crosby's state of health to *anyone*. Every single one of our clients will suffer if we lose volunteers or if funding dries up because of harmful gossip. We hope to see you again next weekend."

Her tone made it clear that the meeting was over, but as soon as the group stepped outside, Trish gestured for everyone to gather around her car.

"We're not going to spread rumors about what's happening here, but I don't think we should just drop the subject, either," Trish declared firmly.

"Let's give the police the benefit of the doubt," Savannah suggested. "If there's any evidence of misconduct, they'll find it."

"And if Lali still thinks the clients might be at risk, we could implement Plan B," Nathan said.

"What's that?" Jake asked.

"Hosting a potluck," Cooper replied. "So we can get to know the volunteers working on Fridays and Saturdays better."

"Excellent idea! I'll call around and see where we can rent a space for our social event," Trish offered. "Just in case we need to throw this thing together at the last minute. I'm thinking one of the community centers would do nicely. After all," she grimaced, "I don't want a thief and potential murderer running around inside *my* house. See you in church tomorrow!"

As the Bible study members dispersed, Nathan walked Cooper to her truck.

He opened her door with a smile. "So how's that pair of kittens we saved?"

"Grammy found homes for them right away." Cooper avoided meeting his eyes, still mortified over how their last date had ended. "A little girl down the road had to put her cat to sleep last month and she was feeling real lonely, so the timing couldn't have been better. 'Course, I don't know if the cats are going to be happy about being called Bella and Edward."

Nathan laughed. "You're always full of surprises! I'll see you in the morning."

Cooper waved good-bye and then drove home in a funk. She knew Nathan was busy preparing the Big Man site for its upcoming launch, but she had wanted to return to the way she had felt during their last date before it had been interrupted by the discovery of the stray cats.

Guess this gives me time to buy another bra, Cooper thought wryly. *And this time, I'm getting the plain cotton kind from Target. After all, Ashley doesn't need to know what happened to the one she bought me.*

"So how'd your new lingerie work out?" Ashley whispered as she and Cooper set the table for Sunday supper.

"Just fine," Cooper mumbled and then gestured toward the hall. "Can we not talk about that right now?"

"Talk about what?" Grammy demanded as she shuffled into the kitchen. "Somethin' juicy?" Her white eyebrows wiggled suggestively as she examined Ashley's flat stomach. "Like baby-makin'? You sure you're tryin' hard enough, girl? You're not on one of those crazy diets again, are you? A woman can't fill her womb eatin' celery and rice cakes. Trust me on that one."

Ashley developed a sudden interest in folding the paper napkins into fan designs.

"I bet you're readin' too many books." Grammy sank into a chair and immediately unfolded the napkin fan. "You can't be science-like about this whole thing. Say a prayer to the Maker, pour yourselves some wine, and celebrate bein' young and in love. That's how you make a baby. It's right simple."

"It's supposed to take couples an average of six months to conceive," Ashley informed Grammy.

Grammy pointed at the wall calendar hanging near the kitchen phone. "Well, when did you start?"

Taking a hesitant step toward the calendar, which the Lees received every year at Christmas time from their State Farm agent, Ashley reached her hand toward the month of October and then froze. Bowing her head, she seemed to be fighting to gain control over her emotions, and when it seemed as though she was on the verge of tears, she pivoted and walked briskly through the kitchen and out the back door. She didn't bother to close the door behind her and a crisp wind bearing the scent of burning leaves mingled with the aroma of the mustard-and sage-covered ham baking in the oven.

"Grammy," Cooper admonished as she held onto the open door. "Ease up on the baby stuff, okay? Nobody wants to have a child more than Ashley, and since she's used to getting exactly she wants, this wait is awful hard on her."

Unperturbed, Grammy reached for the classified section of the *Times-Dispatch*. "I'm just tryin' to shake somethin' loose in that girl. She holds everythin' so tight inside. It ain't good for her. Think about it, granddaughter.

When's the last time you saw her cry or get mad or shout at anybody? I wanna peek under that mask of hers—see how she's really doin'."

"I'll go talk to her. I think that's a better way of finding out what's going on with her than provoking her." Cooper stared at her grandmother in hopes she would get the point.

"Suit yourself," Grammy answered and then yelled, "Maggie! I think your ham's about done!" She then hid herself behind the newspaper and didn't so much as rustle a page until her eldest grandchild stepped outside.

Saffron-edged leaves crunched beneath Cooper's tennis shoes as she crossed the patio toward the cluster of spent Rudbeckia bordering Earl's vegetable garden. Ashley sat on a stone stool, examining one of the golden cone-shaped heads, her elegant fingers tracing the serrated edges of the leaves just below the crown of flower petals. When Cooper drew near, Ashley turned her face toward the woods, but not quickly enough to disguise the tear tracks on her cheeks.

Saying nothing, Cooper squatted next to her sister and put an arm around her waist. They stayed like that for several minutes as a woodpecker hammered into the birch tree bordering the patio.

"Why does Grammy have to be so mean?" Ashley sniffed. "It's bad enough that Lincoln and I have been trying to conceive for over a year and I didn't even realize it 'til she made me look at that damned calendar."

"Grammy just wants you to be happy," Cooper answered, and when Ashley snorted in disbelief, added, "I think she wants to see that our family's growing. You know, that life is going to go on when she's gone. The idea of us being settled is a comfort for her."

"She's still laying it on thick about catching Nathan?" Ashley asked as she swatted away a tear clinging to her jawline.

Cooper smiled. "Not any thicker than you do, Ashley." She searched in the birch tree for the woodpecker and saw his gray-and-black-speckled body flitter around the upper part of the fraying trunk. "To answer your question from earlier, Nathan and I were having a great date until we found those two stray kittens Grammy gave away last week. They, ah, kind of interrupted us. We were, um, heading back to his place when one of the cats ran across our path."

Ashley gave her sister a curious stare. "Good thing you're not superstitious. And what's happened since then?"

Cooper shrugged. "Let's grab Columbus and give him a chance to stretch his wings a bit while we're talking." She fetched the hawk from his cage and walked a safe distance from Ashley toward the split-rail fence. Columbus flapped his wings the entire way and Ashley eyed him warily.

"He won't fly at you," Cooper told her sister. "He's just excited to be out in the open." She raised her arm and the hawk took off.

As Columbus alighted on a tree in the brilliant sunshine, Cooper leaned on the fence rail and sighed. "Maybe Nathan and I aren't meant to be together. We just can't seem to connect. I didn't think falling for someone again after Drew would be . . . such hard work."

Ashley shielded her eyes from the glare as Columbus circled about the field of dry grass.

"Work. Funny you should use that word. That's what Lincoln told me the other night—that I've turned our time with one another into work." Tears pooled in her eyes again. "He says that he's got two jobs now. One running his daddy's dealerships and the other . . ." She trailed off. "Is making *me* a baby. He doesn't say *us*, Cooper. As if it's all about *me*! It's not like we could even be a family without him."

Cooper touched her sister's corona of sunlit hair, which shone like warm honey beneath the open sky. "I'm sorry, Ashley."

"I *need* this baby, Coop. Lincoln's hardly home at all. When he's not working, he's out golfing with other bigshot car guys. And what about me? I'm sick of shopping and I've had every spa treatment this city has to offer. I want more!" She snatched a twig from the ground and began snapping it to pieces. "For years I've done all kinds of charitable work. Habitat for Humanity, United Way, American Cancer Society, American Heart Association, the Children's Hospital, every animal shelter within three counties, a trillion museums, and what for?" Anger appeared in the clench of her jaw. "I just want this *one* thing."

Cooper was silent for a moment. With extreme gentleness she said, "I don't think it works that way, Ashley. You can't earn yourself a baby."

Her sister sighed. "I know, but it's how I feel sometimes. Other people get pregnant and they don't even want to be, and I want a child more than anything and can give a baby such a good life, so how does that make sense?" She picked at a piece of loose pine on the fence rail. "My church friends tell me that God has a plan, or that this might be a test of my faith, or that I should be patient. Well, I think a year's long enough to wait, unless this is a test I'm just plain going to fail."

At that moment, partway across the vast field, Columbus cried out in frustration. He swooped just above the tall grass and rose slowly toward the horizon, his talons bare.

"He almost had something," Cooper murmured. "It must have slipped away."

"That's how I feel about time," Ashley said sadly. "It's just slipping past and I can't hold onto it."

Cooper rubbed her sister's back as the breeze made waves in the sea of grass before them. Together they leaned against the fence, each lost in unhappy thoughts as Columbus attempted another unsuccessful dive. Finally, Maggie called them in for supper.

Ashley brushed a few seeds and nettles from her ochre-hued cashmere sweater and smoothed her pleated skirt. Drawing in a deep breath, she squared her shoulders and gave a little toss to her head, as though shaking off the feelings she had revealed a few moments before.

Cooper reached her forearm into the air, signaling for Columbus to return. He landed in a flutter of creamy white and walnut feathers, blinking rapidly as though agitated. Cooper soothed the bird with her free hand as they made their way back to the house. She returned the raptor to his aviary and hung the thick glove on a hook fastened to the side of his cage. "It'll be okay, Ashley," she said before reentering the kitchen. "Things will work out."

"They'd better," Ashley replied with a frown. "Or I'm going to demand my money back from that fortune teller at the State Fair."

Cooper laughed. "How on earth would you find her again?"

Ashley tapped her temple. "Even *I* could track down someone named Madame Zoofu, Ms. Detective. Now let's get our dinner over with so we can have dessert. Daddy said Mama made apple crisp tartlets with hard sauce—my favorite fall treat! She must've known I needed some extra TLC today."

"That's 'cause she's a mother," Cooper said. "You'll have that kind of instinct about your own child one day, Ashley. And I hope you have a boy. We've got plenty of estrogen in this family as it is."

Ashley shot a wary look in Grammy's direction as she turned her wrinkled face toward the kitchen door. "We've got plenty of what?" she demanded.

Before Cooper could answer, Ashley plopped down in her seat and chirped, "Spirit, Grammy! We've got lots of spirit!"

"Glad to hear it," Grammy replied and then gestured at the ham. "Now somebody cut me off a nice, thick piece. I got a new kind of denture cream and I plan to see if it's as good as the commercial says. We should expect the best outta life, girls." She eyed both of her granddaughters. "Sometimes you gotta believe you deserve the riches of this world first, before they can be given to you. And I'm not talkin' about money in the bank, but all things great and beautiful." She reached across the table and grasped Ashley's left hand. "I'm your grandmother and I'm tellin' you, you deserve these things."

"Thanks, Grammy," Ashley whispered.

Grammy released Ashley's hand and plopped her napkin on her lap. Now, let's say grace so we can eat. Bow your heads, children. I know a short one."

Wednesday morning at Make It Work!, Angela called Cooper on her cell phone and asked her to pick up the company's lunch order from Casa Grande.

"I ordered you cheese enchiladas with refried beans and rice," Angela informed Cooper. She sounded especially chipper. "I know what everybody's favorites are, 'cept for Emilio. He says he likes to try new things all the time. I can only *imagine* what he means by that." She giggled.

"Is Mr. Farmer treating us again?" Cooper asked as she loaded her toolbox into the back of the van and closed the double doors.

"Yes, ma'am! That makes two times this week. He's been mighty friendly to me, too. Brought me a pack of gum Monday, a candy bar yesterday, and this mornin' he brought me a little pumpkin with a painted face. It's the cutest thang."

Cooper pulled herself into the van's high driver seat. "I guess you managed to make him jealous."

"Reckon so." Angela sounded smug.

"So what now?" Cooper tried to refrain from sounding judgmental. "You wanted Mr. Farmer to pay attention to you and he is. I don't see him getting the rest of us little tokens of affection. Are you going to keep flirting with Emilio?"

"It depends where that gold Godiva box Emilio brought with him to work ends up. If I find it on my desk sometime today, then I know he's interested and hey, I might as well give him a try." Angela sighed theatrically. "Maybe then Mr. Farmer will see that he shouldn't have waited so long to decide whether or not he wants me."

"How do you know Emilio's got chocolates with him?" Cooper adjusted her phone headset as she turned onto Broad Street.

"Oh, I just happened to peek in his bag before he went out to empty the shredder boxes."

"Angela!"

"I just wanted to see what cologne he wears," Angela protested innocently. "He always smells *so* good."

Cooper pulled into a strip mall and found a space for the van at the far end of the parking lot. "I've got to go. I'm at the restaurant."

After collecting their order, she returned to the office and laid out the lunches in the break room. As she leaned over to place a pile of napkins on the far side of the table, Emilio entered the room and greeted her enthusiastically.

Cooper swung around and immediately blushed. "Oh, hi. I didn't hear you come in"

"Can I help you set the table?" he offered gallantly. "Because there's somethin' I'd like to give you when you're done."

Pretending to be too busy arranging plastic cutlery to meet Emilio's eyes, Cooper mumbled, "Oh, yeah?"

Emilio sidled closer. "Some chocolate-covered cherries. They smell sweet and melt in your mouth. And they're the best, because some women deserve only the best." His voice had become deep and husky.

Cooper could feel his breath on the back of her neck. She tried not to grimace as his musky cologne nearly overpowered her nostrils. "That's really nice of you, Emilio," she answered, still refusing to look at him. "But you really shouldn't get me anything. We're just coworkers."

Emilio placed his hands over his heart. "But we could be so much more." His words sounded like a low growl. "Did you like that perfume I got you? Are you wearing it right now?"

Feeling trapped in the small kitchen, Cooper prayed for some way to escape from Emilio's hulking presence, but her well-built coworker kept inching toward her until she was backed up against the cabinets with no retreat in sight.

"Look." Cooper held her hand out in front of her. "I'm kind of seeing someone, Emilio."

"I know all about him, but if you were with that guy, you wouldn't say 'kinda.' He must not be treatin' you like the queen you are, but I will. Go out with me this Friday and I'll show you what it's like to be with a man who really understands what a *fine* prize you are. What do you say, babe?"

Shocked, Cooper realized that Emilio intended to kiss her. Spurred by panic, she ducked under his arm and popped up behind his back, twitching like a hunted rabbit. At that moment, Angela and Ben stepped into the room. They paid no attention to their coworkers already in the kitchen. Angela was good-naturedly berating Ben for lapses in his paperwork and he rolled his eyes in exaggerated annoyance.

"Well, I'm starvin'!" Angela declared once she had finished with Ben and sat down, unaware of the charged air within the room.

Ben seemed to sense that something was amiss, for he threw a questioning gaze at Cooper before dumping a mound of tortilla chips on the lid of his takeout container. "Is there any salsa?" He searched inside one of the paper bags sitting in the center of the table. Cooper lurched toward her seat—eager to create more distance between herself and Emilio—and popped the lid off one of two salsa containers and handed it to Ben.

"You're gonna need an extra workout after *that* lunch," Angela said and pointed at Ben's loaded plate with her fork.

"This is the only decent meal I eat," Ben mumbled as Emilio sat down next to Cooper.

"Doesn't your wife cook?" Emilio asked. "I won't marry a woman who doesn't know her way around a kitchen."

Ben glared at Emilio. "Let's just say my *wife's* not feeling up to cooking these days."

"Men are perfectly able to make their own meals anyhow." Angela directed her comment to Emilio. "You're a bachelor. What do you do for supper?"

"I buy it!" Emilio laughed. "'Til I can get me a girlfriend who will fry me up a nice steak, it's all takeout for this man."

Angela dabbed at her crimson lips with a napkin and leaned on her elbows as she gave Emilio an appraising look. "So when you find this girlfriend, what else are you gonna have her cook for you besides steak?"

Emilio pulled at a string of cheese protruding from the edge of his beef enchilada and shrugged. "Stuff my mom made. You know, Italian stuff. Lasagna, veal Parmigianino, gnocchi, cannoli. None of this Southern fried chicken and grits; I can't stand that kind of food."

Angela bristled. Cooper knew that the perky secretary prided herself on the perfection of her fried chicken.

"What if she can't cook like your mama?" Ben inquired.

Emilio pulled another long strand of cheese from his fork, twisted it around his index finger, and pushed it into his mouth with a laugh. "There's lots of fish in the sea, right? And I'll do anythin' for a woman who takes care of me. That's how a good partnership works, right, my man?" He knocked Ben's arm with his elbow, causing his uniform sleeve to submerge in a puddle of guacamole.

"Well, good luck finding a woman who'll slave for you twenty-four/seven!" Angela stood up from the table and gave her chair an angry shove backward.

"Oh, I've already got the perfect lady in mind." Emilio smiled enigmatically.

Cooper also rose and tossed the remainder of her lunch in the garbage.

"Where are you goin'?" Emilio inquired with concern. "Somethin' wrong with your food? Want me to get you somethin' else?"

"No, thanks. I'm not hungry anymore," Cooper assured him hastily. Hurrying to the restroom, she washed her hands and then paused at her locker, almost afraid to look inside. She opened it a hesitant crack, but even the weak fluorescents overhead were sufficient enough to illuminate the gold Godiva box.

"Oh, no," Cooper moaned and slammed the locker shut. She quickly left the room and headed for the front door, thinking that she had never been so eager to perform maintenance on the machines awaiting her at a medical office park across town.

Angela waved a piece of pink memo paper at Cooper with her left hand while holding the phone against her shoulder and taking notes with her right.

She looks cross, Cooper thought. She mouthed a thank-you at Angela and examined the message. It was from Trish. Angela had taken down the Realtor's cell phone number and made it clear that Cooper should return the call ASAP.

Donning her headset once again, Cooper hopped into the van and called Trish.

"You're the last one I needed to get a hold of," Trish

began. "I called Lali to see what happened on Saturday and it's a good thing I did. The police have nothing to go on because Mr. Crosby wouldn't talk to them. I mean, the man didn't say a single word, he just waved them away so he could watch TV. Despite his lack of cooperation, the officers also paid visits to all the folks who claim to have had things stolen from their homes."

"Oh, good," Cooper said, heading for the interstate in hopes of avoiding the hundreds of traffic lights on Broad Street.

"No, not good," Trish countered. "Apparently, all of the victims have suffered memory lapses over the last six months."

Cooper scowled as a minivan eased into her lane without bothering to signal. "So?"

"So they don't make very reliable witnesses," Trish explained impatiently. "Basically, the police told Lali that there's not much they can do until more proof of a crime can be provided."

"Oh, dear." Cooper was discouraged. "I was hoping they'd figure out who was responsible for all these bad things and we wouldn't have to get involved."

"Well, they're not doing anything else, but *we're* going to."

Instantly anxious, Cooper pressed down on the gas pedal and the van lumbered forward in the center lane, gaining on a yellow bus from one of the county's elementary schools. "What do you have in mind?" Cooper asked and then frowned as children sitting in the back seats pressed their faces against the glass and began contorting them for her benefit.

"We're having our potluck party. This Saturday evening at the Deep Run Park Recreation Center. Can you bring one of your mama's wonderful desserts? I'm in charge of the wine."

Cooper was thrown for a loop by that statement. "Can you even drink wine at the park?"

"I'm getting a temporary alcohol permit. We're going to need the wine, Cooper. We've got to loosen some tongues."

"It's kind of short notice, Trish," Cooper remarked as she exited the highway. "Do you think all the volunteers will come?"

"We only need the ones who work Fridays or Saturdays."

"Why?"

"Because the missing items were always found after a weekend and Lali let something *else* slip." Trish paused to build suspense. "The folks who died this summer were all declared dead on a Saturday or Sunday. That means someone's been messing with the clients on a Friday or Saturday."

Cooper tried to digest Trish's logic. "Still, do you think everyone will show up just for a potluck?"

"I know they will," Trish affirmed. "Lali gave me their numbers and I've been on the phone all afternoon. They're all coming—probably because I made a big deal of emphasizing that it was an appreciation dinner in their honor and that someone was going to win two tickets to *Hairspray* at the Landmark Theater. How could they say no?" Trish sounded harried, but pleased. "The only one I can't reach is Leo. Seems he doesn't have a phone at the moment."

"He's the one I'd least expect to see at this dinner."

"Oh, he's going!" Trish declared. "If I've got to tie him up and carry him on my shoulders, he's going."

Cooper laughed at the image Trish's words conjured. "Then I'd better make some extra pumpkin bars. Leo looks like he could pack away some food."

"Let's just hope that's all he's packing," Trish muttered.

"Trish," Cooper admonished. "You've got to stop watching so much *Law & Order.*"

9

Then the land will yield its harvest,
and God, our God, will bless us.

God will bless us,
and all the ends of the earth will fear him.

Psalm 67:6-7 (NIV)

Cooper arrived at the Deep Run Park Recreation Center carrying two baskets lined with autumnal tea towels. Each basket was brimming with fragrant pumpkin crisp squares and she couldn't help but feel a small measure of pride over how perfectly the golden crumb topping and the fluffy cakelike texture of the pumpkin layer had turned out. Of course, every one of Maggie's recipes resulted in a mouth-watering dessert, but not all were as simple to reproduce as the pumpkin squares.

Grammy had watched Cooper bake throughout the afternoon, sampling the unbaked crisp and insisting on more butter or brown sugar in the crumb mixture. Finally, she had declared that every bachelor in the room would propose marriage based on the pumpkin squares.

"You must take after your mama in the kitchen," Grammy remarked. "She ain't stretchin' the truth by namin' her goodies Magnolia's Marvels. Guess I'm the lucky one, since all I seem to have a taste for these days is loaded with sugar or salt. 'Course, I had to find out the hard way that my denture paste can't stand up to peanuts."

As she cut the pumpkin crisp into squares, Cooper noted that Grammy was skinnier than ever and marveled over how she continued to diminish in size despite the fact that she snacked on cookies all day long.

"You feelin' okay, Grammy?" she had asked her.

"Just a mite tired," Grammy had replied and patted Cooper's arm. "Now go on and have a fun supper with your friends. I don't need you frettin' on my account. Leave your worries in this kitchen, ya hear?"

That had been easier said than done, however, for Trish had telephoned all the Sunrise Bible study members and informed them that they were each to pay particular attention to two of the volunteers on Saturday night. Cooper was supposed to glean as much information as possible about Warren and Brenda and then, once she returned home, write down all of her observations to share with the group on Sunday after church.

Cooper didn't expect any difficulty in chatting up Brenda, but drawing Warren out would be a challenge. After all, he was pleasant, but he was also quite shy, and Cooper knew that conducting small talk was a skill in which she was not very accomplished.

I hope I'm not too obvious, she thought as she stepped through the sliding glass doors of the recreation center.

According to Trish, Nathan had been assigned to Warren as well. He and Bryant were also supposed to subtly interrogate Penny until they had a complete picture of her life outside of Door-2-Door.

"By investigating in pairs, we'll have two views on all

the regular Saturday volunteers," Trish explained authoritatively. "Except for Leo, that is. *If* he ever shows up, Savannah wants to be seated next to him and then she wants all of us to leave her alone with him. Can you imagine?"

Cooper could. If anyone could break through Leo's tough exterior, it was Savannah. There was a gentleness about her; a soft quietness that created a feeling of safety. Their group leader was adept at listening, was never judgmental, and always looked for the good in people. This serenity of spirit was infused in all of her folk art paintings and Cooper remembered how she felt when she saw one of Savannah's works for the first time. She had been moved and delighted by the faceless figures of Savannah's Biblical scenes. Whether she was painting Adam and Eve in the Garden or Jesus walking on water, Savannah managed to capture the feeling behind the words of Scripture each time her brush met the canvas.

"Let me take one of those baskets," Jake offered as Cooper entered the room Trish had rented for the occasion. The circular tables borrowed from the community center were covered with mustard-colored cloths and had centerpieces of garnet-hued chrysanthemums in terracotta pots. Red, yellow, and orange balloons were tied to the back of each chair, and oversized leaves sprinkled with glitter dangled from the ceiling, pivoting lazily above the sounds of conversation and laughter.

"Trish, you did a wonderful job in here!" Cooper complimented her friend.

Trish smoothed her helmet of copper hair and grinned. "Thank you. My girls helped me set up this afternoon. They really wanted to stay. They even tried to get my husband to convince me." Her smile grew smaller. "But they've got a piano recital next week and they simply *must*

practice. I promised to bring them some dessert instead."
She leaned toward Cooper's basket. "Are those the pumpkin crisp squares?"

"They smell *so* good!" Quinton put his face close to the basket Jake held and inhaled deeply. Trish reached out for both baskets.

"I'll just put these on the buffet table. Quinton, why don't you see if any of the volunteers would care for a glass of apple cider? We've got nonalcoholic and a spiked version as well. I added apple brandy to the punch bowl on the right. Gotta get those tongues wagging!" Trish swiveled toward the door. "Oh, there's Lali and Anita. Good luck, friends." Trish hurried away in a click of maroon heels.

"Does that woman ever rest?" Jake mumbled in admiration. "And her family seems like the same type of go-getters. The husband and those two cute little girls worked their butts off setting up and then didn't so much as ask Trish to bring home a doggie bag full of brownies. Just kissed her good-bye and went on home."

Cooper watched Trish welcome Lali, Anita, and a man she assumed was Anita's husband. "I'm glad Trish sent the girls home. I'm sure she didn't want them exposed to someone dangerous. After all, there's a wicked person among us, Jake."

"I see what you're sayin'." Jake nodded thoughtfully.

"Did Trish hire a band?" Cooper pointed at a raised platform in the corner, which held three microphones, an amplifier, a keyboard, and a drum set.

"That would be so cool!" Bryant said, having arrived a few minutes behind Cooper. "And here I always thought Trish was so uptight, but I must be wrong. We've got spiked punch and maybe some rock music. What a gig!"

Jake laughed. "Before you get your *Saturday Night Fever* on, I asked her about the little stage over there. It's just been set up for some guy's surprise birthday party. They're usin' this room after us for some late-night bash to celebrate him turnin' twenty-one."

Bryant sighed. "I remember my twenty-first. It was awesome."

"If Trish were standing here, she'd tell you that you still believe you're twenty-one," Cooper teased.

"You're only as young as you think you are," Bryant quipped.

"Or as young as the girls you date." Jake nudged him playfully in the side. "Did you ask out that woman you work with yet?"

Nodding, Bryant smiled. "And her kids! I took them bowling. First of all, I never realized how much food kids can pack away. Popcorn, pretzels, hot dogs, pitchers of soda, and then ice cream for dessert. You should have seen the debris scattered across the table! Secondly, I've never been so badly beaten by an entire family during a casual game of knock-down-the-pins. Paige outscored me by twenty and somehow still managed to make me feel like I was the best bowler in the room."

"She sounds like a real special lady," Jake said. "I think you're gonna have a lot of fun with her and her kids. I'm right glad you took her out, my man."

"Me, too." Bryant grinned sheepishly.

"Okay, friends." Quinton gestured toward the tables. "Let's start socializing. I've been assigned Madge and Eugene. Eugene ought to be easy enough to cross off the list. He always has to go along with someone who can drive, so unless he's been stealing things on the sly during deliveries, he's in the clear." Quinton glanced at the young man, who was putting a face on a pumpkin using a permanent marker, his tongue sticking out of his mouth as he concentrated. "Not that I can see him hurting anyone. He seems completely content, so what would be his motive for taking other people's treasures?"

As Quinton walked away, Cooper reflected on his comment. What *was* the thief's motive? Money? Did they sell the objects they stole? Did they feel humiliated or overlooked and needed to prey on folks they could overpower? Were they seeking revenge against the elderly?

Cooper watched as Jake and Quinton seated themselves at different tables and began to strike up conversations. Shaking her head, she wondered if any of her friends truly possessed the ability to determine whether one of the volunteers fit the profile of a thief and possible murderer.

"You all right?" Nathan whispered, placing his hand on the small of her back. "You look lost in thought."

"This just feels wrong. We should be saluting these folks and celebrating all they do, but we're here to wring out their secrets, hang them on the line, and then examine them with a magnifying glass."

"I know," Nathan replied softly. "But think of Mr. Crosby. He's all alone, as are so many of the old folks relying on Door-2-Door. If we don't protect them, who will?" His hand slid up her back and squeezed her shoulder, sending a tingle along the knobs of her spine. "Just let your heart listen, Cooper. It'll know what to do."

Buoyed by Nathan's pep talk, Cooper joined Warren as he made his way to the food table. Picking up a paper plate covered by designs of a fruit-filled cornucopia, Cooper observed that Trish had also used coordinating cornucopia note cards to identify the dishes. The buffet line began with a cheddar-and-bacon dip accompanied by thin slices of homemade rye bread. Next was a green salad tossed with walnuts and goat cheese. Beyond that, a Crock-Pot filled with simmering corn chowder stood adjacent to a bowl of long-grain rice mixed with dried cranberries. The entrée, which Trish had had catered from a nearby restaurant, was an elegant platter of sliced pork tenderloin in a wild mushroom sauce. A deep bowl of tri-colored pasta salad with black olives came next, followed by a colorful squash medley. A wooden bowl overflowing with autumn succotash was at the end of the long line of mouthwatering food.

Cooper loaded up a spoon with succotash, admiring how beautifully the hues of the lima beans, corn kernels, and bacon slivers complimented one another. When her plate could hold no more, she followed Warren past the dessert table, which contained her pumpkin crisp squares along with an apple strudel and a chocolate pecan pie.

"What a spread," Warren stated with admiration. "Seems like everyone in your Bible study is a great cook."

"We've gotten pretty spoiled on homemade baked goods," Cooper agreed. "Most of us can bake something. Except for Jake. He always picks up Krispy Kremes. Oh, and Trish. She doesn't cook anything—not even brownies from a box. She says she's got the cleanest oven in Richmond."

Warren laughed and Cooper felt herself relaxing. This wasn't so hard. All she had to do was make some jokes and ask some questions. Judging by the way Warren smiled at her between bites, Cooper felt certain that she'd at least glean a snapshot of Warren's life.

Placing his hand on the arm of an elderly lady wearing purple bifocals, Warren turned to Cooper. "This is my

Nana Helen. She's got Alzheimer's. Don't mind her if she doesn't say much. This has been one of those days where she's been revisiting memories in her mind."

"Does she live with you?" Cooper asked, her heart warmed by the tenderness in Warren's eyes.

"Yeah. We're out in Louisa on what's left of their farm. My grandparents' farm, that is." Warren placed a cup of cider in Helen's hand. "But don't worry, it's not one of those sad, we-were-forced-to-sell-off-the-family-farm stories."

"That's good," Cooper said with relief. "'Cause I hate those kind of farm stories."

"Me, too," Warren agreed. "My grandparents sold it so my dad and his brothers could go to college. A businessman made them an offer they couldn't turn down and now most of the land is covered by a subdivision called Fox Run."

Cooper took a sip of the spiked cider and enjoyed the feeling of its warmth flowing down her throat. "Why do they always name subdivisions after foxes or eagles or other creatures that wouldn't be caught dead living in the three trees left standing in the yards of those houses?"

"Or horses. There's got to be a thousand neighborhoods named after steeple chases or thoroughbreds or other equestrian terms, even though there hasn't been a horse within fifty miles of the place in this century." Warren laughed and waved at Campbell, Door-2-Door's kitchen manager, as the giant man passed by them on his way back to the buffet table. "I'd name my subdivision something honest, like Box Hall or Pre-Fab Villas." Warren cut up Helen's pork into bite-sized pieces as she silently fed herself corn chowder. "There you go, Nana," he said, removing her empty soup bowl and placing the pork in front of her.

Cooper smiled at Warren. "Have you been volunteering at Door-2-Door for a long time?"

"A little over a year now," he answered. "I can remember exactly when because it was about the same time Nana's mind started drifting. I started to think about what life would be like for her if she didn't have family around her and I wanted to help people who didn't have that support." He replaced Helen's napkin, which had slid from her lap to the floor. "She's been inspiring me to give to others my whole life."

"And you do give up every Saturday?" Cooper felt a prick of guilt over persisting in her line of questioning. "Don't you need rest after your workweek?"

Warren thought about this for a moment and then shook his head. "I'm a delivery guy for LabTech. I pick up test samples all over town and bring them to the lab. I also bring supplies to the medical offices we run. I have no stress, I'm paid pretty well, and I'm off by four-thirty every day. No complaints. I figure I can spare a few hours on Saturday. I get up early on Saturdays, anyway, so I can check out the most promising garage sales."

"So Saturday's the only time you can drive a route?"

Warren nodded. "Yeah. I wish I could do more, but that's all I can do with my schedule right now. LabTech's got me on a split shift on Friday so I can pack coolers at Door-2-Door. I like going there twice a week. Everyone is really nice. Even Campbell. He's just a big bear with a loud roar." He smirked. "It took me a while not to tremble every time I made a mistake packing coolers. It was like I half-expected Campbell to strap me to the back of his Harley and drive me to the nearest cliff."

At that moment, Brenda arrived at their table trailed by a young boy wearing glasses and holding a library book.

"Darik!" Brenda barked at him affectionately. "Put that book on the table and take your plate from your mama. I ain't gonna stand here all day waitin' on you."

Without replying, Darik seated himself at the table and held out his hands for a plate.

Brenda handed her son a napkin and then sat down between Darik and Cooper. "This is my son, y'all. Darik, say hello."

"Pleased to meet you," the boy said softly, keeping his eyes fastened on his plate.

"You stole one of our clients, Warren?" Brenda joked as she waved at Helen.

Warren explained who she was and Brenda beamed at him. "You're a fine grandson, Warren. This is how it's supposed to be—folks takin' care of the old instead of shuttin' them in some home with a bunch of strangers or leavin' them to fend for themselves." She glanced sideways at Darik. "Oh, I'm sorry, baby. Let's thank the Lord so you can eat." She and Darik bowed their heads, clasped their hands on the table, and whispered a prayer. "And thank you, Jesus, for so *many* reasons to celebrate! Amen!" Brenda ended by saying and Darik echoed her amen with an equal amount of enthusiasm.

"What did you make at that glorious table?" Brenda asked Cooper.

"One of the desserts," Cooper answered. "If anyone has room after the rest of the meal."

"Honey, I'll have plenty of space!" Brenda declared, gesturing at her formidable belly. "You'd think I'd get tired of food, bein' that I work as a cashier at Kroger and see nothin' but things to shove in my mouth all day long." She sighed. "But heaven help me, I love to eat!"

"Being a cashier's got to be hard," Warren commented. "You're on your feet for so many hours."

Brenda's fork bobbed up and down in agreement. "You've no idea, sug! By the end of my shift my back hurts, my feet hurt, and even my arms hurt from pushing those heavy things like Tide and big 'ole cases of beer across the scanner. I work like an ox and am still barely hangin' on." She put her arm around Darik's shoulders. "Good thing this one don't eat too much, but he's little now. I've seen how teenage boys go at their food, and it's somethin' that'll put the fear of God in you! Three burgers, a gallon of milk, potato chips all night. Shoot, I'd better have made shift manager by the time Darik goes to junior high!"

"I'll get a job, too, Mama," the boy declared seriously and Brenda's smile was filled was pride.

"Yessir, you're a good worker, too, but I'd much rather see you read your books, son. That's the secret to movin' up in this world. Books." She eyed Cooper. "You work with books?"

Cooper held out her calloused hands. "No. I work with these." She told her tablemates about her job and the conversation flowed smoothly for another thirty minutes. Warren and Brenda offered to fetch enough dessert for all to share while Cooper refilled cups with apple cider. As she poured some of the nonalcoholic cider into Darik's cup, he looked at her curiously.

"How'd you get different-colored eyes like that?"

Cooper touched the skin just below the green eye. "I had an accident playing sports and I was given the green eye to help me see again."

"Wow," Darik breathed. "Do you have X-ray vision? Like Superman? I saw the movie at Jamaar's house. We don't have a TV. Mama says we can't afford one."

With a laugh, Cooper replied, "I can't see through walls, but that would be pretty cool. Still, if I could have magic powers, I'd rather fly." She told Darik about their family pet Columbus and the little boy listened raptly.

"That hawk got shot?" His dark eyes were round. "That's what happened to my daddy, too. But he's in heaven now. I mean, maybe he's in heaven." The boy looked doubtful. "Mama says Daddy wanted nice stuff but didn't wanna pay for it. He did bad things, but she won't tell me what. Then he got shot right here." He touched his chest and then clamped his lips shut as his mother approached.

"Lord, Darik! I'm gonna need to buy a bigger pair of pants if we stay here much longer!" She handed her son a plate of desserts and then dug the side of her fork into a large slice of apple strudel. "Mmm," she moaned and fanned her face with her hand. "I don't know what we did to deserve this party," she said to Cooper. "But I will bless the day you all decided to show up at Door-2-Door that Saturday. It's the only day I volunteer and if Darik didn't play with his cousin every Saturday, I'd've missed out bein' invited to this feast! We are sure grateful to you all."

"Yes, indeed," Warren said and toasted Cooper with his cider cup. "Thank you for showing us such generosity and appreciation. It's really nice to make new friends."

Flushing at their words, Cooper felt a wave of shame flood through her. How would Warren and Brenda react if they found out that the purpose of the dinner was to seek out a villain?

She stared at the slice of chocolate pecan pie on her plate and sighed. Her stomach was too replete with rich food to squeeze in another morsel. Warren murmured to Helen as he named the selection of desserts for her. Her eyes twinkled as she picked up a bite-sized piece of strudel and then leaned into her grandson, who gave her a brief hug.

Suddenly, five men wearing shiny gray suits walked into the party. One of them carried a saxophone, one had a trumpet, and another held a clarinet against his chest. They headed directly for the stage, only to be intercepted by Trish, who gesticulated angrily between the raised platform and the tables filled with diners. It seemed as though one of the band members was desperately pleading with Trish and it was only when Bryant joined the fray that Trish's grimace finally melted away. Shrugging her shoulders in resignation, she returned to her table.

The band members fidgeted with their equipment and caused everyone to jump to attention when they conducted a sound check on the microphone.

"Good evening, folks!" The lead singer's voice filled the room. "We appreciate the opportunity to warm up before the birthday party begins in an hour. Rockin' Rob here has had a cold all week and we've gotta make sure he can play. Otherwise, we're gonna have to call in some backup. Anyone out there play the sax?"

Several of the Door-2-Door volunteers laughed as Eugene raised his hand.

"All right!" The band member nodded his head. "We'll keep you in mind, brother. And now, without further ado, we'd like to bring you the jumpin', jivin' tunes of Tommy Ziegler and the Capital City Swing Band!"

Instantly, the trumpet and saxophone burst into life, accompanied by a high-energy drumbeat. Tommy Ziegler began to sing, snap his fingers in time to the zippy music, and shake his hips behind the microphone stand. All around the room, heads began to bob and hands began to clap in time to the rhythm.

"Come on, baby!" Brenda shouted to her son. "Let's shake our stuff!" Darik bounced after his mother to the small square of clear flooring in front of the stand and the twosome began to dance, their faces shining with delight.

Inspired, people abandoned their desserts and joined Brenda and Darik. Bryant took Trish in his arms and began to perform complicated swing-dance steps with her. At first, she seemed stiff and unrelenting, but after a few minutes, she was kicking up her heels like a Rockette. Nathan also made his way to the dance floor, and Cooper felt a fresh bout of jealousy as she noticed he was holding Lali's hand.

Where is Lali's husband? she wondered crossly and then saw that he was already dancing with Anita.

In order to avoid staring at Nathan, Cooper looked at Helen instead. She was smiling and clapping her hands, and as Cooper's eyes met Warren's, he stood up and offered her his hand. "I'm not much of a dancer, but I'd love the opportunity to step on your feet if you're willing."

"I am." Cooper laughed and took Warren's hand. Just as they made their way to the crowded space between the tables and the stage, the frenzied swing song ended and Tommy and company began to sing a slow, romantic tune instead.

"Now I can *really* step on you," Warren said with a shy smile as he slipped his arm around Cooper's lower back.

Noticing that Nathan was now slow-dancing with Lali, Cooper allowed herself to move even closer into Warren's chest. He smelled pleasant, like a mixture of wet grass and soil. It was a scent that reminded her of her greenhouse and she felt surprisingly comfortable in his arms. Warren guided her into a graceful turn and then effortlessly reeled her back toward him.

"Whoa! You got some moves there, girl!" Jake shouted as he gently held on to Savannah and rocked her from side to side like an awkward pre-teen at a school dance.

"It's all my partner," Cooper confessed with a blush. "He's a strong leader."

Now Warren's cheeks turned pink. The song ended and Cooper thanked him, and then returned to her seat. Tommy Ziegler took a brief bow and then he and his bandmates set their instruments down. Glowing with exertion, Trish ran forward and invited them to partake of their potluck feast.

As the Capital City Swingers loaded their plates, several of the Door-2-Door volunteers gathered their coats and handbags and after thanking each member of the Sunrise Bible study, left for home. Cooper picked up her empty pumpkin square baskets and said good night to her friends. When Nathan offered to accompany her to her truck, she waved him off politely, longing for some fresh air and a few moments of silence in which she could ask God for forgiveness for practicing deception on such a fine group of people.

"There must be someone else to blame for these thefts," she spoke into the quiet as she drove the dark, one-lane road leading to her house. "Because if all the volunteers are anything like Brenda and Warren, we're accusing angels of being demons."

The next day, Cooper hurriedly dressed for church, anxious to hear what her friends had to say about the Door-2-Door volunteers they had spoken with the night before. She'd completed the last segment of her *Amazing Joseph* homework just before going to bed, but had felt distracted by remembrances of the party as she flipped through chapters of the Bible or scribbled terse answers in her workbook.

When she walked into the classroom where the Sunrise group always met, she was pleased to note that her friends were already assembled there and waiting on her to begin.

"Who provided us with this lovely breakfast?" Savannah asked as Jake presented her with a flaky croissant brushed with melted butter and a salad made of strawberries, blueberries, and raspberries topped by a dollop of crème fraîche.

"I did," Nathan answered. "I was still full from last night's dinner, so I thought I'd avoid our usual fare of iced pastries with a side of coffee cake. I know these croissants look heavy, but they're actually whole wheat and won't settle in your stomach like a pile of bricks."

"You oughta start your own cable show." Jake took an appreciative bite of croissant. "How many guys can come up with somethin' this good made out of wheat?"

Savannah smiled as she tore off the end of her croissant with her elegant, paint-stained fingers. "Maybe Bryant can propose it to his network."

Bryant mumbled something unintelligible and Nathan nudged his elbow. "Late night, Bryant?"

"Sometimes it's hard to keep pace with Paige. I don't know how she has so much energy after spending all day with her kids," Bryant admitted reluctantly.

"A single mom has no choice. She's got an entire family's worth of responsibility on her shoulders." Trish scrutinized Bryant over her coffee cup. "I know Paige is over thirty, but she sounds like she's really got it together. Are you considering getting serious with her?"

Bryant shrugged and Savannah took advantage of the

momentary silence to change the subject. "Let's begin, shall we? Any prayer requests?

Quinton asked for a prayer for his nephew to heal quickly from a broken toe. "He shut it in the car door, poor kid," he explained. "Second time he's done that, too."

"I'd like to ask for some clarity in regards to a new client I've recently taken on," Nathan requested. "He brought me his product to photograph for the website and when I examined it, I don't know, let's just say I have my doubts about it."

"What's he hockin'?" Jake wanted to know.

"Muscle-building products," Nathan answered. "He says his goal is to help little guys bulk up and gain confidence. I like the idea of his product, but I'm just not sure it is what he says it is. However, I have no experience with herbal medicines."

"Maybe they're some kind of harmful steroid," Trish suggested, looking aghast at the idea.

Nathan held out his hands in supplication. "Everything appears to be above-board with his business. It's just a feeling I have about this particular product. I don't know anything about this type of item, so I have no right to assume that there's something wrong with it, but I can't seem to shake the possibility that my client and his goods aren't all that they appear."

Savannah nodded. "We'll pray for the Lord to guide you in this matter, Nathan. Anyone else?"

After a brief hesitation, Cooper spoke up. "I have a prayer request for my sister, Ashley. She and her husband have been trying to start a family for about a year now. Things are . . . getting tense between them. I just worry about her, well, getting depressed because she's not pregnant yet."

Several of Cooper's friends uttered sympathetic murmurs.

"I've got one, too." Jake sat forward in his chair and clasped his hands together over his closed workbook. "You know, when I was readin' about Joseph this weekend—when he gets thrown in the Egyptian slammer for somethin' he didn't even do—do y'all know the part I'm talkin' about?"

"Yes, the first part of Genesis 40, after Joseph is falsely accused of fooling around with Potiphar's wife," Savannah said.

"Yeah!" Jake tapped on his Bible. "Anyway, I remember that Joseph asked his cellmate, the cupbearer guy, to mention him to Pharaoh when he got called to give his defense. Joseph was hopin' the cupbearer was a decent man and could help him get sprung from jail. Y'all with me?"

Everyone nodded in unison.

"Well, the cupbearer gets out, but he forgets about Joseph. Man, readin' that burned me up! And right away, I started thinkin' about the old folks Door-2-Door helps who have been left alone for whatever reason. My prayer is that the Lord won't let us forget about them. I want to allow Him to just go on and work through our brains and our bodies to protect these folks and find the devil among them." He glanced at his friends, his eyes fiery. "I know we're talkin' all this out after church, but I think we need to arm ourselves with prayer, kinda like we learned durin' our Ephesians study."

"Sharpen your weapons, maties." Bryant swiped his Bible through the air as though wielding a sword. "People of faith can be tough guys, too."

Nathan stood and pretended to parry with his own Bible. "Arrrgh! The Good Book is mightier than the sword."

"Okay, Pirates of Pentecost!" Cooper laughed. "Watch out for the coffee cups."

As no one else had prayer requests, the Sunrise members linked hands and bowed their heads while Savannah led them in prayer. They then spent the rest of the hour drinking coffee and sharing their views on Joseph and his prediction of Egypt's seven years of plenty and seven years of famine. Afterward, the group adjourned to the auditorium for worship service and promised to reunite at Quinton's townhouse by quarter of one.

Quinton's Tudor-style town home on South Harrison Street was located beneath the shadow of Richmond's venerable burial ground, Hollywood Cemetery. The cemetery rose in a steep hill to overlook the James and several of Richmond's downtown neighborhoods. Quinton had told his friends many times that he loved living near the historic landmark and often took evening walks through the cemetery.

"When I think I've had a bad day because the stock market's down or a client has left our brokerage firm for a competing firm, it only takes a stroll around that place to put things in perspective," Quinton had once told them. "And it's strangely peaceful to read the loving epitaphs people have written for their family members."

Cooper had never been inside his home before, but she was impressed by the cleanliness of the walnut wood floors, glass-topped tables, and plush, leather furniture. Quinton had decorated his apartment using a multitude of brown and cream tones, punctuated by splashes of red and green, which appeared in the rugs, throw pillows, and in the lithographs grouped on his off-white walls.

"Quinton, I wish you'd come over and make my place look half as cool as this." Jake pivoted around and around, impressed by what he saw. "I've still got my mama's old flowered sofas and a coffee table that's piled so high with magazines and tools and junk that its legs are startin' to give."

"I can't take any credit for the décor in here. My sister's an interior designer and I just gave her my Visa card and she took over." He led his friends into his kitchen, which was illuminated by a series of pendant chandeliers with jewel-toned shades made of glass. "I bought sandwich fixings for our meal." Quinton began pulling lunchmeat out of his gigantic Sub-Zero fridge. "And fresh bread from Montana Gold." He looked to Trish for help. "Would you arrange the food on this platter?" He handed her an oversized brass platter. "I had to save all my exertions for a special dessert."

"Hard salami!" Jake grinned as he hovered behind Trish. "I liked you before, my man, but I love ya now. This is my favorite."

"I'll stick to turkey and muenster," Bryant said, assembling his sandwich. "You have any pickles, Quinton?"

"Oh, sure. And three kinds of potato chips." He ripped open a bag of barbeque chips and dumped them into a wooden bowl. "I've also got brownies." He whipped the tin foil off a tray of brownie squares. "But these aren't your run-of-the mill Duncan Hines boxed stuff. For you, my dearest friends, I've made fudge brownies with peanut butter frosting."

"Quinton, thank you so much for providing for us today," Savannah said as Jake helped her settle on one of the stools tucked beneath the kitchen island. Trish and Cooper also sat while the rest of the group leaned against the cabinets to eat.

They chewed in thoughtful silence for a few moments and Cooper wondered if they all felt as reluctant as she did to share their observances on their fellow Door-2-Door volunteers.

Nathan, who was standing near Quinton's double sink, suddenly put down his ham and provolone sandwich and aggressively dusted crumbs from his large hands. "I've got to admit that I'm not looking forward to the work set out for us this afternoon. The two people I talked to last night were delightful—just as they've been at the Door-2-Door headquarters the past few Saturdays. It's how I imagine they are all the time. Totally great."

"*Somebody's* only pretendin' to be good," Jake reminded Nathan. "This ain't gonna be a smooth road we're treadin', but we've got to walk it to find out the truth."

"Should we get started, then?" Savannah asked the group.

At that moment, Trish's cell phone rang and strains of Pachelbel's *Canon* echoed throughout the kitchen as she removed the cacophonous instrument from her purse and glanced at the Caller ID. "It's Lali," she said with surprise and answered the phone.

The Sunrise members watched with a tense curiosity that quickly turned to alarm as Trish's violet-tinted eyes grew round with shock. Her hand flew over her mouth, but not before she murmured, "No!" She listened for another moment; her expression growing more and more dismayed, and then slowly closed her phone.

Trish placed her right palm on the countertop to steady herself. "Lali called . . . she wanted us to know . . ." She took a deep breath and began again. "She wanted to tell us that Mr. Crosby is dead. The paramedics believe it was heart failure at this point." She looked up, her eyes meeting Cooper's briefly before traveling around the room. "And I'm afraid they found him sitting up in his chair."

10

Make plans by seeking advice;
if you wage war, obtain guidance.

Proverbs 20:18 (NIV)

Quinton's brownie tray clattered to the counter. "Not another one."

"That makes three Door-2-Door clients that have been found . . ." Nathan forced the word out. "Dead. Sitting in their chairs."

Cooper stared at his stricken face, but her mind was miles away inside Frank Crosby's small, disheveled house. She visualized his quivering hands—the loose and wrinkled skin, the blue-purple of the swollen veins on the backs of his palms, the irregular speckles of brown from wrist to knuckle. She saw Frank clutching his borrowed newspaper, the wobbling letters scratched inside each crossword square with the nub of a pencil. The scent of urine and stale sweat invaded her memory, forcing her to wince involuntarily, but the remembered odor was quickly supplanted by the picture of the old man alone, releasing his last breaths into the musty air of his decaying room.

Cooper couldn't stop her tears from falling.

She was not alone. Savannah had her head bowed and

though her hands covered her mouth and nose, the liquid pooling in her dark blue eyes trickled over onto her fingers. Trish and Jake had their arms around one another—their expressions a mixture of sorrow and fresh, bright anger. Bryant and Quinton gazed dully at the floor while Nathan twisted a paper napkin around and around his thumb as though it were a manacle.

After a moment, he placed a hand on Cooper's arm. "You just met Mr. Crosby the other day. This must be especially tough for you."

Bryant's head snapped up. "And I *found* Mrs. Davenport!" He turned to Trish, his eyes uncommonly hostile. "I suppose Lali's told the police? They've got to conduct an autopsy and find out what this fiend is using to send these old folks off to sleep. And don't tell me that we're not involved, because from where I'm standing, *we are definitely involved*!"

Startled by Bryant's vehemence, Trish shrugged helplessly. "She called the police. I have no idea what's going on beyond what she told me."

"No sense leavin' this mess all in *their* hands," Jake stated firmly. "I say we go ahead with our suspect lists. We've helped the cops before and you know these Door-2-Door folks are gonna be more themselves with us than with a bunch of tough-lookin' uniforms carryin' guns and wooden sticks."

The group members all looked to Savannah to gauge what she thought of Jake's suggestion. Their leader closed her eyes and murmured an inaudible prayer. At first, everyone watched her lips move, nearly hypnotized by the serenity that immediately flooded her features, but soon each of them followed suit by bowing their heads and shutting their eyes.

Several minutes passed before Savannah let out a restorative sigh. "One of the names for God is the Ancient of Days. I think that title came to my mind because I was asking God to help me understand why someone would be preying on these helpless, ancient souls. I asked Him to help quell my emotions, to give me the clarity of insight and to release my anger, as it does us no good."

"It's hard to think at all considering what we're up against, but here's a thought: Lali told us that Mr. Manningham and Mrs. Davenport were both in their nineties." Nathan frowned. "Do you think this person believes he's releasing them from pain or the indignities of becoming old so they can find peace?"

"Like some kind of mercy killer?" Jake shook his head. "Except for bein' old, they didn't have diseases or painful cancer or anything. Maybe he thinks they're poor and lonely and are better off bein' with their loved ones who have already gone on to heaven."

"*If* he believes in heaven," Trish snorted. "No one can decide on behalf of another person that it's their time to die. That is the Lord's prerogative!"

"He's a merciful killer, because he kills gently, but I doubt he's doing this out of pity. More like greed. Or fear." Cooper drummed her fingers on the countertop. "I don't think Mrs. Davenport was too troubled by loneliness. Lali told us that her daughter visited regularly. They used to polish her jewelry and try it on, right?" She turned to Nathan. "And Mr. Crosby was in his late seventies. I know that's no spring filly, but it's not the kind of old where people start feeling that their bodies are rotting while their minds are still sharp. He could have lived for two more decades for all we know."

"But maybe the murderer thought that Mr. Crosby

wasn't living at all," Nathan argued. "That he was miserable and longed to let go of life."

"I agree with Cooper. These are not acts of kindness and we are not going to figure out the *why* until we figure out the *who*," Quinton asserted as he cut a large brownie square for himself. "I know this looks callous, but I need to eat when I'm anxious." He bit off half the brownie. "And I'm *really* anxious right now," he mumbled through a mouthful of chocolate and peanut butter.

Savannah held out her hand. "Come stand by me, Quinton."

He hastily complied and she leaned her petite body against Quinton's large, thick torso, and he was clearly comforted by her nearness.

"The Ancient of Days is eternal," Savannah intoned. "He has the power of judgment. We do not." Her voice was infused with the strength of conviction. "But I believe we can work our hardest to do His will and I am quite certain that we have a role to play in making sure justice is done. We can begin by sharing what we discovered at the party, putting together a list of who might have the strongest motive to steal from these elderly people, and continue to get to know them. If the police solve the case—wonderful. If they reach a dead end, then perhaps we can raze some of the obstacles in their path." She turned her warm blind gaze upon her friends. "We are a community. We must help one another, trust one another, and shield our neighbors from harm."

Bryant laid a briefcase on the counter, removing a legal pad and a ballpoint pen from inside. "Anything relevant from last night's party can be immediately shared with the police."

"If there *is* anything relevant," Quinton said gloomily.

"I wonder if anything's missin' from Mr. Crosby's house," Jake mused as each member retrieved the notes they had recorded on their fellow Door-2-Door volunteers. "Did Brenda say anythin' about him havin' family?" Jake asked Cooper.

"He's got a son—" Cooper began.

"Then he's sure to look into his father's death!" Trish declared, smoothing a creaseless sheet of creamy cardstock covered by florid handwriting. "Personally, I think a relative is better suited to help the police search for clues than we are." Trish touched a lock of carefully placed copper hair and continued quickly, as if to forestall all possible argument. "Being Mr. Crosby's son means that he can ensure an autopsy is performed and he's certain to know if his father owned anything valuable. We can hardly rummage through his house."

Cooper opened her mouth to disagree with Trish, but before she could speak, Quinton said, "You're assuming quite a lot about the son." His hand inched toward the brownie pan. "Father and son may not even be close. Does the kid even live locally? If he's in the picture, why did Mr. Crosby need the services of Door-2-Door every single day? Why didn't he visit—?"

"It's *not* possible for him to visit his daddy!" Cooper stated forcefully before the conjecture could continue. "The son's in jail."

Nathan's eyes widened. "Why?"

Cooper tried to recall what Brenda had told her. "He's a drug dealer. I believe he tried to sell heroin to an undercover cop. I got the impression that this wasn't the first time he'd been caught, either."

The friends exchanged dejected looks. Quinton polished off a second brownie and then began to pour coffee beans into an electric grinder. "I predict we're going to need a caffeine boost to get our minds churning. Cover your ears, everyone." He pressed on the plastic lid of the grinder and the noise of the beans being pulverized into grounds prevented further conversation.

Cooper inhaled the pleasant, homey odor of the fresh coffee as Quinton shook the contents of the grinder into a paper filter. It was comforting to watch the big man move about his kitchen. His nimble fingers were both delicate and precise as he poured filtered water into what appeared to be an expensive and complicated coffee machine. Afterward, he laid out several stainless steel ramekins and carefully poured both white and raw brown sugar into two of the small bowls. The third contained several brands of sugar substitutes. Next, Quinton produced a pair of porcelain creamers and filled one with half-and-half and the other with low-fat milk.

As the coffee percolated, all eyes remained fastened on Quinton as he set out diminutive silver spoons next to the ramekins and displayed porcelain cups and saucers in a neat rectangle to the right of the creamers. Steam erupted from the top of the coffee carafe and surrounded Quinton's head in a halo of thin mist.

"Quinton, I could watch you move around this kitchen all day," Nathan commented. "And you're just brewing coffee. I can't fathom how magical it must be to watch you bake."

"Less quiet," Quinton replied, his round face pink with pleasure over Nathan's compliment. "I always bake to the strains of classical music. The big symphonies in particular. Dvorak's *New World* is my favorite."

While the last hiccups emanated from the Cuisinart coffeemaker, Quinton retrieved a set of glass shakers from his cupboard. "I've got cinnamon, nutmeg, or dark chocolate curls should you like a little extra something in your coffee."

"Would you marry me?" Bryant asked and then offered to prepare a cup for Savannah. Once they were all armed with caffeine, Quinton led them into his living room where they exchanged details on the Door-2-Door volunteers. Nathan volunteered to act as secretary by inputting any relevant information into his laptop.

An hour later, the coffee cups were drained, the brownies were gone, and Nathan had created a master list summarizing their findings.

"I can hook this up to your printer and make copies for all of us," Nathan suggested and, by the time Trish and Bryant had loaded Quinton's dishwasher with the lunch items, Cooper held the summary in her hands. She read it over carefully.

Warren—Courier for LabTech. Likes to go to garage sales on weekends. Bachelor. Lives with his grandma Helen on family farm in Louisa. She has Alzheimer's. Warren volunteers at D2D Fridays and Saturdays. Has been there for over a year. Dresses in casual, inexpensive clothes, and is careful with his appearance. Drives a Toyota Corolla (not new, but very clean). A bit reserved but seems content. Good dancer.

Erik—Retired principal. Divorcee in his early seventies. Attractive. Good sense of humor. Lives on pension. Seems determined not to move from current D2D route. Flirts with female volunteers and D2D staff. Freely admits to wanting a wife who will cook and clean. Loves to do lake fishing by himself and play Internet poker late at night. Drives an aged SUV rigged with fishing pole holders.

Brenda—Works as a cashier at Kroger. Finds her job tiresome. Young son Darik is a bookworm. She really wants him to go to a private school outside the city as his district is full of young gangsters. She worries son is not getting the education he'll need to get a college scholarship. She barely makes enough to feed and house them. Volunteers at D2D because she feels blessed and wants to pass that on by delivering food and friendship. When Brenda was out of earshot, Darik said that his daddy was shot in the chest and killed. Was likely a criminal. Brenda drives a rusty, dented Caddy.

Madge—Sweet, rather fragile woman in her late sixties. Imagines herself in similar position to those D2D serves. Retired nurse. One daughter who lives in London as a stage actress—she is wild and has had issues with drug and alcohol abuse. Madge doesn't think she can count on her to take care of her when she gets old. Seems a bit afraid of everything. Works at D2D because she and Penny go to same church and Penny convinced her to come. She's glad that Penny asked her, as she doesn't have much going on other than church functions. Misses excitement of hospital work. Drives a Saturn sedan.

Penny—Works part-time selling ad space for mailbox coupons. Married an older man who died and has two sons, both of whom are well off. One is a dentist and the other a hematologist. Both live outside of D.C. and are very busy with their own families and work. She says she's addicted to QVC and has gotten into hot water buying things from the show. Admits to getting lonely. She says D2D is a main part of her social life. She gets sick of the bossy ladies at her church. Too much like a high school clique, she says. Drives a station wagon.

Campbell—D2D kitchen manager. Always has Mondays off. Rides his Harley Davidson to VA beach as much as he can. He's got a serious crush on a female bartender there who has been rejecting his advances for over a year. He's determined to win her heart by Christmas by "doing something big." Wouldn't say more. Loves his job. Is very close to his parents who live in Petersburg. Says the D2D clients are all like the grandparents he never knew.

Leo—Forced to work at D2D as part of court sentence. Started in the middle of summer. Angry. Violent tattoos. Doesn't have a car. Uses bus to get to D2D. Job? Hobbies? Family?

Cooper jotted several notes on her sheet of paper as she read. She then reviewed the document one more time, doing her best to pretend that the names listed there belonged to strangers instead of the likable group of volunteers.

"What are you circling?" Nathan asked her.

"I think we should consider the possibility that the killer is motivated by money." She held up her hand before anyone could protest. "I know that sounds strange in a way because the Door-2-Door victims were poor, but if these aren't mercy killings, than what else could the killer's motive be?" Cooper was clearly thinking out loud. "I'm circling any indications that the volunteers have money issues. Perhaps someone who's desperate would hope that each client had something of value tucked away somewhere."

"Good thinkin'!" Jake nodded. "We can circle Erik right off. If he's playin' poker on the Internet, he could be deep in the hole. My brother got sucked into one of those cyber-money pits a few years ago. He'd come home from work, type in his credit card number, and boom!" He slammed his hand on the coffee table for emphasis. "Six months later my sister-in-law finds out that he's taken a second mortgage on the house. Man, he slept on the couch for a *long* time after *that*!"

"I bet." Trish smirked. "I hate to be the one to point it out, but Brenda's got motivation then, too. She wants her son to go to private school, and take it from me, tuition is *very* expensive. Why, if my business weren't doing so *well*, my girls would be going to our *local* school for certain." She shook off the objectionable idea of her progeny attending public school. "But there isn't much a mother won't do to ensure a good future for her child, and Brenda's Kroger paycheck is *not* going to change Darik's future. Selling pricey jewelry or gold coins to a pawnbroker could add up over time, assuming that's what they're doing."

"I hate to circle anyone on this list." Quinton sighed despondently. "But Penny might be in debt due to her QVC sprees. Campbell may also be trying to accumulate a big pile of money to buy some . . ." He turned to Bryant. "What do teenagers call glitzy jewelry these days?"

"Bling," Bryant answered authoritatively. "He might plan to dazzle his girlfriend with some bling."

"And Madge could be trying to stockpile a nest egg for her old age," Nathan added. "She seems fearful of being unable to care for herself and is truly terrified of the idea of a nursing home."

"Can't say that I blame her," Cooper murmured, grateful that Grammy was firmly established in the Lee house. Still, she couldn't help but wonder what would happen if Grammy should get sick. None of the Lees had medical training and could never afford to hire a full-time nurse. Even Ashley's coffers might not be full enough to prevent Grammy from entering into some kind of assisted-living program. Feeling grim, Cooper returned her attention to their suspect list. "Warren may want extra money, too," she said, her face flushing with guilt as she recalled how pleasant it had been to dance with him. "His grandma has Alzheimer's and must need special care during the day. He's at work, so someone must be looking after her."

"Everyone on this list needs money! We're gettin' real far real fast," Jake muttered darkly.

"Fighting the devil is never easy, my friend," Savannah said softly. "And what's especially difficult here is that no one appears to be *spending* any money. From what you've all told me, the volunteers wear inexpensive clothes, sport little or no jewelry, and drive fairly old cars. They take care of what they've got and try hard to make ends meet." She rubbed her chin in thought. "Whoever is committing these crimes has a way to sell the stolen items and has been doing something that's not obvious to an outsider with the cash."

"Like hiding it in the hen coop." Cooper was reminded of where Grammy's parents hid their money instead of entrusting it to the bank. Absently rubbing her right hand over the names on the list, she said, "I wonder if this person wants to acquire a certain amount or if they're going to just keep going, even though the police are involved now." She shook her head. There were no easy answers.

No obvious clues. "I think we're going to have to wait and see what drugs were in Mr. Crosby's body. Then we can narrow down our suspect list to a person who has access to drugs *and* needs cash."

Nathan abruptly left his seat and strolled over to the window that overlooked a hill of patchy grass belonging to the cemetery. Shoving his hands deep into his pockets, he paced back and forth, his reflection in the large panel of glass flickering as his body passed through the curtain of sunlight.

"It could take days for Mr. Crosby's test results to come back and that's *if* an autopsy's even performed. I know Lali's talked to the police about her fears that her clients are being sent to their graves earlier than scheduled, but we need to know what Mr. Crosby's most valuable possession was. It would be the freshest clue."

"Well, there's only one person who we could ask. Frank Crosby's son." Bryant grimaced. "And I can't be seen hanging out with a guy in an orange jumpsuit. I've got a reputation to consider."

"Me, too!" Trish echoed, placing her hand over her heart as though the very idea of being seen with an inmate would instantaneously cause her business to go up in flames.

Nathan turned from the window and looked intently at Cooper. "I'll go see his son. My knees will knock the whole time, but I'll do it."

Cooper felt a rush of tenderness sweep through her. She knew that Nathan was offering to visit Frank's son because he wanted to solve the mystery of the older man's death, but also because he knew how saddened Cooper was over the news that Mr. Crosby's life had been stolen away by someone he trusted. "You won't be alone," she whispered to him as though they were the only two people in the room. "I'll be with you."

Jake and Quinton also volunteered to be present, but Savannah suggested that too many people might cause the son to clam up.

"We'll focus our attention elsewhere," she told the remaining group members. "Quinton, you see what you can find out about everyone's financial situation. Perhaps you can call them under the guise of proposing investment strategies."

Quinton nodded his head in agreement. "Actually, I might be able to help them save more judiciously. Every penny counts and I'm sure very few of them have spoken to financial consultants about how to make the most of their money." He held out his hands. "I just hope I don't aid the murderer too much."

"You'll just have to take a chance with your kindness," Savannah replied. "Trish, you keep in contact with Lali. If she hears anything from the police, let us know." Savannah fell silent, pulling the length of her long, black braid through her right hand over and over as she ruminated.

"What about me?" Jake asked, looking hurt.

"I need you with me," Savannah answered and Jake immediately smiled at her in adoration. "You and I are going to pay a visit to Leo," she continued firmly. "Since he didn't come to our little party, we're going to bring one to him."

Looking uncertain, Jake mumbled, "I'd better make sure I got plenty of metal pipes in the back of the Mr. Faucet van. You never know how these parties are gonna end."

* * *

The next day Cooper was struggling to replace the fuser assembly on a Canon copier so that it would no longer produce double images when her cell phone rang. Since her hands were dirty, she ignored the melodious burst of her phone's *Love Me Do* ring. When it began to ring again, the Beatles crooning rather loudly in boisterous harmony, the manager of the clothing store swiveled around in her chair and frowned.

"Can I get that for you?" she asked Cooper acerbically, tapping her pencil with impatience. "I'm trying to fill out my hours schedule and I just can't do the math when I'm distracted."

"Sorry, ma'am." Cooper hastily wiped her hands with a rag, grabbed her phone, and stepped out the back door, which was reserved for deliveries, smoke breaks, and banished service people, such as herself.

Noting that both calls had come from Ashley, Cooper immediately grew annoyed. "*Some* of us have jobs to do!" she blurted out as her sister answered the phone.

There was a moment of silence. "Coop. I need a favor."

Surprised by Ashley's tone, which was uncommonly quiet and edging toward timidity, Cooper quickly agreed.

"I've got an appointment with Dr. Easter this afternoon," Ashley explained. "He's the foremost infertility doctor in Richmond."

"I thought you decided to give yourself more time before seeing a specialist," Cooper noted gently.

Ashley sighed mournfully. "The time it takes most couples has come and gone. Something's wrong, Cooper. I can feel it inside and I need to know what the problem is. I'm going to get one of those 3-D ultrasounds this afternoon and Lincoln won't, well, he can't . . ." She trailed off.

"Of course I'll come."

"You won't even miss any work," Ashley hurriedly explained. "I took the last appointment of the day so Lincoln wouldn't have to cut his weekly staff meeting short, but now he says he's got some Fall Madness Sale coming up and has to be there to fire up his salesmen." She sniffed. "I can't believe he thinks that talking one of his employees into wearing a werewolf suit for Halloween is more important than us having a baby. I *need* to see Dr. Easter, but I just couldn't go alone, Coop. I'm . . . I'm scared."

Trying to suppress the anger she felt toward Lincoln for being so unsupportive of her sister, Cooper kicked at the concrete wall she was leaning against with the point of her black boot. "Don't be. Everything's going to be all right. I'll even hold your hand if you want me to."

"Gross!" Ashley uttered a characteristically theatrical squeal. "I don't want grease all over me!" She let loose a small giggle. "Besides, who knows what parts of me are going to be exposed. Your neck would be red as a fire truck!"

The sisters laughed and said good-bye. Back inside, the manager's scowl had deepened. "I'm ready to use my copier now," she whined while straightening one of her five necklaces. "When will it be fixed?"

"In just a few moments, ma'am," Cooper replied politely through gritted teeth.

"Like the *few minutes* it took you to talk on the phone," the woman muttered nastily under her breath and then walked out of her office with her nose in the air. Cooper heard her bark a series of curt orders to the salesgirls on the floor who were already busy assisting customers, folding sweaters, or steaming crinkled blouses.

Retrieving a pair of pliers from her toolbox, Cooper said a quick prayer of gratitude for working at a job she loved. Her thoughts turned to Ashley, who wanted a career in motherhood so desperately. Resuming work on the fuser assembly, Cooper reflected that there were certain things people wanted so badly that they'd do anything to get them. For Ashley, it was a baby. For others, it was fame. The person preying on the Door-2-Door clients would cross any line in order to attain items possessing high retail value, which could either be sold for profit or hoarded as some kind of twisted secret collection.

"Why are you doing this?" she whispered in quiet anger and then positioned the fuser assembly into the copier's cavity and replaced the surrounding mechanisms. The copier emitted a rumbling hum as power was restored to its system and Cooper sat beside it for a moment, enjoying the small victory of bringing a machine back to life.

She packed up her tools and forced herself to smile kindly as she asked the petulant manager to sign off on the work order. "If only humans were as easy to fix," she murmured and headed off to her next assignment.

11

God sets the lonely in families,
he leads forth the prisoners with singing;
but the rebellious live in a sun-scorched land.

Psalm 68:6 (NIV)

Seated in Dr. Easter's office, Cooper did her best to feign interest in an old issue of *American Baby* magazine. However, it was impossible not to glance around the waiting room, for its occupants were far more captivating than an article on potty training.

Cooper's gaze traveled first to the woman seated one seat over who steadily rubbed her protruding belly in wide, concentric circles while humming to herself. She was a marked contrast to the slim, pale-faced woman who stood next to the aquarium, biting her nails in agitation and occasionally tapping on the glass so that the fish darted away, startled. Directly across from Cooper, a couple sat with their hands clasped and their heads bent toward one another. Their downcast eyes, tense whispers, and hunched shoulders made it clear that they were frightened, and Cooper hoped that the perinatal physician could ease their fear.

Lastly, there was a young family that occupied half a

dozen chairs next to the exit. Children between the ages of seven and two chewed on graham crackers, suckled noisily on juice boxes, clambered onto the swollen lap of their pregnant mother, or hung from the belt loops of their father's pants. Despite their parents' incessant requests that their brood whisper, the children filled the waiting room with squeals, whines, and giggles.

"This place is a circus," Ashley murmured crossly. "If I have to watch that little boy take apart that uterus model one more time, I'm going to brain him with it."

"According to this magazine, you should try to talk to young children about disciplinary issues before resorting to violence," Cooper teased in an attempt to lighten her sister's mood.

"We've been sitting here for almost forty minutes." Ashley tapped her faux leopard-skin ankle boot impatiently. "I'm sick of waiting. I've been waiting months and months to get pregnant and now I can't stand to waste another second wondering what's wrong with me!"

Before Cooper could reassure her sister, the receptionist pushed open the glass window dividing her file folder–lined enclosure from the rest of the waiting room. Sliding on a pair of reading glasses, she examined the inside of a manila file and called out, "Ashley Love?"

"Present!" Cooper smiled as Ashley held up her right arm as though she were in a classroom. Folding her suede coat over her arm, Ashley approached the nurse in pink scrubs who held open the door leading to a warren of examination rooms. Cooper was inches behind her, practically treading on her ankles.

"Will this take long?" Ashley asked, her blue eyes anxious.

The nurse shook her head. "No, dear. We're just gonna

do an ultrasound. Shouldn't take too long and nothin's gonna hurt." Taking Ashley's elbow, she began to steer her into the hallway. "Your sister can come on back once Dr. Easter's ready to talk to you in his office, all right, sug?"

As Ashley nodded like an obedient child, Cooper's cell phone rang from within the interior of her purse. The nurse pointed at the "Please Turn Off Cell Phones In Waiting Room" sign posted on the surface of the door she was propping open with her wide derriere and scowled.

"I'll be right here waiting for you. And don't be nervous, Ashley. Everything's going to be fine," Cooper assured her sister as the nurse closed the door.

The Beatles continued to sing from the depths of her bag, so Cooper hustled out the office's front door and pulled her phone out of her purse just as it fell mute. Noting that the missed call was from Nathan, Cooper settled herself on a bench overlooking a circular bed of fluffy purple dahlias and clusters of tall snapdragons with two-toned petals of gold and orange and called him back.

"Are you sitting down?" Nathan immediately inquired.

"Uh-oh," Cooper moaned. "Not more bad news."

She could sense Nathan choosing his words carefully. "Trish heard from Lali. The police are definitely viewing Mr. Crosby's death as suspicious and have ordered an autopsy."

"But that's good. An autopsy will show how Mr. Crosby was poisoned or doped or whatever. That should help the police find their guy," she stated with relief.

"I don't know if you heard about the double murder that happened over the weekend, but it's all over the news. Between that and the high-profile suicide, or *apparent* suicide, of the former Olympic gymnast, I don't think the toxicology lab will move Frank's case to their top of their list."

"I did hear about the gymnast on the radio this morning," Cooper said. "Irina Korolev, right? She won four gold medals in her career but recently got caught shoplifting from the petite's section at Saks." She watched as another pregnant woman waddled into Dr. Easter's office. "Why do you say 'apparent' suicide?"

"The *Times-Dispatch* mentioned a theory that illegal steroids might be the true cause of death. Tobey showed me the article this morning after I corrected some minor errors on the Big Man site. He really wanted to emphasize that his products will remove the dangers of people coming to harm through the misuse of steroids. I've got to say, Cooper, he was really convincing, too. I believe I was wrong in questioning his sincerity."

"You're just being a prudent businessman," Cooper assured him. "So do you think the double murder and Irina's cases will get pushed ahead of Frank's?"

Nathan sighed. "Yeah. In fact, I called the medical examiner's office and found out that it takes as much as eight weeks for a complete tox report, so even though Mr. Crosby's, um, body has been viewed, his cause of death could remain a mystery for another two months."

"Eight weeks? The killer could easily strike again in that amount of time!" Cooper jumped up from the bench, her alarm growing. "There's got to be something we can do!" She began to pace around the circular flowerbed and the answer suddenly came to her. Swallowing hard, she said, "What are you doing for lunch tomorrow, Nathan?"

Nonplussed by her sudden change in tone, Nathan hesitated before answering. "I don't have any plans and I'd love to see you. Is this a 'date' date or a quick lunch so we can come up with a brilliant plan to foil the Door-2-Door killer?"

"We *have* had some unusual dates, haven't we?" Cooper murmured, a smile playing at the corners of her mouth. "But this one might be our oddest one yet. I'm going to call Lali and get the details on the whereabouts of Mr. Crosby's son and you and I are going to visit him."

"Ah, I'm almost afraid to ask, but exactly where are we going for this romantic interlude? We've already covered dates in dark alleys, hospitals, and being held at gunpoint in an elevator." Nathan laughed. "What's left?"

"Oh, we haven't been to *this* place before," Cooper stated flatly. "Nathan, we're going to jail."

"Can someone explain Ashley's problem to me in plain English?" Grammy demanded that night as the Lees gathered for supper.

"She's got a bicornuate uterus, Grammy," Cooper explained patiently. "That means it's heart-shaped and she could have some challenges carrying a baby to term."

"Can't they fix that? Cut away the part that indents or somethin'?" Grammy speared a meatball with her fork and popped the whole thing in her mouth.

Cooper grimaced at the thought of a surgeon cutting away bits of her sister's body as though removing undesirable pieces of fat from a roast beef. Staring at her plate of linguini and plump meatballs drenched in tomato sauce, she felt her appetite wane. "I don't think they can fix it like that, Grammy, but Ashley will need surgery to remove the polyps she's got in her uterus. The procedure is scheduled for next week."

Maggie placed a basket of fragrant garlic bread in the center of the table. "She seemed mighty upset on the phone. I'm glad you went with her today, honey. It warms my heart to see you lookin' after your baby sister."

"Unlike that rotten man of hers!" Grammy grunted, her cheeks still stuffed with meatball. "I'd like to get that boy on the phone and give him a piece of my mind!" She stabbed at the air with her sauce-stained fork.

"Have some salad, Ma." Maggie slid a bowl of greens mixed with Italian dressing toward her mother-in-law. "Let's give Lincoln the benefit of the doubt. I'm sure he didn't figure on Ashley bein' scared of goin' to the doctor. After all, she's never been afraid of anythin' except for spiders." She sprinkled canned Parmesan cheese on top of her noodles. "I'm right sure Lincoln'll be there for Ashley's surgery. After all, she'll need someone to drive her and look after her when she's back at home."

"You'll see to it, won't you, son?" Grammy turned to Earl. "That your daughter is taken care of by her man? He won't make much of a daddy if he can't even make time for his wife."

Earl pushed his plate away, slowly finished chewing, and folded his hands together. "I don't aim to interfere in either of my girls' relationships." He held up his finger to stop Grammy from interrupting. "But don't you fear. I will make certain that Ashley has the help she needs during this time, even if I've gotta take off work to do it." That being said, Earl pulled his dish back within reach and resumed the deliberate consumption of his supper.

"And what about you?" Grammy's steely gaze settled upon Cooper. "Any big dates in your future? You haven't been spendin' as much time with that Nathan boy as I thought you would." She pointed her fork at her granddaughter. "You ain't playin' hard-to-get are you?"

"Absolutely not! And I'll have you know that we are

seeing each other tomorrow—for a *really* hot date!" Cooper declared as she wiped her mouth with a dramatic flourish using a *Casper the Ghost* paper napkin. "I'm taking Nathan to visit an incarcerated drug dealer at the county jail. Now, if *that* doesn't make him fall head over heels for me, I can't imagine what will."

If Cooper had been hoping to shock her grandmother, she failed entirely. Grammy's only reaction was to shrug and reach for the garlic bread. "First you spend time packin' food for a bunch of old coots and now you're gonna hang out with the jailbirds." She waved an aromatic heel of bread at Cooper. "And you wonder why you ain't married?"

The next day, Cooper spent the commute into work praying for an extremely busy morning. She hoped to be so caught up in the business of collecting copiers from a large furniture chain undergoing bankruptcy that she could momentarily forget her plans to visit the local jail during her lunch hour.

Upon her return from the furniture store's Southside location, she backed her van into one of Make It Work!'s garage bays to find Emilio waiting for her on the loading dock.

"Thought I'd give you a hand unloadin'. I know you can haul these big machines as well as any guy, but I can't have you hurtin' yourself when I was close enough to help." His mouth split into a wide, confident grin, making it clear that he expected Cooper to respond to his charm.

Cooper gestured from the ramp attached to the back of the van to the heavy-duty hand truck parked against the side wall. "That's nice of you, Emilio, but I've been loading and unloading copiers for years. I've got a system."

Emilio leaned against the van, crossed his arms so that

his fists pushed his well-developed biceps into even larger masses, and snorted. "Fine, fine. I'm down with all that women's lib stuff. If you wanna be Miss Tough Cookie, I'll just hang out and watch you do your thang." He smiled again. "But I'm right here if you need me."

"Don't you have shredders to empty?" Cooper asked as she pushed the hand truck up the ramp.

"I finished early. I wanted to ride with you and pick up the rest of the machines from that furniture warehouse. It's so cool that that business is completely broke. All that over-priced, ugly stuff is gonna get sold for what it's really worth. And I can't stand their commercials, you know?" Emilio snorted derisively. "Every freakin' football game I have to sit through five minutes listening to the BIG, BIG SALE! What a bunch of bull—"

"You're right. Their ads *are* annoying," Cooper agreed. "And I don't know why everyone's trying to use penguins to sell stuff these days. They're cute, but I don't see the connection to dining room sets." She pushed the edge of the hand truck beneath the first copier. "Still," she grunted as she eased straps around the bulk of the machine. "Dozens of folks are going to lose their jobs because this chain of stores is closing. And in this economy, it's going to be tough to find new work."

Emilio shrugged, unconcerned. "They're always hiring at Burger King."

Before Cooper had a chance to remark on her coworker's lack of empathy, Angela arrived at the loading dock, her heels clicking a sharp staccato on the cement floor. "What are you two up to in here?" she demanded, eyeing Emilio with suspicion.

Cooper was too focused on maneuvering the copier

down the ramp to be polite. "What does it look like?" she snapped. "Unloading the van."

Angela pretended to be hurt. "There's no need to get all huffy. I was just gonna take lunch orders and I thought I heard voices in here."

"Lunch? You're on, beautiful!" Emilio sidled over to Angela and held out his arm. When Angela took it, he suddenly whisked her around so that she was facing him and began a spontaneous waltz across the floor. As they returned to where Cooper stood next to the empty hand truck, Emilio dipped Angela so low that her platinum-blonde bob swept the ground. Holding her there, he gazed into her eyes, smiled charmingly, and then kissed her lightly on the cheek.

"Has anyone ever told you that you've got the grace of a ballerina?" he whispered, gazing at Angela with what Cooper assumed was feigned devotion.

Over the top of Emilio's bent head, Cooper noticed Mr. Farmer's stocky shadow suddenly disappear from the doorway leading into the garage.

"Oh! You are too, too much! And lunch is *my* treat," Angela cooed to Emilio, the look of adoration that had disappeared last week having instantly resurfaced in her eyes.

Disgusted, Cooper ignored the pair and finished emptying the last copier from the van.

I'm going to have to have a chat with Mr. Farmer, she thought. *Or Angela will end up heartbroken.* And *broke.*

"Nervous?" Nathan inquired as Cooper met him outside the Henrico County Sheriff's Office.

Cooper glanced at a small placard positioned alongside

the sidewalk. It had an arrow pointing to the closest set of double glass doors and simply read: JAIL. Gripping her trembling fingers, she tried to control the feeling of nausea that had plagued her since she'd pulled into the visitor's parking lot.

"I'm terrified. I've gotten my share of speeding tickets, but that's as far on the wrong side of the law as I've been." She observed the stream of lawyers, uniformed deputies, and civilians marching in and out the door. "This is like a city within the city and it's kind of overwhelming."

"You've only got an hour, right?" Nathan prodded gently.

Cooper nodded. "I ate a Subway sandwich in the van after a midday pick-up. There was no way I was going to make it 'til three-thirty. Angela thought I was totally bonkers for taking such a late lunch hour, but I didn't feel like explaining to her that visiting hours at the county jail don't start until later in the afternoon."

Nathan held the door open and Cooper passed into the lobby, where a long line of people waited to sign up for visitation. "I take it you haven't told Angela about our current case," Nathan said as he fidgeted with the car keys in his right pocket. "I thought she was one of your closest friends."

"She is, but she's been so wrapped up in Emilio worship lately that she can't think about anything else." Cooper noticed that once people reached the front of the line they were asked to present their driver's license to the woman behind the counter. Relieved to have something to do as they waited, she removed her license from her wallet, her hands still shaking as though she were incredibly cold.

Nathan snatched it from her and examined her picture.

"Whoa! Did you spend all day at the DMV before they took this?"

"No!" Cooper reclaimed her license. "Actually, this guy walked past me and let loose the nastiest gas cloud I'd ever smelled. *That's* when the DMV employee decided to take the picture. And no matter what I said, she wouldn't do a re-take."

"Ah, government agencies." Nathan swept his arm around the room. "So who's Emilio?"

"Our new coworker. Thinks he's God's gift to women and apparently, Angela agrees," she replied sourly.

Nathan nudged her playfully as the line moved forward. "And you don't?"

"No way. *I* prefer guys who collect *Star Wars* figures," Cooper stated in a low voice and was pleased to see a flush of pleasure color Nathan's cheeks.

All too soon, they arrived at the front of the line. "We, um, we're here to see Edward Crosby," Cooper informed the young woman seated at the desk, repeating the name Lali had given her over the phone.

Without looking up from her computer, the sheriff's office receptionist stated, "Your identification, please." She typed so quickly that it seemed as though she were playing a challenging piece on a concert piano instead of inputting data regarding inmate visitation schedules.

Nathan handed her their driver's licenses and leaned over the tall desk in order to see exactly what she was typing. After shooting him an irritated look, the woman returned their IDs and called, "Next, please."

"Um." Cooper edged closer to the desk instead of backing away. "What do we do now?"

Hesitating, as though she was surprised to be asked such a question, the woman replied, "Wait until the deputy calls Edward Crosby," and then turned her attention to the next person in line.

"But what if, um, Mr. Crosby's not expecting us?" Cooper blurted.

"They never know who their visitors are," the woman explained as the other visitors grumbled with impatience. "They're just told they have a visitor and are brought to the visiting area."

"So he might not talk to us," Cooper said to herself, her fingers twisting in agitation. "After all, he doesn't know us from Adam." Too flustered to sit down, she and Nathan stood to the side of the check-in desk, listening as the next woman in line shouted in outrage after being informed that the inmate she wished to see had lost his visitation rights.

"What you mean? He been tossed into isolation again? He *told* me all y'all got it out for him! He shouldn't be here in the first place. The man's innocent!" The woman placed one hand on her hip and pounded on the receptionist's desk with the other. Within seconds, a sheriff's deputy appeared from nowhere and, gently taking hold of the woman's elbow, steered her away from the line. No matter how much she ranted at him, the deputy remained quietly courteous. Without breaking eye contact, he described the infraction that had caused her boyfriend to be placed in isolation, but the woman was incapable of listening. After interrupting his explanation with a guttural, animalistic snarl, she threw up her arms in disgust and stormed out the front door, leaving a trail of expletives in her wake.

"I couldn't have handled that woman half as well he did," Nathan murmured to Cooper. "But I guess these deputies have seen and heard it all."

From the far left corner, a bass voice suddenly boomed out, "Edward Crosby!"

Nathan raised his arm and grabbed Cooper's sleeve.

A short, bulky deputy holding onto a clipboard gestured for them to follow him into the visiting room. As they entered the long, narrow room filled with twenty cubicles, the deputy gestured at the fourth chair facing the room-length wall of glass. "Thirty minutes," he reminded them and then turned to collect more visitors.

Cooper took a moment to get her bearings. Finding that she wasn't quite ready to come to terms with the significance of the large glass wall, the mounted black telephone handset, or the plastic chair facing an identical chair on the other side of the wall, she focused her attention elsewhere. She looked at the wooden bench along the entire right wall, the cameras jutting out from the ceiling corners, and the baby stroller parked behind the cubicle at the very end of the row. Behind her, a toddler began to push two Matchbox cars across the carpet while his mother hissed into the phone at a young man wearing dark blue scrubs.

A buzz resounded in the room and a diminutive Hispanic man wearing white scrubs entered the room from a hallway obscured from view. His face immediately broke into a jubilant smile as his wife held a sleeping infant up to the glass. The father held up an index finger toward his son's face as though he longed to stroke the soft skin, but could only mimic a tender touch. As he gazed at the baby, his smile dissipated, to be replaced by an expression of sorrow and regret. His wife shifted their son to her right arm and, after picking up the handset with her left, began to release a torrent of angry Spanish into the phone as she tapped her wedding ring against the glass. Her husband wouldn't meet her eyes. He rubbed the script tattoo on his forearm, stretching and smoothing the black ink reading "Rosa," which was enclosed by a circle of red, thorny flowers. Beneath the largest bloom was the name Alfonso. Multi-hued sunrays and a soaring eagle surrounded the name of his infant son.

As Cooper continued to absorb her surroundings, an elderly African-American woman entered the visitor's room and was seated in the neighboring cubicle.

"You sure I can't give Dwayne his glasses?" she asked the deputy directing her to the correct chair. "My boy likes to read right much, but he can't see nothin' without his glasses."

"I'll send them to medical, ma'am. If they think he needs them, they'll get them to him," the deputy assured her.

"Please tell 'em to hurry. He can't even read his Bible right now and nothin' settles him down like a dose of the Word." She fiddled with her purse, her eyes growing moist. "If only he'd *listen* to our Savior more, he wouldn't be here in the first place!"

Cooper stared at the concerned mother until the buzzing noise reoccurred and a Caucasian man in his mid-thirties wearing beige scrubs entered the inmate's side of the room. He looked around, perplexed, and passed his palm over his buzzcut until the deputy on duty directed him to the cubicle where Cooper was supposed to be sitting.

"Do you want me to talk to him?" Nathan whispered from behind Cooper's shoulder. "There's only room for one person in that cubby hole. You don't have to do this, you know."

Seeing that Nathan was paler than usual, Cooper was sure that he felt just as unnerved as she. She waved off his suggestion with a grateful smile and then forced herself to sit in the rose-colored chair. Removing the black phone from its cradle, she met Edward Crosby's confused stare. Slowly, he eased into his chair and picked up the handset on his side of the glass.

"Who are you?" he demanded tersely, studying her face as though he wanted to capture it forever in his memory.

The intensity of his gaze nearly made Cooper flinch, but she squeezed the handset instead and the firmness of the cold metal calmed her enough to be able to reply. "I'm a volunteer with Door-2-Door Dinners. Your daddy got his meals from them. I . . . I saw him just a few days before he died."

A flicker of sadness crossed the man's gunmetal gray eyes, but was quickly replaced by a blank look that betrayed no emotion whatsoever. "So? What do you want from me?" he asked flatly.

"First, I want to offer my condolences. I only met your daddy once but . . ." Cooper drew a blank in searching for complimentary phrases in which to describe Frank Crosby.

"He didn't impress ya much, now did he? When you showed up, he was probably still sittin' around in his skivvies, watching football on that piece-of-shit TV, and goin' off about yellow this and yellow that. The world's sure gonna miss him."

Cooper had cautioned herself that Frank's son might not be overwrought by his father's death, but Edward's callousness moved her to anger. "Whatever he did or didn't do, Frank Crosby was *still* your father, Edward."

"Don't you EVER call me that name!" A hostile palm slapped against the glass in front of her face and Cooper let loose a startled whimper. "My *name* is The Colonel. You got that? *The Colonel!* Now say it!"

"The Colonel," Cooper hastily whispered, her heart in her throat.

The belligerence seeped from The Colonel's face and he relaxed in his chair, crossing his arms over his chest. "Frank's dead. They told me. Even asked if I wanted an escort for his viewing. I don't." He bowed his head and began to rub it and Cooper noticed that the flag of Dixie had been tattooed across the width of his scalp. "Me and the old man weren't exactly tight, you got it? And you didn't know him for shit, so what are you doin' sittin' in that chair? He was an old man and he died. End of story."

"Your daddy's death was suspicious. Did anyone tell you that?"

The Colonel looked bored. "Probably overdosed on some meds. Lots of old farts do that. Can't read the label or they do it on purpose 'cause they wanna check out."

"Not Frank. And he wasn't on any medication," Cooper insisted. "But someone has been stealing and poisoning Door-2-Door clients. This person is probably a volunteer. I'm here to ask you what valuables could have been stolen from your daddy's house. He was *very* upset about a 'secret' being stolen." Cooper leaned toward the glass. "It truly caused him heartache when he discovered that this thing was taken. He was actually grieving over it." She placed her hand over her heart for emphasis. "Do you know what it was?"

The Colonel waited until the inmate two chairs over murmured a cryptic good-bye to the woman with the toddler. The child turned away from his toy cars and began to wail, giant tears rolling down his cheeks as the man disappeared into the unseen depths of the jail.

"Some whack job is rubbin' out old folks?" The Colonel asked into the phone, his gray eyes narrowing. "That ain't right. Me? I sell drugs. But I don't sell to no kids or to no pregnant women. There are still rules. I sell to sorry-ass punks who can't stay off the stuff. It's easy cash money and I was never no good at school." His eyes turned cold. "The old man knew what I did. Told me I brought shame on our house, but he was big into shame."

Cooper shifted her grip on the phone, as its weight seemed to have increased over the course of their conversation. "What do you mean?"

"Some family member from the Civil War acted like a pansy and *Frank* never got over it. Read everythin' he could about the guy and the battles he fought. Waste of fu—" He cut himself off, passing his palm over his head while his mouth turned down in a grimace. "Look. We ain't seen each other for years, but the old man had this soldier's sword and some kinda book. A diary or somethin'. He kept the sword in his closet. He liked to take it out now and again. Polish it up and stuff."

Glancing at her watch, Cooper noted that her time with The Colonel was quickly running out. "I guess a sword from the Civil War could be valuable."

"Damn straight it was!" The Colonel spat indignantly. "I coulda used that money. Coulda started my own business! I had this kick-ass idea but I needed start-up cash. Would the old man give it to me? No. So I found my own way to make money. He didn't even post my bail when I landed in juvie the first time." He pounded the counter in front of him. "Screw this trip down memory lane!" The deputy monitoring the inmates rose to his feet, casting a fierce glance at The Colonel.

"Sorry, Sergeant." The Colonel held up his arms in submission and the deputy issued a curt nod and then resumed his seat, his gaze still fixed on their cubicle.

Cooper heard a whisper from the bench behind her back. "You still okay?" Nathan's voice instilled her with a needed measure of calm. She nodded, never breaking eye contact with The Colonel. "I'm sorry to bring up unhappy memories," she told him sincerely. "But I hope you understand that I can't sit by while someone harms the innocent elderly."

The Colonel indicated that he understood her motivation by jerking his left thumb in the air. "There are rules," he muttered a few moments later.

Grateful for his cooperation, Cooper eagerly asked, "Do you know where he kept the diary?"

The Colonel shook his head at first and then he closed his eyes and absently rubbed his head, back and forth in a hypnotizing rhythm. Cooper felt that he was once again walking through his father's house as a boy, not as the incarcerated drug trafficker he had become.

"I bet it's in my mama's rocker," The Colonel said, suddenly raising his head and gesturing animatedly. "Nasty old cushioned thing that I could never sit on. Even our damn cat couldn't go on there and it never made no sense, seein' as how it was full of rips and stains anyhow. I never saw the book. I only heard about it when I got one of Frank's lectures about honor." He shrugged. "If it ain't there, then it's gone. Feel free to poke around the place. The lock on the back door's been broke since I was a kid. I doubt the old man bothered to fix it."

Retrieving a small pad of paper from her purse, Cooper wrote "check rocking chair for diary" on the first line and then held her pen aloft.

"Was he always . . . freaked out by the color yellow?"

"Wasn't allowed in the house. Ever." The Colonel

scowled. "How'd you like to grow up with a nut case like that?"

Ignoring the question, Cooper pointed at the bench behind her. "My friend Nathan told me it could take eight weeks to get lab results on which drug poisoned your daddy. If I told you the symptoms, do you think you might be able to identify the drug?"

The Colonel laughed. "I'm a dealer, lady, not a freakin' pharmacist. I know how to make people feel good. I know how to make them forget their pain. But I don't sample my own products." He leaned back in his chair in a posture of superiority. "That's bad for business."

"Frank was experiencing short-term memory loss. He seemed really anxious and confused," Cooper plowed on. "He lost a whole day just sitting in his chair and he thinks he saw someone go into his bedroom."

"Time's up, Crosby!" The deputy stood up from behind the desk again.

Cooper placed her hand against the glass. "Please!" she pleaded into the phone. "If you could just give me an educated guess!"

"Could be ecstasy," The Colonel replied and stood. "You find out, let me know. Maybe I could expand my product line." He winked at her.

Ignoring the barb, Cooper removed her hand from the glass. "I'll write you if we discover anything. I promise."

For the first time, a glimmer of something resembling hope entered The Colonel's eyes. "That'd be the first promise someone hasn't broken, then," he replied, hung up the phone, and strutted from the room.

Cooper watched the doorway through which he

departed, relieved that the interview was over. As she and Nathan left the visitor's room and crossed through the boisterous lobby and out into the October air, Cooper was overcome with the sorrowful realization that Frank Crosby's son seemed every bit as friendless and alone as his father had been.

In the parking lot, Cooper reached for Nathan. She buried her head against his neck and listened to his melodious baritone as he prayed for Edward Crosby. Outside of Bible study, she had never heard him pray aloud before. The intimacy of this act, of him sharing his concerns for a complete stranger while she bore witness was immeasurably moving.

You have placed such a good man in my path, Cooper spoke a silent praise and held onto Nathan until finally, time forced her to let go.

12

Hail fell and lightning flashed back and forth. It was the worst storm in all the land of Egypt since it had become a nation.

Exodus 9:24 (NIV)

Following her visit with The Colonel, Cooper called an emergency meeting of the Sunrise Bible study. Savannah led a couples group on Wednesday, so they were unable to congregate right away, and since both Quinton and Bryant had professional commitments on Thursday, they couldn't gather until Friday evening. Nathan had suggested they assemble at Cracker Barrel, as their unusual conversation was likely to go unheard in the eatery's customary din.

Quinton and Trish were contentedly established in two of the rockers on Cracker Barrel's veranda when Cooper arrived. Having come straight from work, she was still in her Make It Work! uniform and felt underdressed in comparison to her friends. Trish looked like a coiffed cardinal in a bright red suit, white blouse, and black heels while Quinton was elegantly attired in a checked blazer, a royal blue button-down, and dark brown pants. His loafers were polished to a high shine and an ironed handkerchief poked out from his front jacket pocket, displaying four, perfectly folded points.

"Aren't you dapper?" Cooper smiled at him. Trish wiggled her fingers in greeting but then returned her attention to her mobile phone.

"I *told* you, dear." Trish turned her body away from Cooper and Quinton. "I'll reschedule when I have time. It's probably just a calcium deposit or a cyst. Anyway, I've got two open houses this weekend and am closing on the Bowers house *and* the Markus estate tomorrow." She frowned. "Just get the girls to their piano lessons before they're late and let me worry about my own doctor's appointments," she snapped and then said good-bye.

Cooper and Quinton exchanged uncomfortable glances and were relieved to see Bryant and Nathan arrive at the end of the row of rockers.

Bryant bowed gallantly and helped Trish from her chair. "You should take his advice, milady," he said. "If you're talking about a lump then there's no time to waste."

Trish opened her mouth to issue a curt reply, but before she had the chance, a car pulled into the handicapped space right in front of them. Savannah emerged from the passenger seat, her cane clicking on the asphalt as she stood up, still holding onto the open car door.

Out of nowhere, Jake appeared by her side, prepared to guide her onto the porch. "Oh, Pearl, I smell Jake's aftershave! I'll see you Monday, my dear!" Savannah waved at her housekeeper and held out her arm for Jake to tuck under his own.

The pair joined the others and walked inside the restaurant, wading their way through spinner racks of candy, Halloween decorations, and old-fashioned toys toward the hostess station. By miraculous circumstance, they only had to wait a mere fifteen minutes for a table to come free.

"I'm gonna get the Country Boy Breakfast," Jake declared, rubbing his work-worn hands together. "Three eggs, pork chops, some grits, Sawmill gravy, fried apples, hash-brown casserole, and buttermilk biscuits. That should keep me 'til mornin'."

"There's always the chocolate pudding pie if you've room left over," Quinton informed his friend.

Once their hostess seated them at a large wooden table in the center of the dining room, Cooper flipped right to the menu's breakfast page. "Jake, you've got me craving pecan pancakes and some bacon."

"Ever since I knew we were coming here I planned to order the meatloaf, but now I've just got to have Eggs-in-the Basket instead. See how I crumble in the face of peer pressure," Nathan said with a chuckle. "Let's get a big ca-rafe of decaf and start our day all over again!"

"No, thank you." Bryant looked horrified by the idea. "That grad student I was dating a few months ago has turned into a psychotic stalker. She weaseled her way into the studio today by introducing herself to everyone as my *fiancée*. If it weren't for Paige, my deranged ex would have jumped right in front of the blue screen with me!"

"Paige is a single mom, remember? I bet some young, unworldly grad student is no match for her!" Trish re-marked after the waitress had taken their breakfast orders.

Bryant's eyes glimmered as he described how Paige had handled the determined ex-girlfriend. "She was firm, but really sweet at the same time. She gave the girl a hug, told her to find someone who was available and that lots of guys would kill to date someone as lovely and intelli-gent as her, and then walked her to the door. By the time she kicked her out, my ex was hugging her like Paige was her best friend." He shrugged in befuddlement. "Women."

"I told you Paige sounded like someone you needed to

get serious with. And fast!" Trish chided. "And *she's* a woman, not a girl. Maybe that's what you need, Bryant."

"Yeah. Mother, career woman, *and* bouncer. What more could you want?" Quinton teased as he poured three sugar packets into his coffee cup.

"I'll make you a deal," Bryant said to Trish. "I'll ask Paige to join me on a weekend getaway *with the kids* once you've rescheduled your doctor's appointment." He reached over and took her hand. "A lump could be serious. Assuming that it's nothing could be a big mistake and I'm only being a nag because I care what happens to you."

Moved by Bryant's concern, Trish smoothed her copper hair and shifted in her chair. Stacking several unopened creamers on her butter plate, she blinked innocently and said, "I could have already been to the imaging center for all you know."

Bryant eyed her keenly. "I heard the tail end of your phone call and I've been married enough times to sense that you were being nagged by your husband. He means well, Trish. And he's right. You need to schedule an appointment right away. Now, shake on our deal." He held out his hand and Trish reluctantly accepted it.

"Okay, Cooper." Jake gestured at her with his coffee cup. "What's goin' on?"

After taking a quick survey of the nearby tables, Cooper determined that none of the other diners were the slightest bit interested in eavesdropping on their conversation, so she told her friends about her visit with The Colonel. They listened carefully, their coffees growing cold as she described The Colonel's appearance and attitude. Cooper had just finished describing the Civil War items Frank Crosby had owned when their food arrived.

Jake sprinkled salt over every inch of his plate and then zealously carved into his pork chop. Simultaneously, Quinton drowned his French toast in a puddle of warm maple syrup while Savannah covered a piece of toast with a thick layer of apple butter. Bryant cut his smoked sausage patties into equivalent chunks and then looked up at Cooper. "Go on and take a bite before you finish. Cold pancakes aren't very savory."

"I'll finish up for her," Nathan volunteered as Cooper spread a pat of butter over the surface of the pecan pancake on the top of her pile. In between bites of egg sandwich, Nathan told his friends about The Colonel's theory that ecstasy was the drug behind Frank's overdose.

"I just can't imagine any of the Door-2-Door volunteers walking around with a Ziploc full of ecstasy," Trish shook her head in disbelief. "I thought—not that I know much about illegal drugs—that ecstasy was a party drug. You know, for the rich, hip, club-going crowds." She patted Bryant's arm playfully. "And I'm not taking a potshot at you for hanging out at those places with your twenty-something girlfriends, either."

"Thanks." Bryant smiled ruefully. "But I think you're on the money about the drug's reputation. I remember when a few of our investigative reporters went undercover to learn more about ecstasy. It didn't take them long to see that popping these pills has become the thing to do for the young crowds at concerts, dance clubs, or those rave parties they're so into. That's why it's called a designer drug, because it's supposed to give you a high that can go on for days."

Cooper nodded. "I read about it online. Ecstasy or E or X can give folks hallucinations and create short-term memory loss." She paused to accept Nathan's offer of a piece of bacon. "Ecstasy is also available in powder form, so it'd be easy to mix with food or dissolve into a liquid, like Mr. Crosby's hot tea."

Savannah put down her triangle of toast and sighed. "We need to have a more intimate gathering with our volunteer friends. I pray the police discover the identity of the killer soon, but if they aren't successful, we'll have to keep digging."

"That's where we arrive at the emergency part of this meeting." Cooper hesitated and then confessed, "I want to go into Frank's house and check around for the sword and the diary. If our bad guy tries to sell those things, there won't be too many sources available to him. Or her. They'll have to consign them with a local auction or antique store or sell them outright using an online auction site. If the diary contains the name of the soldier, than searching for the items will be much easier."

"Why don't you just tell the police about the diary?" Trish demanded. "They've got more manpower than we do to monitor eBay and interview Richmond area antique dealers. I, for one, am totally swamped this week, so why don't we do our jobs and let them do theirs?"

Cooper hesitated. Trish had raised a solid point, so why did she suddenly feel the desire to defend her plan, to argue that in some way, it was her responsibility to search Frank's house for clues? "Look. If the diary's there, I'll read it and hand it over to the police. I guess I'd just like the chance to see what caused Mr. Crosby such anguish over the loss of the sword, if that's what was stolen, and I want to know the secret about this relative of his. It seemed to have ruined his relationship with his son and created this irrational hatred of the color yellow."

"You know what they say about curiosity," Quinton

warned. "Sorry, Cooper, but I'm with Trish on this one. You may have found out about an important clue, and that's great, but let the people experienced in these things figure out what to do with it. Like Savannah said, we've got to concentrate on the volunteers."

Jake nodded. "Yeah, 'cause if this slime ball is hoarding all the stolen loot at home or knows other scumbags to hawk it to, we're not going to find 'em that way. We gotta get a look at these people's souls somehow. That's what we need to puzzle out right now."

Chastised, Cooper ate the rest of her meal in silence. She knew that her friends were right and that she should turn matters over to the police, but after talking to The Colonel she felt that she owed it to him to personally find some answers.

After filling their stomachs with eggs, pancakes, sausage, bacon, hash browns, and biscuits, the Sunrise members were too stuffed to even contemplate dessert. They settled their bill and then waddled outside into the crisp evening air. No one had arrived with a clever idea on how to get closer to the Door-2-Door volunteers.

"I'll see you all at Door-2-Door this weekend. Try to talk to the volunteers as much as you can while you work. See how they act with the clients. Watch where they go inside the house if they suddenly separate from you," Savannah advised as she accepted Jake's arm. "I'm hoping to have some information to share with you come Sunday morning as Jake and I are calling on Leo Saturday night."

"You're a brave woman," Bryant praised Savannah.

Jake scowled. "Hey. *I'm* gonna be there, too, remember?"

"With your vanload of pipes!" Trish laughed.

The group exchanged good nights and dispersed to their cars, but Cooper and Nathan lingered behind.

"What's on your mind?" Nathan asked, slipping his arm around Cooper's waist.

Cooper gently pushed him away in order to look into his eyes. "I know what they said about letting the police look for the Civil War stuff in Frank's house is right, but I just can't hand it over without seeing for myself. I want to better understand the man who died. I want to be able to provide some answers to his son." She hesitated and then decided to trust Nathan with her decision. "I'm going over there tonight. To Frank's house."

Nathan didn't speak right away, but his expression showed his internal conflict. His warm brown eyes searched her face for a few moments and then, finally, he nodded. "You aren't going alone."

"We can take my car." Cooper smiled in gratitude. "I've got two flashlights in my toolbox."

They drove to Frank's house without speaking, letting the easy-listening station fill the silence with Celine Dion and Michael Bublé's melodic crooning. As they headed east on the Interstate, Cooper noted a bank of ominous thunderclouds in her rearview mirror. She felt a sick feeling in the pit of her stomach as the memory of her dream of floating on a rushing river toward the fearsome storm returned to her with fresh intensity.

Unlike her dream, however, Cooper was moving away from the storm at a rapid pace. Still, she knew that once they reached Frank's house and spent time searching inside for the sword and diary, it wouldn't take long for the cloud mass to catch up.

Feeling on edge, Cooper gazed out at the blue-black

highway, trying not to pay attention to how much the road resembled a meandering river or that the dark trees encroaching toward the shoulder looked awfully similar to the sinister pines from her nightmare.

By the time she brought her truck to a stop two blocks away from the sad white house where Frank Crosby had died, a persistent breeze had sprung to life, carrying with it the scent of rain. Cooper retrieved the flashlights and she and Nathan walked hurriedly toward the house, looking over their shoulders to make sure they weren't being observed. Nathan headed straight for the front door, but Cooper grabbed his arm and shook her head.

"Not that door. Around back."

Nathan followed her through the overgrown strip of grass bordering the sagging chain-link fence dividing Frank's property from the adjacent house. As they passed between the two bungalows, Cooper noted the illuminated window on the side of the next-door neighbor's home. The consistent flickering light and intermittent sounds of canned laughter suggested that its occupants were watching television. Based on the volume of the set, Cooper felt confident that there was little threat that the neighbors would overhear any activity taking place inside Frank's residence.

The warped wooden planks that made up the staircase leading to the back door creaked as Cooper set her work boots upon them. Flinching at the noise, she reached out and turned the flaking, brass knob. It rotated, but the door remained firmly closed.

"Is it locked?" Nathan whispered.

Cooper tried the knob again. "I don't think so. I can turn it clockwise as far as it can go, but it's like the door is stuck to the frame—like it was painted shut or something."

"Let me give it a shot."

Stepping back onto the grass, Cooper watched as Nathan leaned his right shoulder against the door. Holding the knob with his left hand, he slammed his weight against the door. "Ow," he muttered and then repeated the motion several times.

Cooper glanced around nervously. To the west, a curtain of lightning set the sky aglow and then quickly disappeared. A fat raindrop fell onto the crown of her head as Nathan paused to rest.

"I've almost got it. Let me try something different." He placed his foot in the center of the door and gave it a mighty kick. The warped wood splintered at the top corner and, being off-balance, Nathan practically fell inside the house.

Stale air rushed from inside as they hustled into the shadowy kitchen. Cooper switched on her flashlight and moved around Frank's metal table and folding chairs, keeping the beam of light pointed at the floor. Even in the minimal brightness it was apparent that every cabinet, drawer, and shelf had been rifled through.

"This place is a mess," Nathan mumbled, stepping over a saucepot. "I'd hate to have the cops search my house."

"They'd probably knock all your action figures out of alphabetical order and damage the original packaging," Cooper replied in a lame attempt at levity. "You'd be in therapy for years."

She led Nathan from the kitchen to the bedroom, frowning as her flashlight revealed an unmade bed covered with crumpled clothes. A sour, putrid odor filled the room, as though none of the fabrics had been washed for years.

"Ugh. Smells like a men's locker room in here," Nathan commented. "I don't see a rocker. Let's go!"

Pulling her shirt up over her mouth and nose, Cooper said, "Not so fast. The Colonel told me that Frank kept the Civil War sword in his closet." She passed Nathan the flashlight. "Hold this while I look through these clothes."

As Cooper rooted through soiled garments and mud-encrusted shoes, she wished she had thought to bring along the work gloves from her toolbox. Every time she shifted a mound of clothes, the stench of spoiled food and body odor assailed her nostrils, but her search was in vain. There was no sword hidden on the floor or among the two moth-holed sweaters or the outdated blazer hanging limply from the wooden rod. The single shelf above the rod contained a few shoeboxes filled with random objects such as yellowed postcards, clip-on bowties, Christmas tree ornaments, a belt with cracked brown leather, and an assortment of old magazines.

"The sword is definitely gone." Cooper backed away from the closet and exited the bedroom. She passed the only bathroom, relieved that there was no need to search there, and returned to the front room where she had met Frank Crosby for the first and only time.

She stared at the chair where he had taken his last breath and noticed a folded newspaper on the floor beneath the seat's right arm. Bending over, she picked up the page containing the comic strips and word puzzles and saw that the crossword was incomplete. The empty boxes seemed to emphasize the vacant house and the sudden absence of its owner. As she stared at the newspaper in reflective silence, the rain began to patter lightly, almost timidly, against the window and Cooper wished that it would fall with a violence forceful enough to mask her sniffles.

Nathan squeezed her shoulder. "You holding up okay?"

"I'm fine, thanks," she replied without turning toward him.

After wiping her face with her sleeve, Cooper continued toward the television set in the corner of the room. The appliance was positioned on top of a scratched bureau and next to the chest was a chairlike shape covered by a multicolored afghan. Cooper whipped the blanket from the rocker and beckoned for Nathan to bring the light closer.

She pressed her fingertips into the floral fabric, ignoring the dust being coaxed from between the tight stitches as she worked her way across the seat. Finding nothing, she and Nathan upended the rocker and discovered a four-inch piece of brown packing tape covering up the upholstery across the back of the chair. Cooper eased the tape away and slipped her hand inside the rent in the material. As she reached upward, her fingers knocked against a hard edge. Pushing her hand further into the chair, she winced as the tear in the fabric grew wider, but the damage allowed her to grasp the hidden book and pull it free from its fibrous prison.

"This is it." Cooper exhaled. She examined the parcel, which appeared to be wrapped in a thin, yellow towel.

"That's got to be the only yellow thing in this house," Nathan commented.

Cooper unfolded the old material to reveal the brown leather cover of a small book. She opened to the first page and read the fluid, black script: "The Diary of First Lieutenant Aaron Crosby."

"You did it!" Nathan reached for the book. "Here. I'll put it down my shirt so it doesn't get wet. Now let's get out of this place before the storm hits."

Together, they hastened from the house, closing the

back door as firmly as possible. Despite the splintered wood, the door seemed to reinsert itself in its frame as steadfastly as before. For some inexplicable reason, Cooper was reassured by the fact that Frank's house wouldn't be exposed to the rain or other intrusions for the time being.

The flickering light from behind the next-door neighbor's curtained window echoed the lightning flashes above the roofs. Crouching low, Nathan and Cooper sprinted toward her truck as the rain intensified.

"What the—!" Cooper exclaimed, coming to an abrupt halt in front of the driver's side of her truck.

She stared dumbstruck at the words sprayed onto her door. Even as she processed the meaning of the letters written in fingerpaint, the rain was mutating them, dissolving them, erasing them.

But Cooper had had a chance to read them first.

SEEK & DIE

And then the rain began to fall, the large droplets thoroughly obliterating the threat scrawled onto the crimson paint of her truck.

Nathan insisted on driving Cooper directly to his house.

"You're in shock," he told her, removing the wet car keys from her hands and leading her to the passenger door of the truck. "Now get out of the rain and let me drive."

The trip to his downtown row house passed in a blur. Vacillating between rage and fear, Cooper couldn't think straight. Her hands were shaking and she would have killed for a cigarette, but she had given up smoking months ago.

Twenty minutes later, she stood mute in Nathan's living room, squeezing moisture from the ends of her hair.

"If we were in a movie, I'd be offering you a glass of brandy and forcing you to drink it," Nathan opened a small cabinet next to the fireplace. "But my bar's not that well stocked."

Cooper sank down on the couch and listened to the clanking of bottles and the clinking of ice cubes hitting glass. Nathan handed her a tumbler.

"It's whiskey. Just a shot's worth, but it'll make you nice and toasty inside."

Numbly, Cooper swallowed the contents without pausing for breath. The alcohol burned a trail down her throat, warming the pit of her stomach and allowing her to gain control over the tremors moving through her body.

Gently, Nathan pried the tumbler from her hands and pulled her to him. At first, he wrapped his arms around her and held her close, saying nothing, but then he began to stroke her hair. When he kissed her on the smooth skin of her forehead, she raised her lips and captured his in her own.

Nathan's response was light and tender, but Cooper kissed him hungrily, opening her mouth greedily while pressing her body against his chest. Abruptly, she broke her lips away and began to kiss his neck, nibbling the soft flesh beneath his ear. Roughly tugging on his shirt, she slid her eager hands upward along the bare skin of his back, her mouth returning to meet his.

He denied her his lips. Instead, he kissed her in the soft depression between her collarbones as his fingers deftly unbuttoned her uniform shirt. He yanked the fabric free on one side, exposing her shoulder, and she groaned as he traced a slow line with his fingertips from the ridge of her shoulder to the swell of her right breast.

They kissed again, heatedly, discarding their shirts

onto the living room floor. Nathan unhooked Cooper's bra and, pulling it free from her body with one hand, cupped the base of her neck with the other in order to crush her torso against his. He lay back on the couch, allowing Cooper to fall on top of him, her hair forming a curtain against the light of the room's single lamp.

Breathing hard, Cooper brushed her fingers against Nathan's belt buckle. As she did so, he broke away. "Are you sure?" he asked her, his voice hoarse with desire.

Cooper nodded, but didn't speak.

They stared at one another for a moment and then Cooper looked away, embarrassed by her conflicting emotions. She wanted Nathan, but she knew that having been in such close proximity with a murderer was clouding her judgment.

"I want to do this for the right reasons," Nathan whispered into her ear, his breath sending shivers through her body. "I don't want to have sex with you." He pushed a strand of hair from her face. "I mean, I do, but I want it to be . . . not sex but . . ." He sighed in frustration. "This sounds so corny, but I want us to make love. I don't want to do this as a reaction to what we went through tonight."

Grasping the hand touching her hair, Cooper kissed the inside of Nathan's palm as tears welled in her eyes. "You're amazing," she murmured.

"No, you are." Nathan reached behind his head and, grabbing a chenille throw, used it to cover their exposed upper bodies. "I would have freaked out back at Frank's if you hadn't been so calm. Do you want to talk about it? The message?"

"What's there to say?" Cooper stated wryly, her heart still thudding double-time in her chest. She gazed up at the ceiling, her hand tracing slow, lazy circles across

Nathan's chest. "The killer we're *supposed* to be tracking down knows our every move. We thought we were collecting clues, but this person's probably been one step ahead of us the whole time." She frowned. "How can we stop someone like that?"

Nathan sat up and gazed intently into Cooper's eyes. "For starters, we don't let them get to us. We're not going to put off by some threat written in paint. I'm going to brew some coffee and then we'll check out the diary you found. Tomorrow, you'll turn it over to the police. Whoever wrote that message on your car will be back at Door-2-Door on Saturday . . ."

"So we're going to have to find a way to ask all the volunteers where they were tonight and hope we can narrow down the suspect list," Cooper finished his thought.

"Exactly." Nathan collected his shirt from the floor and then handed Cooper her clothes. "As for tonight, I think you should stay here. I don't want you to be alone after what's happened."

Cooper gestured at the balled-up uniform shirt on her lap. "I'll have to put my uniform in the dryer. It's soaked. And I'm going to have to drive home pretty early to change or everyone'll wonder why I'm showing up at Door-2-Door dressed for work!"

"Why don't you take a hot shower? I'll make coffee, start a load of wash, and lay out a pair of my pajamas for you." Nathan smiled. "I'll even make you one of my famous omelets in the morning."

Laughing, Cooper wrapped the blanket around her chest and tossed her shirt at him. "What woman could resist that offer?" Then, more soberly, she added, "I'm so grateful you were with me tonight, Nathan. If you weren't there, I would have been really scared. I feel . . . I feel like nothing bad can happen when you're with me."

"Then I guess I'll have to be with you a lot." He gazed at her tenderly and then jerked his thumb toward the stairs. "Now, go up there and get naked. I've got a lot of work to do."

13

And in my dismay I said,
"All men are liars."

Psalm 116:11 (NIV)

When the Sunrise group gathered in Door-2-Door's kitchen on Saturday morning, they were all grateful to be out of the cold and damp. It had been raining since dawn and the precipitation was tinged with a winter's chill that drove all the volunteers directly to the coffee station.

Following Quinton's suggestion, each of the Bible study members made plans to ride with a volunteer they hadn't talked with much. Cooper chose Erik, the retired principal with a penchant for lake fishing and online gambling.

"Can we take your car? I'm a bit low on gas," Cooper told him once their coolers were packed, flushing slightly at the lie.

"Sure thing," Erik replied amiably. Even though Cooper was half his age, he insisted on pushing the cart bearing the coolers and Sunday food boxes down the steep loading ramp.

Outside, the rain pecked at their exposed skin as they filled the back seat of Erik's SUV. As Cooper opened the door to the passenger side, anticipating the dry warmth of the car's interior, she nearly sat on a bouquet of pink carnations arranged in a cushion of purple tissue paper. Luckily, Erik snatched them out from beneath her bottom in the nick of time, laying them down on the floor of the back seat with the deliberate gentleness of a mother placing her newborn in a bassinet.

"Those flowers are lovely," Cooper commented, hoping to discover who they were intended for, but Erik deflected her question by complaining about the weather and the astronomical price of gas.

"Over three bucks a gallon!" He shook his head in disgust. "Drives up the price of everything else, too. Food. Services. Our heating bills are going to shoot through the roof over the next couple of months." He waved at a driver looking to change lanes. "I remember when my cost of living was half what it is now and I had a salary back then. Now, I've just got my pension."

"Is that enough to live on these days?" Cooper asked as casually as possible.

Erik shrugged. "I do okay. My house is paid off, so I don't have to worry about a mortgage anymore. I'm pretty handy and that keeps me from having to write checks to the repair man." He sighed. "I don't spend a lot on my hobbies, either, but I'll be buying gas for my boat even if it goes to five bucks a gallon."

"I can guess what one of your hobbies is." Cooper gestured out the water-splattered windshield at the fishing pole holders strapped to the front of Erik's SUV. "What are the others? I could use some cheap hobbies. I've gotten totally addicted to pedicures."

"Well, I can't say that's one of mine." Erik laughed. "I like to play poker on the Internet. It's free and I wouldn't waste good money on a card game where I can't see the other players' faces, in any case." Erik parked at their first delivery stop. "And I guess Door-2-Door is a hobby. I've been doing this since I retired. Only costs some gas and time, but I've worked for my community my whole life, so it wouldn't feel right to sit around and only see to my own needs now."

"And you seem to really like this route, too," Cooper stated, watching Erik carefully for his reaction. Although he quickly got out of the truck in order to retrieve one of the coolers, he couldn't disguise the rush of blood tingeing his cheeks red.

"Nice folks on this route," he murmured cryptically.

They delivered a meal to a Mrs. Lockhart, who lived in a tidy, one-bedroom apartment off Broad Street. Mrs. Lockhart was in high sprits and informed Erik and Cooper that her son and daughter-in-law were relocating to Richmond and had invited her to live with them.

"I won't be needing Door-2-Door much longer," she told them proudly and then reached out to Erik. "But I'll miss seein' you. You've always been so kind to me. I wish we had gotten to know one another better."

Erik squeezed the old woman's hand and smiled at her tenderly. "I'm glad to lose you to your family. We've got to move on now, ma'am. You take care of yourself, you hear?"

At least that'll be one less client for the Door-2-Door killer to prey on, Cooper thought with relief, hoping that Mrs. Lockhart's son would relocate his mother with alacrity.

During the next three stops, Erik conducted his deliveries with polite efficiency and Cooper realized that even though he had stuck with the same route for over a year, he wasn't exactly on intimate terms with the clients.

I don't think he's the one, she thought. *The murderer has to get to know these folks well enough to learn about their valuables. Erik isn't big on small talk.*

Cooper was a bit surprised by the route Erik chose in order to reach their final stop. Though she wasn't overly familiar with Richmond's East Side, her sense of direction was keen enough to recognize that Erik had doubled back, practically passing right by their second stop, in order to pull into the gravel driveway of a light blue ranch.

The house looked very well-kept in comparison to most of the other clients' residences. The lawn was meticulously trimmed and free of weeds, the bushes lining the front path were neatly pruned, and it looked as though someone had recently replaced the mounted mailbox and polished the brass knocker and kick plate on the front door until they shone.

Tucking the remaining food box under his arm, Erik asked Cooper to carry the cooler. He then removed the bouquet from his back seat and cradled the flowers carefully in his free hand. Whistling as he walked up the front path, Erik gave a proprietary glance around the yard. He knocked jauntily three times on the front door and then let himself in without waiting for an invitation.

"Is that our knight in shining armor?" a woman's voice called from within.

Erik was smiling widely. "Yes, milady. 'Tis me!"

"We're on the sun porch, watching the rain fall," a second female voice said.

Beckoning Cooper to follow, Erik set the food down in the kitchen and then, hiding the flowers behind his back, hustled through the living room to the narrow sun porch where the two women, who were clearly sisters, awaited him.

Though both females were slight of figure and had thick, bobbed white hair, there was an obvious age difference between the two. They produced identical smiles when Erik entered the room and there was no way to miss the brightness illuminating his features.

"Cooper, this is Velma Crick." Erik gestured at the older sister, who was probably in her early eighties. "And this is Violet," he spoke the other woman's name with tender affection. Cooper noted that Violet was at least a decade younger than Velma.

"Ooooh! Someone's brought a surprise!" Velma cooed.

Erik produced the carnations with a flourish and handed them to Violet. "To the most beautiful flower in Richmond."

Violet giggled and thanked Erik effusively. After offering the volunteers tea, which they accepted, Violet, Velma, and Erik settled in for a good, long chat.

Watching Erik intently as he complimented the sisters on their tea, the china cups, and the shade of their sweater sets, Cooper felt like an intruder. After several moments of ordinary conversation, Velma insinuated that the sink in their bathroom seemed to be leaking from the faucet base and Erik leapt up to examine the problem.

"I'd better show you," Violet said with a mischievous smile and she and Erik sneaked from the room like lustful teenagers.

"That man is right smitten!" Velma cackled. "Our house has never been in such good shape."

That explained Erik's bizarre route. He saved this house for last in order to spend the most time here. There was no doubt he was on intimate terms with both occupants, but Cooper believed that he had absolutely no intention of hurting these women. Erik was obviously in love with Violet and didn't pretend to conceal his interest in her.

"How long has he felt this way?" Cooper asked.

"Ever since he stepped foot inside this house over a year ago. Our middle sister, Vera, still lived here then, but she's had to go into a home. We couldn't take care of her anymore." Velma's face creased in sorrow as she gestured at a collection of framed photographs clustered on a nearby table. "Doesn't even know us most days. It's a right shame." She leaned forward and stared at Cooper's face. "You've got some interestin' eyes, missy. Like you're part husky and part jaguar. Lovely."

"Thank you." Cooper moved to the table and examined the photographs. Mostly black and white, the photos depicted three lovely young woman in a variety of hometown settings. The sisters posed in cheerleader outfits in what was likely their high school gym, showed off ice-cream sundaes at an old-fashioned soda fountain, and posed gracefully at skating rinks, bowling alleys, and from the leather seat of a Mustang convertible. Cooper's favorite shot was of the sisters dressed in their holiday finest, planting kisses on the cheeks of a delighted Santa Claus. None of the photographs showed the sisters in their old age—it was as if their youth together was all that mattered. At least, until Erik appeared on the scene.

The sound of muted laughter came echoing down the hall from Violet's bathroom. "They're so sweet," Cooper whispered to Velma.

"I told her to go on and marry the man, but she won't leave me." Velma clucked her tongue. "He's even bought her a ring. Showed it to me once. It's a single amethyst. Not very fancy, but lovely. It'd suit my sister just right and so would he."

"Couldn't he . . ." Cooper hesitated to interfere.

"Erik move in with us?" Velma completed Cooper's thought. "I've suggested that, too, trust me, missy. We all get along like a gaggle of geese and I'm too old to be en-vyin' Violet's happiness, so why not?" She pointed down the hall. "He's already doin' most of the chores 'round here and he could use a woman to keep his clothes tidy and his belly full. We pay for our Door-2-Door meals," Velma added proudly. "But if we had a man to run to the store for us, Violet would start cookin' again and her food is miles better that what y'all bring. No offense intended."

"None taken." Cooper gave Velma a quick bow. "What's your sister's objection to his moving in?"

Velma stirred her tepid tea. "She's afraid it's not proper. That she'd be breakin' her weddin' vows, but her man's been under the ground for two years and he never treated her like he should have, anyhow, so I don't know why she's letting him hold her back. Now Erik, he's a good man."

At that moment, Erik and Violet reentered the room. Violet declared that the sink was fixed and that once again, she and her sister were in his debt.

"I'd do anything to make sure your days were filled with ease," Erik whispered to Violet. They exchanged flirtatious grins, and then Erik bent over and kissed her hand. After giving Velma a chaste peck on her wrinkled cheek, he and Cooper bid the ladies farewell.

"Velma approves of your marrying her sister," Cooper stated simply as they headed back to Door-2-Door. "She says there's plenty of room for you in their house."

Taken aback, Erik blinked at her in surprise. Then he frowned. "Velma's not the problem. It's Violet I've got to convince. I know she loves me, but she feels guilty about marrying again. She said she made a vow and has never broken a promise in her life."

Cooper mulled this hurdle over. "Is Violet a religious woman?"

"Well, she goes to church every Sunday and she and Velma read the Bible to each other every night. Why?"

"I think Savannah might be able to give you some advice on how to show Violet that she's not doing anything wrong by remarrying," Cooper thought out loud. "She leads our Bible study and always seems to know the answers to life's most difficult puzzles."

Beaming, Erik parked his truck, turned off the ignition, and grabbed Cooper by the hand. "I'm not getting any younger, so if you can offer me some hope, I'd be really grateful. Can we ask her right away?"

Hurrying inside, Cooper found Savannah in conversation with Leo. She had just finished eliciting directions to his apartment as the truculent young man muttered that she'd be wasting his valuable free time. Unperturbed by his hostility, Savannah smiled at him and said that she was looking forward to their visit and promised to arrive with a homemade maple-apple cream pie as well as other surprises.

Once Leo had stalked off, Cooper propelled Erik into the seat next to Savannah's and explained the older man's dilemma.

"I believe God approves of widows remarrying," Savannah stated carefully. "If you love one another, you should celebrate that love through the bond of marriage."

"But what about Violet's former marriage vows? Would she be betraying them?" Erik wrung his hands together.

"Romans chapter seven, verse three states that if a woman's husband dies, she is released from the law of marriage and is not an adulteress, even if she marries another man." Savannah touched Erik on the arm. "Perhaps you can share that passage with your Violet. If she still has doubts, I'd be available to talk with her. I also run a couples discussion group at Hope Street Church on Wednesday nights, should you two care to join."

Erik leapt from his seat. "Thank you! Romans seven, verse three. Romans seven, verse three. Got it!" He smiled like a schoolboy. "I'm heading back to her house right now! I'm going to read her that verse and then hand her the ring. I bought her a violet gem, because I can't see the color purple without thinking of her. I'd give anything to slip that ring on her finger this very day!" And off he raced, his truck wheels screeching as he tore from the parking lot.

"I don't think he's our killer," Cooper spoke into Savannah's ear.

"It certainly seems like he's focused on something other than money," Savannah agreed quietly. "I rode along with Brenda today. The woman is devoted to these clients and to her son. I doubt she'd risk having him placed in foster care while she was sent to jail for murder." She sighed. "The brutal death of Darik's father seems to have made her repulsed by violence, not attracted to it." Savannah placed her cane on the floor and stood up. "I hope our friends have discovered a deep, dark secret about one of their partners because you and I certainly haven't."

Thinking of Erik's hope-filled face, Cooper smiled. "You know, it was kind of nice to be in on a romantic adventure instead. I hope Violet says 'yes.'"

After leading Savannah out to the Mr. Faucet van, Cooper cornered Nathan in the walk-in fridge and invited him to join her for lunch followed by an afternoon reading through Frank Crosby's Civil War diary. Nathan had stayed behind to help Campbell in the kitchen, but the biker had been too preoccupied with work to exchange more than a few polite sentences.

"A chance to check out the treasure we stole? Of course I'm in," Nathan whispered as Quinton and Bryant walked past. "But I'm not looking forward to making a confession during Bible study tomorrow about our activities Friday night."

"At least I have faith that our friends will forgive us," Cooper frowned. "I'm not so certain the cops will be as merciful."

Cooper entered the classroom where the Sunrise Bible study met and inhaled an enticing aroma. Quinton had baked pecan cinnamon coffee cake muffins and had kept them warm using the oven in the teacher's lounge while Nathan had provided a healthy side dish of a bowl of sliced red Anjou pears mixed with golden raisins and Trish had supplied them with fresh-ground Kona coffee.

"This was an exciting week for Joseph," Savannah said as she waited for her friends to sit at their desks and turn to the appropriate workbook page. "In our reading, Joseph has been promoted to one of the highest available positions in the Pharaoh's court. Joseph's pretty much the right-hand man and because his predictions about the seven years of plenty followed by seven years of famine were spot-on, Egypt will be able to survive the lean times."

"But the rest of the world wasn't as prepared," Bryant added.

"Too true." Trish pointed at a verse in Genesis forty-two. "Joseph's brothers were forced to travel to Egypt in hopes of buying grain. When they got there, they didn't even recognize the brother they had sold into slavery. What a role reversal!" She reviewed a segment of Scripture and then shook her head. "Can you even imagine how conflicted Joseph must have felt when he saw them again?"

"Especially when his brothers call themselves honest men in verse eleven. What a joke!" Jake spluttered. "'Bout as honest as a bunch of pawnbrokers!"

"Let's address one of the key questions from our homework," Savannah suggested after casting a bemused smile in Jake's direction. "How do you feel about Joseph's treatment of his brothers when they came to seek help for their folks back home?"

"He messed with them," Nathan answered. "He put the silver they had used as payment for the grain back in their saddle bags and then demanded they return to Egypt with their youngest brother, Benjamin. All the brothers knew Jacob would go insane when he heard that an overseer of Egypt wanted to see his youngest son, but they were terrified of being accused of stealing the silver so they had no choice."

Quinton frowned. "I was torn. On one hand, I thought it was fair for Joseph to cause his brothers some anguish. On the other hand, I wanted him to just reveal himself and have a big-time reunion banquet right off. Personally, I don't think he was able to get a grip on his conflicting feelings. I think he felt angry and hurt that they didn't know him, but relieved and happy that they were alive and well and there was hope for them to become a family again."

"Cooper, anything to add before we move on to the next point?" Savannah inquired mildly.

Starting guiltily, Cooper found that she had been so focused on the contents of Frank Crosby's Civil War diary that she hadn't been following their discourse.

"Page 181," Nathan whispered.

Glancing quickly at her workbook, Cooper said, "I loved the end of chapter forty-three. I could just picture the scene where Joseph hears that his father is still alive. That news must have made his heart swell." She flipped the thin pages of her Bible, enjoying the rustling murmur as she found the section in Genesis she wanted to discuss. "Joseph meets his brother Benjamin in verse twenty-nine, and verse thirty says, 'Deeply moved at the sight of his brother, Joseph hurried out and looked for a place to weep. He went into his private room and wept there.'" Cooper looked at her friends. "My eyes didn't stay dry, either. You can just sense how overwhelmed with love and longing Joseph was. It drove me crazy that I had to wait 'til Genesis forty-five for Joseph to finally tell his brothers who he was!"

Trish dabbed at her eyes with a tissue, leaving blotches of mascara on her upper cheeks. "And then they hug each other and cry. These grown men—all of whom have made so many mistakes! It just goes to show us that there's always time to make amends." She sniffed. "And when Jacob and Joseph are reunited, it was so beautiful. It made me think of you, Jake, and I prayed that one day you'd see your daddy again and you could forgive him and weep together."

Now it was Jake's turn to become misty-eyed. Unable to speak, he hoarsely whispered "Thank you" to Trish and then got up from his desk under the pretense of refilling his coffee cup.

"From deception, fear, and doubt, Joseph and his family

are brought to a place of reconciliation and renewal through God's will," Savannah declared quietly. "I was very moved by our lesson this week as well. Does anyone want to share their answer to the life-reflection question on page 183?"

"Before we go on," Cooper cleared her throat. "I need to tell you about something, um, deceitful I've done. Nathan was with me, too, but only to make sure I didn't get hurt. The decision to search Frank's house for clues and ignore your advice was all mine." As she absently picked the crumb topping off her muffin, Cooper described how she and Nathan had gained access through the back door, retrieved the diary from inside the rocking chair, and were made aware that the killer had followed them. Lastly, she repeated the words that had been written on the side of her truck.

"Seek and die!" Trish shrieked. "That's a pretty serious threat!"

"Why didn't you tell us before we showed up at Door-2-Door yesterday?" Bryant demanded. "We could have asked everyone what they were up to Friday night!"

Jake's mouth formed a crooked smile. "Yeah, sure. I could have just turned to Penny and said, 'Hey, lady. Were you out in the rain last night, writing threats on my friend's truck?'" He waved off the notion. "Give Cooper a break. She did something she felt she had to do. Didn't we all just read some lessons from Scripture about makin' mistakes?"

Quinton studied Cooper and Nathan, his eyes lit with interest. "Did you read the diary?"

"I did, and now we know why Mr. Crosby had such an aversion to the color yellow." She paused to look over at Nathan. "Lucky for us, we decided to bring the diary to the Tuckahoe Library to read and one of the reference librarians recognized this." She pulled the rectangle of yellow fabric from her purse.

"It's shaped like a flag," Bryant said.

"You're a clever guy." Nathan was impressed. "It's a hospital flag from the Civil War. It was flown outside the hospital tents to clearly identify them. And Frank's relative, Lieutenant Aaron Crosby, spent some time in a Union field hospital."

Jake nearly choked on his coffee. "He was a Yankee?"

"No, but he was shot in the back by one during a retreat," Nathan explained. "So he took the coat and sword from a dead Union soldier lying nearby and, because they thought he was one of them, he was taken to their hospital. Aaron wrote that his own army was on the run and his only chance of survival was to pretend to be a Yank."

"That seems a bit dishonorable," Quinton said.

Trish's violet eyes narrowed. "The man just wanted to live. Maybe he had a family he wanted to see again—a future he dreamed about."

"He did," Cooper opened the diary and read Aaron's words:

April 18
Sunrise. I dreamed of returning to our farm. Annie must be awake by now. The cows will need milking. I hope the boy is helping her with the chores. I wonder if he's taller than me now. I'm tired. Will write more tomorrow.

April 19
The doctors are beginning to wonder about my muteness. I will have to leave here soon. My wound is healing well and it is a luxury to rest in a soft bed again, so it will be

difficult to leave. My feet are still clotted with blood and I've lost four nails from my right foot. That is no surprise considering the shape of my boots. Most of our men were barefoot in our last skirmish and we haven't had enough food to fill our bellies for months.

The South cannot win this war. She is like David fighting Goliath, but with no stone to throw. All I want is to return home, to look upon the faces of my dear ones and to watch my cornstalks grow.

I have forgotten what it is we have been fighting for . . .

"The poor man," Savannah said. "I'm glad to know Lieutenant Aaron must have reunited with his family or there wouldn't have been a Frank Crosby. I wonder how he ended up with the hospital flag."

"He stole it," Nathan informed her. "The hospital tent was in a state of chaos as a large group of wounded soldiers was brought inside. Aaron used the confusion to his advantage by leaving his bed. He grabbed a pair of discarded boots but had no socks, so he ripped down the hospital flag to wrap around his right foot, which was in pretty bad shape." Gesturing at the flag, he added, "Must have been washed since then."

"So Frank was ashamed of his relative for retreating and then deserting?" Bryant wondered aloud.

Cooper nodded. "That and more. Apparently, the field hospital fell under cannon fire and everyone inside died."

"Because the yellow flag had been taken?" Trish's violet eyes were wide with horror.

"There's no way of knowing," Nathan answered. "But Frank was obviously greatly ashamed of being related to this man and wanted to keep all ties to Aaron Crosby a secret."

"*That* part of our mystery is now solved," Savannah spoke with quiet authority. "It's time to turn the diary over to the police, and Cooper, you *must* tell them about the message written on your truck."

"I will. I'm going to call them right after church. But first, I'd like to ask for your forgiveness." Cooper looked at her friends in appeal. "Something inside me just wouldn't rest until I understood Frank better. Thoughts of him have been kind of haunting me since I learned of his death. I'm sorry."

"Of course we forgive you!" Trish announced. "And who knows? Maybe the killer will stop now that they realize it's not just the authorities out there looking for them. Maybe what you did will save lives."

The sound of music drifted into the open door of the classroom. The praise song *Come and Worship* was a signal to individual classes to wrap up their discussion and make way to the auditorium for worship service.

"The police are likely to interview the regular Saturday Door-2-Door volunteers about their movements Friday night," Quinton said as he began tidying up. "I guess we no longer have a role to play."

Bryant looked disappointed. "So there's no need to snoop into the volunteer's lives any more?"

"Oh, I wouldn't say that," Savannah argued. "I have no doubt that God, through Trish, placed us in the path of those volunteers. If He hadn't, then Leo wouldn't be joining us for worship this morning. We should always take an interest in those around us."

"Leo's coming here?" The alarm in Trish's voice made Jake grin.

"You can relax that grip on your purse," he teased. "That boy's all bark and no bite. Tell 'em the story, Savannah. Quick, before we have to go."

"First of all, Leo was arrested for disorderly conduct." She couldn't hold back the smile that appeared on her face. "Turns out, our friend had a bit too much to drink one warm spring evening and found himself with a full bladder. He went in search of the closest tree—"

"But found the leg of a horse instead!" Jake hollered. "The horse belonged to a mounted cop and let's just say that our man Leo didn't have very good aim that night! Both horse and rider were sprayed by somethin' warm and smelly and wet."

"Oh, dear." Trish giggled behind her hand.

"Leo works for a moving company and lives in the same apartment building as his mama. We met her and she's a fine, upstanding woman," Savannah continued. "I also brought our new friend a copy of T.D. Jakes's *Speaks to Men* on CD. Leo must have been influenced by the book because he called me at seven this morning to ask if there was a bus stop close to Hope Street."

"Savannah was perfect," Jake said with enthusiasm. "She just listened to Leo talk and then told him that everyone makes mistakes and that we can learn from them and be changed by them. His mama is going to be in seventh heaven when she finds out that he's goin' to church today."

"Then we'd better get a move on." Savannah stood. "We'll pray for you, Cooper. I hope that you don't get in too much trouble for poking around in Frank's house."

"Maybe The Colonel and I can be cellmates," Cooper joked, but her heart was filled with trepidation as she followed her friends down the hallway and into the large chapel, where a sea of joy-filled faces was lifted toward the glow of two enormous projection screens.

"This next song was written by two our very own members," the band leader announced. "Lyrics by Quinton Enderly and music by Jake Lombardi. Here's *Teach Us How to Pray*."

The drums and guitar burst into life and immediately, the congregation began to clap. Quinton was staring at Jake in astonishment, but his friend was too busy responding to Savannah's questions. Jake's face was animated with delight and Cooper wondered how long he had been planning this surprise. When the band began to sing, Cooper did her best to add her voice to the rising swell of sound within the room. They sang:

> *There's a little church*
> *Down a long dirt road*
> *It's packed from door to door*
> *Hands are lifted to the rafters*
> *And feet stomp upon the floor*
>
> *These are your children, Lord*
> *These are your children, Lord*
> *Gathered beneath this roof to say*
> *Our hearts are open to your presence*
>
> *Can you teach us how to pray?*
> *Can you teach us how to pray?*

Toward the end of the fourth verse, Cooper stole another glance at Quinton and Jake. Both men looked incredibly pleased by their joint composition. She also noticed that Leo had arrived sometime after the song's opening and had taken a seat next to Savannah. He swayed his shoulders and sang as though he had known the song since birth.

Sometimes my favorite church
Is a canopy of indigo blue
I bow my head, get down on my knees
And have a good long talk with You

And as the warm breeze blows
'Cross my face and I am bathed in Your light
I become infused with Your holy presence
Awed by Your tenderness and might

One of Your children, Lord
One of Your children, Lord
You walk beside me every day
Everywhere I go
Can You teach me how to pray?

During the moment of silent prayer, once the congregation had finished offering a hearty round of applause to Quinton and Jake, Cooper prayed that Ashley's surgery would go smoothly the next day. She then asked for forgiveness over being angry with Lincoln for insisting that he be the only one at Ashley's side while she was at the hospital. Finally, Cooper prayed that the Lord would be right beside her as she walked into Henrico County Police Department's Headquarters.

14

True to her word, Cooper left Hope Street Church and, after grabbing a bagel with honey-almond cream cheese at Einstein's, drove north toward the cluster of governmental buildings located on Parham Road. She had to explain herself to several officers before a gruff woman wearing an extremely form-fitting uniform took her name and phone number. The female cop reluctantly took the diary from Cooper's hands, flipped it over and, not finding anything interesting on the front or back covers, tossed the Ziploc onto her desk.

"That's it?" Cooper was incredibly relieved that she had gotten off so lightly.

The woman snorted. "No, it isn't *it*. Investigator Rector will be calling you tomorrow. I'm sure he's gonna want to hear your colorful story in person."

"Do you think I'm going to," Cooper gulped, "be arrested?"

Smiling maliciously, the woman shrugged. "Who knows? You broke into a crime scene, tampered with evidence, and maybe compromised a police investigation.

It'd sure be within our rights to read you your Miranda warning." She pointed a stubby finger at Cooper's chest. "Just don't go anywhere. You come marching straight here the second he calls, no matter what you're doing. Investigator Rector doesn't like people to be late."

Beads of perspiration dotted Cooper's brow. "Yes, ma'am. And I'm really sorry. It wasn't my intention to make things harder for the police. I mean," she quickly amended the latter statement, "I wasn't trying to mess things up. I just wanted to find out what happened to Mr. Crosby. I *was* actually hoping to help you all."

The female officer hitched her weighted belt higher on her round hips. "Save your speeches for tomorrow. Lucky for you, I'm not the one you need to convince."

And with that, Cooper was dismissed.

Monday morning was unusually fair and mild. The weather was at odds with the displays of Halloween decorations, chrysanthemums, hay-stuffed scarecrows, and pyramids of rotund pumpkins gracing every storefront Cooper passed during the course of her commute.

Cooper had barely stepped foot through Make It Work!'s front door when Angela rushed over, grabbed her by the hand, and pulled her toward the magnificent assortment of cut roses bursting from the dark brown wicker basket. The professional arrangement, which was the size of a picnic basket, took the customary place of the rose bouquet Angela purchased every Sunday afternoon from Costco.

"I'm going to go out on a limb and assume you didn't get those from a discount warehouse," Cooper said as the secretary sniffed the lustrous petals of the red, pink, and fuchsia roses.

"Look at the tag!" Angela thrust a label bearing watering instructions into Cooper's hand. "This design is called The Kiss." She pulled a florist's greeting card from its plastic fork in the center of the group of roses with a flourish. "Now read this!"

Obediently, Cooper examined the card. " 'Because I dream of kissing you.' "

"Who do you think it's from?" Angela clutched the card against her heart. "Emilio? Did you see the way he danced with me in the garage the other day?"

"It's not him!" Cooper immediately responded. Seeing the hurt on her friend's face, she softened her tone. "I'm sorry, Angela, but this is way too classy for Emilio. Take the wording of the note, for example. It doesn't sound at all like how he talks." She lowered her voice. "I think it's from Mr. Farmer. You made him jealous and he's trying to tell you that he cares."

Angela rolled her eyes. "I doubt it. I told you before, he's had a bazillion chances to reel me in." She crossed her arms defensively and stared at Cooper from beneath her fake eyelashes. "What is with you today? Your tongue is sharp as a lightnin' bolt and you look like you haven't had a wink of sleep. Is it Nathan?"

"No. Everything's going fine with him." Cooper felt queasy just thinking about the phone call she would inevitably be receiving from Investigator Rector. "Ashley's having surgery today," she provided Angela with a partial truth. "I'm a little worried about her. I just won't be able to concentrate until Mama calls and tells me she's okay."

"Oh, honey. She's gonna be right as rain." Angela threw her arms around Cooper. "And I'm sorry that I've been so self-centered lately. It's gettin' older that's doin' it. I wanna take care of somebody and I want somebody to take care of me." She smiled and her eyes turned misty. "Now. I want you to take the white roses from Costco to your sister with best wishes for a speedy recovery from all of us. I've got a drawer full of Hallmark cards and I'm gonna get everybody to sign one for her. And you tell me if you need to leave early today. I'll rearrange your schedule in a flash." She snapped her manicured fingers.

Cooper felt a rush of affection for her friend. "Enjoy your flowers, Angela. No matter who they're from, someone obviously recognizes what a catch you are."

A flicker of genuine sadness passed across the secretary's face and it was that brief glimpse of Angela's fear of aloneness that propelled Cooper to march right into Mr. Farmer's office. Her boss was bent over a spreadsheet, an adding machine close to his right hand and the latest issue of *Popular Mechanics* next to his left. He looked up at her, blinking, as though surprised to see another human being in his lair.

"Good morning." He removed his glasses, drew his hand away from the adding machine, and waited for her to speak.

Cooper shut the door behind her and, after removing a pile of newspapers from the only other chair in the room, sat down and faced her boss. "Sir. Have you been sending Angela roses?"

Mr. Farmer blushed from the bottom of his cheeks to the bald spot in the center of his head. "Well, I—"

"Because I know you care about her and that you might believe she has feelings for Emilio. In a sense, she would like him to have feelings for her, just for vanity's sake, but the truth is that she wants a man to share her life with. The man she's waiting for is not Emilio." She stared intently at Mr. Farmer. "It's you."

Flustered, her boss's fingers twitched erratically and his pinkie hit the total button on the adding machine. Numbers appeared on the thin strip of white paper as the machine buzzed in a wild frenzy of ink. Mr. Farmer reached out to turn it off, but he couldn't control the trembling of his hands, so Cooper walked around the desk and flicked the switch for him.

"You've got to make a bold statement, sir. Not roses. Something that declares how you feel in a *big* way. Prove to her once and for all that you're willing to take the risk and ask her to be with you." Cooper paused, wondering if she was making a grave mistake by issuing orders to her boss. "Forgive me for butting in here, sir, but she's been miserable lately and I think you have, too."

After a pregnant pause, Mr. Farmer issued the briefest of nods. Finally, without meeting Cooper's eyes, he murmured, "What should I do?"

For the moment, Cooper forgot her own troubles. Perhaps she could balance out her reckless act of breaking into Frank's house by finally bringing Angela and Mr. Farmer together. With a grin, she resumed her seat across from her boss. "Don't worry, sir. I have an idea."

Cooper's first appointment after lunch was at an unexpected location. Lali Gupta had phoned earlier in the day and requested an annual service contract with Make It Work!

"The director asked for you personally." Angela handed Cooper a work order. "They've got a busted copier and fax machine. Get her to sign our annual contract form before you leave, too. Mr. Farmer is going to give them a special rate 'cause they're a nonprofit. He's got such a big heart, that man." Opening the makeup compact that was never far from reach, Angela reapplied a layer of scarlet lipstick. "He asked me to stay late tonight. We've never worked a minute past five before. I can't imagine what he's up to."

"Me, either," Cooper replied innocently. "But he's got some nasty-looking spreadsheets in his office, so it can't be anything fun."

Frowning in disappointment, Angela returned to her desk while Cooper slid the Door-2-Door paperwork onto her clipboard and headed out to a work van. Emilio intercepted her before she could open the driver's door.

"Hey, gorgeous." Emilio leaned against the van, his knuckles pushing his biceps outward. "How was the weekend? Did you sit around, eat bonbons, and maybe wonder just for a minute what *I* was doin'? 'Cause I was thinkin' about *you*. Let's go out tonight. I became good buddies with one of the chefs at Ruth Chris. We could eat like kings. What do ya say?"

Emilio was the last person Cooper wanted to see at the moment. Hoping to run him off, she opened one of the van's rear doors, planted her toolbox firmly on the floor, and slammed the door shut. Giving him a wide berth, she walked back to the front of the van. "I had a lovely weekend, thank you. I ate a bunch of fried food, broke into an old man's house with my boyfriend, received a threatening note from a serial killer, went to church, and then turned myself into the police because I broke the law and I damned well knew it. In fact, I'm waiting for a phone call from one of the detectives who's probably going to tell me to get my ass down to the station before his coffee gets cold, so if you'll excuse me, I'd like to get to this next job as quick as I can."

Instead of being repelled by Cooper's caustic demeanor, Emilio inched closer to her. "You don't need to make up stories to impress me. I already think you're awesome."

"Well, the feeling's *not* mutual!" Cooper snapped and then jumped into the van and locked the door.

As she sped off, Emilio stared after her. "She likes this cat-and-mouse game, but I'm not a patient guy." His mind conjured a fantasy scene in which Cooper served him a gigantic rib-eye while modeling skimpy lingerie. "Time to get rid of this so-called boyfriend. She needs a *real* man."

Emilio turned back to the office, hoping to flirt with Angela until she gave him some useful information about Cooper's boyfriend. Whistling *Wild Thing*, Emilio strutted across the parking lot, his wavy, dark hair blowing in the wind and his eyes narrowed in determination. At that moment, he looked more like a wolf than a man.

When Cooper approached Lali Gupta's desk, she was shocked by the woman's appearance. Lali was a wreck. Her black hair was stringy and dull, her eyes were puffy and bloodshot, and her blouse was wrinkled and had been buttoned incorrectly. Even her nails had been chewed into jagged fragments. Cooper wished she could find a way to comfort the unhappy woman, but she knew that only the police could offer Lali the kind of resolution she desperately needed.

Despite knowing the answer, Cooper asked the volunteer director how she was holding up. Lali sighed heavily. "There was a story in Sunday's paper about the suspicious deaths of our clients. I knew it would come out sooner or later, but the timing is really awful because we just sent out our quarterly requests for funding last week. We've had two corporate accounts already call this morning to say that they'll be donating to a different cause in the future as they don't want their names connected to our *troubles*."

"That's awful."

"If we lose any more benefactors, we're going to have to turn away clients." Lali rubbed her temples. "I can't stand the thought of saying no to people who have a true need for our services. I don't even know where we're going to scrape together the money to pay for our current clients."

Cooper observed the men and women seated in nearby cubicles. Every one of them was engaged in a phone conversation, and as Cooper worked on the broken fax machine located in the middle of the row, it became obvious that the Door-2-Door staff was putting every ounce of their energy into garnering donations. Even though their pleas were replete with passion and conviction, most of them hung up their phones without having secured any funds.

Angrily twisting a screw into place, Cooper reflected that the Door-2-Door killer had already stolen the lives of several helpless elderly men and women, but now, the villain was also diminishing the chances for other aged Richmonders to receive the meals they desperately needed.

"It's out of our hands now," Cooper reminded herself with a whisper.

When her repair on the fax machine was complete, she packed up her tools and relocated to a hallway outside the conference room. The copier, a refurbished Canon image-Runner 6000, looked as though it hadn't been serviced since it left the factory. Cooper accessed the interior of the machine and began her analysis of the existing problems. She was so absorbed in her work that she didn't notice a pair of black boots appear behind her toolbox. She gazed up to see Campbell standing there, his massive arms on his hips and a playful smirk on his face.

"Well, well. So *you're* our repairman, eh? A woman wielding tools is a cool thing. It's easy to forget that our volunteers have lives outside of my kitchen." He stroked the braid hanging down from his beard. "I won't be seein' you guys this weekend." He blinked and the amused glimmer vanished. "Keep an eye on things for me, would you?"

Cooper's mind raced. *Did Campbell realize that the killer was likely one of his Friday or Saturday volunteers? Was he leaving town because* he *was guilty?*

"Of course I will," she assured him. "But I don't quite give off the same vibe of authority as you do. Guess I could rent one of those muscle suits, but there's no chance of me growing a Fu Manchu by Saturday." She wiped her hands on a rag. "So where are you off to?"

"I've gotta run to the beach. There's this girl there. Aurora. She's a bartender at one of the big hotels on the strip. She rides a Harley, she sings like an angel, and she's tough as nails."

"And pretty?"

The light returned to Campbell's eyes. "The most beautiful woman to ever walk this earth. And I'm gonna meet her folks for lunch on Saturday. She wants to be serious about our relationship and if this is what it takes to officially make her my own, then I'll meet her family, her preacher, her high school teachers, her Girl Scout leader—anybody!"

Cooper wiped some ink from her wrench and smiled. "I heard that you've liked this woman for a long time but she didn't really, um, return your affection. How'd you get her to change her mind?"

"With this." Campbell turned his back on Cooper and then yanked his tight black T-shirt over his head. A spectrum of colors covering the skin of his back was suddenly revealed. Cooper found herself staring at the biggest tattoo she had ever seen. It began as blue waves on his lower back—an ocean filled with tropical fish and fingers of coral. Above the curls of white foam in the middle of Campbell's back, porpoises leapt from the surf. An enormous sunrise, created with dazzling yellows, oranges, and hot pinks, spread from shoulder blade to shoulder blade. Striped sunrays radiated outward from the edges of Campbell's shoulders to the base of his neck. Doves carrying red roses in their beaks flew upward toward the ornate black letters spelling out the name *Aurora*.

"Wow," Cooper breathed.

Campbell pulled his shirt down over the taut muscles of his back and swiveled around. "That's what Aurora said. She figured I must really want the real thing with her to do what I did."

Cooper nodded. "Yeah, I would say so! That's a pretty permanent gesture."

"She's all I ever wanted." Campbell held out his hands as though he meant to grab the handlebars of his bike. "In a few days, it'll be time to ride to my lady. Anita's filling in for me this weekend, but help her keep an eye on everybody. If I catch the piece of scum that's been messin' with my food, I'm gonna think of all new uses for that deep freeze."

"I'll do my best," Cooper promised him and then watched as he walked away, his burly figure buoyed by a litheness that could only be attributed to happiness.

He's not the killer, she thought. *Like Erik, Campbell is motivated by love instead of money. So who wants money, or to deliberately hurt old folks, more than anything else? That's our murderer.*

Before she had the chance to review her mental list of remaining suspects, her phone rang. Swallowing, she saw that the number belonged to a Taylor Rector. She was being summoned.

Nathan happened to call her cell right after she got off the phone with Investigator Rector and he insisted on accompanying her to the police headquarters. Although Cooper argued with him over his decision as she drove toward Parham Road, he wouldn't take no for an answer.

"I was with you, remember?"

"You wouldn't have been there if I'd just kept my big mouth shut about what I was doing. I refuse to let you get in trouble with the cops because you were trying to be a good boyfriend."

"It took me long enough!" Nathan countered. "I kept putting work before you. Not anymore, Cooper."

Though pleased by his comment, Cooper couldn't let Nathan share the blame for her rash behavior. "I'm pulling into the parking lot and I refuse to tell you who I'm here to see. *Please* wait for me out in the lobby, Nathan. Just knowing you're close by will mean the world to me."

Nathan mumbled something noncommittal and said good-bye.

After checking in at the front, Cooper was led through a warren of desks by a stern-faced and uncommunicative officer until they reached a wooden door bearing Investigator Rector's name on a brass plate.

The investigating officer was not what Cooper had

expected. He was about her age and, due to his ruddy cheeks and freckled nose, had a boyish appearance. His hair was roguishly wavy and his brown eyes, tinged with green, were framed by a sweep of dark eyelashes that most women would kill for. A file folder was open in the center of a disheveled desk and, by pointing at one of the two empty chairs pushed against the back wall, Rector indicated that Cooper should sit while he wrapped up his phone conversation.

Swallowing nervously, she noticed that Aaron Crosby's diary had been transferred to an official plastic evidence bag and was placed in a prominent position on the policeman's desk.

"Ms. Lee, I presume?" Investigator Rector said rhetorically as he replaced his phone receiver with a firm click into the cradle.

"Guilty as charged," Cooper replied and then silently cursed herself for such a poor choice of words.

Rector raised his brows, unamused by her quip. "Breaking into a sealed crime scene is a felony, Ms. Lee. In certain circumstances, you could be looking at a steep fine." He held up a thin sheaf of stapled papers. "I've checked you out. Fortunately, you've got a clean record. Not even a moving violation in the past six months, so what made you suddenly decide to tamper with evidence and hinder a police investigation?"

Cooper took a deep breath. "I wasn't trying to interfere with your case, sir. I paid a visit to Frank Crosby's son and he told me about the existence of a diary and a sword. Until then, it didn't seem like there was anything valuable in Mr. Crosby's house and that he had been killed for no reason." She gazed at the diary. "It had been a long time since The Colonel, I mean, Edward Crosby, had been in his daddy's house. He and Frank didn't get along and I didn't want to waste your time unless he was telling the truth about those items, so I went to look for them myself."

Rector's eyes flashed, but his lips curved into the hint of a smile. "You were just watching out for us, is that it? Didn't want us to waste valuable manpower?"

Cooper's falsified tale withered under Rector's scrutiny. "I met Frank Crosby. He was nervous, and bitter, and, I'm ashamed to say this, but a little disgusting, too. His house was a mess, his clothes were gross, and he had no one to care for him. The biggest highlight of his day was when he could get his hands on the neighbor's newspaper so he could work the puzzles."

After a pause, Rector said, "Go on."

"I pitied Frank. I wished for a better life for him." Cooper gazed at her hands. "And I was grateful to him, too, for he made me realize that I had so much to be thankful for. With his son in jail, I felt a responsibility to find out what happened to him. I know that might not make sense to you, but when I thought about someone stealing from and then . . . poisoning my own Grammy, I just couldn't sit by and wait. Something . . . inside drove me to act."

"Tell me about the sword," Rector prompted.

"Edward told us that his father kept Aaron Crosby's sword in his bedroom closet. It was supposed to be in excellent shape and Frank liked to take it out of its scabbard every now and again to clean it. I don't know any other details about it, but maybe Edward does."

Rector pivoted in his chair and turned his attention to his computer keyboard. "Let's see." His fingers worked rapidly. "According to this auction site, Civil War swords complete with scabbard sell for a range of six hundred to three thousand dollars."

"That's it?" Cooper was shocked. "Frank got killed for that amount of money?"

"People have been killed for much less, Ms. Lee. Still, it makes me wonder if money is this guy's main motive after all," Rector mumbled to himself. "Our killer is angry with senior citizens for some reason. He or she wants to get rid of them, but doesn't have what it takes to do it with his own hands. Therefore he poisons them so they just slip away."

"He can feel less guilt that way," Cooper suggested quietly. "As though he's done them a kindness by relieving them of their sad lives. It's almost as though he hates them, but cares about them, too."

Studying her again, Rector folded his hands together. "And were you alone when you went to Frank's? I'm just asking out of curiosity."

"My boyfriend was with me. I . . . I didn't want him to come but he was worried about my safety. Truthfully, I should have tried harder to convince him to stay home," she confessed hurriedly. "He tried to talk me out of going, though. He and my friends were in agreement that we should leave everything in the hands of the police."

"Nathan Dexter is another member of the illustrious Sunrise Bible study, right?"

Stunned at the amount of information the investigator seemed to have gathered, she nodded. "Yes."

"Don't be too impressed." The officer grinned, shuffling papers around. "I ate lunch with Investigator Mc-Namara today. I'm sure you remember him. He had a lot to say about you."

McNamara had been the lead investigator in the murder case Cooper and her friends had been involved with during the spring of last year. The officer had treated them courteously, and had even shared Scripture quotes with them, but, when all was said and done, had sternly ordered them to cease their sleuthing. McNamara was older than Rector and had a fiercer intensity about him, but Cooper knew that Rector's youthful face could easily belie an unbending determination to uphold the law, no matter what explanations she provided in her own defense.

"There's something else I should tell you." Cooper inhaled and then hastily described the message left on her truck.

The policeman jerked upright in his chair, his eyes alert and excited. "The killer was following you! We might be able to use this." He twiddled his thumbs as he thought. After a few moments, he seemed to recall that Cooper was in the room. "All right, Ms. Lee, you're free to go. I merely wanted to discover if you'd found anything that might prove useful to us and it seems that you have." His expression turned pensive. "I may call on you to do something for me in the immediate future. Something to bait our suspect into revealing his identity. Would you be interested in cooperating with us?"

Cooper exhaled in relief. Standing, she grasped the investigator's outstretched hand and pumped it heartily. "I'll help you any way that I can!"

"No so fast," he added sternly. "I'd also like your word that you and your friends are officially off the case. Should some *clue* or piece of useful information come your way, you are to contact me directly. Otherwise, until I get in touch, the Sunrise Sleuths are officially retired. Is that crystal clear?"

"Yes."

Rector raised his left brow. "I'm sure, being that you're

a faithful churchgoer, that I can take you at your word. Have a nice day."

Cooper walked down the hallway with a much lighter step, uttered a quick prayer of gratitude for being able to share what she knew with the young investigator without reprisal, and then burst through the lobby doors.

Nathan, who had been pacing back and forth near a row of plastic chairs, looked at her anxiously. She responded by swiftly closing the distance between them. Throwing her arms around his neck, she smiled. "It's okay! We just had a nice, civilized discussion."

"Good!" Nathan lifted her from the ground in celebration. The movement caused her purse to drop from her shoulder. Though its contents spread across the marble floor in a noisy clatter, Cooper still clung to Nathan.

"Watch out!" he cautioned, releasing his hold. "You're about to step on your phone." He scooped it off the ground and then watched as Cooper shoved her wallet, car keys, sunglasses, a packet of tissues, a lip gloss, and a roll of Life Savers back into her purse.

"I've got to grab a drink of water," she said and shrugged her purse back onto her shoulder. "My mouth went so dry back there." Spying a sign for the restrooms, Cooper squeezed Nathan's arm. "Be right back."

By the time she turned the corner and headed off to where the restrooms, pay phones, and water fountains could be found, Cooper was too far away to hear her cell phone's customized Beatles text message alert go off.

Nathan looked at the vibrating phone in his hand and, out of sheer habit, pressed the button that would allow him to read the incoming text message. Staring at the display window, his face fell as he read the black letters that appeared in the field of silver:

Can't W8 2 B alone w/ U in the break room again. I want 2 smell the perfume I gave U. XOXO Emilio

The cell phone went quiet and then, as Nathan tried to fully comprehend the message, the phone broke into song for the second time and a second message appeared on the screen:

I'M WAITING

Nathan jabbed the end button until the screen went dark. He experienced such a tumult of mixed emotions that he didn't know what to feel. At that moment, Cooper returned, wearing an exuberant smile. She locked her arm in his and together, they stepped outside.

Leaves tripped down the sidewalk and the flags whipped back and forth in the late afternoon breeze. Cooper inhaled the crisp air with renewed appreciation and sent a wayward stick scuttling into the grass with a playful kick.

"Now that the interrogation is over, I've got to call Ashley," Cooper stated. "As long as her surgery went well, then this has turned out to be a pretty good day after all."

As they walked toward the parking lot, Cooper told Nathan about seeing Campbell at Door-2-Door. When she was finished, Nathan gave her the phone he had been gripping so tightly in his right hand.

"It's amazing what a guy will do to impress a woman," he remarked wryly, but Cooper was too happy to notice the acerbic tone to his voice. She kissed him, thanked him again for standing by her, and then got into her truck, her thoughts already focused on Ashley.

At home, Grammy and Earl were arguing over the

directions Maggie had written regarding the preparation of their dinner.

"It's a chicken pot pie, son. Just stick it in the oven for a spell. If you poke your finger in the middle and get burnt, then it's ready to eat."

"I'm right sure this is a three." Earl pointed at a sheet of notepaper. Seeing Cooper, he thrust the instructions at her. "What do you think?"

Reading over her mother's hasty scrawl, Cooper set the oven, pulled a tossed salad from the fridge, and then shook up a mason jar containing homemade poppy seed dressing. "How's Ashley, Daddy?"

"Just fine," Earl answered, spreading open his newspaper. "Your mama's gone to fix her supper. Says your sister's a bit tired, but in high spirits. I take it they mended everythin' that needed fixin'."

"Was Lincoln there?" Cooper placed a pair of wooden salad forks in the center of the table.

After nodding, Earl turned his attention to his paper. Meanwhile, Grammy had settled herself at the kitchen table and was giving Cooper one of her eagle-eyed stares.

"*You* never came home Friday night, girlie," she said with a cackle. "You and that boy are *finally* startin' to act your ages. 'Bout time you took a roll in the hay. You've been chaste as a nun for far too long."

No one responded. Earl pretended to be absorbed in an article about declining interest rates while Cooper gathered silverware from the drawer next to the sink, her neck flushing pink.

Grammy had erroneously assumed that Cooper and Nathan had had sex, but Cooper decided not to bother correcting her. After all, she hoped that she'd have more sleepovers with her boyfriend in the near future. Until then, it was time to follow Aurora's lead. The woman was right in inviting Campbell to meet her family in order to cement the seriousness of the relationship.

"Any plans this weekend, Daddy?" Cooper asked and handed Grammy an orange napkin.

Earl shrugged. "Nothin' special." He looked sideways at his mother. "You'd know better than me."

Grammy shook her head. "Just another bake sale at church. Why, granddaughter? You got somethin' excitin' in mind?"

Cooper sat across from her and smiled. "Exciting to me. I'd like to invite Nathan here for Sunday dinner. It's time for you all to meet each other."

Rubbing her hands together with glee, Grammy exclaimed, "Oh! I'm gonna make it a point to mention that nice diamond engagement ring gatherin' dust in our bank box!"

Knowing that it would do no good to ask Grammy to refrain from mentioning the subject of marriage during Nathan's first visit to the Lee home, Cooper removed the pot pie from the oven with a defeated groan.

15

The last enemy to be destroyed is death.

1 Corinthians 15:26 (NIV)

Cooper had the storm nightmare for the third time.

As in the other dreams, she found herself inside the small boat as it raced toward the low thunderclouds, but this time, she could practically feel the chill of the rain as it hit her skin. The drops were sharp as needles and Cooper longed to take cover, but she had no control over a single element in the environment. Her feet were stung by the rain and when Cooper looked down at her raw, red toes, she noticed several objects floating in a shallow puddle in the stern of her boat.

She recognized Frank's diary and a black-and-white tintype of a young man in uniform. The face had been partially scratched off as though someone had been intent upon erasing the image completely. There was also a bouquet of purple flowers. Primroses or violets. It was hard to tell.

As the boat cut through the water, Cooper's dream self looked down at the rolling gray river and saw the yellow hospital flag drift past. She reached out to grab it, desperately wanting to rescue it from the water, but a stray current pushed it just beyond her grasp. Though it seemed impossible, the boat picked up even more speed, practically hurtling itself forward.

This was the closest the dream had ever taken Cooper to the storm. The tongues of lightning that had once lingered in the distance now seemed to hover directly above the trees flanking the river. Several of the tallest pines were already aflame. Abruptly, the scene changed, and every single tree was on fire. Cooper stared at the conflagration in fear, feeling the heat on her face and watching as pieces of ash began to drop from the sky into her boat. The rain had ceased and the air burned her lungs. She crouched lower in her boat, breathing in wet wood and the smoking cinders of pinecones.

As though mocking the danger, the current slowed and began to bear Cooper to the shore. Trees, their needles lit with scarlet and orange flames, crashed into the water, sending a burst of sparks into the black sky. Looking back over her shoulder, she saw that the wilderness behind her was pristine and unharmed, but the daylight had faded completely. When she turned to face the forest again, the fire was gone. All was still.

The bow of her boat bumped gently against a pebbled bank. The sand was so white it glowed and the small stones winked like starshine. Cooper sighed. She was safe. The storm had passed. She was preparing to leave the small craft when a stick snapped somewhere in the forest ahead of her. A shape began to materialize from the shadows. It was a man.

Wordlessly, he moved toward her, malice preceding him like a perfume borne by the wind. Frantic, Cooper pushed her boat back into the water, clawing at the liquid with her arms, but the man kept coming toward her. She paddled desperately, edging backward inch by agonizing inch, the cold water splashing onto her face and hair. But there was no way to escape him. Her heart grew frigid as she watched him wade effortlessly into the water. He reached out for her and she woke up.

Cooper waited until eight-thirty Tuesday morning before calling Nathan to ask him to join her family for dinner that weekend. He broke into the recording on his answering machine, only to inform her that he'd been at work for an hour already, as his email inbox was filled with several irate messages from dissatisfied Big Man Product customers.

"Why are they writing you?" Cooper asked, perplexed. "You're the webmaster. It's not your business."

"Try telling *them* that. According to these customers, the toll-free number listed on the contact page is bogus." Nathan sounded extremely cross. "And I'm having no luck getting in touch with Tobey on his cell. The whole thing is giving me a bad feeling. His customers are claiming that his muscle builders have made them sick. Really sick."

Deciding that it wasn't the best time to invite him to supper, Cooper turned her attention to Nathan's problem. "I hate to mention this, but has Tobey paid you for your work?"

There was a brief silence, and then Nathan said, "He paid the deposit I require for setting up a commercial website and I've billed him for the rest of the project, but his payment isn't officially late until, let's see . . ." Cooper could hear the *tap tap* of computer keys. "It's due tomorrow, actually. I give everyone the standard turnaround time of thirty days."

"Do you have a credit card number on file?"

"No," Nathan growled. "Listen, I've got to run. I need to look into this before I can focus on my other projects. I just received another two emails while we were talking, damn it."

"Maybe you could do one of those online background checks," Cooper suggested, thinking that Nathan would be grateful for her cleverness and desire to help. "Though Tobey Dodge sounds a bit like a fake name, now that I think about it."

"Thanks," Nathan answered sourly. "I wish that had crossed your mind the night the three of us went out to dinner."

Stung by his demeanor, Cooper blurted, "That's unfair!"

"I know. I'm sorry," Nathan hastily responded. "But I do have to take care of this mess right now."

Cooper was still smarting from his cutting remark, but she managed to control herself from prolonging the argument. She scowled, however, when she saw that Emilio was once again waiting for her in the office parking lot. "I'm sure everything will get straightened out," she assured Nathan. "I've gotta run, too. I see a coworker I need to deal with."

"You bet," Cooper thought she heard Nathan grumble, but what he really said was, "*I* bet." Then he hung up.

Emilio was propping the door open for Cooper, giving her one of his winning salesman smiles when the mail truck pulled up and came to a stop with a squeal of sudden pressure to the brakes. A woman in her early twenties with big hair and tight pants sashayed past Emilio. Her jaw, which had been furiously working over a piece of pink bubble gum, momentarily paused in mid-chew as she looked him over with interest.

"Hey, handsome!" she greeted Emilio in a nasal voice that reminded Cooper of Fran Drescher's character in *The Nanny*. A fog of perfume surrounded the confident postal carrier and Cooper coughed as she sidestepped the younger woman and headed for cover behind Angela's desk.

Emilio had forgotten about Cooper completely. He stared at the heavily scented newcomer as though his eyes had never beheld such an enticing vision.

"Where's the regular guy?" Cooper whispered to Angela as a bundle of mail was unceremoniously dumped onto the desk.

"Vacation. For the next two weeks." Angela grinned as the mailwoman sauntered to the exit. "Honey, you look close at that man and that woman. What you see before you is Cupid at work. That little cherub is havin' target practice right before our eyes."

Cooper and Angela watched in amusement as the mailwoman, whose name was Carla, seduced Emilio in a mere twenty seconds. She began by telling Emilio she was tired from having stayed up to watch Monday Night Football and then she complained that her girlfriends refused to stay at Buffalo Wild Wings for the whole game. On top of those tidbits, which had already caused Emilio's eyes to glimmer, Carla managed to let slip that *Victoria's Secret* had just released its winter line and that her mail truck was full of hundreds of copies that would no doubt end up in the garbage.

"Except for mine, of course." She winked at Emilio, picked up the newspaper lying near the front door, and pushed it into his arms. "I'm gonna be ordering a little silky thing or two. Too bad there's nobody to see me model them."

Saucily, wiggling her fingers good-bye, she sauntered back to her truck while blowing a bubble the size of a dinner plate.

"Wow," Emilio murmured as Carla peeled off. "What a woman!"

"I think she liked you," Cooper said quickly.

Emilio looked at her as though he had never seen her before. "You do?"

"Heck, yes!" Angela chimed in. "Carla'll be here for the next two weeks. Better make the most of it, boy. 'Specially if you want to get a peek at the latest underwear fashions." She slapped him on the back and handed him a pile of work orders.

Still in a daze, Emilio took a step toward the locker room and then, after hesitating, jogged back to Cooper and whispered, "You still got that box of chocolates?"

She nodded. "They're in my locker. Please help yourself."

"Thanks." He suddenly seemed to have remembered that he had given Cooper the chocolates as a token of his esteem. "Hey. It wouldn't have worked out between you and me anyhow, right? I mean, you've already got a guy. I wouldn't wanna get in the middle of you two."

"I appreciate that," Cooper replied with a smile. "And I don't think you and I are very well matched. I don't watch football. And that *Victoria's Secret* catalogue I had in my work bag a few weeks ago? That was actually my grandmother's."

Emilio shivered in distaste and walked away. As soon as he was out of earshot, Angela and Cooper nearly fell over laughing.

"I cannot *believe* he asked for those Godivas! I sure hope he doesn't want that God-awful perfume back, too.

Then again, Carla seems to like the smell of flowers mixed with kerosene!" Angela said once she managed to calm down. "Oh, look at me! I've gone and cried off all my mascara!"

"So it doesn't bother *you*?" Cooper examined her friend carefully. Angela seemed to have an ethereal glow about her this morning. "You're totally fine with the fact that Emilio is obviously smitten with the mail lady?"

"I don't care a fig about that boy. I've got me the most wonderful man in the world." Angela snapped open her compact and began to make repairs to her makeup. "Last night, a bit of magic happened right here in this office." She blushed. "Well, back in Mr. Farmer's office, if I'm gonna tell the tale right."

"I remember that he asked you to stay late." Cooper played dumb.

Angela sat on her chair and spun herself around giddily. "There was no work involved, sugar. Why, he had the biggest surprise for me! I could never have dreamed up what happened. It was like a scene from a romance book!"

"Stop keeping me in suspense. What did Mr. Farmer do?"

Planting her heels firmly on the floor, Angela stopped going around in circles and leaned toward Cooper. "He bought tickets to the Sara Bay Kennel Club Dog Show next month. In Sarasota, Florida! Not just that, but he got us *two*, *first-class* airplane tickets." She clapped her hands with glee. "He's takin' me to the Sunshine State in style! It'll be the fanciest, most romantic date I've ever had! Isn't he just the Eighth World Wonder?"

Cooper hugged her friend. "Oh, I think that title belongs to you."

"We'll see about that," Angela replied with a mischievous smile. "After all, he booked two hotels rooms. I sure hope they've got one of those doors leadin' from the one to the other, 'cause this girl is gonna get gussied up and go a-knockin'!"

Angela handed Cooper her first assignment of the day and then focused her attention on her own billing duties, humming as she reviewed the monthly accounts.

Spirits lifted, Cooper sat in the Make It Work! van waiting for the longest traffic light in Richmond to turn green. She dialed Ashley's home number and then slipped on her headset.

"Tell me something interesting," Ashley whined. "I'm already bored. There is absolutely *nothing* on TV in the mornings. What *does* Grammy find to watch every day?"

"*Judge Judy. Animal Planet* reruns," Cooper said. "It sounds like you're feeling well."

"I'm great! Can't wait to start practicing once I'm all healed. Now, lay some juicy gossip on me."

"Love is in the air, Ashley." Cooper told her sister all about Emilio, Angela, and her decision to introduce Nathan to the family.

Ashley made a strangling sound.

"Are you okay?" Cooper was alarmed.

"Yes! But I just spilled my coffee all over my sofa. Thank goodness I paid for that extra stain protection." Ashley muted the television. "We're going to meet him this weekend? Oh, I'll have to find something nice to wear. I hope Lincoln won't have to work. What's Mama going to cook? Do you think Grammy will behave herself?" Without pausing, she answered the second question before her sister could. "Of course she won't behave. She's going to eat him alive. Have you prepared your boyfriend for this grand occasion?"

Cooper laughed. "You make it sound like he should expect the Chinese Water Torture treatment or something. It's just dinner."

"Oh, no, it's not," Ashley responded in all seriousness. "When you're over thirty and you bring a steady boyfriend over to meet the folks, it's never *just* dinner."

The workweek sped by, and though Cooper awaited word from Investigator Rector, he never contacted her about playing a part in the investigation. According to the *Times-Dispatch*, no one had been apprehended as of yet, but police were busy interviewing Door-2-Door volunteers and employees.

The buoyant mood Cooper had experienced on Tuesday slowly gave way to gloom. As the days passed, Nathan had become increasingly distant and though Cooper knew he was struggling with the mounting number of angry Big Man customers and had yet to speak to Tobey Dodge, his coolness toward her was hurtful and confusing. Worst of all, his reticence to make weekend plans with her made her feel as though their entire relationship was on shaky ground.

"I don't think I can schedule anything until this situation is resolved," Nathan finally responded to her repeated invitations on Friday evening. "According to the background check I purchased, Tobey Dodge from L.A. doesn't exist. I've shut the website down temporarily, but I'm out of my league here. One of the Big Man clients is a lawyer and he plans on filing a civil suit. We're going to meet for coffee Saturday afternoon so I can find out what's wrong with the product and figure out where I stand." Nathan sighed. "These folks want their money back, and I'd like to get paid for all of my work, too, or I'll never get my furnace fixed."

Cooper didn't see why Nathan's afternoon appointment should preclude him from coming to her house for dinner, but she sensed that cajoling him into meeting her family might not generate the casual, relaxed atmosphere she had been hoping for. It also bothered her that his professional problems could transfer to his personal life to such an extent that he could barely be civil to his own girlfriend.

Is this the way he handles job-related stress? Cooper wondered worriedly and then headed downstairs to her parent's kitchen in order to tell Maggie that their special dinner was off.

"Oh, Grammy's gonna be so disappointed," Maggie said and then eyed her daughter keenly. "Is everythin' all right between you and Nathan?"

"It's fine. He's just tied up with a big project right now. Maybe next weekend will work out better." Cooper made a hasty escape before her grandmother could give her the third degree, knowing she'd never be able to hide the truth about Nathan's inexplicable coolness from Grammy.

Back in her tiny apartment, she cooked a quick dinner of macaroni and cheese with a side of green beans and went to bed early. Lying in the darkness, she prayed that the police had successfully identified the killer as a result of the weeklong interviews.

"And please guide Nathan through his trouble," she added. "So that we can go back to the way we were. Things were going so well, Lord. If it's Your will, can You knock aside this invisible obstacle that's come between us? I don't know what it is, Lord, but I know *You* do. I'd be very grateful, and I think You put us together for a reason. Thanks. Amen."

* * *

The volunteers were not their boisterous selves Saturday morning at Door-2-Door. They all looked tired and scared. Conversation was stilted and the kitchen echoed with nervous whispers and the sounds of soft jazz coming from the radio near the front door. The radio had always been on, but the energetic noises emanating from the volunteers typically eclipsed all other sound.

Cooper positioned herself next to Brenda to pack coolers. After her partner dropped one of the lunch trays on the floor for the third time, Cooper placed her hand on Brenda's thick arm.

"You doing okay?" she whispered, noting that Brenda's hands were shaking.

Brenda's eyes welled. "No, I ain't okay! I got called in to talk to the police in the middle of my shift. I told the boss all about it but he's been lookin' at me sideways since then—like I might've actually hurt old folks!" She gripped the tray and tried to control her voice. "I almost worked today to make up the hours, but then I started thinkin' and do you know what I thought?"

Cooper shook her head.

"I thought I might look guilty if I didn't show up here this mornin'. This is a mess, I tell you! I ain't been sleepin' right. I've been frettin' about Darik. What if he hears about all this? He's had enough bad news without worryin' that his mama's on the cops' short list."

"I doubt you are," Cooper argued, hoping to soothe her agitated friend. "What kind of questions did they ask you?"

"All kinds of stuff. How I felt about the elderly. Did I take any prescription drugs? Where was I Friday night last week?" She sighed. "Praise Jesus, I was at church. We had choir practice and then a cold chicken dinner. I picked

Darik up from a friend's house, so a whole bunch of people were able to tell them I wasn't lyin'."

"They asked all of us the same questions," Penny added as she pushed a cart of fresh lunch trays to the middle of the room. "Unfortunately for me, I didn't have much of an alibi. I ate a bowlful of popcorn in front of an Audrey Hepburn movie Friday night and then went to bed."

"Where's Madge this morning?" Bryant inquired, looking around the kitchen.

Penny handed him a rectangular steel tray filled with sandwiches and red apples. "She's under the weather. I think having to go to the police station really upset her. I'm going to drop by her place when I'm done here. The poor thing. It's bad enough that her daughter's in trouble again. It's just too much for her to handle at once."

"Her daughter?" Quinton gathered several sandwiches into his hands. "The one living in London?"

Nodding, Penny looked aggrieved. "She was fired from the play she was in. Apparently, she went onstage after taking some kind of drug, botched all her lines, and was booed by the audience. Madge is just devastated, so the timing of all this . . ." She gestured around the kitchen. "Well, it's been a very rough week for her."

"We'll be certain to add her, and all of you, to our prayers," Savannah said from nearby, where she and Leo had been chatting quietly in a corner.

"I think we're ready, people!" Anita clapped her hands with forced enthusiasm. "Let's load our cars! I'm gonna take route twelve and Eugene has offered to be my navigator. It's the longest route and I drive fast! Now I know we're short-handed today and some of us are making two trips, so let's get rolling."

"Do you want us each to drive our own routes to save

time?" Nathan asked her. He had been packing alongside Erik throughout the morning. Neither man had spoken half a dozen words to each other or anyone else, but at least Erik wore a secretive smile and seemed to be lost in happy thoughts whereas Nathan looked tired and cross.

His question seemed to make Anita anxious. "No, no. You go on with Erik, Nathan. We're not changing our partner routine now. Trish, will you help Penny out? Most of y'all are gonna have to take two short routes since we don't have Madge. That all right?"

The volunteers nodded and quickly loaded their carts. Nathan didn't even glance in Cooper's direction as he slipped on his navy blue barn coat and headed out into the brisk air.

"Care to tag along with me today?" Warren asked Cooper with a shy smile. He had a few crumbs clinging to his strawberry-blond beard, undoubtedly from the coffee cake laid out in the lobby.

Cooper pointed at her own chin. "I'll need to vacuum you off first."

"Oh, sorry!" Warren blushed. "I can't help it. I love the food they give us every week. Don't tell anyone, but that's why I volunteer." He whispered, "I don't want to help anyone—I just want free cake and cookies."

Cooper felt Nathan's eyes on her. "Sounds like you were deprived as a kid," she teased Warren as they loaded a wheeled cart with coolers. "My mama must've baked a million cookies while I was growing up but I'm still not tired of eating them. The thing about living in the country is that it's easy to exercise. If you walk to the mailbox, you've done a quarter mile just like that."

Warren nodded. "You've got that right. Seems my chore list is never-ending. Still, when I was a kid,

Grandma Helen baked a mean pie and we had fresh eggs for breakfast every morning, so don't start crying for my sad childhood yet." He pushed open the door to the outside. "Ladies first. Especially beautiful ones."

"Thank you." Cooper smiled, hoping Nathan had overheard the compliment.

Together, they loaded coolers and Sunday food boxes into Warren's spotless Corolla. Their route consisted of ten stops, in which all of the clients recognized and welcomed Warren warmly. He spoke with a gentle politeness that seemed to put them all at ease, but he was efficient also. He put their meals away, gave them instructions regarding the contents of their Sunday food box, and then, if they had any, inquired about their pets. He never left a home without ensuring that the dog or cat in residence had fresh water and a bowlful of food.

When one owner, a Mrs. Tilden, began to weep because she had run out of dog food, Warren assured her that he had brought supplies along with him.

"I'll be right back," he promised the old woman and jogged out to his car. He popped the trunk, grabbed a large Ziploc bag filled with kibble and two cans of moist dog food and returned to Mrs. Tilden's kitchen. Her canine, a mixed breed named Buddy Boy, began to thump his tail on the floor as Warren replenished his empty bowls.

"You go on and eat now, Buddy," his owner directed and the dog sprang toward his dinner. Warren seemed pleased to watch Mrs. Tilden's pet devour his meal. He then brushed a few of Buddy's hairs from his pants and said good-bye to Mrs. Tilden.

"I don't know what we'd do without you, dear man!" she called after Warren, a grateful smile on her face.

"Do you have a dog?" Cooper asked him on the way to their next stop.

"No. I'd like one, but Grandma Helen's afraid of them now. She didn't used to be. We had all kinds of dogs on the farm when I was a kid." He glanced in Cooper's direction as they paused at a four-way stop sign and she noticed that his eyes seemed sad.

"You take really good care of her. Even if she can't tell you that all the time, she's grateful." She smiled at him. "Do you have any help? Your parents? Siblings?"

"Whoa! You sound like that police investigator who interviewed me." He laughed. "Are you wearing a wire inside that leather jacket or something?"

Cooper was embarrassed. "I'm sorry. I've always been lousy at small talk. It couldn't have been too much fun to have been interrogated by the cops and here I am, doing the same thing."

"But hopefully for different reasons. Like you just want to get to know me," Warren answered flirtatiously. "And that Rector guy wasn't nasty or anything. He was really polite, actually, and he didn't ask me anything unreasonable, considering what's going on. Background stuff, mostly. And where I was last Friday night."

"I hope your alibi's tighter than Penny's. She's worried because no one saw her. She was just at home, watching TV."

Warren nodded. "That's what half of America does most nights. I was lucky, because Friday night is bingo night and I took Grandma Helen to the Columbine Center to play. She doesn't always know what's going on during the games, but she smiles like a kid at the circus when she hears those tiles being spun around. We go at least once a month, so people recognize us." He wiped his hand across his forehead in a dramatized gesture of relief. "I was never so grateful for bingo in my life!"

"Maybe the police are overlooking something. I keep thinking that there's no way it's a Door-2-Door person." Cooper sighed in frustration. "When I consider the people I've met, well, you're all too nice!" She looked at him as he pulled in front of their final delivery stop. "You've been there almost a year, so you've stood beside the same people week after week. Doesn't it blow your mind that someone could be a murderer?"

Warren parked and then dropped his eyes to his lap. "I just hope they're wrong. That's all I can do." He looked at her, his face pinched and drawn. "Because the other possibility is too hard to accept. This could be the end of Door-2-Door. People will stop donating and others will be too afraid to volunteer. Without gifts of money and time, this organization can't make it."

"And hundreds of clients will suffer."

"Hundreds," Warren repeated softly.

They delivered meals to their last stop quickly and then drove back to headquarters in gloomy silence. As the square building came into view, the gray walls facing the parking lot were highlighted by flashes of blue. Three Henrico County police cars and a pair of City of Richmond cruisers had parked in a fanlike pattern within steps of the front door.

Warren, whose face had gone pale, seemed to freeze behind the wheel at the intersection across from Door-2-Door.

"They're bringing someone out," Cooper breathed. "I can't tell who, though. We're too far away."

Blinking, Warren pressed the accelerator and they pulled into the parking lot. Cooper jumped out of the

Corolla just as one of the police car's rear doors was slammed shut. The vehicle was obscured by the bodies of a dozen uniformed officers. Rector was there, too. He gesticulated briefly to several of his men and then walked briskly toward a black mustang.

Cooper looked at the scene Rector had left in his wake. Most of the Door-2-Door volunteers had completed their delivery routes and were posed in positions of open-mouthed shock on the building's front steps. Trish was standing on the loading ramp, her hand clamped over her mouth.

Cooper ran up to Trish and blocked her vision of the police cars. "What's happened?"

"I just don't believe it," Trish murmured and then pointed at the cruiser in the center of the pack. "They've arrested Erik."

"The police think *he's* the killer?" Cooper was astounded.

Trish nodded numbly. "There's been another murder. A woman named Vera. She's not a Door-2-Door client, but she was given food from here."

Vera? The name sounded familiar to Cooper. She turned her attention to the parking lot. The policemen had disappeared inside their cars and were slowly beginning to drive off, blue lights still ablaze.

"Violet!" Cooper exclaimed. "Vera is Violet's sister! There are three Vs. Violet, Vera, and Velma."

Trish swallowed hard and stared at Cooper in horror. "He murdered his own fiancée's sister?"

"No." Cooper rejected the idea immediately. "No way was it him."

Trish put her hand on Cooper's shoulder as Warren joined them on the ramp. "I heard two of the policemen explaining things to Lali. They found Vera dead in her chair. Just like the others." Trish spoke softly, reluctant to press the point. "Her watch was taken right off her wrist. It was the only valuable thing she owned."

"And she was poisoned?" It didn't make sense to Cooper. She struggled to understand how Erik could have gained access to a woman living in a center with round-the-clock care.

"They think it was in her milk carton," Bryant said. "It looked like it had been opened a bit and then resealed. Lali's been asked to review all the victim's dietary records to see if they were milk drinkers."

Cooper ran her hand through her hair. "How could the Door-2-Door killer have gotten milk into a senior center? You can't just waltz into those kind of facilities, can you?"

"No. There's usually a check-in at the front door." Trish stared into the distance, equally puzzled.

Cooper grabbed her friend's hand. "Oh, Trish. This is so awful!" She looked around for Nathan, longing to be taken into his arms, but he was nowhere to be seen.

The volunteers began to slowly drift back inside, but Cooper didn't want to be in the midst of the speculative talk about Erik's guilt. Suddenly, she recalled an image of him and Violet giggling together, heads drawn close, shoulders touching. She remembered his contented smile earlier in the day. It was not the expression of a murderer recalling his sordid deeds, but of a man dreaming of his future with the woman he loved.

Without really thinking about her actions, Cooper raced toward Cherry-O and headed for Violet's house. She knew that she'd be of little comfort to Violet, but perhaps having another person present who believed in her fiancé's innocence would be a balm to the older woman.

Cooper didn't pause long enough to consider that the poor woman who had lost her sister and her future husband within hours might not be interested in receiving visitors.

Cooper was in need of comfort, too, and an inner voice told her that she was driving in the right direction to find it.

16

*For such people are not serving our Lord Christ, but their own appe-
tites. By smooth talk and flattery they deceive the minds of naive
people.*

Romans 16:18 (NIV)

Halfway to Violet and Velma's, Cooper noticed that her
truck was almost out of gas. Even in her numb state of
mind, she deliberately risked driving past the higher-
priced stations like Shell and Exxon and headed for one of
the lesser-known names in order to save two cents per gallon. Out of habit, she pulled into the closest Wawa and,
after affixing the nozzle to its automatic pumping setting,
wandered over to the temporary tent erected next to the
vacuum station. A young man wearing a green apron and
a boyishly charming smile was selling cut flowers and
plush animals.

While he was busy assisting another customer, Cooper
ran her fingertips over the rose bouquets, deciding that
they were too formal and stiff to bring the grieving sisters.
Instead, she chose an arrangement of red, yellow, and orange Gerbera daises that had been artistically mixed with
a cluster of Bittersweet. The boy wrapped the flowers in
green tissue and tied them with a white ribbon, his long

fingers deft and graceful. He small-talked and smiled gratefully throughout the transaction and though Copper wanted to be friendly, she felt too detached from the scene to respond, as though her body were floating miles above the gas station and the cheerful flower vendor's tent.

It didn't help that she felt repulsed by the toothy grins of the purple, pink, and bright blue rabbits, spotted dogs, and teddy bears. To her, their frozen smiles bordered on leers, so she accepted the flowers with a murmur of thanks and retreated to the silent safety of her truck.

There were no cars parked in front of Violet's house when Cooper arrived, but the porch light was on. She didn't know if it had been burning throughout the night and, even though it was weak competition for the autumn sun, she took it as a sign that she should pursue her decision to visit the women inside.

Velma answered Cooper's gentle knock, but only after peering hesitantly through a crack between the wooden door and the locked screen door.

"Do you remember me, ma'am?" Cooper said, holding the flowers in front of her like a peace offering. "I was here with Erik last week."

"Of course, child." Velma unlocked the outer door and shuffled backward. "Come in, come in."

There were no lights on inside the house and the air felt heavy and still. Velma led her out to the sun porch and sank into the same chair she had occupied during Cooper's last visit. The old woman seemed to have been reduced in size since that time. Her body looked shrunken, her face especially pale, and her sharp eyes dull and somnolent. Cooper laid the flowers carefully on the table and took the seat facing Velma.

"I am so sorry for your loss," she said, wishing she could think of a more original expression of condolence. "For everything that's happened. Can I do anything for you? Get you some groceries or run errands? I've got the whole day free and I'd love to help."

Velma turned toward the window as if she hadn't heard a word. "I gave her the milk, you know. Brought it with me durin' our visit like I always do. Vera wanted it. Had to have it. You see, the center doesn't serve Richfood milk, so Vera won't touch it. We've been drinkin' Richfood milk since we were little girls and it's the only brand Vera recognizes. She'd get real put-out with me if I didn't bring her that milk. Why, she even threatened to snitch to our mama if I didn't hand it over fast enough!" Her profile was etched with pain. "So I brought it to her every visit. How she smiled when she took that first sip," she added ruefully. "You'd have thought it was a bottle of Coca-Cola. We weren't allowed to drink soda pop until we lived on our own, you know."

Cooper reached over and touched the old woman's dry, bony hand. "You didn't do this to her, Velma. Someone else did. It's not your fault."

Velma's eyes flashed and Cooper caught a glimpse of the woman she had met a week ago. "I'll tell you one thing—Erik didn't do this! I know that man and it wasn't *him*. Those police—they wouldn't listen to me!" She gripped Cooper's arm. "You gotta talk to them!"

"I will," Cooper promised. "I believe he's innocent, too. But why do they think he's guilty?"

"Because he came with us to visit Vera. Violet wanted the two of them to meet since she and Erik were plannin' on gettin' married in a couple of weeks." Velma sighed. "Vera wouldn't have understood who Erik was, but it was important to Violet that he shake hands with her other sister. But you know—Erik never *did* get to meet her. The nurses were helpin' her take a shower and we decided to bring him back later."

"And that was on Friday?" Cooper wanted clarification.

Velma nodded. "Right after lunch. They found Vera the next morning. She left this earth sometime in the night, but she was sittin' up in bed with her magazine on her lap, like she was just takin' a rest from readin' a long story."

"And you told the police Erik never actually saw your sister?"

"I certainly did, but he was in her room and that's all they seemed to care about!"

Cooper fell silent, feeling that the only service she could provide at the moment was to listen to anything Velma wanted to talk about. She rubbed the older woman's hand gently, to reassure her that she had all the time in the world to sit with her.

"Vera was an old woman," Velma said matter-of-factly. "Her mind hadn't been right for a long time and now she's with our Lord. If someone hadn't sent her to heaven before her time, I could be at peace with her passin', but my heart is heavy. I've got Violet laid out in the bedroom, refusin' to eat or speak to me, and the wrong man's bein' held accountable." A single tear rolled down her wrinkled cheek. "What can an old lady do about such mighty troubles besides pray?"

"I wish I had more comfort to give you, but I can tell you that this is not an open-and-shut case for the police," Cooper assured Velma. "All of the other victims have been robbed. They're going to search Erik's home and they're not going to find any of the stolen items. They're not going to find extra money in his bank account, either. Most importantly, Erik has no motive. He'd gotten his dream-come-true when Violet agreed to become his wife."

Velma dabbed at her eyes with the corner of her sleeve and looked at Cooper hopefully. "But he could've messed with our milk or given it to Vera himself durin' our visit. Isn't that enough?"

"To hold him for questioning, but that's it," Cooper answered, unsure of the accuracy of her statement. "Of course, it would be better if they had someone *else* to question. I hate to picture Erik in a cell." She paused to once again consider the desires and behaviors of the other volunteers.

"I'm gonna get these flowers a drink," Velma whispered and walked away, and though Cooper observed the woman's slow gait, she didn't offer to assist her. Thoughts whirled around in her mind and she tried desperately to sort through sundry ideas in search of something that could be of tangible use.

"Is there a visitor's log at Vera's living center?" she asked when Velma returned bearing a white pottery pitcher and a pair of scissors.

"There sure is. Durin' the day, you sign your name and put down the name and room number of the person you're gonna visit. There's a gal workin' up front and she waves folks through unless she doesn't recognize them. We never have to sign in, of course, and neither do delivery-men and folks like that. Things shut down more in the evenin'. I believe they lock the outside door after eight at night, but we never visit that late, anyhow."

Cooper frowned. "I'm not so sure if reviewing those sign-up sheets will help much, but I'm confident the police will look them over closely." She sat back in her chair and crossed her arms, thinking hard. "What about the nurses? Wouldn't they have noticed a stranger going into Vera's room?"

Velma shrugged. "I'd imagine so, but there's so many shifts, and then they rotate the halls they work every day. I guess so they're sure to know all the residents. And there aren't enough of them to see what goes on in every room. Someone could drop off a milk and be gone awful quick."

"I certainly hope the police show photos of all the Door-2-Door volunteers to the nurses. Maybe they'll recognize the real killer, *if* he or she is really a volunteer." Cooper angrily ripped the tissue paper apart in order to release the cut flowers. "Why would someone go after Vera? It doesn't make sense. The other victims have lived alone and owned something valuable that this crazy person wanted to possess."

Velma reached for one of the flower stems. "We don't have anythin' worth takin', but Vera's watch was special. Her husband gave it to her on their wedding day in the forties. It was from Tiffany's and was real gold. I suppose it's worth a pretty penny by now."

Cooper whistled. "I imagine you're right." She scowled. "But how would the killer know you'd share your milk with her?"

"Someone knew I'd done it lots of times before, I reckon."

"Did Violet drink her milk?"

"Nope. She left hers with Vera, too. I suppose the police have got it now."

As Velma eased the daises into the pitcher, Cooper stared at a hairline crack running beneath the handle to the base of the pottery container. The true killer was not unlike the damaged pitcher. He or she looked and acted completely normal, but in some way they were damaged. There was a crack in their psyche that compelled them to steal and to commit the most grievous crime against another human being: murder.

"I need to review that suspect list we made at Quinton's house," she muttered to herself. "There's got to be something we've overlooked."

At that moment, Violet appeared at the end of the hallway leading into the sun room. For a second, Cooper thought she was seeing a ghost. Dressed in a white bathrobe with a white shawl wrapped around her narrow shoulders, Violet's slippered feet made no noise. Her white hair was loose and tumbled over the ridge of her collarbone like a wave of snow. She clutched something against her chest and her amethyst engagement ring winked as she passed through a slim sunbeam.

"Violet. Our new friend has brought us daises." Velma held her hand out for her sister. "And hope."

Cooper jumped up from her chair and offered the seat to Violet, who dropped into it without saying a word.

"She believes in Erik, too, Vi. She doesn't think the police will be able to keep him too long." Velma touched her sister's knee. "We should get ourselves together. They're gonna want to talk to us more. If you want to help him, we gotta trust in the Lord and shake off our despair."

"It's always been the three of us," Violet whispered, looking down at the framed photograph she grasped so tightly. "Maybe it was a sin to love another. Look what's happened since I gave in to my feelings."

"That's hogwash and you know it!" Velma spoke sharply. "If anyone's to blame, that'd be me. It was my milk, after all."

"The fault lies with the horrible person who poisoned the milk—not with either of you!" Cooper interjected before either sister could continue the blame game. "You are victims, just as Vera was a victim. Just like the other older folks and their families have been victims." Cooper lowered her voice. "I believe God delights in love, Violet. I saw the joy in Erik's eyes and anyone could tell that his heart was singing. How could that not please every ear in heaven?" She smiled. "I bet the angels were dancing a jig when you said 'yes' and agreed to join your life with Erik's."

"She's right, Vi, and you know it." Velma crossed her arms and sat up straighter in her chair.

Violet looked at Cooper and nodded in gratitude. "Thank you for coming today. You must have been sent here by the Maker Himself." She held out the photograph so that the light fell onto it. "I'm just havin' a terrible time thinkin' about the years to come without Vera bein' with us. I feel like part of my *self* has been ripped away. Even though she didn't always know us, we were still together. We were family." She traced a thin finger along the wooden frame. "Now someone's taken her from us and I'm so damned mad! It's *God's* right and His *alone* to call His children home."

"I'm angry, too," Cooper said softly. "Someone has worn a mask of goodness and charity in order to do evil, and my friends and I haven't been able to see the true face of this person. I can't understand why I can't *see* more clearly!"

"That's what Vera used to say when we were girls," Violet said with a hesitant smile. "She had glasses all her life. Always picked out the wildest ones in the store, too, didn't she, Velma?" She held the photograph out for Cooper to see. "This was taken last year by one of Vera's nurses. Look at those beauties my sister's wearin'!"

Cooper cradled the picture carefully in her hands and examined the image of the three sisters. Unlike the ones on display in the living room, this photograph, which Violet had brought out from someplace in her bedroom, showed the women in their old age. Velma and Violet were seated in hard-backed chairs on either side of their sister, who was comfortably ensconced in a peach-colored upholstered chair. Cooper's eyes absorbed the gentle visage of the middle sister and the frame nearly slipped from her paralyzed fingers.

"Oh, God!" she gasped.

Thrusting the photograph into Violet's startled hands, Cooper shifted inside her purse until she came up with Rector's card. She jabbed his number into her cell phone and began to pace as it rang and rang. Finally, he picked up.

"Investigator? This is Cooper Lee," she panted. "I have an idea who it could be. I think I know who the killer is!"

Rector listened carefully to what she had to say and then admonished her to stay put. Without another word, he abruptly ended the phone call. Cooper held the phone in her hand and then glanced back at the photograph of the three sisters.

Could I be right? She stared at the similar smiles, the crinkles of skin at the corners of their eyes, the age-spotted hands holding onto one another. *How could someone be that vile? Someone I thought was truly good.*

Suddenly, she knew she was going to be sick. "Excuse me!" she called out to the bewildered sisters in a panicked voice and dashed down the hall, knowing from her previous visit that there was a bathroom at the end of the corridor.

She made it just in time, kneeling in front of the toilet as her stomach purged itself of the morning's coffee and pastries. When the nausea eventually passed, she sat back against the wall, as though requiring its support to remain upright. Her skin was clammy and she pushed back strands of sweat-dampened hair from her forehead.

"Lord, how we've all been deceived!" she whispered weakly.

Closing her eyes, images of her Saturdays at Door-2-Door flooded her mind. She recalled the celebratory atmosphere of their potluck dinner, the playful dancing, the feeling of partnership in accompanying the volunteers on their routes. The pleasant memories were immediately darkened by the troubled countenances of Frank Crosby, The Colonel, and now, of Velma and Violet.

Finally, after what seemed like hours, there was a gentle tap and Violet's head appeared around the door.

"Are you okay, honey?"

Cooper managed to drag her body to a standing position. "Yes, ma'am. Let me just wash up and I'll be right out."

She scrubbed her hands vigorously with a bar of Dove soap and then leaned over and rinsed her mouth directly from the tap, gurgling to remove the foul taste from the surface of her tongue.

Upon her return to the sun porch, Violet handed her a cup of hot tea. "This'll settle you down."

After taking a tentative sip, Cooper blew a mist of steam from the surface of the milky tea and drank some more, marveling at the restorative powers of the tea. "Thank you. I feel much better already." Allowing her body to relax a fraction, she looked at the stricken faces patiently awaiting an explanation. "When I saw that picture," she quickly pointed at the photograph so as not to hold the sisters in suspense another second, "I knew which of the volunteers was the murderer. One of them—a man—introduced us to a woman he claimed was his grandmother. When I looked at Vera's face and saw her purple glasses, I knew that this man had introduced us to your *sister*."

"Are you sure?" Violet seemed dubious.

"It wasn't just the purple rhinestone glasses, though those are pretty unique," Cooper told her with confidence. "It's Vera's eyes. They look out on the world like this man's Grandma Helen's did. The gaze, it's, it was . . ." Cooper didn't know how to describe the feeling of vacancy implied by Vera's stare without offending her sisters.

"Like she wasn't all there?" Velma suggested.

Cooper nodded. "Kind of absent, yet content. I met her at this potluck dinner my Bible study group hosted for the volunteers. Erik was there, too, but since he hadn't met her before or seen a current photograph of her, he also thought she was this . . . man's grandmother." She gave the sisters a weak smile. "Vera seemed perfectly happy. I want you to know that she wasn't abused in any way. In fact, she enjoyed the food and tapped on the table with her fork and knife when the band played."

Violet grinned, reminiscing. "Vera always loved music. Any loud sounds, actually. Even after she started forgettin' things, she'd still love to hear a strong rain or a bowling ball strikin' pins."

"Or bingo tiles?" Cooper asked, trying to keep the revulsion she felt about Warren's duplicity out of her voice.

"One of her favorite noises," Velma said with grin. Then her humor vanished. "So what you're sayin' is that this person, this man who . . . killed my sister, actually led her around like she was some kind of pet before he took her life?"

Cradling her tea cup in search of warmth, Cooper was reluctant to answer. "I don't know what his motives were, ma'am. And I'm sorry if I've caused you more grief by revealing all this. To tell you the truth, and I know this sounds crazy, but he acted like he really cared for your sister. It was like he really saw her as his grandmother. I can't explain what caused him to turn from the conscientious guy who cut up Vera's food for her into the monster who ended more than one life."

"Of course you can't, dear." Violet touched Cooper's shoulder. "None of us can wrap our minds around how such a twisted soul operates and it's likely we never will. The Lord will judge this man and he will be found wanting, I'm sure of that!" She returned her hands to her lap and tried to steady their trembling. "Are the police goin' to get him now?"

"Yes," Cooper whispered soberly. "He lives in his family's farmhouse out in Goochland. They're on their way now."

The three women fell silent, each lost in their own thoughts. Cooper finished her tea and a heavy drowsiness seemed to fall over her. She longed to go home and collapse in the cozy shelter of her apartment. Perhaps she'd call Nathan and ask him to drive out to see her. She'd like nothing more than to lie in his arms for a few hours, listening to the comforting sound of his heartbeat.

"I'm going to wash this tea cup," she said and stood. "Can I bring you anything?"

Velma shook her head. "We're gonna sit here for a spell. I imagine we won't have much quiet later on, so we should rest while we can." She reached out with both of her arms and Cooper put down the tea cup and accepted the old woman's tender embrace. "They'll release Erik 'cause of you. Bless you, child."

Cooper then turned and hugged Violet. All three women had tears running from their eyes. Shock, grief, anger, and the desperate desire to cling to hope was too much to hold inside.

"I wish I had known sooner," Cooper whispered into Violet's hair. "Your sister could have been spared. Forgive me." She sniffed and then, drawing away from Violet, pressed a napkin against her red, blotchy face.

"There is nothing to forgive." Violet managed a tremulous smile. "You brought daisies, and kindness, and justice into our home today. What more can we give you in return but our love and friendship and a lifetime's worth of prayers?"

Velma wagged a finger at Cooper. "You stay in touch now, young lady. We've got a weddin' to invite you to once we're done grievin' for our Vera. There will be laughter yet in these rooms if I've got any say in the matter."

"Yes, ma'am." Cooper dried her eyes, cleaned up the tea things, and showed herself out.

Standing on the cement walkway, she was temporarily blinded by the brilliance of the afternoon sun.

"It's over." She raised her arms upward toward the fiery yellow and crimson-tinged treetops. A wind rushed through the leaves like a murmur of fast water over rocks and Cooper lifted her chin until her face was awash in cleansing light.

"It's over," she repeated and then turned her thoughts toward home.

17

The cords of the grave coiled around me;
the snares of death confronted me.

2 Samuel 22:6 (NIV)

Cooper climbed the steps to her apartment as though her legs were made of cement. She looked back over her shoulder and noticed the warm and welcoming light spilling from the kitchen window of her parents' house below. It was a comfort to imagine her mother moving around inside, humming as she added ingredients to bubbling saucepans on the stovetop and then knocking the oven door closed with one of her round hips. Every now and again, she'd wipe a smear of dough or brown gravy onto the front of her favorite apron, which was decorated with bright cherries on a field of navy.

Columbus squawked from within his aviary, and Cooper yelled down to him that she'd walk him later. Her promise seemed to excite the raptor further and it was with a twinge of guilt that she ignored his complaints and ducked inside her apartment to retreat into the pleasant quiet of her bedroom instead. However, Columbus's screeches did not subside as they usually did, so Cooper relocated to her sofa and switched on the television, hoping some background noise would block out the hawk's clamor.

HGTV provided the perfect pictorial balm. As the cameras panned over banks of perennial beds blooming alongside a quaint stone cottage nestled somewhere in the English countryside, Cooper felt her body sink deeper into the couch cushions. Her lids grew heavy and by the time the show's narrator turned his attention to the charming home's herb garden, Cooper was on the cusp of sleep.

When The Beatles burst into song from the speaker of her cell phone, which was buried at the bottom of her purse, she decided to ignore it. Repositioning herself on the sofa, she slipped her arm under a throw pillow, pulled a crocheted afghan over her legs, and prepared to take a restorative nap.

Her cell phone sang again.

"Damn it," Cooper muttered crossly. She opened her eyes, but didn't stir her body in any other way.

This time, the caller left a message and Cooper's phone, which had an annoying habit of repeatedly chirping whenever it received a new voicemail, issued its first alert signal. Cooper counted to ten, slowly, and could just hear the sound of the message beep again.

"So much for a rest." She swung her legs onto the floor and sat upright for a moment, reluctant to stand up. When the alert sounded for the third time, she threw off her blanket in irritation and grabbed her purse from the kitchen counter.

Bringing the phone to life with the touch of a button, Cooper noticed that the calls had both come from Rector. Regretting that she hadn't answered him the first time, she was just about to prompt her phone to dial his number when a voice commanded, "I'd like you to put that down. Right now."

Cooper swung around. Warren was leaning against the doorframe that led into her bathroom. He held a snack-sized plastic bag filled with what looked like crushed brown leaves in his hand and his eyes glinted with a strange and ominous light.

Without breaking eye contact, Cooper's thumb edged toward the send button. Warren shook the bag and gave her a crooked grin. "Don't do it or your family will suffer. You see, we had a little tea party while you were out."

The phone clattered onto the floor as the implications of Warren's words hit home. The phone's battery, dislodged by the impact, skated into the shadows beneath the kitchen table. Cooper's voice was taut with anger and fear. "What have you done to them?"

Warren shrugged. "I just introduced myself as one of your volunteer friends and invited them to share in my unique blend of Lipton's Cranberry Pomegranate and Jimson weed." He held up three syringes. "But don't worry, a shot of this lorazepam and they should make it to the hospital without having a seizure. Jimson weed can make some people really agitated. Not good for the heart, you know."

"Jimson weed?" Cooper was confused, and that made her feel even more frightened. "Is that some kind of poison?"

Again, the crooked smile. "It can be. But I'm disappointed in you, Cooper. You're a country girl. And a gardener. I thought I could count on you to recognize the beauty and versatility of my favorite herb."

"Sorry, but I'm not familiar with it."

Gesturing at her kitchen chair, Warren moved forward a step. "Well, take a seat and I'll tell you all about it. It's understandable that you don't recognize my plant because while you live in the sticks, you don't live near any farms. When I was a kid, Jimson weed grew all over the edges of our cow pastures. It produces pretty purple or white bell-shaped flowers, but my grandparents warned me never to touch them, because the seeds hold power."

"The power to make people sleep?" Cooper guessed. "All they need to do is ingest them somehow."

Pleased, Warren dipped his chin in recognition of her reasoning skills. "The Indians—oh, excuse me—the *Native Americans* used Jimson weed in their sacred ceremonies. I think it was the Navajo who had a little chant about it." His voice changed to a childlike singsong. " 'Eat a little, and go to sleep. Eat some more, and have a dream. Eat some more, and don't wake up.' That's pretty accurate."

"That's why Frank Crosby lost a day. You didn't give him enough to kill him, but he slept for almost twenty-four hours." Cooper looked away in disgust.

"It wasn't my intention to have him sleep any longer. Not *that* time. I was trying to get him to tell me where he'd hidden the rest of his Civil War treasures. I knew he was holding out on me and folks will spill their secrets once they've swallowed a bit of my brew." Warren fondled the bag of tea leaves. "I got bored of trying to understand his gibberish about yellow this and coward that, so I decided that he needed to move on. He was tired of life."

"Is that why you killed all those people? Because you thought they were done living?" Despite her fears, Cooper wanted to hear Warren's motives. If she could pretend to be sympathetic and learn about how the poison worked, she might be able to save her family.

"Of course they were *done*!" Warren spat. "They were poor, lonely, pathetic. No one should end up in such an undignified state. That's what happened to my grandparents. They were the ones who raised me. Then age started getting the better of them. They got stupid and weak and gullible and sold our land for nothing." His hands gripped the tea bag until the leaves were crushed beneath his fingers. "I've had to work two jobs since I turned sixteen. All through my twenties, when I should have been having fun and seeing the world, I worked to keep the three of us going! And when they got so that I couldn't take care of them, I figured out how much it would cost to put them in a nursing home and I knew I just couldn't take any more!" He relaxed his hands and made a clear effort to calm himself. "I gave them a gentle way out."

"But Mrs. Davenport wasn't lonely," Cooper argued tentatively. "She had her daughter."

"That bitch!" Warren spluttered. "All she wanted was her mama's jewelry. I was over there once when she was cleaning it. She asked to try on that necklace every time, saying that it looked better on her and that her mama was too old to wear it, but Mrs. Davenport liked to remember her husband by looking at it. She wanted to be with him. She'd told me that a dozen times, so I granted her wish." He smirked. "And there was no way in hell I was going to let that greedy, miserable leech of a daughter get the jewelry, so I took it."

"Please," Cooper spoke plaintively. "*I* care about my family more than anything in the world. They're not ready to let go. We're happy the way we are. Please let me help them. I'm begging you for mercy."

"Tell me the story behind your butterfly pin," Warren

said instead, sitting down at the table next to Cooper. "I've never seen you without it."

Cooper stroked the filigree wings as if she could draw strength from the thin silver. "It was my grammy's. She gave it to me when I was going through a rough time. My grandpa gave it to her for the same reason."

"Would you say that it's your most prized possession?" Warren leaned closer to her and Cooper tried not to flinch.

Instead, she cupped her hand over the pin, obscuring it from Warren's covetous gaze. "That's how you decided what you were going to steal. You took the one thing each person valued most. Mr. Manningham's coin, Mrs. Davenport's necklace, Frank Crosby's sword, and Vera's watch."

"I had to collect a fee for my services," Warren stated blithely. "And I needed to have portable wealth in case I had to relocate in a hurry."

"But no one here needs your services. My parents and my grammy make the most of every day." Seeing that her words had no effect on Warren at all, Cooper took surreptitious glances around her kitchen in search of a handy weapon. To distract him while she tried to concoct a plan, she asked, "Why Vera, Warren? Why did you treat her like your own grandmother and then murder her? I saw you with her at the volunteer dinner. You were so gentle, so attentive to her. I admired how you cared for her."

For the first time, Warren seemed uncomfortable with their discussion. He picked at the red crust of a tomato sauce stain on the edge of Cooper's table. "I missed Grandma Helen. She and Vera were a lot alike. I could tell Vera anything and she was always happy to see me. Even when she couldn't remember my name, she'd smile like she knew me."

Cooper tried to recall the specifics of Warren's job.

"And as the pick-up guy for LabTech, you visit nursing homes. That's how you met Vera in the first place."

"Nursing homes, hospitals, medical office parks. I see old people everywhere I go. Half of these people have no spirit left. They sap up the government's money, make it necessary for thousands of able-bodied adults to give volunteer time and money to keep them alive, and all *they* do is look to their past—to loved ones that are long gone."

"How did you get Vera off the grounds of her center?" Cooper wanted to interrupt his train of thought. "Didn't anyone challenge you? After all, if her sisters found out you were borrowing her, they'd surely have reported you."

Warren waved off the suggestion. "Oh, please. One of Vera's regular nurses has a thing for me. I told her how much I missed my grandmother and that I'd like to bestow my affection on someone like her, and this woman practically rolled out the red carpet and packed the wheelchair into my trunk. She's how I came to find out about Vera's milk quirks and which days her sisters would visit. Such an agreeable lady—the nurse—but a bit old for me." He laughed dryly.

Cooper could feel the seconds ticking by. What was happening to her family? Were they asleep? Hallucinating? Having heart issues as Warren had insinuated? "It's not our job to decide when people are ready to die," she told him firmly.

Warren resumed his arrogant, straight-backed posture. "Eventually, we'll all be turned off like a light when we reach a certain age. I've read about that notion in dozens of science fiction books. It's the humane thing to do and my teas are such an inexpensive and painless way to administer a dose of everlasting peace."

"You're crazy," Cooper whispered and then quickly

covered her mouth with her hand. She couldn't afford to upset the man sitting beside her. He was a calculating, unhinged murderer and the lives of her beloved family members depended on her remaining calm and rational. "What I mean," she hastily adjusted her tone, "is that you could have had your *real* Grandma Helen, but you . . . let her go. Why do that to Vera when you felt like you had a relationship with her?"

"She begged me to end it!" Warren exclaimed. "Vera had lucid moments like Helen did, and just like Helen, it made her sick to know how mixed up her mind was. She knew she was a burden on her two sisters. She talked to me about how they'd spent all of their savings paying her medical bills. The guilt was eating her up." He turned to Cooper and she was surprised to see that his eyes were wet. "Vera knew about the others. She knew about the Jimson weed. She told me I had done right. She asked me to put it in her milk, so I did."

"The poisoned milk wasn't from Velma or Violet's Sunday sandwich bag?"

Warren shook his head. "No. It was just a milk carton I took from Door-2-Door's cooler. Jimson weed doesn't taste too good, so I was forced to use smelly herbal tea on everyone else, but Vera knew what she was drinking and didn't care. She wanted her last drink to be milk because it made her feel like a girl, so that's what I gave her." He picked at the tomato sauce again. "I'm going to miss her. We understood each other." His eyes bored into Cooper. "I knew you'd find me out if you ever saw a picture of Vera, so I've been following you. I saw you go into the house where her sisters live, so I crept around back and watched all three of you through a window. I know the cops are probably at my place right now, because you told them all about me."

"So why are you here?" Cooper asked, and looked around her kitchen for something to use as a weapon.

Placing an unnaturally cold hand over hers, Warren answered, "For you. I'm hitting the road and I'd like some company. You're smart and funny and damned pretty. I'd be proud to have you with me as I start my next adventure." His look hardened. "Come with me and your family lives. It's as simple as that."

Cooper swallowed. Her time was running out. Warren had told her his motives and his methods. Eventually, he was going to grow bored with talking and then he'd have to act. She had little doubt that he'd let her family succumb to the effects of the Jimson weed, so she had to agree with his warped notion that he'd provided a service to the elderly he'd murdered in order to survive this ordeal.

"I see what you're saying about senior citizens. I fought against it at first, but now it makes more sense to me," she spoke softly after taking a deliberate pause. "My grammy misses everyone who's gone on ahead of her, too. Especially her husband. I guess when you spend most of a lifetime with someone and then they're not there, you feel like half a person." Cooper met Warren's curious stare. His hand slid away from hers. "She hasn't been eating well lately and she's getting pretty depressed. Maybe she'd want . . ." She trailed off, acting uncertain.

"What Vera wanted? Maybe you're realizing that it's her time? Before you have to put her in a home where someone has to help her go to the bathroom, take showers, or even feed herself? Before her care uses every dime your parents have? Or even your savings?" Warren's expression was wolfish. "See? I'm not so crazy now, am I?"

Cooper hesitated and then mutely shook her head. "No. You've released people from suffering. I'm sorry that your good intentions weren't clear to me before." Reaching across the table, she touched his sleeve. "I could help you," she whispered. "I'll come with you. No protests, no games."

He eyed her distrustfully, but a spark of hope ignited his face at the same time. "Why should I believe you?"

Unpinning the silver butterfly from her shirt, Cooper placed it in Warren's cold palm. She closed his fingers around the wings and held onto his hand. It was one of the most difficult things she had ever done. Touching his flesh repulsed her to the core, but her desperation to aid her family forced her to return his suspicious stare with as much sincerity as she could muster. As they sat this way, Cooper was silently shouting a passionate prayer for God to rescue her from the wicked man assessing her so closely.

"The cops will be here soon. Since you informed them about me, they're sure to call in and check on you when my house is empty," Warren finally remarked, his voice flat and almost disinterested. "But that's okay. My bags have been packed for a while." He glanced around the kitchen. "Since you're coming with me, I think I'll have to put you to the test before we go. I don't want any dramatics once we're on the road." He gestured at the cabinets behind them. "Get me a coffee cup and fill it with water."

Hastening to do as she was told, Cooper selected a white mug covered by Van Gogh's irises.

"Now, a spoon," Warren ordered pleasantly as he opened the Ziploc. "The seeds are very toxic. A small bit will cause hallucinations and short-term memory loss," he explained as he measured out his blend of Jimson weed and tea. "My little plant has so many names. So many faces. Did you know that when Virginia was an English colony we used this stuff against British soldiers at Jamestown? Grown men in their prime ran around like lunatics. Dancing naked. Spilling all their secrets. The next day, they couldn't remember a thing. Aren't Virginians crafty?" He stirred the mixture until the clear water mutated into a pale brown that resembled beef broth.

Cooper watched his movements with morbid fascination. "So you didn't give my family enough tea to kill them?"

Warren shook his head. "No. They're just taking naps, like you were going to do before your cell phone started ringing. But this cuppa tea will release your grammy for good." He tapped the butterfly pin, which was within reach of his left hand. "And I will keep this to remember her by. The other things I'll sell when we get where we're going."

"And where's that?" Cooper's voice was much lighter now that she knew her parents and grandmother weren't in immediate danger. Of course, Warren could well be lying. He was a master of deceit, but she felt as though he had revealed himself to her and had no cause to tell her partial truths after confessing with such calm pride to his host of crimes.

"First, I need to believe that you and I understand each other." He eased the hot mug into Cooper's hand. "Careful. Don't spill any."

Leading Cooper to her front door, he jerked it open and then stepped back in surprise. A tall figure darkened the doorway and before Cooper knew it, Warren was falling backward onto her. She pressed herself against the wall and flung the cup of tea from her hand in order to prepare her body for the impact of Warren's weight. Unbalanced, she didn't watch as the tea formed an auburn arc of scalding liquid before it landed on Warren's scalp and face.

He didn't even cry out.

Before she could make any sense of what was happening, Cooper was knocked flat. Her head banged against the floor with a commanding thud and she moaned as pain splintered from the point of contact and instantly radiated through her skull and down the vertebrae of her neck. It was so sharp that she squeezed her eyes shut until she felt she could draw in a few shallow breaths. A wave of nausea rolled over her.

She felt a pair of large but gentle hands touch her face. A familiar voice whispered softly near her still-ringing ear. She couldn't make out the words, but when she opened her eyes, she saw Nathan bending over her. He smiled as their eyes met and then he brushed her hair from her forehead and kissed her tenderly on the revealed skin above each eyebrow and then again on her lips.

Cooper was content to lie motionless as the sound of other voices filled her apartment. She hadn't been aware that Warren's torso was still covering her legs until he was lifted off her. She closed her eyes again, noticing that the pain had become duller; its jagged edges had softened and the nausea she had briefly experienced had receded.

"I'm going to carry you to your bed," Nathan murmured softly to her. "Do you think it's okay for you to be moved? I don't want to hurt you."

Cooper glanced at the hand he was using to stroke her hair and saw rivulets of bright blood easing downward from his knuckles.

"What happened?" she whispered.

Instead of answering, Nathan gathered her into his arms with infinite care. She held onto his neck and rested her head against his shoulder. The smell of his body, the feel of his wool sweater against her cheek, and the motion of his muscles as he walked infused her with feelings of safety and solidity.

"I thought I'd lost you," Nathan said as he laid her down. Cooper felt a tear fall onto the bridge of her nose and was startled to recognize that her boyfriend was weeping.

"Shhh. It's all right now." She cradled his face in her hands and then pulled his mouth to hers. She kissed him deeply until the sound of someone clearing their throat interrupted their embrace.

"Daddy!" Cooper shouted in surprised embarrassment and then winced as the ache in her head intensified for a moment.

Earl blushed and then gave Nathan a little smile. "Reckon she's gonna be right as rain. We got our *uninvited guest* all trussed up. Mama spoke to the police and they're on the way." He looked over his shoulder. "What are you doin', Maggie?"

"He's wakin' up!" Cooper's mother called out. "I'm just makin' sure you tied these knots good and tight." Maggie appeared in the room seconds later and put her arm around Nathan. "Your man's got a powerful right hook, Coop. He knocked that boy flat! 'Course, we were there for backup, but Nathan had no need of us." She held up a rolling pin. "It's too bad, though. Grammy really wanted to take a shot at him with this, but she didn't feel like climbin' the stairs."

Immensely relieved to see her parents in perfect health, Cooper began to laugh at the absurd image of Grammy thumping Warren over the head with Maggie's rolling pin. It was so cartoonish that soon they were all giggling at the visual.

"We should have let her at him," Nathan interjected. "A little payback from the senior citizen community would have been totally appropriate."

Earl cocked his head. "I hear the cavalry comin'. Guess I'll go meet them downstairs before Mama starts tellin' them how to do their jobs." He saluted Nathan. "Nicely done, young man."

"Thank you, sir."

Maggie beamed at him. "And here I thought we were just gonna have supper together," she teased and then walked to the other side of Cooper's bed. "Now lemme take a look at that bump."

Cooper allowed her mother to inspect her bruised head.

"No blood," Maggie declared. "Seems to me you took bigger lumps than this learnin' to ride your bike. I'll get you some ice." She removed Cooper's butterfly pin from her apron pocket and frowned. "And I'll put *this* in a hot vinegar bath. Get rid of the germs on it and all."

"But Mama? Aren't you feeling sleepy after drinking Warren's tea?"

Maggie blinked in bewilderment. "Maybe you should see a doctor," she said as Earl led a group of policemen into Cooper's apartment. "We didn't eat or drink anything with that awful man. In fact, we never set eyes on him 'til Nathan punched his lights out." She glanced at his wounded hand. "And don't think I'm gonna let you go anywhere without gettin' cleaned up, too, mister. We're gonna have a nice supper and get ourselves calmed down."

"I don't think Investigator Rector is going to allow us

to eat a leisurely dinner." Cooper sighed at the disagreeable idea of spending an evening at the police station. "He'll want to take our statements right away."

Tapping her rolling pin against the flat of her palm, Maggie prepared to close the bedroom door so that Cooper and Nathan could have a moment alone. "You two have done enough for now. You leave that policeman to me."

"I like the sound of that!" Nathan waited until Maggie was gone and then stretched out on the bed. He slid his arm around Cooper's waist and rested his head on the pillow.

"Sounds good to me, too. Besides, I need *something* to distract me from thinking about my throbbing head and all the rest of today's unpleasant events." Cooper reached for him. "And I have an idea of what might just do the trick."

18

Dear friends, let us love one another, for love comes from God. Everyone who loves has been born of God and knows God.

— *1 John 4:7* (NIV)

For the first time since the inception of their group, the Sunrise Bible study members ignored the usual array of pastries and carafe of aromatic coffee. They all spoke at once, asking Nathan and Cooper question after question about the events of the previous evening.

"I know you tried to tell us everything on the phone," Bryant said during a brief lull in the conversation, "but I still can't get over the visual of Warren waiting for you in your apartment. And look at you! You seem totally normal despite what you went through."

"It's too, too creepy," Trish muttered. "Like a scene from *Psycho*. How did you ever get to sleep last night? I would have needed *something* to help me rest after someone threatened my entire family."

Cooper touched the sore spot on the back of her head. "Having supper with my family was the best medicine. And of course, Nathan offered to sleep on the couch, but by the time we'd all had our second cup of decaf and another serving of my mama's roasted apple tart covered in warm caramel sauce, I was too full to be afraid. All I did was change into my pajamas and fall into bed." She glanced around at her friends. "Tonight may be a different story. I expect that certain things will run through my mind over and over again for days."

"You must have been really scared." Quinton drew Cooper against him in a one-armed hug. "We're so glad that you're safe."

Bryant nudged Nathan in the side. "How did you happen to be there, Mr. Knight in Shining Armor?"

Nathan colored. "It's a really strange story, actually. I was in the Kroger parking lot when I noticed that a Make It Work! van had been damaged by a yellow Hummer. For a second, I thought Cooper might have been driving the van, so I jumped out of my car to see if she was okay."

"Was it you?" Jake asked Cooper.

"No," Nathan answered. "It was her boss and one of Cooper's coworkers, a woman named Angela. Anyway, the Hummer driver obviously had plans to leave the scene, but his exit was blocked by a woman in a minivan waiting for a choice parking space to come open. Because she was kind of sitting in the middle of the road, no one could go around her. Between the minivan and a line of shopping carts, he was penned in."

Bryant grabbed Nathan's sleeve. "Did you do something to stop the Hummer? Can't those things drive over small cars?"

Nathan shrugged. "Maybe. But apparently *this* Hummer couldn't straddle those shopping carts. Believe me, the driver tried, but he got totally stuck. So he left his truck and took off running, but Angela's little dog chased after him. The thing probably weighed three pounds, but it tripped him up. By the time the cops arrived we had the guy immobilized in the back of the Make it Work! van."

"Tell them the best part!" Cooper prodded.

"Turns out I knew the driver," Nathan added enigmatically.

Savannah, who had been listening quietly to the morning's rambunctious discussion, suddenly shook her cane at Nathan. "I can't take the suspense, my friend!" She smiled. "Sorry, but I feel like I've been on the edge of my seat since we started. Any more anticipation and I'm going to fall off!"

Following Savannah's request, Nathan went on with the remainder of his tale. "Do you remember when we started studying Joseph and I was having that dream about a person outside my door?" His friends all nodded. "I believe that person was Tobey Dodge, the client I took on with some reservations. As I've now discovered, God was trying to warn me about this man, but I didn't listen closely enough to what He was saying. Tobey is a crook and a low-life swindler. And I totally fell for his act."

"I did, too," Cooper interjected and then added, "He was a real smooth-talker—making us believe that he wanted to help people with his products. I didn't hear any alarm bells go off when we met, though I didn't particularly like him."

"Anyway, I'd been searching for him all week," Nathan continued. "A bunch of clients wanted refunds because the Big Man muscle builders didn't work. A few of them wanted to sue him because his products had actually made them sick. Two men ended up in the hospital."

Trish frowned. "If you ask me, no one should take steroids in the first place."

Nathan shook his head. "Tobey's clients believed they

were buying all-natural products, but according to one of the clients who needed hospitalization, the Big Man muscle builders were actually animal steroids. They're quite dangerous, but a heck of a lot cheaper than steroids made for humans."

"What a snake!" Quinton declared. "You know, I've bought plenty of weight-loss products that made me feel pretty awful. Looking back, it's a wonder I didn't require medical care myself! Remember when all the diet stuff used to contain too much ephedrine or that dangerous fen-phen stuff? I think I've tried it all."

Seeing the glum expression on Quinton's face, Jake smiled at his friend. "I wouldn't want there to be a pound less of you, my man."

As the two men exchanged affectionate high-fives, Trish's attention remained focused on Nathan. "How does Tobey fit into the Kroger story?"

"*He* was the guy in the Hummer. By the time the cops arrived and Cooper's boss, the Kroger manager, and I had finished coming up with a list of the con artist's activities, we all felt like old friends." At this point, Nathan seemed to be at a loss for words.

"Go on," Bryant prompted.

"Well, I don't know if you're aware of this, but Cooper and I . . . we . . ."

Jake finished the sentence for him. "Have the hots for each other? We know, my man."

As Cooper flushed bright pink, Nathan hurried to finish. "I'd been giving Cooper the cold shoulder all week because I thought, in a moment of total insanity, that she and the new guy at work had kissed."

"Which would *never* happen!" Cooper exclaimed. "Emilio is the perfect man for someone, but not for me.

He's the type of guy who thinks all women want him. Yes, he tried to kiss me once but I wouldn't let him. Of course, he then thought I was playing hard-to-get so he sent me a text message saying that we could try that kiss again. The problem was that Nathan read the message."

"And you didn't give Cooper a chance to explain?" Trish swatted at Nathan. "You bad boy."

"I know." Nathan's voice was contrite. "But I was so tortured over the whole thing that I asked Angela if Emilio and Cooper had anything going on between them. That woman sure set me straight! I think I still have the scars from where she dug her nails into my arm!"

"And then you went flying to Cooper's house to apologize, right?" Savannah guessed.

Nathan nodded. "I passed a car parked on the side of the road about a half mile from her driveway. I knew I'd seen that car before, so I pulled over to check it out. A Door-2-Door cooler was on the front seat and a bunch of boxes and bags were in the back. It looked like someone was ready to go on a long trip."

"And you just knew it was our killer," Jake whispered, entranced.

"Yeah. I felt like all the blood in my body surged through my heart at once. I don't think I even remembered to breathe as I drove the rest of the way. During those last few seconds I was imagining the worst. If I had gotten there too late . . ." Nathan's voice cracked and he had to pause and collect himself. "I practically crashed through her parents' screen door. I can't even remember what I told them. They knew who I was and they trusted me immediately, and the next thing I knew, we were storming up the stairs to Cooper's apartment. As I ran, I kept wishing I could fly . . ."

"It's okay, Nathan," Savannah spoke up. "We would have all been just as afraid. When we care about another person, our love is often mixed with fear. Look at Joseph's father. Jacob loved young Joseph so much that he kept him by his side. Joseph didn't tend the flocks or do the chores his brothers did. Fear and love prompted Jacob to hold Joseph close, but too much fear is destructive. Joseph was betrayed by his brothers and sent far from his homeland because Jacob treated him differently from the rest."

Jake touched the cover of his *Amazing Joseph* workbook. "And only God's love could reunite the family in the end. Jacob was able to die right there with his son and his son's sons gathered 'round his bed. That felt so right to me."

"I was so moved by Genesis forty-eight," Trish said. "When Joseph places his two sons on the bed with Jacob and he hugs and kisses them just like any grandfather would do. Oh! It's such a sweet ending."

"And a dignified one," Quinton added. "Jacob prophesied the future of the tribes of Israel, blessed everyone, drew up his knees, and breathed his last." Looking aggrieved, he sighed. "Warren's victims weren't fortunate enough to die like that. I feel so much anger toward that man for robbing those folks of their last years. He took away precious time—the opportunity to experience life in all its joys and sorrows."

Cooper bowed her head. The image that repeated itself most while she soaked in a warm tub, ate breakfast with her family, and drove beneath a sky filled with narrow clouds outlined with pearly sunshine that morning was of Vera. To Cooper, it was the photograph capturing the old woman's contented smile, the purple rhinestone glasses, and the childlike innocence that radiated from her eyes that haunted her thoughts.

Separating herself from the others, she walked over to the food table and mechanically poured a cup of coffee. She could feel her friends watching her, their stares filled with compassion and concern.

"There is grief in this life," Savannah spoke in a hushed tone. "Wrongs are done to good people every day. Sometimes it's hard to understand the world we live in—the motives that drive folks to commit acts of such malevolent violence. But if we set aside our reasons to mourn for a moment, what do we have left? What have *we* gained by being placed in the center of these trying events?"

Bryant cleared his throat. "I vow to respect and appreciate my mother. It's just hit me how I don't know her as well as I should. What was she like as a little girl? Is there something she'd like to do or a place she'd like to see before . . ." He stopped himself. "I want to let her go like Joseph let his father go. I want her to be at peace, and now I realize that I need to find out what that means to *her,* not me."

"I learned that we're part of a bigger picture," Quinton said. "We hear that in church all the time, but until this happened, it was just a phrase. Because of Trish, I've met neighbors that needed my help. And in helping them, *I* was the one who received a gift."

Jake touched Trish on the hand. "We'd better get a bunch of folks on board if we wanna rescue the sinkin' ship called Door-2-Door. I'm gonna talk to my boss about a sponsorship, but can your company swing a few more weeks sponsoring a route? Those folks aren't gonna make it unless we act and we act now!"

"Of course I'm going to help." Trish pointed at Quinton.

"I'm sure your firm can afford a month or two as well. I hope you can talk some of your clients into donating, too. I've never approached my own clients about a cause, but it wouldn't hurt to have some flyers and a collection box at our office."

Savannah listened in approval. "I spoke to some of the elders last week. Hope Street is going to organize a group of volunteers immediately. They're also discussing creating a mission trip that'll stay right here in Richmond and assist Door-2-Door clients with home repairs and such."

"I think I'll offer to spiff up their website. It could use an update." Nathan seemed to be thinking out loud. "And from now on, I'm going to try to pay better attention when God is doing His best to give me advice. I could have avoided this Tobey mess altogether."

Cooper smiled at him. "As for me, I've been feeling like I have something left to do for Frank Crosby and I think it involves his son. I'm going to visit him tomorrow afternoon, so please pray that I'll find the right words to use when I tell him about Warren and about the secret his daddy had been trying to keep for so long." She cupped her coffee mug in her hands. "I'm kind of intimidated by The Colonel. We're from such different worlds, but I understand what you said about the bigger picture, Quinton. I think we need to venture away from our safe places and take some risks in order to truly be changed."

"Well said, all of you." Savannah closed her workbook. "I realize we didn't review the homework questions, but I believe you have all grown incredibly during this study. I also want to say that I have never felt so united with a group of people in my life. When I think of the word *family*, your faces float before my mind's eye. I smile when I think of you or whenever I speak your names." She reached out and automatically, her hands were grasped, and then everyone took hold of their neighbor's hand. "It is scary to love, but I love you, my friends. Now, let's pray to the One who loves us most."

Cooper had invited her friends to join her after church in order to experience Sunday supper Lee-style.

Maggie had gone all out—roasting a turkey, making green bean casserole, homemade oyster stuffing, cranberry relish, mashed potatoes, caramelized yams, corn in butter sauce, sunflower rolls, and a smorgasbord of desserts. Though the food was formal, like a special holiday dinner, the actual meal was not. The Lee table could only seat six, so the rest of the diners ate standing up, sitting in the living room, or, in Nathan and Cooper's case, seated cross-legged on the floor.

"We ain't seen this much company since Ashley's weddin'!" Grammy yelled with a mouthful of yams. "How you feelin' these days, little darlin'?"

"Just fine, thank you." Ashley leaned over Grammy's chair and kissed her wrinkled cheek. "I'll give you those grandbabies you want yet." She then stood and winked at Cooper. "And if my body doesn't want to grow a baby, Cooper will just have carry one for me. Right, sis?"

Cooper nearly choked on a bite of roll.

"Are you tryin' to scare the pants off that Nathan boy?" Grammy snarled at Ashley. "Let him think about marriage before his mind skips ahead to the diaper-changin' part. Now go get yourself another plate. Babies like to grow in a belly filled regularly with food."

Maggie was all too pleased to ladle several servings of starch onto her youngest child's dish.

Once the supper plates had been cleared, desserts sampled, and coffee poured, Savannah whispered something into Jake's ear and he exited the house expediently. Upon his return, he handed a rectangular packaged wrapped in butcher paper to Cooper's grandmother.

"What's this?" Grammy demanded, eying Jake with suspicion.

"It's one of my paintings," Savannah answered. "A while back, Cooper told us how much the pin you gave her means to her. During that moment, I sensed such love and gratitude in her story that I have thought about that little butterfly many times since then." She smiled. "This is my way of thanking you for enriching our lives with your story of hope and courage."

Grammy squirmed in the face of such an overt compliment. "Well, I've never done a single thing to merit that kind of praise, but I won't say no to a present. I haven't got enough years left in me to reject kindness, so I thank you."

Ripping off the paper with glee, Grammy seemed transformed. Suddenly, she was a little girl tearing the gift wrap from a joyfully anticipated birthday or Christmas present. Cooper watched as her grandmother's expression became illuminated with pleasure as she gazed at Savannah's work.

"Come on, Grammy," Ashley complained. "Turn it around and let us all see."

"Keep your socks on, granddaughter. I'm havin' a fine time just soakin' in the colors and feelings of this picture." She handed the painting back to Jake and shuffled over to Savannah. "It's right lovely. Thank you." As the two women embraced, Maggie burst into tears.

"Isn't the Lord amazing? Look how He's brought all of us together!" she cried, dabbing at her brimming eyes with the corner of her apron. She then took a step closer to Cooper so she could examine Grammy's painting. Cooper slipped an arm around her mother's waist and simultaneously, they bent down in order to properly examine the artwork.

The scene was a familiar one in that it depicted Noah and his family stepping onto dry land for the first time in forty days and nights. The family members held hands as they raised their faces toward the sun-filled sky, seemingly oblivious to the stampede of freed animals bursting past them. Birds and insects filled the air and Cooper was amazed at the energy Savannah had managed to infuse into the movements of every creature, from a pair of ants to the magnificent grace of an antelope couple. Lions roared in rejoicing, elephants trumpeted in celebration of their survival, and a group of primates launched themselves into the trees with rapturous animation.

The most personal detail of the painting, however, had to do with the rainbow stretching across the horizon as a reminder of God's covenant. Unlike most rainbows, which seemed like hesitant, ephemeral blurs of pale color, Savannah's rainbow was alive—literally. Brilliant shades of violet, indigo, emerald, saffron, pumpkin, and crimson were represented by dozens and dozens of butterflies. The beautiful insects had been designed so that their delicate wings touched one another, but not so completely that pinpricks of light couldn't find their way through the openings.

"Amazing," Maggie breathed. "You gave Mama more butterflies than she's ever dreamed of havin'. And what these stand for . . . oh, it's too lovely!" She began crying all over again.

Maggie wasn't the only one shedding tears. To everyone's surprise, Trish was weeping as well.

"I'm sorry. I don't mean to subtract from this moment, but I've been trying to keep my worries inside for days now and I just can't. I've never felt so scared before!" She buried her face in her hands.

Maggie rubbed Trish's back. "What's wrong, honey?"

"I had a biopsy on Friday," Trish whimpered. "And I won't get the results back until Wednesday. The waiting is tearing me apart. Breast cancer runs in my family and I've been pretending like it can't touch me. Not *me*, the successful businesswoman, wife, and churchgoing mother of two. But it *can* and I'm really, really frightened!" Trish hid herself in Maggie's comforting bosom.

Cooper watched as Maggie stroked her friend's copper hair and murmured into her ear.

"No matter what the results are," Bryant spoke firmly to Trish, "we'll be here for you. We'll lend you strength and pray for your health and even come with you to the doctor on Wednesday."

Jake nodded. "Yeah, you tell us what you need and we'll be on the job."

"When you face a time of trial, know that you're not alone," Savannah whispered. "Let love and faith outweigh your fear."

Trish pulled away from Maggie and looked at her friends, her expression anguished. Grammy rubbed at her chin and then locked eyes with Cooper. Immediately comprehending what Grammy's hazel eyes were telling her, Cooper unpinned the silver butterfly from her cardigan and gently fastened it onto Trish's umber-hued suit jacket.

"We're with you," Cooper promised and took her friend's hand in hers. "Wherever you go. We're right there."

Later, after Cooper's friends had gone home, Cooper and Grammy took Columbus out for his final flight of the day. With the hawk on her left arm and her grandmother clutching her right, Cooper felt amazingly balanced considering the experiences of the past few weeks.

"I hope this doesn't sound weird," Cooper began once the hawk had jumped from her arm and circled skyward. "But this tragedy with the Door-2-Door folks has got me thinking. You've been such an important part of my life, Grammy, and—"

"Now don't go pushin' me in the grave yet, girlie!" Grammy interrupted with a cackle. "I walked all the way out to this here fence in case you weren't payin' attention. No need to talk about me like I'm on the way out."

Cooper smiled at her grandmother, soaking up the laugh lines fanning out from the corners of her eyes, the soft white curls of her hair, the delicateness of her hands. For once, she didn't notice age spots or wrinkles, the shiny track suit or mismatched argyle socks, but only a strong, determined, and loyal woman who placed her family above all other things.

"I just wanted to know if you felt like you'd missed out on something. Is there anything I could do to, I don't know, to fulfill a wish?" Cooper finished, feeling a bit lame in her inability to express what she wanted to say.

Grammy snorted. "Like takin' me to climb a pyramid or toss a quarter into that famous fountain in Rome? That sort of thing?"

Cooper shrugged. "Yeah. Kind of."

"Girlie, I got everythin' I want right here. I got a heart that beats, a mind that thinks, and two arms to put around the folks I love, and, for some mysterious reason, love me right back." She squeezed Cooper's arm. "My only wish is for you to be happy. Do that, and I've got everythin' I ever wanted."

As Columbus called out a cry of delight, his tawny feathers tinted gold by the waning light, Cooper hugged her grandmother. She held onto the small and bony frame until the first star winked into life above the ridge of trees.

The following Tuesday, when Cooper checked in at the lobby of the Henrico County's Jail West and requested a visit with Edward Crosby, she discovered that she wasn't nervous at all.

Earlier in the day, Mr. Farmer had spontaneously declared that he was taking all of his employees to a well-deserved lunch at Ipanema Grill, where they could spend an hour gorging on Brazilian cuisine. Though Cooper would have enjoyed such a sumptuous free lunch, she knew that keeping her promise to The Colonel was more important.

"Ipanema? That's the place where they keep bringing ya giant slabs of meat!" Emilio had exclaimed when he heard the news. "They carve it right there at your table. Beef, lamb, pork, chicken. And they don't stop until you tell 'em to. Man, I've got the best job *and* the best girl in Richmond. Awesome, huh?" He clapped Mr. Farmer on the back.

"I don't know about the best girl part," Mr. Farmer had replied, shooting a coy grin in Angela's direction, "but I'm glad you're happy at Make It Work!"

"What about you, Cooper?" Ben had elbowed her in the side while Angela blew kisses at their boss. "Aren't you just dying to watch Emilio polish off a barnyard's worth of cow, pig, and fowl?"

"I'll leave that pleasure to you," she said, shoving him aside with her shoulder. "Though I wouldn't mind hanging out with you for an hour."

Ben grinned. "You mean, now that I'm not acting like a total grump?"

"I mean, now that you're more like your old self."

"I'll never be that again," Ben confessed without ire. "But the guy I turned into after going through this with Melissa might make it worth the grief. I'm learning a lot about myself by supporting her."

Cooper stopped organizing the morning's work orders and looked at Ben in astonishment. "You know—that's the first time I've heard you say her name! Ben and Melissa. Has a nice ring to it, doesn't it?"

Nodding, Ben smiled. "It does. It really does."

Waving good-bye to her coworkers, Cooper unwrapped the peanut butter and jelly sandwich she had brought from home and enjoyed a quiet lunch alone in the office kitchen. After a fifteen-minute break, she got busy with her afternoon repairs, which included removing a jammed paperclip from the inside of a scanner, fixing a malfunctioning stamp machine at the post office, and reprogramming a copier so that it chose eight-by-eleven sheets of paper instead of the legal-size documents it had insisted on producing no matter what paper tray had been selected.

Once every Make It Work! client had been completely satisfied, Cooper took her official lunch break at two-thirty. That left her less than an hour to drive to the government complex and see The Colonel before visiting hours were over.

When he appeared in the portioned room, Frank's son seemed stunned by the realization that Cooper had actually returned.

"So the cops nailed the bastard who killed my dad?" he asked, his eyes fierce.

"Yes." Cooper wondered how much detail to go into.

"I read about it in today's paper, but a little birdie told me they picked him up at your place. You meant what you said, didn't you? That you were gonna make things right and figure out the truth about Frank's death." He gazed at her with respect. "You're the first person I've met that means what they say. You. A total fu—ah, freakin' stranger. Why do you give a rat's ass? Why are you even here?"

Momentarily taken aback, Cooper wasn't sure how to respond. Even though The Colonel had asked the question with no hostility, she felt offended. "I wanted you to know why your daddy hid that diary and why he was so obsessed about honor." She then described the incidents surrounding Aaron Crosby's history. "I thought if you knew, you might be able to forgive your daddy."

The Colonel rubbed his stubble in bewilderment. "Who cares about Aaron Crosby? It all happened a hundred years ago. Why'd Frank have to let some relative destroy *this* generation of Crosbys? You gotta admit—he was completely whacked."

Cooper disagreed. "He may have taken things too much to heart, and his fears no doubt hurt you and your mama, but there's no reason why you can't make the Crosby name shine again. It's not too late."

The Colonel smirked, unconvinced. "You gonna pour holy water over my head and whisper some Bible mumbo-jumbo and expect that my life will be all nice and pretty? Just like that?" He snapped his fingers. "Damn, woman! I'm gonna get out in six months and go right back to the street. It's what I *know*."

"And end up back in here!" Cooper replied angrily. "Where's the honor in that plan? All you need is for *one person* to believe in you—in your ability to change, to take a chance at a life that includes a regular job, an apartment, a few friends. Maybe even a girlfriend."

Smiling for the first time since he sat down, The Colonel leaned forward. "You applying for the job?"

"Sorry, Colonel. I'm spoken for." Cooper relished how wonderful it felt to utter that phrase. "But you can put me down on your list as a friend. As someone who truly believes in your potential."

The Colonel seemed to withdraw and Cooper hoped that she hadn't been too pushy. When he remained silently staring at her even after the guard warned him that his visit would be over in sixty seconds, she began to despair that she had mishandled the situation completely.

With only seconds remaining, The Colonel abruptly whispered into the phone, "If we're gonna hang out sometime, then you'd better call me Edward." He raised his hand to prevent her from speaking. "As for livin' the *straight* life, it'll take a sign from God to make *that* happen."

And with that, he hung up the phone and disappeared.

A sign? Cooper remained immobile in her seat for a few moments longer. *What kind of sign would it take? I don't think God's in the business of performing on demand.*

Suddenly, she had an idea. Approaching the nearest guard, she asked him to deliver a folded piece of paper to Edward Crosby.

"I'll see he gets it, ma'am."

Later that afternoon, Cooper clocked out and headed for one of the dozens of strip malls on Broad Street. She and Nathan had planned a quiet evening lounging around his house. Nathan had volunteered to cook a pizza and throw together a salad if Cooper promised to arrive bearing a movie for them to watch after dinner.

"I can tell you already that I'm renting *Love, Actually*," she informed him over the phone as she pulled into Blockbuster's parking lot. "I need to watch something with a happy ending."

"I'm a fan of those kind of endings myself," Nathan answered. "And I know I'm going to be seeing your beautiful face in person soon, but did everything go okay during your visit with The Colonel?"

Cooper paused. "He told me he'd be looking out for a sign—something to encourage him to live a different life once he's released."

"That's a bit beyond our power, isn't it?"

"But maybe not Quinton's," Cooper replied with a smile. "I think his most recent song was meant specifically for Edward Crosby."

"Cool. I hope Jake sets that one to music, too. That is, if he has time. Yesterday, he told me that he's spending the next few days cleaning every inch of his house. He's finally done it, Cooper."

"Asked Savannah on a date?" Cooper inquired hopefully.

Nathan laughed. "I guess his feelings for her are as obvious as mine are for you." Then he softly added, "See you soon, sweetheart."

In a group jail cell, populated by thirty men in beige scrubs, there was little opportunity for privacy or quiet. One of the few times the men fell silent and minded their own business occurred after the arrival of the mail each day. When the letters were delivered to the eager inmates that Tuesday evening, Edward Crosby was surprised to hear his name called and have a folded sheet of paper handed to him.

"Who's this from?" he asked as he glimpsed the bottom of the page in search of a signature.

The guard shrugged. "No idea."

Edward retreated to his cot. He smoothed the slightly creased paper flat and then began to read.

My heart was like a winter storm
Frozen hard with ice and cold
Blanketed in piles of snow
I was lost among the shadows

I wondered:
Is it too late
To find the light?
Is it too late
To make things right?

I hoarded riches, I gathered pride
I knocked down others
To feel big inside
I gave in to envy
I surrendered to hate
While an inner voice whispered
Is it too late?

Is it too late
To know the Lord?
Is it too late
To hear His word?

I wandered into a house of prayer
A group of strangers were gathered there
They welcomed me as one of their own
My spirit stirred in a way I'd never known
As the light streamed through the panes
My soul began to rearrange

Now my future rests in His hands
On my knees I've come understand
The bounty of my Lord's sweet love
Forgiveness delivered from heaven above

It's not too late
It's not too late

"It's not too late," Edward murmured to himself. He then closed his eyes, leaned against his pillow and whispered to someone he had never addressed before. "I got your sign, God. Show me what to do next and I'll do it."

In his heart, he felt a sudden and powerful feeling of calm—a measure of peace that he had never experienced before.

"What you grinnin' about like some fool? Huh, Colonel?" one of the other inmates demanded.

Edward Crosby stood and slapped the man affectionately on the back. "The future," he said and snapped his fingers as he had earlier while talking to Cooper. "Just like that, I got cause to smile."

Magnolia's Marvels

ICED LEMON COOKIES

Cookies:
   1 cup butter
   2 cups sugar
   3 eggs, beaten
   1 cup buttermilk
   4 cups flour
   2 tsp. baking powder
   2 tsp. baking soda
   1 tsp. pure vanilla
   1 tsp. lemon flavoring

Lemon Icing:
   1½ cups confectioner's sugar
   2 tablespoons water
   1 tablespoon lemon juice

Cream butter and sugar, add beaten eggs and then buttermilk. Stir in flour, baking powder, soda, and flavorings. Refrigerate overnight. Drop by teaspoons on greased sheets. Bake at 400 degrees until cookies are lightly brown (approx. 10 minutes). Frost with lemon icing.

SOFT GINGER MOLASSES COOKIES

> ¾ cup unsalted butter
> 1 cup dark brown sugar, packed
> 1 egg
> ¼ cup molasses
> 2¼ cups flour
> 2 tsp. baking soda
> 1 tsp. cinnamon
> 1 tsp. ginger
> ½ tsp. salt
> ½ tsp. cloves
> Granulated sugar for rolling

Cream butter and sugar. Add egg. Gently mix. Add remaining ingredients and mix well. Form dough into small balls and roll in granulated sugar. Bake at 375 degrees for nine minutes. These cookies will be very soft to the touch, but don't fret. They'll harden to the perfect consistency when they cool.

PUMPKIN CRISP SQUARES

Squares:
> 1 can (15 oz.) pumpkin
> 1 can evaporated milk
> 1 cup granulated sugar
> 1 tsp. pumpkin pie spice
> 3 eggs
> 1 box yellow cake mix
> 1 cup chopped pecans
> 2 sticks butter, melted

Frosting:

 1 pkg. (8 oz.) cream cheese
 1 stick of butter
 3½ cups confectioner's sugar

Mix pumpkin, milk, sugar, eggs and pumpkin pie spice together. Pour into 9 × 13–inch greased pan. Sprinkle dry cake mix over pumpkin mix. Pat nuts onto surface of mixture. Melt butter and pour over the top. Bake at 350 degrees for 50 to 60 minutes. Cool and frost. To make frosting, combine cream cheese and butter and mix on low speed for one minute. Add sugar and mix until all the sugar is incorporated.

READ ON FOR AN EXCERPT FROM

THE WAY OF THE GUILTY

The Next Hope Street Church mystery
from Jennifer Stanley and
St. Martin's / Minotaur Paperbacks!

Trust in the LORD with all your heart
and lean not on your own understanding;

in all your ways acknowledge him,
and he will make your paths straight.

Do not be wise in your own eyes;
fear the LORD and shun evil.

This will bring health to your body
and nourishment to your bones.

Proverbs 3:5–8 (NIV)

Cooper was excited about starting a new Bible study with her friends from Hope Street Church. Except for Nathan, she hadn't seen any of them since the Christmas Eve candlelight service. Every member had left town in order to visit family. Savannah Knapp, the legally blind folk artist who led their small group, had stayed away even longer in order to conduct a painting workshop for an artist's colony, so they'd been unable to commence with a fresh study until she returned.

Feelings of pleasant expectation coursed through Cooper when she finally received a phone call from Quinton Enderly, the successful investment banker and talented amateur pastry chef, announcing that it was his turn to choose the next study. He'd picked *Directing Our Passion: Corinthians I and II.*

"Whoa!" she'd teased him. "Sounds steamy."

"I've been praying for a wife for over ten years now," Quinton had replied solemnly. "But suddenly I realized that I've got to have a clear relationship with God before I can even attempt to form one with a woman. This study just spoke to me."

"Trust me, Quinton. We could *all* use help in the relationship department. Besides, you're a real catch. Some girl is going to celebrate the day she found her way to your doorstep," Cooper said to her portly and kind-hearted friend before speeding off to LifeWay to buy the study guide.

She loved opening an unblemished, stiff workbook, uncapping her favorite purple pen, and rustling the pages of her Bible as she prepared to complete the first homework lesson.

"Sounds like the wings of dove, doesn't it?" Her mother had once said while flipping through her own Bible. "How the angels must rejoice over the music made by the turnin' of those pages."

Cooper had felt a bit lost during the break the Bible study group had taken. She'd gone to church, but her focus had wandered during each service, her eyes roaming the congregation in search of the faces of her friends. Now, on the third Sunday in January, it was time to reunite. Humming to herself, she was the first one to arrive in the Hope Street Christian Academy's Biology class-room. She set out a basket of her mother's meringue pecan bars, brewed a pot of coffee in the teacher's lounge, and placed a stack of snowman napkins alongside a plate of plump red seedless grapes.

"Now *this* is an interesting room," meteorologist Bryant Shelton declared as he entered, flicking a solar system model suspended from the ceiling into orbit. "I'm glad we got booted from the English classroom. I was getting kind of tired of being stared at by those Shakespeare and Virginia Woolf posters." He sidled up to the life-sized skeleton and slung an arm around its bony shoulders. "Sorry to keep you waiting for our dinner date, sweet cheeks. You've practically wasted away!" He laughed, displaying his famous television smile. Twin dimples appeared in his tanned cheeks as he released the skeleton and walked over to embrace Cooper. "I've missed our meetings."

Cooper smiled at him, knowing that dozens of women longed to be the recipient of Bryant's attention and would have gladly locked her in the classroom's supply closet if it meant the gorgeous weatherman would hug them instead. Cooper cared deeply for Bryant, but only as a friend. The two of them had quickly bonded a year ago over their experiences with failed relationships. Bryant was a divorcé three times over and Cooper's only serious boyfriend had left her for another woman. Together, they'd vowed to forgive those who'd hurt them and focus on the future instead.

"I smell cookies!" Jake Lombardi bellowed as he stepped into the classroom. "Yours or your mama's?" He stripped off a pair of worn leather gloves, dumped his aged barn jacket onto one of the student desks, and began to remove tissue-wrapped coffee mugs from a grocery bag.

"Magnolia's Marvels," Cooper admitted. "She made an extra two dozen for us this morning."

"Lucky us." Bryant pointed at the coffee mugs. "What are those, Jake?"

"I saw 'em online," Jake answered. "I wanted to get somethin' for our first meetin' of the year. I may be a plumber, but I got good taste. Check these out." He handed Cooper a mug. It showed a rising sun and the words COFFEE HOUR: THE THIRD SACRAMENT.

"We're the Sunrise Bible Study group and we sure like our coffee," Jake explained. "Figured these were made for us."

"Did you come bearing gifts, Jake?" a mellifluous voice asked from the doorway. Savannah held a white cane in one hand and several books in the other. Quinton was guiding her by the elbow with Trish Tyler, an ambitious realtor and mother of two, following closely behind. Nathan took up the rear.

"These are cute, Jake." Trish said as she picked up one of the mugs. "Even if they're a *tad* cynical."

"Get your caffeine on and be grateful, lady." Jake grinned at her. "After all, I could've picked the ones that said *God Only Loves You 'Cause He Has To!*"

Nathan chuckled. "Oh man, that is *so* mean!"

The members exchanged small talk about their various trips and then settled down to begin Day One of their study.

"The first book of Corinthians addresses the people of Corinth. Imagine that!" Savannah took a bite of one of the meringue pecan cookies and sighed in delight. "This Greek city was a bustling and wealthy port," she stated. "All kinds of exotic goods came in and out of this place and its people were as mixed as its goods. There was plenty of entertainment to be found there, including athletic competitions like the Olympics. And according to my audio guide, there was a tavern on *every* street corner."

"Sounds like Americans and our Starbucks," Bryant remarked.

"In this city filled with immorality, the Apostle Paul appeared more than once to preach to the people," Savannah continued with a smile. "Does this setting remind you of another Biblical place?"

"Babylon," Nathan answered quickly. "Both cities have the lure of glamour, wealth, and greed."

Savannah nodded. "We live in a modern Babylon, so we face similar temptations every day. I don't know about you all, but I give in to these kind of trappings on a regular basis." She held up her cane. "I can't even *see* and I've got a house loaded with *stuff*!" She laughed. "I admit to enjoying too many material things. You probably didn't know that I listen to QVC even though I can't see the products clearly—only fuzzy colors! But I like how the hosts describe everything. It's a seductive show, I tell you!"

"My Corinth/Babylon problem is the same one as always," Quinton spoke next. "I want more food than I need. Portion control. Overindulgence. I can't seem to get a grip on it."

Jake patted the large man on the back. "I hear ya, man. Over the holidays I slipped and had a smoke. And then a second one. Now those cigarettes are callin' to me night and day."

"Boy, I know that feeling." Cooper sympathized with Jake. "Even though I quit months ago, any time I get stressed the thought of just taking a few drags seems like a great idea. Hang in there." Glancing at her own workbook page, Cooper recalled that she'd written that her weekly pedicures were an unnecessary luxury, but that she had no intention of giving them up.

Savannah raised the next discussion point. "In verse nineteen of chapter one, Paul quotes from Isaiah. How do you respond to the phrases 'destroy the wisdom of the wise' and 'the intelligence of the intelligent I will frustrate'?" Savannah looked around the circle of faces, as though she could see everyone's features through her nearly sightless, navy-blue eyes. Cooper noticed that she'd loosed her braid, allowing her dark brown hair to spill over her shoulders. The light from the windows caught a few strands of silver framing Savannah's unlined face. Once again, Cooper was struck by Savannah's loveliness. Though only forty, their group leader possessed a level of grace, poise, and self-awareness that made her seem wiser than her years.

"I don't think Paul is trying to compliment smart people," Trish said, and then paused to rub her glossy ruby-tinted lips with her pinkie. "Sometimes, the biggest brainiacs are the biggest atheists too. Like they've figured out all of life's riddles and therefore have no reason to believe in God."

Bryant rubbed his chin thoughtfully. "Like Benjamin Franklin? I think he was the one who said, 'Lighthouses are more helpful than churches.'" He waved his hand around the room. "Here we are, in a place filled with the evidence of man's scientific discoveries and they really are great, but even this level of wisdom doesn't give us what we *need*."

Quinton nodded. "Take Adam. He had everything he needed, but he wasn't satisfied. Look where *that* got us."

"Good point!" Jake exclaimed with a smirk. "That ole serpent knew what he was doin' when he told Adam he could know as much as God if he'd only take a little nibble of fruit." He nudged Trish playfully with his elbow. "Thanks a lot, Eve."

Trish scowled, her pencil-drawn eye brows furrowing. "No one twisted Adam's arm. He made his own choice. Besides, women have *paid* for Eve's bad decision." Her voice rose. "You *men* don't have any idea what labor pains are like! That damned *fruit* cost us plenty." Her eyes dropped to her book and fixed upon the page as the rest of the group exchanged startled glances.

Savannah recovered first and steered the conversation back to the subject at hand. Cooper shared her thoughts that human wisdom was different from divine wisdom, for one had limits and the other had none, but felt that she needed to say something else to lighten the mood.

"I've definitely acted dumb when I *thought* I was being clever," she told her friends while trying to block out images of a party she'd attended recently. "When I started fixing office machines, I thought I was some kind of female Da Vinci. One of my first jobs was to repair a printer in the nurse's office of a nearby grade school. I tried everything, but I couldn't get it to work. Then this seven-year-old boy comes in and tells me that it's not plugged in. Sure, there was a nest of cords and wires under the nurse's desk, but I never even checked the most basic step because I *wanted* to solve a complicated problem." She shrugged. "Guess I needed a dose of humility."

"Arrogant is not a word that I'd associate with you." Nathan winked at her. "And you're awesome at problem-solving. Do I have to point out that you've helped solve two murder cases?"

"Well, arrogant *is* a word people might use to describe me," Bryant commented with a self-effacing grin. "Once, when I was working at a station at the beach, I showed up too late to review the latest weather data before I went on the air at six A.M. Because of that, I failed to warn commuters that they'd be dealing with a serious fog. There were dozens of accidents that day and lots of people called the station to complain about my crappy forecast. My boss reamed me out with a hurricane-force lecture."

"At least you didn't punch a hole in somebody's septic tank." Jake screwed up his face in disgust. "On Fourth of July. Durin' a family reunion. Do you know what sewage smells like in the middle of a ninety-nine-degree day?"

Quinton squirmed in his chair. "Eew! No more details, Jake, *please*. You'll put me off my cookies. Did I ever tell you guys about the time—?"

"ENOUGH!" Trish shouted and the Bible study members jumped in their seats. "*I* win the blue ribbon for being stupid! Hands down, no contest, game over! I win!" She hit the desktop with a closed fist, her crimson fingernails digging into the flesh of her palm. "I always thought I was the type of person who couldn't get sick. People who smoked or drank or never exercised got sick. Not *me*! I eat balanced meals, work out four times a week, and only drink a glass of Chablis when the mood strikes me. But I'm sick, all right. Look at this." She raked her fingers through her copper-colored hair and then showed her friends the red clump resting on her palm.

"What's happening?" Savannah pleaded, unable to witness the unsettling act.

"She's losing her hair," Cooper whispered, her eyes never leaving Trish's tormented face.

"I'll be lucky if that's all I lose," Trish muttered hoarsely and then her mouth began to quiver. "Do you remember that biopsy I had back in the fall? The one that came out benign?"

Her friends nodded fearfully.

"Well, I've had another one since then and it's *not* benign." She spat out the word as though it were an enemy. "I, Trish Tyler, have cancer. Right here." She folded her hands across her heart and then fanned them out across her chest. "I have breast cancer. The serious kind."

Jubilant music calling people to worship tripped down the corridors of the church wing housing the school, but none of the Sunrise Bible Study members responded to the enticing melody. The unhindered shrieks of children racing down the hall toward their Sunday School classes, the cheerful shouts of adults greeting one another, and the increasing volume of the drumbeat emanating from within the chapel produced a cacophony of cheerfulness that seemed to mock the atmosphere in the Biology classroom.

"I'm sorry." Trish hid her face in her hands. "I didn't mean to let it out this way. I'm so mixed up right now. I go from brave to being scared out of my mind, to angry, to yelling curses in the privacy of my shower, to crying so hard I've got to pull the car off the road and park. Right now, I'm just really, really tired."

Savannah eased herself from behind her desk and

walked carefully over to where Trish sat. Putting both arms around her distraught friend, she whispered, "Tell us everything."

"I've got Grade Two cancer, which means that they couldn't just cut the bad cells out and send me on my way. I had surgery right after Christmas—I didn't want to spoil things for the girls so I insisted on waiting a few days—and they removed the masses, but it's not enough."

Jake gave her a stern look. "You should've told us, you stubborn woman. 'Least we could've prayed for you while you were goin' through all that."

Surprisingly, Trish smiled. "I was in serious denial three weeks ago. I figured if I didn't tell anyone it would just go away."

"Do you need chemo?" Quinton asked, his kind eyes filled with concern.

Trish picked up the loose strands of hair and began winding them around and around her index finger. "I've already started. Had my first dose on Thursday."

"Oh, Trish." Cooper felt like crying, but forced back the tears.

"I get another dose next week. Through an IV. It takes about an hour. That should finish off what's left of my hair. And here I thought my auburn color, the blow dryer, and flat iron would be the ones to fry my gorgeous locks." Trish offered up a crooked grin. "Guess it's a good thing I had the photo taken for my Tyler Fine Properties billboard last summer."

"Woman, you're gonna look smokin' hot with no hair," Jake teased. "Like that singer, Sinead somethin' or other. Or Demi Moore when she shaved her head for that *G.I. Jane* movie."

"I think you'd like nice in a wig, too," Nathan added kindly. "You could look like Princess Di one day and Cleopatra the next."

"Thanks, you two, but either way, the hair is going." She gripped Savannah's hand with sudden desperation. "I don't want to do it myself, though. I know I'm going to get upset when I see the results. Would you . . . ?" she faltered.

"We'll come over whenever you're ready," Savannah declared and gave Trish's hands a compassionate squeeze. "Though you might want to pick someone other than *me* to do the shaving!" She smiled. "We'll all be there to help you through this. Not just the losing your hair part, but every single moment of terror, anger, doubt, and grief."

Bryant also got up and walked over to Trish. "That's right. We'll cook for you—well, the rest of them will cook and I'll buy takeout—and drive you places, go to the doctor with you, and listen to you vent."

"Thank you." Trish sniffed and sat in silence for a moment. "Listen, I'd rather not talk about this anymore if that's okay. Let's go worship now."

"*After* we pray for you," Cooper insisted and everyone immediately reached out for a friend's hand.

Savannah closed her eyes. "I am too unsettled to come up with any words of my own, so I will rely on scripture. Please turn to Isaiah forty-one, verse ten and read aloud with me." She pulled Trish's hands towards her own and bent over them, so that her breath fell directly onto the sick woman's skin.

"*So do not fear, for I am with you;*
do not be dismayed, for I am your God.
I will strengthen you and help you;
I will uphold you with my righteous right hand.' "

One by one, the members of the Sunrise Bible Study stood up and placed their hands on Trish's body. They touched her shoulders, her back, her arms, her hands, the top of her head, and her face.

"You will not face this alone," someone whispered. "We are with you."

"Amen," Trish murmured through her tears.